blue: season

blue: season

Chris Lombardi

MUMBLERS

Published by Mumblers Press LLC, San Francisco CA USA

ISBN 978-1-7362444-6-3 (e-book) | 978-1-7362444-7-0 (paperback)

LCCN 2022919833

To Rachel Rawlings, who loved this book long before she married me.

Contents

Is there one who understands me?

Not many people heard the impact: a car hitting a human body doesn't make that much noise.

But everyone heard the girl singing.

The station wagon had disappeared silently, invisibly into the night, leaving other people or vehicles unaffected. (Besides, at two a.m. most people were in bed and not after trouble—not in 1993, not on a hot August night in East Baltimore, not in a neighborhood with two drive-by shootings in the past three weeks.) But the spiraling, whistle-like cries were distinctive enough to bring people out of their skinny row houses.

"My word, who is that crying so loud, waking the dead."

"That fool girl jogger . . . !"

They gathered around her in robes and blue jeans, carrying flashlights and baseball bats, ready to fight or help. She lay on her side, bleeding from her left elbow—her cries coming out staccato as she gasped for breath.

"Miss? You all right?" a brave teenager knelt beside her to ask. "My mom just called 911, is there somebody else?"

"You leave her alone; can't you see she's too hurt to talk?" An

1

older man, putting down his baseball bat to examine the girl's ankle.

"Hey, I know her—she runs all over Baltimore, didn't you see her down by the harbor that time? Hopkins kids think nothing will ever hurt them."

The young woman fell silent; then quietly, her lips began to move again, her upper body still shaking. From her throat came almost inaudible, unpleasantly high-pitched sounds.

"Hey listen!"

The group stopped talking to listen to the new sound—a feeble soprano wail, the words incomprehensible, the melody slow and wavering within its own rhythm. Each time she stopped to take a breath she would begin to cry again, and then stop quickly, the weeping merged and then submerged in her song.

"Anyone know Spanish?"

"No, Dina speaks Spanish, that's something else."

The siren of the ambulance, though far louder than her voice, screamed a similar pitch, as if it had been summoned not by a phone call but by her otherworldly, off-key cries

"Well, his affect is flat, so we're titrating his lithium—carefully, so he doesn't flip into mania."

"Oh please . . . one rerun of last week and it'll be Xanax all around!"

Anne-Marie Krieger bent her head, as if to protect herself from the volleys of jargon being tossed across the conference table. She wrote on her legal pad in a careful, rounded hand. "What happened last week?" she asked.

The head nurse grimaced. "Oh, a fight at Chatham over some TV program. Chairs overturned, a couple black eyes. Welcome to Pearlstone, Miss Krieger."

"Do they have their TV rights back?" asked a student nurse.

"And how! You can hear it all the way here."

Anne-Marie stared at the intern, before she realized he was joking. Even she knew it was impossible to hear the locked ward from this paneled conference room: five hundred yards of pathway and a stand of weeping willow trees separated Chatham Hall, the former younger boys' dorm of Hillsdale Preparatory Academy, from the school's former classroom building, now the main building of Jacob Pearlstone Psychiatric Institute. In 1993, the smell of chalkboards a half-century earlier seemed to linger.

Anne-Marie had nearly gotten lost on her way to her very first daily briefing; she'd had trouble finding the conference room, a wax-polished enclave that seemed still to smell of faculty cigarettes. The air conditioning enclosed the group in its quiet, white noise, drowning out even the murmurs from the few birds still braving the August heat; the assembled non-psychiatric staff (senior nursing staff, volunteers, therapists, social workers like Anne-Marie) similarly quieted. It was all quite the contrast to where she'd interned before graduating, an underfunded, chaotic city mental-health center full of noise and need. Here, she hoped, the treatment plans were as resourced as staff salaries. The only sound under Gail Ryan's words was the soft, occasional "beep" from a secretary's word processor next door.

The nameplate on Gail's silk blouse said G. RYAN, THERAPY COORDINATOR. She turned a page in her blue binder, going on to the next patient. "Frank Morrison still refuses lithium, says it slows him down. Doesn't object to the Mellaril—"

"What's the dosage on that?" one of the student nurses asked, cramming her notes on a steno pad in tiny handwriting.

"1240 milligrams, right now. We think it's halting the thought insertions, but he's still sullen, uncooperative. Calls his lawyer a lot." Gail issued a careful, tolerant smile and closed her blue binder.

"Is that it?" The head nurse was looking at her watch. "Didn't we have a new admission?" Anne-Marie wrote in her legal pad, *current patients discussed first.*

Gail grinned, opening the red binder. "Oh yes . . . our mystery patient."

"The singing jogger?" asked a volunteer with a PORSCHE T-shirt, whose arm muscles boasted of hours at the gym.

"Ah! You've met her, Steve?"

"I moved her in," he said. "Got the whole morning concert."

Gail addressed the rest of the group. "New patient: they called her 'the singing jogger' over at Homewood Hospital, where she was brought last Friday at three-thirty in the morning—appeared to be a hit-and-run accident. They have her down as Lucy Doe, and so do we, for now."

"Hoo-ee, bet the legal department loves that. Not to mention accounts payable!"

Gail nodded and read aloud. "Caucasian woman, mid-twenties, with a fractured arm and bruised ribs. Accident occurred while patient was out jogging by Clifton Park."

"At three o'clock in the morning? That's a 622 right there!"

Amid the scattered laughter in the conference room, Anne-Marie whispered to the nurse next to her, "622?"

"Danger to self or others," the nurse replied, not looking at her.

"Oh right." Anne-Marie underlined the words thickly, circling the phrase as if drawing a highway exit sign.

"Patient couldn't seem to stop crying . . . She was in physical pain, of course, but mixed with her crying was this singing."

"Real off-key, too," added Steve, the volunteer. "A nurse recognized it from some Italian opera."

"Which one?" Anne-Marie asked. Gail looked at her strangely, as if it were an odd, irrelevant question.

"I don't know, but the nurse said she was singing, *Death is good for me, Death is good for me, Death is good for me.*" The translation passed a collective "oh" along the table, a few half-suppressed laughs.

"Bingo," said a volunteer. "Then the car accident—"

"Is down as a suicide attempt."

"Are you sure?" asked an intern. "Not organic damage from the accident itself?"

"Patient wouldn't cooperate with a neuro exam, but they did get a drip into her and took a CAT scan. It came up negative, no brain or spinal cord injuries. So they sent her here, with a 21-day certification—long enough for us to take a look at her."

"How do we plan on learning who she is?"

Gail sighed. "Police have taken a description; they'll try to match it with missing-persons reports."

"Oh great—in summertime, how long's it gonna take for some student to get reported missing?" The head nurse shook her head. "Meantime, why Lucy instead of Jane?"

"Because when they asked, the only name she kept saying was 'Lucia,' over and over."

"Could she be Italian, some immigrant?" A student nurse with long legs and large gestures, his Louisiana origins betrayed by his "Eye-talian."

"No. Dan Kepler's her doctor here, and he says she's as American as you or I. Speech—" Gail squinted to read the admission report. "God, Kepler's handwriting—speech is bizarre, dissociative: neologisms, clang formations, the works. Prelim diagnosis is schizoaffective or schizophreniform disorder." The air conditioner stopped, having brought the room to its desired coldness: her voice was suddenly loud in the silence.

Anne-Marie was still getting down the three phrases when an intern asked, "Treatment plan?" Everyone at the table seemed to lean forward at the question.

"To start: Trilafon, 500 mg t.i.d. and Prozac, 200 mg, b.i.d. Level D for now; she's pretty low-functioning but we can try her in some very simple groups."

"Like what?" asked Anne-Marie.

Gail turned to the hospital's newest staff member, noting to herself to assign her only to female patients for a while: the young redhead was short and a little too curvy. "The most logical, of course, would be to invite her to our weekly sing-alongs." Gail's smile turned elfin. "If she'll consent to sing along with the rest of us." Anne-Marie nodded her thanks, writing more quickly.

"So the state's paying for all this?" The head nurse's voice was skeptical. "Some student from out of town?"

"At least until we find some family for her." Gail sighed and turned the page in her binder. "Onward, my friends . . . it looks like it's gonna be a long week."

Anne-Marie took a deep breath, while all around her briefcases closed, chairs were pushed back from the table. The laser printer from the office next door began to churn out pages, a soft whoosh! the only response to Gail's words.

"My eyes are blackened by the punch of sleeplessness." Lucy Doe's words were soft, blotted by the noise in the corridor. "I toss . . . on the couch of separation."

Chatham Hall, the locked unit, had once been a boys' dorm. Its hallways were cloaked in patients' voices, shouting over the TV in the dayroom, and soft imprecations from the nurses.

Anne-Marie Krieger stood shyly, uncomprehending, in the doorway of Lucy Doe's room, facing the former "singing jogger." She moved closer to the tall, angular patient lying on her back, one leg hanging over the edge of the bed, her left arm rigid in a cast from wrist to just above the elbow. Through the thin T-shirt, her ribs were clearly visible. Lucy looked back up at Anne-Marie, singing softly under her breath; her gray-blue eyes were both fatigued and questioning, some sort of private plea.

Anne-Marie felt clumsy clutching her legal pad, a pen, and a copy of one of the intake questionnaires. "I'm sorry you haven't been able to sleep, Lucy . . . do you remember meeting me yesterday? I'm Anne-Marie." When Lucy gave no reply she continued, "I'm kinda new here—so they thought they'd let me meet you and do some of the nurses' work for them. Is it okay if I ask a few questions?"

She had to bend to hear the other woman's reply, and almost missed it. "You can," Lucy sighed. "You or anyone at all can."

Anne-Marie sat shyly and opened the questionnaire. "These are questions to help us figure out how to help you get better," she read aloud from the prepared script. Then she looked down at the patient and took another deep breath. "Could you sit up for me?"

The girl pulled herself up, slowly, grimacing. The plea was still there, in her eyes, in the tentative hunch in her shoulders. She spoke slowly, her eyes scanning Anne-Marie's face. "Help me, help me, so that's your mission." Dark cynicism in the soft murmur, "Talk of molniacs' manias and missions for mades!"

"I'm sure we can help you," Anne-Marie heard her mouth say, before she saw the young woman's hands held tightly to the bedframe. "Don't be scared," she said, whether to Lucy or herself she wasn't sure. "Listen, it's up to you—if you don't feel well enough for this right now, I can come back later."

The young woman sighed. "And tomorrow and tomorrow and tomorrow." She motioned to Anne-Marie to come closer, as if she were disclosing a secret, and looked very carefully and directly into the social worker's eyes. She was still asking, still pleading, but her request had grown in intensity, become all-encompassing. "Listen. What can't be coded can be decoded, if your eye seizes what no eye ere grieved for." Anne-Marie wished she could do it, wished she could decode Lucy's song.

Instead, she noted those words as "fractured speech," using the COMMENTS space on the form's third page. Then she flipped to the beginning, feeling a little foolish. "In doing daily activities," she read aloud, "do you have difficulty with any of the following aspects of task performance—now here's a list."

Lucy sighed, and sat up straighter; no longer pleading, she seemed simply to be observing.

"Attention span, concentration?"

Lucy Doe shook her head, then lowered it to her chest and began to move it in a slow circle, a yogi stretching before a sun salutation. She reversed the direction, her eyes closed.

"Following directions?"

She opened her eyes and shrugged, a quick gesture that then repeated in another stretch—a slower, elongated lifting of both shoulders. She was singing again: Anne-Marie tried to screen out the TV noise from the dayroom next door, recognizing a few of the Italian words: "questa vita disperata." She scribbled on the last page of the form, *desperate life?*

At the next item, Anne-Marie had to fight the urge to put the form in her pocket and go away. "Task planning and organization?" At Lucy's blank stare she elaborated, raising her voice over the girl's song. "Do you have trouble deciding when to do what you need to do?"

As if on cue the door opened and a nurse entered, followed by Gail Ryan. The nurse held a small cup of water, two tablets and two capsules. "Should I come back?" she asked Anne-Marie. Anne-Marie looked at Gail, who waved her on with a big smile.

"No, no, go ahead." The words in her own voice seemed to come from somewhere else.

Lucy took the pills into her hand and looked at them, holding her hand to the light so that the blue gelatin capsules glistened. The capsules were nearly the same shade of blue as the walls of the room, both lightening her eyes. "C'mon honey," the nurse said in her bright voice, "bottoms up." "They might make you feel a lot better," Gail added.

"What are they?" Lucy asked. "Thorazine?"

Anne-Marie was startled; *Familiarity with meds: previous*

hospitalizations? While Anne-Marie wrote, Gail squatted by the girl's upraised palm. "Those two are Trilafon," she said brightly, "they're sort of like Thorazine. The other two are Prozac. Because you've been so sad."

Lucy Doe closed her eyes as she took the pills, her eyelashes casting black strokes against her creamy skin. "Ti abbracio, Lucia," a half-whispered prayer.

Anne-Marie took a deep breath. "Who is Lucia? Can I find her for you?" Behind her Gail smiled hugely, sat in a chair in one corner of the room.

When Lucy opened her eyes, she looked up, beyond Anne-Marie, and met Gail's eyes: her voice was playful, challenging. "Look around you . . . we are all Lucia."

"Really?" Anne-Marie wrote in her notepad, huge question marks curling the red lines of the margins on yellow paper. "Why do you say that, Lucy?"

Lucy shrugged. "Annie died the other day," she said, as if that explained what she meant.

Anne-Marie looked at her notes before she persisted, her words slow, measured. "So . . . were you Annie, and now you're Lucia?"

Lucy Doe smiled; her manner had changed markedly, as if the Prozac were taking instantaneous effect. She tossed her head, as if her razor-short hair were instead a mane. "According to recent rumors," she declared, "I'm the insufficiently malestimated notes-natcher. I'm Shem the Penman!"

Anne-Marie shook her head. "I'll stick to Lucy for right now, okay?" Under COMMENTS she wrote: *Gender confusion? Multiple personality disorder?* She looked down at the form, wondering if she should bother to try to complete it: she looked over at Gail and saw her supervisor nod. "I was asking if you had trouble managing your time."

"Of course not, my deepseep darling," Lucy's voice now lilting, the quick trill of a flute. "You do it for me! You know, *Take this pill, It's breakfast time.*"

9

"I mean outside the hospital. Before you came here."

Lucy closed her eyes again and was still for so long that Anne-Marie feared she had lost her; when she spoke her voice was younger, a wounded child. "That's up to them, isn't it?"

"Up to who, Lucy?" Anne-Marie saw Gail shake her head: those questions were for psychiatrists.

"My mother and father, of course. Time we started: train won't wait. Going to London to get married." She opened her eyes and began to chant, tears in her throat. "Woo me, win me, wed me, ah weary me!"

On her way out, Gail gestured for Anne-Marie to skip to the last page of the questionnaire. Anne-Marie looked down: of course, this was the answer they were all waiting for. "Lucy, before you came here, where did you live? And with whom?"

Lucy Doe lay back on her bed, fixing on the ceiling again: this time the answer came from deep in her throat, the voice of a French café singer at two in the morning. "Boulevard Raspail, number two, Paris, France. Square Robiac. Zurich. Back to Paris . . . Rue Galilee." She turned on her side and looked at the floor, her words slower. "Nyon, at Les Rives des Prangins. Ivry, near the Bois de Vincennes." Anne-Marie wrote furiously, dredging up her undergraduate French.

Then Lucy sat up, looking directly at Anne-Marie. "No! Try Ravenswood Castle, Scotland. Bray, Ireland." She pointed to the wall, as if there were a window to the outside world. "Baltiskeeamore." Then suddenly, angrily: "Boston, Mass."

Anne-Marie folded the assessment form, feeling stupid, useless. "Maybe we should try this another time, Lucy. It's been very nice meeting you."

Back in the corridors Anne-Marie breathed shallowly, still unused to the ward-smell of sweetened ammonia, disinfectant masking excretions. Gail was waiting for her; a cacophony of voices swirled through the hallway that separated the dayroom and the nurse's station. A dramatic, childish moan grew louder as Anne-Marie passed, coming from a slight woman who looked no older than seventeen. Gail gestured to keep moving, until the girl pulled on her blouse.

"Shana, is there something I can do for you?" Gail asked.

Shana stopped moaning and said in a high-pitched wheedle, "My baby."

"Your baby's safe, Shana."

"My baby's birthday. Today!" Her voice singsong, suddenly cheerful.

"Is it really? How old is she?"

"Two!" The eyes huge, the smile revealing perfect teeth.

"She's two today? That's exciting!"

"Yes, two." She pointed at Gail's eyes. "And two eyes. And two legs. And two thighs. And . . . Tuesday!"

"It's Friday, Shana. And Anne-Marie and I have to go now. I hope you're coming to art today. After lunch."

Leaving was an exit into suffocating humidity: Gail fanned herself as she turned to Anne-Marie. "Boy, is it silly season at Chatham today."

Anne-Marie was silent, pulling her hair behind her.

"I haven't seen Shana's little-girl act in a while—and my lord, is Lucy Doe grossly psychotic! Even with all that Trilafon." Gail fanned herself with the papers she carried.

After Anne-Marie finished pinning up her hair, she turned to her supervisor, her voice low. "When does she get assigned a psychiatrist?"

"Should be soon, maybe today. Listen I gotta sprint, there's a meeting about the Harvest Picnic. I'll see you back there."

Anne-Marie watched Gail move down the path, the senior therapist walking briskly, as if she were in some other climate. Then Anne-Marie walked more slowly among the weeping willow trees, letting the humid air envelop her, an invisible bath washing the locked ward from her skin.

The patients' lunchroom was in the basement of the main building, a few floors below the conference room and directly underneath the main therapy rooms. Patients' chatter mingled with the noise of lunch carts; the radio was tuned to "soft favorites," Shana dancing in her seat to the sound of the Supremes.

It was Steve, the hefty volunteer, who escorted Lucy Doe into the lunchroom, lagging behind the others from Chatham. The mingled chatter of the lunchroom stopped dead as they walked in, the new patient following slowly, holding her left arm in its cast like a heavy foreign object.

"Sit here! By me, by me," Shana cooed.

Lucy Doe's appearance at the lunchroom was brief, that first day: as Steve lifted the tray and began to cut her meat, her chest began to heave. In a seeming instant they were on their way out, as if they had never arrived. "It's okay Lucy, do you need a bathroom before I take you back?" As soon as they were out of earshot, the review of the new arrival began.

Frank the sociologist was impressed by her height, while others favored her figure or her shining (if messy) short black hair. Soft voices and loud, slow comments and fast, theme and counterpoint to the sound of lunch trays being taken away.

"She's so young, so pretty, I'm surprised to see somebody like that here."

"Too skinny . . . I bet she has AIDS."

"No, her color's too good. Remember Fred, how pale he was? And those leg muscles! The singing jogger, remember?"

"A Jane Doe, did you hear? Like on TV."

"Jane Doe, with skin like snow," Shana rhymed, her voice close to an actual song. "Lucy Doe, who I don't know." Shana's brown eyes were soft, her smile always on the verge of a grin; she stood up cheerfully as the volunteers came to return the groups to their respective wards or therapy appointments.

"Give Lucy Doe my love," Frank said to Shana, as he was led to his psychiatrist.

"Lucy Doe-oh," Shana sang, echoing the radio. "Lucy Doe-oh, where did our love go?"

The first two times a resident came to evaluate Lucy Doe, she was throwing up: first at the foot of her bed, then into the toilet, Steve holding her head. These incidents produced one line on her chart: Trilafon contraindicated. New regime: Prolix 1000 mg. t.i.d. and Haldol 50 mg. b.i.d. . . . watch Prozac.

The third time she was sitting up, staring at the cast on her left arm. She didn't meet the doctor's eyes, but he was used to that.

"Lucy, I'm going to ask you to do some things so we can make sure your nerves are working. We're wondering if maybe you're feeling bad because your head got hurt in the accident." He spoke slowly, as to a child. No response.

"Come on, Lucy. This won't be hard, I promise."

"This is hard." The blue eyes closed, and Lucy's slim, long-fingered hand was at the back of her neck.

"Do you mean a squeezing feeling, Lucy?" No answer, but the young medical student wrote on a clean new page, *dystonic reaction?* While he was writing, Lucy stood up, her motions suddenly quick, determined. "Lucy, where are you going?"

"Loonely in me me loneness," she sang out, not looking at him, "I am passing out." Her voice rose as she exited the room, calling out, "Nuee! Nuee!"

Entry in chart: *Mania, resistance to evaluation. Rec. Li 40 mg. b.i.d.* The next day, there was a new pill in the nurse's hand; after that, the new girl slowed down, and slept even more.

Three days later the police officer arrived, a quiet, small-boned woman in plain clothes walking softly as a spy into Lucy Doe's room. The patient's cast had been removed, arm now in a sling; she flipped through a women's magazine, staring as if struggling to focus her eyes. Before saying a word, the police officer took out a small camera and clicked the shutter, one, two, three times.

Lucy's hand went to her face at the first click, shading one eye for the second and third shots. As the officer sat in a chair near hers, together they looked at glossy models playacting, laughing, and women in wisps of silk kissing men in tuxedos. "You're thinner than they are," the police officer observed.

Lucy ignored her, reaching across her for a sip of water as if the other woman did not exist.

After a few moments, the officer tried again. "My name is Nancy Hamilton. How's your arm?"

As if she'd heard the word "arm" from the soap opera next door, Lucy Doe reached over and massaged her wrist, absentmindedly, leaving the magazine in her lap.

Deep breath. "Where'd you get those clothes?" pointing to her baggy jeans and Radcliffe T-shirt. No response.

Finally, Officer Hamilton reached over and placed one hand over the magazine, looking straight into Lucy Doe's eyes. "Lucy. I'm trying to talk to you."

Lucy Doe looked at her blankly, then pointed to the camera. "Alis, alas, you broke the glass!" she said softly, looking at the camera lens. "But ours," she shook her head, "ours is a mystery of pain."

"I'm just trying to help," said Nancy Hamilton. "So your family can find you. Wouldn't you like that?"

The eyes widened, met the policewoman's eyes for the first time. "My father," Lucy said slowly and distinctly, "had blood in his eyes. I cannot but choose to weep, to think they should lay him in the cold ground."

"Lucy? Do you mean that your father's dead?"

Lucy Doe did not reply, instead closing her eyes. Then she began to sing, "Those are pearls that were his eyes. . . ."

The police officer waited patiently, but the singing did not stop.

When an aide came to get the patient for lunch, he said, "Oh, she's at that again.

Good luck, ma'am, she can keep it up for hours."

Hamilton looked at her watch, shaking her head. "I'm running forty-five minutes late as it is . . . Listen, tell them I'll come back when you guys have managed to run a full psychiatric evaluation. I need more to go on than this mumbo jumbo." She handed him a slip of printed legal instructions, stapled to the green sheet Gail Ryan had given her. "Meantime we'll spread her picture around, now that school's starting again. You got that?"

As Officer Hamilton's steps faded down the hall, Lucy continued her song, the melody simple, almost liturgical despite the secular words.

Full fathom five thy father lies
Of his bones are coral made;
Those are pearls that were his eyes.
Nothing of him doth fade
But doth suffer a sea-change
Into something rich and strange, into something rich and
strange.

Five days of slumber and singing, five days in which Lucy Doe seemed either not to notice people speaking to her or to examine them with unnatural concentration, as if she were trying to recognize a half-remembered friend. Sometimes she would stand and run her fingers lightly over the edges of the furniture, trace the walls with her slim fingertips, hold the cool surface of a glass to her cheek before she drank gratefully, washing down her medications with the relief of an addict. Then she would return to bed, to sleep with her head under blankets, defying both heat and the air conditioning.

On the sixth day the singing jogger got out of bed and went to the nurses' station, surprising them by saying a normal sentence. "I want pen and paper," she said, as if she talked like that every day.

The nurse's eyes widened. "I'll ask Nurse Diamond."

"We don't get pens," Frank called from the pay phone. "They're afraid you'll stick the tip through your wrist or up your nose into your brain or something."

A few minutes later Gail arrived, red binder under one arm. "Lucy, it's so nice to see you feeling better! And it sounds like you're finally ready to talk to your doctor—don't you think?"

Daniel Kepler, the youngest of the staff psychiatrists, dressed like an extra in the recent movie Wall Street: sandy hair slicked back, his tie a startling red. When he arrived at Lucy Doe's room, she was absorbed with the notepad in her lap, her reward for agreeing to see him. When he finally got her attention, he asked her to put the pads aside; instead, she agreed to let them lay still in her lap.

The doctor asked Lucy to touch his finger, then her nose, then his finger, then her nose: then he watched the young woman's eyes follow his finger as he traced a wide arc in the air. Lucy laughed.

"What's so funny?"

"The music. Mozart. I think, it's in two. *Zauberflöte?*" Kepler turned and wrote in his own small spiral notebook.

She laughed harder. "No, no! You're a conductor, get it?"

Kepler wrote *all neurological signs normal, but tangential thought patterns.* She responded docilely when asked about the food, the temperature of the ward. Then the doctor risked it, asked her name, using the same smooth voice, smooth enough for a TV commercial.

Lucy shook her head. "I told you—Shem the Penman. You'd better find some more abcedminded practitioner to talk to me—No, that's a-b-c-e-d minded, there, there now you've got it, scrib-bledehobble!"

Kepler was writing quickly, in large aggressive strokes. *MPD with schizoid features?*

When he left, she turned again to her large drawing tablet,

writing with the long, very soft pencil they had given her—more like a crayon or pastel stick.

A quick rap on the door and Gail Ryan entered, not waiting for a response. "Coming to group this afternoon?" Her voice was energetic, verging on frantic.

Lucy's back stiffened. "Will we sing?"

Gail's smile was a wide, high-caffeine grin. "No, this morning we're just going to do a little movement." She waved both arms, to demonstrate.

"I used to love gymnastics," Lucy said. "I could do the long jump."

By the end of the sentence she was lying down and whispering the word "jump."

Gail sat at the edge of Lucy's bed. "If you come," she coaxed, "I'm sure you'll have a wonderful time."

Lucy opened her eyes abruptly, this time speaking with a girlish lilt. "My teacher danced better than Isadora Duncan herself," she said. She sat up with a deep sigh, running her fingers through her hair. "And Samuel Beckett said I danced very well."

Gail's report the next morning held a barely-suppressed laugh. "So she gets up in the middle of group," the therapist stood to demonstrate. "She kind of leans back, one arm arching around, the other one's in the sling, it was ridiculous, she kept trying to demonstrate some special dance."

"What did she say?" Anne-Marie asked, but she was interrupted by the dance therapy intern saying, "She also got to show off her French . . . she kept saying over and over, *Rythme et Couleur*, 'rhythm and color.' Her accent was pretty good."

"Italian, French, what next?" Gail's smile was faint, tolerant. "What a mess, what with Frank Morrison doing his Motown thing again . . ."

Steve grimaced. "God, that man . . . is he cheeking his meds, or what?"

The head nurse sighed. "We think so. That's why Russell ordered the blood tests."

"You mean not swallowing?" asked Anne-Marie, yielding to the knowing smiles all around her.

"I'm curious to see how his blood levels turn out," Gail said. "As for Lucy Doe . . . so much for her so-called improvement."

"What can we do to help her?" Anne-Marie's voice sweet inquiry, her poised pen peeking from between her red curls.

Gail looked back down at the binder. "Kepler might up her lithium. At least we seem to have stopped the crying, if not all the singing."

"What do we do if the 21 days runs out and we still haven't found out who she is?"

"She walks, Ms. Krieger. Into the streets, unless she tries to hurt herself—then we can try to find a judge to let us keep her." Gail's voice was stressed suddenly, a warrior preparing for a fight. "Speaking of which, did anybody here actually see Frank Morrison smash that lamp against the dayroom wall?"

"I know this one." Frank Morrison led Lucy Doe into the dayroom, the former jogger following on slow, halting steps; he gestured for her to sit down on the sofa near the door, before he sat beside her. "I saw this movie with my wife, when I had one."

"Well, don't tell us the ending, s'il-vous-plait." Karen Hightower, a tall, elegantly dressed woman with beautifully applied eye makeup, let Shana comb her dyed red hair as they watched. Ever since her admission, Karen had guaranteed a steady stream of rented films at Chatham; she seemed to regard her stay at Pearlstone as a sort of extended restful vacation, while she recovered from the cuts on her wrists. On screen the Manhattan skyline appeared in gracious, black-and-white silhouette, the music of George Gershwin swelling below it.

"Boy, Lucy, you sure don't like the lunch around here," said Shana. "You eat anything besides the lettuce?"

"I eat the air, promise-crammed," Lucy replied, slumping back in her seat. The television showed Woody Allen's familiar, morose face in black and white shadow, his shoulders hunched as talked to a teenage girl.

"Oh no, I didn't mean to rent this one," Karen exclaimed. "I cannot watch that man any more—not especially since le scandale," an exaggerated French accent. She left abruptly, trailing the scent of Obsession behind her.

"How old is that girl? Thirteen?" Shana always talked through movies; everyone was used to it. They watched Woody Allen walk through Central Park with the young woman, her dark eyes alive below strong black eyebrows. Shana pointed to the screen, and then to Lucy Doe. "Look at them eyebrows! Like yours, Lucy, like yours!"

Lucy Doe did not reply: her eyes filled, still fixed on the screen. She whispered something, but it was obscured by *Rhapsody in Blue*, so that out of her mouth instead seemed to come a low, throbbing piano melody.

"I never been to New York," Shana continued. "How about you?"

"Ha! Been there?" Frank laughed. "I would venture to guess that a graceful young ladylike our Lucy usually lives in New York . . . she certainly doesn't seem bred in this burg. Am I right, Miss Doe?"

She nodded, closing her eyes; tears leaked out from under the black eyelashes. When she opened them again, the medication nurse was standing before her. "You want something to take these with?"

"Hey, can I have some?" Shana asked, loudly enough for several of the others to shush her. "C'mon Lucy, you know we're supposed to share."

Lucy received the pills in her palm, looking at them for a long moment before she took them and swallowed. She turned to Shana, her voice tight. "You cannot take from me anything that I will more willingly part withal . . . except my life, except my life, except my life," by the third repetition her voice was down to a whisper.

Frank watched as the nurse left, hurrying to unlock the door of a small side room, lined by shelves packed with thick binders. He turned to Lucy and whispered, "Hurry look, she's writing it in your chart! 'Quotes Shakespeare under stress.' No, she's probably writing 'suicidal ideation,' if I know them. They don't understand educated people."

Lucy ignored him, staring at the screen. After a while, her face slackened as the medication took effect, the pupils dilating till they seemed to fill her eyes.

"You lived there?" Shana pointed to a fancy brownstone, made dreamlike by the film's lighting. Then she looked at Dr. Kepler, who had just appeared behind Lucy's chair. "She lived in that fancy house!"

"Lucy," Dr. Kepler said, "can you come with me a minute, so we can talk?" He remained standing behind her, but she kept her eyes fixed forward. "How are you today?"

Lucy Doe reached for her neck and squeezed it, still facing the screen.

"I can get you something for that, if you'll come talk to me."

"You don't have a choice," Frank explained. "They pretend you do, but you don't."

"Frank, please be quiet," Kepler said impatiently.

Lucy finally lifted her head to look at him. "Oh! It's you, the big white cat." Her voice soft, relaxed, almost dreamlike. "They said you were a doctor, but as long as you're a cat, that's different." She stood up, wobbling as if from the weight of the arm strapped to her chest, and followed him out of the dayroom.

. . .

Lucy Doe's room contained three neatly made beds, two of them vacant. Unlike most of the others', it contained not a single personal item, no photographs or flowers or clothes.

"How are you feeling today, Lucy?"

Lucy sat on the edge of her bed, her eyes closed; when she winced, Kepler called to a nurse, "Benadryl and orange juice, please . . . This should help your neck, Lucy. How's your rib?"

She lifted her shirt and showed him: the body still unnaturally thin, nipples and skin stretched tight over the ribs. She saw his eyes widen, and explained, "When you're bled till you're bone, it crops out in your flesh."

"Is that why you got so thin, Lucy? Because you felt bad?" The secondary diagnosis of anorexia was no longer a question mark on Lucy Doe's chart.

The singing jogger covered her face with her hands, fingertips buried in her hair; she closed her eyes, like a three-year-old hoping it would make him disappear. Kepler watched her from one of the empty beds until the nurse arrived with the Benadryl; then he tapped one of her knees, watched as she drank the orange juice.

Kepler sighed. "Listen to me, Lucy."

Lucy Doe responded by leaning forward, her blue eyes focused on his.

"All I want, Lucy," Kepler said, "is to help you get better. That's the only reason I'm sitting here. But I can't help you if you won't talk to me or cooperate in groups."

"Groups?" Lucy spat the word, standing unsteadily. "They made me stop! Just when I was remembering *Rythme et Couleur!*"

Kepler was careful with the French words. "Rythme? Couleur?"

"I cried a month of tears when I had to leave, you know."

Kepler's right hand twitched, preparing his ballpoint pen. "Then why did you? Why did you leave *Rythme et Couleur?*"

Lucy looked down at the floor. "Babbo needed me."

"Babbo? Who is that?"

21

"My father, the famous Irish writer."

Kepler finally opened his tiny spiral pad, writing furious short strokes. "What do other people call him, Lucy?"

"Sender: Boston, Mass." The girl spat the words as if in heresy or rage. She extended her leg and bent over it, a classic runner's stretch. "What is his name, what is your name, the cool cool water of her Christian name. Dick and Nicole equals 'Dicole.'"

"Who's Nicole, Lucy? Is that you?"

"Oh for God's sake, of course it is. Nicole Diver, haven't you heard of us?" Lucy lay on her back, ignoring him.

Dr. Kepler sat up straight and wrote Nicole Diver on his legal pad. "Any other names I could use for you, Lucy?"

The silence was so long, he thought she had fallen asleep with her eyes open. Finally Lucy rolled over to face him, and whispered, "Christine Beauchamp."

"Can you spell that?"

"Issy-la-Chappelle. Sally. Ophelia. Nuvoletta. Shem the Penman." The chant a song, breathy like her opera excerpts: then her eyes did close, and she retreated from him entirely, her body flaccid, her fingertips brushing the gray steel of the bedframe.

The silence was filled by Gershwin music punctuated by Shana's loud voice; by the competing Mozart coming from the rear dayroom; by Karen Hightower, crying in her private therapy session next door.

Kepler could feel Karen's doctor waiting it out, just as he himself was doing; but the cries just escalated until they seemed to fill the room, became the cries that could no longer come from the catatonic Lucy.

"Nicole Diver! That's F. Scott Fitzgerald," Anne-Marie exclaimed the next morning. "*Tender is the Night*. Maybe he's the famous Irish writer?"

The air was thick with strong coffee: these heavy-caffeine briefings always echoed the students recovering from partying or studying, older staff from trying to juggle multiple responsibilities. Anne-Marie stuck chastely to her apple juice, sipped delicately with a straw from a glass bottle.

"Interesting," Gail wrote a quick note in the margin of the daily report. "But they already checked, and there's neither a Nicole Diver or Christine Beauchamp in the phone book or registered at any of the universities . . . Probably Christine's just another name, she's using, for one of her personalities."

"What a mess!" the head nurse exclaimed. "I've never heard of an MPD with such strong psychotic symptomatology—as if one or two of the selves were schizophrenic."

"I know, this is the case of the dancing diagnosis." Gail drained her coffee mug in one quick gesture. "There's even suspicion of malingering—that for her own reasons, she's somehow faking the whole thing."

"Faking catatonia?"

Gail sighed. "Sounds unlikely to me, too. But until we get a diagnosis, there's a lot that can't happen . . . So Kepler has suggested lowering the Prolixin and the lithium, and see what happens; I think the judge will give us another sixty days with her, perhaps under the 'gravely disabled' clause. I certainly wouldn't trust her to care for herself."

"Then what?" asked Clay Jones, a newer nurse.

"Well, we finally got the evoked potentials test scheduled—that's often a more definitive diagnostic for schizophrenia. Meanwhile, needless to say—" Gail made a dismissive gesture—"she's down at Level E." She wrote Lucy Doe's name in one of the intersecting triangles that made up the daily chart, assigning each patient to the right group—or, as in Lucy's case, consigning the lowest functioning to some never-never land of To Be Watched Carefully.

. . .

Karen Hightower ran a carefully polished fingernail over the croissant on her breakfast tray. "I didn't order a croissant," she said loudly in a faux French accent. "I would never order something so high in fat. What are you all trying to do to me?"

The dietary aide pointed to the menu sitting next to the tray. "That looks like you're writing. See, you wrote no butter. And there it is, you circled croissant."

"Well, I never." Karen folded her arms. "You don't even make good croissant around here. I'd more readily order something like— oh, an ice cream sundae!" She pointed to the mural on the wall just above Lucy Doe's head, a huge collage made by the "low-functioning" group during art class. Lucy Doe ignored them both, head bent to her tray.

Across the top was the word "Summer," above four or five distinct groups of clippings from magazines: balloons, rock and roll stars, ice cream sundaes, and many, many fast cars and women— beach bunnies from lemonade ads, elegant fashion models cut out from Vogue or Elle. Next to one of the models, three words collaged together: "KEEPING Magnanimous Women.

"Awful quiet in here this morning," Frank Morrison said as he walked in. "Where's Shana?"

"She's in seclusion," said the dietary aide.

"In seclusion? Since when?" Frank demanded.

"Last night. And don't ask me why, I couldn't tell you even if I knew."

"Seclusion?" Lucy Doe's eyes widened. "Where is that?"

Frank laughed. "Now there's a hospital virgin. If Shana were here, she'd be dancing around the room singing, she doesn't know about seclusion, she doesn't know about seclusion!"

Karen Hightower spoke softly. "Honey, seclusion is a little room with soft walls and a mattress on the floor. They put you there if you do something like try to climb out the window, make the nurses angry." She stretched an arm to the ceiling. "It's a good place for a nap, anyway."

"I'm gonna ask a nurse why she was put in there," Frank said. "If all she did was talk back to a doctor, it's a violation of patients' rights and I'll talk to my lawyer. She's coming this afternoon anyway, to talk about my lawsuit against the University of Maryland." He leaned against the mural, his elbow touching two phrases collaged together: "TRUE BELIEVER to make it on their own."

After breakfast, Frank and Karen stopped at the nurses' station as they entered Chatham, while the others, including Lucy Doe, went to the dayroom and watched TV, pretending not to listen.

"When did she go in? Last night?" The nurse looked puzzled. "I just came on, let me check." She read the chart carefully, then saying in a neutral tone, "Sometimes Shana gets overexcited. She doesn't know how to be quiet. And she . . . makes sexual overtures when it's quite inappropriate. So we think it's better for her to be somewhere where she can just calm down. "Ah," said Karen, "I see."

"Quite inappropriate," Frank repeated the phrase loudly. "Isn't that what you call hypersexual? I got called that last time I was in here, just for kissing that Italian girl at the end of the hall." His voice, trained for teaching, filled the hallway despite Karen's best efforts to shush him. In the dayroom, Lucy Doe was quietly hyperventilating, her crutch held-close like a long-missed child.

After the nurse had put away her charts, Frank went off to call his lawyer; Karen went into the dayroom, where Lucy Doe had started to cry. "Are you okay, Lucy? Feeling sorry for Shana?"

Lucy Doe lifted her head and stared at the nurse, her lips moving but forming no words.

Karen tried again. "It's one of the things they just don't allow here—they don't let you fall in love." She tossed her head, with a big dramatic sigh; Lucy Doe cried harder, then began to speak in a singsong chant.

"Why, why, why . . . Weh, oh weh! I'se so silly to be flowing but I no canna stay!" She drew her knees to her chin and kept sobbing. Karen stroked her hair, gently.

"No touching, Karen, remember?" The nurse spoke quietly, but with the firmness of an elementary-school teacher. "You know that by now."

Karen's eyes widened; she stood up in a huff and strode out of the room. "They won't even let me comfort a girl in love!" The nurse didn't follow her; instead, she squatted to face Lucy Doe.

"Lucy?" the nurse tried softly, tentatively. Then, remembering the morning briefings, she tried, "Nicole? Christine? Shem?"

That got the girl laughing, her head up. "Lucia," she said, still crying. "Only Lucia, her little breaths and her climbing color." Then she started to sing, this time leaving opera behind for a lower register, the soft raspy moaning sound of the blues.

"Okay here we go, everybody's favorite TV show: the squares." The doctor had dyed blonde hair and big doe eyes. Her nameplate said MERCEDES SOTO, M.D.; her heavily accented voice was soothing and merry at the same time, like that of a kindergarten teacher. Behind her head a window showed North Charles Street, black behemoth buses sharing a street with automobiles and slim racer bicycles: Baltimore, a small urban hospital.

Lucy Doe sat up straight, watching the street instead of the TV screen. A technician was busy attaching electrodes to her head, massaging her scalp with rough white adhesive. He made her turn her head to the attach the last one; Lucy reached up and traced the thin, curly wires, delicate as angel-hair pasta. "Why?"

"Just a test, your doctor requested it a long time ago," Dr. Soto stretched "long" with one slow, sensuous vowel. "A very popular machine, everybody in town want to get into this show. Now just look ahead, think about the weather or something, relax . . . no, no, no,, don't look at the weather, watch the TV."

On the screen a hyperexcited chessboard: dozens of tiny squares in neat little rows, greyish-black and bluish white. Lucy lapsed into silence, the room filling with street sounds, lumbering buses and the conversations of undergraduates. The only sound in the room was the hysterical scratching of the EEG needle, as it recorded the girl's neurologic response to the images.

Finally, Lucy sat up straight, pointed to the machine. "I know! It's the sixth sealed chapter of the going forth by black!" She turned, pointing to the yards of paper pouring onto the floor. "Yes?"

Soto laughed. "No, just a little old squiggle. Just a few more minutes."

As if to amuse herself, the girl began to sing: the singing jogger's soprano was audible only as a high-pitched extension of the "hmmm" of the machine.

> *Ah! Spargi d'amaro pianto, il mio terrestre velo*
> *Ah! ch'io spiri accanto a te . . . appresso a te!*

Each Ah! line sparked a string of attempted cadenzas, dwindling into air as they surpassed her range. Mercedes Soto listened, distracted momentarily by the half-understood words, punctuated by hiccups and gasps for breath. She scribbled notes on the bottom of the form.

Soto turned off the TV. "Show's over! Now the noises." She put a pair of earphones on Lucy Doe's head, with large rubber cups that nestled in her hair.

Lucy stopped singing. "They're too big," she said, pointing to the speakers. "We should use my Walkman. I run every day with its music . . . Bach or the blues."

Soto waited until the patient had finished crying before she turned up the sounds. Lucy Doe's eyes widened.

"Scratch scratch!" She smiled, for the first time. "Tin tin. Fin fin."

Soto smiled back. "I know, them little scratchy sounds drive you—" she bit down on the word "crazy" just as her patient continued her recitation.

"With regards from cinder Christinette!" Lucy bent and made

notes in her little notepad.

Soto checked the printouts. "Okay honey, you're done now. I'll call for someone to come get you."

In the van that took her back from Homewood Hospital, the girl kept her head down, singing and writing. Steve, who had accompanied her, looked down with interest. "What are you writing?" he asked.

She stopped singing to look up at him and say, "My nonday diary, what else? Perhaps someday you'll read it."

"Planning on publishing it?"

"No no no," Lucy shook her head. "But copies might end up in libraries, all over the world."

Steve had begun to keep his own notebook: he wrote a note to Kepler, *delusions of grandeur?*

When they got to Pearlstone, Steve led Lucy along the path toward Chatham. As he unlocked the door, three women were standing in a clump by the nurses' station, talking to Dr. Kepler. One was Nancy Hamilton, the police officer who had come to see Lucy a few times. The other two stared as they saw Lucy Doe enter, jerking a little with her cane, her chin-length hair still full of white adhesive.

Another woman was tall, nearly as thin as Lucy, in black Bermuda shorts, a loose black T-shirt and high-top laced black shoes. Her head was shaven, with an olive-complected scalp that matched her face and dark-lined eyes; she wore four earrings in one ear and large, carved ceramic African bracelets on each wrist. The other's long blonde hair was held back by a braid, her eyes alert behind oversized glasses.

Dr. Kepler was beside them, a half-suppressed smile on his lips. "Is that your roommate?" he asked the blonde woman, looking at Lucy Doe.

Lucy leaned against the wall, closing her eyes for a moment. When she opened them, she looked very, very tired. "Rachel," she said.

"Oh, Molly!" Rachel ran forward and hugged her, holding tight for a minute or two. "We've been so worried about you!" Lucy Doe —Molly—began to shake, soundlessly.

When they separated, Dr. Kepler approached the patient with a genuine smile. "Good afternoon, Molly O'Donnell," he said. "It's nice to finally meet you." He reached out his hand in greeting.

"You know me better than they do," Molly said slowly. "You know Lucia . . . you know Shem." It was then that she shouted, a sudden shock to all assembled, a wail that slammed against the corridor walls. "A hundred cares and a tithe of troubles and is there one who understands me?"

The energy in the shout seemed to exhaust her; a nurse came by, but Kepler waved her away, let the bald woman approach Molly with careful steps.

Rachel took a deep breath. "I've never heard James Joyce shouted like that. Her thesis in school—" She broke off and turned to her friend. "Felicia, do you have the Boston phone numbers?"

Felicia was still looking at Molly; she nodded, without turning her head. "I have Emma's number, anyway." She looked over at Dr. Kepler. "Can Molly and I talk privately for a moment?"

Kepler looked disapprovingly from Felicia's bald head to Molly's tearful face. "Of course," he said. "Molly, do you want to take Felicia into your room, or will the dayroom do?"

Molly raised an eyebrow and pointed at the dayroom, where Karen and the others were watching Wheel of Fortune; then she gestured to Felicia, pointing down the hall to her room. Rachel and Kepler followed at a discreet distance.

"So how long have you known Molly?" Kepler leaned against the wall, his Visined eyes betraying a lack of sleep.

"Lemme think . . . around this time last year, school was just getting started when she moved in." Rachel's eyes were focused on nothing, as if she could see that day she named. "I was happy to have another grad student in the house."

Kepler looked down at his notes, reflectively. "Studying James

Joyce," he said softly, as if to himself. "James Joyce, the famous Irish writer." Molly's words from last week echoed against the glass, bypassing Rachel entirely. "And Lucia was Joyce's daughter?"

Rachel nodded. "I can't believe you've been calling her Lucy—"She stopped as Felicia and Molly emerged from the room, Felicia's hand on Molly's shoulder.

"I want to take her home," Felicia said to Kepler. "That's legal, isn't it?"

"Do you want that, Molly?" Kepler asked. "Are you sure?"

Molly turned her eyes on Kepler, her laugh bitter. "Molly is gone . . . you know better, calling me Lucy Doe."

"Felicia!" Rachel went to Felicia's side, a stage whisper into her ear: "Shouldn't we wait until her family comes?"

"Who, her alcoholic mother?" Felicia's back was tense. "Who's gonna cast the first stone?"

"At least Emma," Rachel said. "Just a few more days. Do you want to be responsible if she gets hurt again?"

And it was then that they heard it: Molly's song, first just as a faint whisper, then growing larger until they could make out the words. "*Ah, mi togli, eterno Iddio, questa vita disperata, che la morte e un ben per me, si, la morte e un ben per me.*" Molly was no longer looking at any of them; she sang to the floor and the walls, the motes of sunlight making their way from the dayroom.

Felicia stared at the floor, its well-polished surface distorting her reflected face while elongating the African images on her bracelets. Then she looked from Rachel to Dr. Kepler. "Okay," she said in a low voice. "You win."

Usually, no one at Chatham took much notice of the sunrise—especially in the summer, when it occurred at five-thirty a.m., just when the nurses on midnight shift were at their most overtired. Sunrise always came too early for most of the patients, still under the influence of their nighttime meds.

The morning after she received her new ID bracelet, Molly O'Donnell left her room at five o'clock and went to the rear dayroom, turning the radio to classical music. The night nurse wrote in her chart, *Slept only 5 hours: li. level ok?*

Molly stood by the window, her fingertips touching the glass; one of the aides sat on the sofa nearby, watching the sun rise on the hospital grounds for, he thought, the first time.

Beyond the weeping willows and hospital buildings the Maryland hills did not roll so much as ripple gently, distant highways and housing tracts teasing the idea of ancient sculptures carved into the land. The main building had huge plate-glass windows, protected now by special double shatter-resistant surfaces that did not reflect the sunlight so much as diffuse it, spinning rose and gold into pale yellows.

When the sun had finally illuminated the hills, Molly turned from the window and looked at the floor, her body still, fingertips shaking. "What's the matter?" the aide asked. "It's beautiful, isn't it?"

"Where is she?" Molly asked.

"Where is who, Molly?"

"Lucia. I used to see her every morning, when I went running by the baseball stadium. Or by the water—the Inner Harbor, the Seine, swimming naked in the sea in Ireland. Where is she? I can help her, when she comes." She pulled out of her pocket the old strip of plastic cut from her wrist the afternoon before, the one that read DOE, LUCY. "See, this is hers."

Then she turned back to the window, crossed her arms and lay them against the glass, to rest her chin. The aide moved closer, in case she intended a violent move. But she was only staring, her eyes urgent, searching, as if she could somehow bring her lost Lucia right into the dayroom—or else herself cross through the woods directly to the baseball stadium, from there to swim in some rough, unnamed Irish sea.

Courting daylight in saving darkness

29 August 1990

A morning drenched in amber—and what a sea-change in my life!

Sea-change from that Purcell song in my Walkman, women singing Shakespeare: "Full fathom five thy father lies . . .' That's the verse I spoke at my father's funeral, death transfigured into beauty—which is, of course, what late summer feels like. Especially today, with amber-gold filling the bay window of my new room. And I just finished a new six-mile running route, the sun rising to Purcell's little chorale.

The new route speeds me through Baltimore's greenest like a first baseman celebrating a home run. Memorial Stadium, then up Loch Raven Boulevard into carefully groomed, middle-class Black neighborhoods before a sharp left at Northern Parkway, past shy, low-slung apartment complexes and an urban-renewal shopping mall. Ending with our mainest of all main streets, Charles Street, before two twists home to this mildly shabby row house, a place to let my muscles stretch and yawn.

As I was curving round the university, headed for home, my father's soft murmur in my mind: *you're getting there, Shem.*

The new route's as much a beginning as the pile of boxes from my basement apartment in Hampden. Though not as much as the transit from Boston, Mass. to New York to this small city by a huge yearning bay. More like my dissertation, patiently awaiting the first round of real work. *Yes, Will, I am getting there.*

After half a year I finally don't get lost any more, and I've seen all Baltimore's seasons: muddy/frozen winter streets fringed with white snow, spring's pale yellows, and the nearly-black green of summer—as well as this hesitant auburn autumn, a pale echo of the season's glory in Massachusetts and New York.

Yes, Will, your daughter has done what none of your other children thought was possible. I got the hell out of New York, away from Colin and the music scene and too much fine wine. I showed up in Baltimore, having gotten myself admitted to a doctoral program; I returned to a nearly-forgotten love, literature—and, inevitably, to your first and only love, James Joyce. When you died, I'm sure you thought I'd be first cello in some orchestra section by now, or carrying on the passionate love affair of a string quartet. How were you to know I'd leave music behind, except perhaps to sing a hesitant soprano?

But you of all people can't deny me the pleasure of James Joyce, you who introduced me to Ulysses at a tender age. And yesterday your old friend Ross Tilden, now my adviser, showed up for our meeting like the proverbial cat half-drowned in cream. "Well, Ms. O'Donnell, you asked for it—'Schizophrenic Thought and Speech from *Portrait* to *Finnegans Wake.*' Go for it, it's all yours." His tone always cool, but I know he was proud—I wouldn't be here at all without our chance encounter in Manhattan last summer.

"God," I said to him, "did you ever think I'd be here today, when you first met me? That 15-year-old kid, Will's water-carrier at Bloomsday?"

"I wouldn't have imagined you anywhere else," when he recognized me at the Plaza Theatre last July, fanning ourselves with *The New York Times* on an hour-and-a half movie line.

Of course, my topic—inspired by one of Carl Jung's observations about Joyce—is barely abstract enough for him. Tilden is one of those people who chose Joyce because his books (or "texts," excuse me) could be a complete escape from life, sort of like mathematics. You can tell by looking at him: lean, bespectacled, constantly wearing the same gray sweater (I'm convinced he has a closet full of them, all frayed at the bottom by some vicious laundromat).

Will would instead ask: Why so abstract? He, of course, doesn't know about Colin, about my failure as a musician and the mess of my life in New York. Will, this is about order out of chaos—about how Joyce made speech that might be seen as mad into an illumination of the human soul.

For that's what I love about this most obscure and difficult of writers. I love his three million charts and diagrams done to structure and explain *Ulysses*, the lists of sigla and cross-references that were his tools for *Finnegans Wake*. That's why my little library carrel is labeled: *How they succeeded by courting daylight in saving darkness, he who loves will see.*

That is what I love, and want to learn. I want to court daylight from now on; I've courted, created, endured enough chaos and darkness, leaving behind me a mess of a life at the ripe old age of twenty-five. I need to learn how to create the order in my life that Joyce that did in his work.

You're getting there, Shem, your private name for me confirming your private place in my heart. And your voice, Will, is conflating with Brahms and runner's high this morning to bring me to this place of peace, with the gold autumn light coming full strength through my window.

Now comes the scary part, of course: delivering. Starting, I suppose, with leaving this journal alone so that I can show up for my office hours. (Is there some fair creature who actually likes being a teaching assistant? Whose dream in life is to nurse perfumed undergraduates who get out of their Volvos just long enough for Tilden's Lit 120 course, in time for their med-school applications?)

After that run, I should shower. On the other hand, it's nearly eight o'clock, there may not be any hot water left: the students who come to see me may simply have to put up with a fragrant post-run instructor. Perhaps it will keep them away.

30 August

Actually, I got nearly three-quarters of the way through before I ran out of hot water. I hate cold showers, but as long as I'm going to keep my hair long, I need to nurse it against Baltimore humidity. My one vanity! I can almost sit on it now.

Then breakfast with the newspaper and Rachel, roomie and fellow doctoral wannabe. (Felicia, the artist roommate, was asleep— as far as I can figure out, she sleeps till noon most days, after nights of playing the most dreadful music right above my head. I have a feeling I'm going to want to ignore her.)

Rachel's in medieval history and dresses the part: long skirts and low-neckline blouses, her hair always one thick blond braid. Her topic is the fifteenth-century European witch-hunts, "the Catholic church sacrificing women on its altar." So far, we seem to get along—I tease her about dressing for the wrong century, she teases me on my fondness for Carl Jung. "You know why you love him," she said this morning. "He writes so beautifully, even when he doesn't know what the hell he's talking about."

"You just be careful," I toasted her with orange juice. "Without him I'd have no dissertation." *While the ordinary [schizophrenic] patient cannot help himself thinking and talking in such a way, Joyce has willed it and moreover developed it with all his creative forces.* C.G. Jung, 1930. In other words, Joyce's genius and self-discipline transmuted madness beyond itself, something beyond the capacity of one of Jung's most famous patients: Joyce's own daughter, Lucia.

"Are you going to write about Lucia?" If I hear that question one more time, I will probably go mad myself.

But I know I'm going to hear it today at yet another English Department reception, this time for our new Shakespearean, Gary diCesare, arrived after years at Grinnell. (Already a full professor, now he's endowed; he probably never has to worry about his job for the rest of his life, even if the rest of the place goes bankrupt.) So more bad wine and mediocre cheese, low-rent echo of Colin's symphony receptions; more of the same questions, from professors, grad students and the inevitable undergraduates, all asking the same fucking questions—like, am I going to write about the littlest Joyce, who spent the last forty years of her life in a mental hospital?

No thank you, no thank you. You can already fill a 747 with all the feminists and Foucault clones already hot on the job, claiming Lucia's failed dance career as evidence of suppressed genius. Myself, I'll stay away from the one who (as Jung himself said, after his fruitless attempt to treat her) drowned in the river into which her father was so gracefully diving. I'm already heartily sick of drowning.

Another question I'm sick of: "When did your father first tell you about James Joyce?" Over and over again I have to say, I don't remember. I think Will must have whispered his name in my infant ear and continued the story from then on—especially after I was allowed to enter his sacrosanct study, up in the attic of our Dorchester house.

James Augustus Joyce, Will's boy-soprano voice whispers to my memory. Born in Ireland, 1882. Left it forever in 1905 with a hotel waitress named Nora Barnacle, who bore two children long before he married her in 1935, in a "secret" wedding noted on London newspapers. Who he would love until he died, in 1941, of a perforated ulcer. Where they lived long imprinted on my tongue: Trieste, Zurich, Rome, and most of all that most blessed of all places and times, Paris in the 1920s and 1930s. Chased back to Zurich by World War II, to die on his least-favorite soil.

His work was Dr. Seuss to the O'Donnell clan: Our adventure stories drawn from *Ulysses*, Joyce's Odyssey retold in a multi-layered half dreamed Irish day in June; our adolescent rebel Stephen Dedalus from *Portrait of the Artist as a Young Man,* and our lullabies songs from that vertigo-ridden Irish dream *Finnegans Wake*, the world and the universe in trilingual puns and multiple allusions.

I was shocked at twelve when I found out that the nuns in my school didn't know about Stephen Dedalus. And I think Will was equally shocked; the protagonist of *Portrait of the Artist* was the true love of my father's life, or at least his work.

Then there's the inevitable "He must have wanted you to become a Joyce scholar, since he named you Molly."

No, il silly professore, he wanted me to be a musician. What I always say instead is "No, he got away with giving us all Joycean names. I have sisters named Anna and Emma, even a brother named Leopold."

"What? No brother named Stephen?" That's what Rosen, the department head, actually asked at the last such reception. I avoided the story of Stephen O'Donnell, my parents' firstborn, how some membrane over his lungs refused to burst at birth, denying him air and life. (I feel sometimes like mine burst only incompletely, since I spent the last six months with Colin feeling as though a balloon had expanded in my chest, preventing me from breathing properly.)

Instead, I said, "No, but there is a Shaun, straight out of *Finnegans Wake*." If Will could have gotten away with it he'd have named him Shem, but my mother would have cried, finding it unlucky somehow. Her Catholicism consists mainly of superstition, and she cries easily, even when she hasn't been drinking.

"Boy, your father would be proud of you now." Comments like that started even back at Barnard, the few "A" papers studded with

"If Will could only see this!" It's amazing how even those who spend most of their time burrowing into Beowulf or John Donne still remember Will O'Donnell, the tall, fragile figure at Modern Language Association conferences with the white cane and the high-pitched Irish voice.

Onward—the reception is at three o'clock and I still have at least two hours' worth of work: dissertation materials to my left, Lit 120 papers to my right. Being Will O'Donnell's daughter is, after all, a double-edged blessing: a golden girl is expected to do no wrong. And that includes getting that first round of essays graded and returned, in time for the students to figure out how to write a paper by the time the semester is over. God knows they haven't gotten a clue yet.

31 August

The anointed endowed diCesare had an entirely different take on this golden girl stuff, and what I inherited from my father.

"You sure know how to get what you want," he said, "but I guess I'd expect that from an O'Donnell."

He murmured it into my shoulder as if it were as much of a secret as my presence in his Bolton Hill apartment, the Courvoisier poured on my breasts, his beard tickling my pubic hair as he nuzzled between my legs. (His wife teaches chemistry at the University of New Hampshire; the photo shows a bosomy Italian with round John Lennon glasses. The chemistry between them must be fabulous—how else would a specialist in lithium compounds come together with a Shakespearean who made his reputation on disease imagery in Hamlet?)

Of course, Joyce was himself obsessed with Hamlet: mothers and sons, there's a whole chapter on it in Will's book.

"I'm going to have to start living Will down," I told Gary, in between bites of his neck.

"And how do you plan to do that?"

"Write some dreadful paper comparing Stephen Dedalus to Errol Flynn. Run naked down Charles Street. Shoot a president. Something to lower these artificially raised expectations."

Gary looked up then. "Oh, you were named well," he teased, "you Molly Bloom. You'll do what you want no matter what." As if to prove him right, I made love to him again.

I think we've fallen into something that will work, here—no promises, no dreams of a future, no Colin-esque fits of temper; just warmth, to get him to the weekend and me through my dissertation without either of us dying of sexual frustration. (Physically he's a totally unusual type for me: a sort of a hippie teddy-bear, big around the middle and with a ponytail hidden under his collar for academic meetings.) The sex was relaxed, pleasurable, nothing stratospheric—no emotional heights, but very hot.

Enough of that: to the dissertation. Oddly enough my first task on this project concerns neither Shakespeare nor Joyce. I need more specific facts about schizophrenic speech, to follow up on the cursory research I did to get the topic approved. I need to learn more of the theory, and find more real accounts of the speech of a person disintegrating into madness. Then I can go back to the work, and really see and feel Joyce's triumph: how he took those speech patterns and created glory from them, multilayered insights into the human condition and the human heart.

Practicing, working toward mastery—Will's hand over mine on the bow, guiding it to the right place. Yes, that's where we need to go, right now. Like doing my scales, counting time, discovering the elements of creation.

With any luck, I can detour around the Lucia story; the various passionate partisans can carry her flag in my absence, thank you very much. Which sounds a little like what I told Emma on the phone the other night, about Margaret. She was imparting the less-than-surprising fact that our mother is smoking again. "Will you talk to her, Molly? She respects you, perhaps she'll listen to you—I see her all the time, maybe she's bored with me."

39

I do talk to her. I always say the same thing: listen to your doctors, Mam, listen to your doctors. "She's a grownup, Em. She smokes for the same reason she drinks—because she likes it. She's sixty-three and if those are her only gratifications, at least she's no longer neglecting five kids to do it."

Emma's voice began to tremble, and I felt myself tighten inside. "But I'm afraid to leave my baby alone with her. And I hate that."

I heard my voice growing harsh, even to my baby sister and best friend. "You knew how hard it might be, back when you were pregnant. We even talked about it." That voice wasn't really for her, it was me, to the New York ex-musician who also knew how to resort to alcohol's warm solace, that liquid blur defining the word "surcease."

I let myself soften, against the tears I could almost hear welling up in those golden-brown eyes. "Listen—I am sorry. But I thought that group of yours was helping you, with Mam and all that."

That quickly brought humor back into her voice. "Hey Molly, I thought my group was bullshit. I believe your words were, 'adult children mewling about Mommy'."

Hoist on my own petard! I told her to "call it useful bullshit, if it helps you feel like you don't need to clean up after her anymore."

Ever since Emma first told me about Adult Children of Alcoholics, I've been noticing all the spinoffs—ranging from Adult Survivors of Physical Abuse to Adult Children of Dysfunctional Families. I even saw some fake advertisement in the April Fool's Day issue of the City Paper, for "Adult Children of Parents . . . Were you unlucky enough to have had parents?" I was lucky enough to have Will and unlucky enough to lose him.

Well, one out of two. It's just too bad about

September 4

Hmmm . . . too bad about what? The state of the economy? familial relations in the United States? on the planet? I assume I was going to write "the other," meaning Margaret—but who knows? I actually fell asleep with the light on and the journal open.

So strange, this fat notebook with nearly too many pages for its metal spirals. I'm finally doing what all the other girls at Sacred Heart were doing while I was busy helping Will and playing cello. I never saw any use for a diary, I hated those silly little locked books bound with flowered cloth, to be filled with bad poetry. I got this one for that Amtrak train from New York to Baltimore, Colin's accusations still ringing in my ears.

At first I needed the journal if only to keep track of how many miles I'd run each day; my weight; how much negotiating with myself had been required to get out of bed in the morning, how many days it had been since I had had a glass of wine. My own, rather pedestrian way of weaving some order out of the chaos of my life.

Now it can help me navigate the divergent streams of Joyce research and schizophrenic-speech research, added to Lit 120 and training for marathons.

To the latter end, this morning I ran five miles, venturing into the unfamiliar territory of the medical school in Southeast Baltimore. It's not a neighborhood I know at all—usually pass right by it to get to Fells Point, Gary's favorite bohemian-yuppie waterfront. The next day, when I went *to* the med school for research, I splurged on a taxi so I wouldn't be full of sweat.

"Was a shooting there last week," the cabbie reported cheerfully, pointing to an anonymous set of homes. "At least six police cars came." I didn't know the terrain, after riding down North Broadway past strip joints, 7-Elevens, and slim rowhouses run down by drugs and crime and sheer neglect.

Just past where the cabbie pointed, a fragile-looking church building: a long line of men and a few young families waited patiently in the September chill by the closed side door. I asked what was going on: he said matter-of-factly, "Lunchtime, ma'am, St. Stephen's serves on Tuesdays and Thursdays."

When I got to my destination, it wasn't hard to find the right library: by the elevator was a poster for a "Mental Health Conference" in San Francisco, declaring "THE 90'S: THE DECADE OF THE BRAIN."

Ten hours later, my head is still spinning. Schizophrenia is a damn family of disorders, from "schizoid personality disorder" to "schizoaffective disorder" (the latter as much an emotional as a thought disorder) to a cluster of full-fledged schizophrenias, including hebephrenic (Lucia Joyce's diagnosis). I laughed out loud when I found "schizophreniform disorder"—brand-new or temporary schizophrenia, meaning the doctor doesn't know yet if the disease will stick around.

And in this decade of the brain, it's all from abnormal brain chemistry. Does this mean that Joyce was perhaps blessed with bad chemistry, just less toxic than what plagued his daughter?

It didn't take long to find Joyce: "loosening of associations," "overvalued ideas" (God, for example?), "preoccupation with an internal world." So far so good—Will told me forever ago that once Joyce began *Finnegans Wake*, its world was more real to him than reality.

Running short on time, I checked out a huge pile of books. Librarian looked me over, was I a budding psychiatrist or just some failing undergraduate? Neither: I am a traveler from an antique land, hoping your doctor-writers will help me chart my uncertain direction.

Then this traveler walked the three-plus miles back up to my house, west on Monument Street till I got to Charles—a few nervous moments going past the housing projects, men brandishing large beer bottles, shouting, "Hey sweetheart." Past the Peabody Conservatory of Music, to which I applied at age 17 sight unseen. What would my life be like if I had come to Baltimore eight years ago, instead of New York? Would I now be performing for thousands, or would I have met another Colin there, hands in his back pockets as he checked the acoustics of a concert hall?

Either way, Will reminds me, I could easily have been doing exactly what I was the night he died: struggling in string quartet rehearsal, trying not to let my personality conflicts with the violist interfere with the pursuit of Haydn. I am so sorry, Will. I may never forgive myself for deserting you, for being so far from you when the blood vessel burst in your brain. To this day I have difficulty listening to Haydn.

I'm now inclined to search out Brett's cheap tape of that quartet, to listen to it as I run tomorrow (the dry-brown autumn leaves are now falling with unnerving rapidity, like a scratchy snowstorm). When I hear the allegro slip, I'll know it's Joan, who never could catch on to a quick time change.

I also get to look down at my body and worry: my weight is at 124, another sign that I've a long way to go before being able to run the New York Marathon next year—part of the long route back from Colin, whose idea of a productive run was one that brought back a carton of cigarettes, a few bottles of Mouton-Cadét, and two grams of cocaine.

12 September

And now a quiz: Are the following symptoms of schizophrenia or merely literary terms? Or accusations hurled at *Finnegans Wake?*

Clang associations: Neologisms
Symbolism: Absurdity
Loose: Queer
Confusion: Autistic logic
Punning: Literalized metaphor
Metonymy: Condensation
Fluidity: Contamination
Fabulized combination: Confabulation
Incoherence

(God, am I getting a headache!)

Most of that's from a chart of "thought disorder" in schizophrenia—the rest whisper through the other books lying all around me. I'm getting crowded out of this tiny carrel, piles of papers and books stacked along each divider and atop the desk.

Psych jargon mimics literary jargon! Metonymy, for example, using some small detail of something to represent the whole—I remember that from Latin, studying Virgil with Sister Catherine. Clang associations, words strings linked more by sound than meaning (e.g., "Czars have their income from bazaars").

What would/do these psychologists do with the *Wake*, with "Talk of molniacs' manias and missions for mades," or "from spark to phoenish!"? Both puns (its own disorder!) are "neologisms," made-up words—but we already knew, kids, that Joyce was constantly and consciously creating his own dialect, layer by layer, asking his friends "Is this obscure enough yet?" And it worked, the result does feel like you've just been awakened for a deep sleep, the dream you just left half-remembered, incomprehensible.

The doctors also tell me that neologisms and clang formations only occur at the final stages of schizophrenia, when the brain is in its final and worst stage of deterioration. Of course, *Finnegans Wake* was the last thing Joyce ever wrote, and it took him sixteen years. So was his brain also warring, dying?

And what do I do with his earlier work, where the word usage is relatively normal, even if the structure and content are dense and difficult? I guess Jung meant much more than speech when he talked about Joyce's schizophrenic thought. He must have had in mind the hallucinations in *Ulysses*, Dedalus' childhood disorganization in *Portrait*.

Which makes clearer my next step: to leave aside thought/language disorder and look at schizophrenia as a whole. It makes no sense to *begin* with language unless I wish only to write about *Finnegans Wake*, and unlike Tilden I have no desire to spend the next year (two?) on a single book, whatever its inexhaustibility. I think when people read the *Wake* too much it makes them a little odd—they forget simple things, like washing their hair. Tilden certainly does.

But then again, so does my roommate Felicia, half the time. The difference between her and Tilden is that she simply smears some sort of plasticized gel over her unwashed dyed-black crewcut, a slick Nazi helmet. God, two weeks in that house and she already drives me up the proverbial wall.

Ok it's true, Felicia's pleasant enough. Cleans up after herself, manages the rent on a part-time bartending job. She never holds up the phone and always takes messages, writing them in a clear if affected hand.

"So what's the problem?" Emma would ask.

Problem A: her room/studio is right over my head, which means I have to hear her piercing rock and roll unless I specifically request that it be stopped. Since she works at night, she doesn't even get home until one a.m.; then she starts painting, or whatever it is she does. To this former cellist, the music of Sister Double Happiness (I asked!) is an unpleasant sound at any time of day: at four a.m. it is akin to root canal without anesthesia.

Problem B: I've never met, let alone lived with, someone who has voluntarily come into contact with so many needles. First, there are the nine earring-holes (artist as golf course?), five in her ears alone. Then there are the tattoos, which go beyond anything my little pedestrian mind had ever thought possible.

At her wrists delicate snakes, curling together head to tail just below the palm, like a perverted Hippocratic staff. A yin-yang symbol on one bony shoulder. And across her entire back, beginning just below her shoulder blades, a reproduction of one of the most grotesque paintings in the entire Museum of Modern Art—a huge rust-brown infant head, a smaller infant in a loincloth coming out of its mouth, surrounded by post-industrial rubble, all silver-grays and reds and smoky browns. "It's called 'Echoes of a Scream,'" she informed me the day I noticed it, as she came out of the shower (the same day I saw the pierced nipple). "David Alfaro Siqueiros."

I didn't bother to ask how someone could contemplate bearing such an image on her back for even a single day, let alone the rest of her life. I did ask, fascinated despite myself: "How long did it take?"

"About five sessions, maybe three hours apiece. It burned, more than hurt, after a while." Fifteen hours being drilled with needles, now that's my idea of a good time. Her arms show no sign that she continues this tradition with intravenous drugs, but who knows? There must be a reason for Problem C: Which is that she never seems quite awake, even though she sleeps till three p.m.

Perhaps it's the fumes, from having to paint and sleep in the same room. Of course, those sleepy eyes could also belong to my mother, after a good solid evening alone with a bottle—or to Colin, crashing down from the fever height of Stravinsky and cocaine. Perhaps Felicia is doing the same, when I see her: maybe she reserves her drug supply for her nighttime finger-paints. Coke would go well enough with that dreadful screaming music.

10 September

Gary when I complain about Felicia: "You're so judgmental, Molly." I've never understood that criticism, and I told him so. Emma says that too, and what does she mean? Isn't she being judgmental when she makes her own baby food? "Aren't you being judgmental when you give a B instead of an A?"

"I don't get riled up about it, do I?" And it's true, I've never seen him show anger at anyone—be it a student who takes up three hours of his time crying about her boyfriend, a faculty committee that won't listen to reason, or the police ignoring fraternity parties that drench university carpeting in beer and urine. His calm sometimes downright eerie.

Like when his wife called at 6:45 this morning, right after we made love.

He reached over to answer it, pulling the phone's long cord so that he could stay in bed while he spoke. At first, I simply turned and faced the other way, writing my to-do list on the envelope of his phone bill. Then he said, "So did you explain to him that these kids are coming in completely ignorant, no matter what their transcripts say?" This indicating an extended conversation, I got up, dressed and came home.

Gary's voice didn't reflect at all the fact that he'd just cried out in orgasm: whereas with me, even if I were trying hard (if it were Tilden or my mother calling, for example), I think my voice would sound a little different. Perhaps it's a difference between men and women. I remember a conductor calling to change rehearsal times on Colin, and he had his little dignified-soloist voice on while he untied the ribbons that held me to the bed.

And yet somehow I cannot imagine James Joyce being that way —not from his letters, not from the characters that flowed from his pen. The physical, the erotic, the cerebral and the everyday all mingle, cross, no dividing lines—no "boundaries," as the psychologists say (e.g., "The schizophrenic knows no boundaries between himself and other people: he will think the man on T.V. is talking from inside his head").

Like the boundaries between teacher and student, violated every time Gary and I make love. Denise's call did get get me out of Gary's bed early enough, enough time for my morning run around the reservoir.

The temp is already descending to the low forties with some regularity—one needs to be layered and armored, ready to pull off gloves and sweatshirt and carry them when my body temp heats up (the hat stays on, my ears are always cold). In my Walkman I had Pictures at an Exhibition, which I love because of the trumpet solo; even for this string player the music of the angels comes from trumpet. Mozart's Ave Verum or Mussorgsky and Ravel's call to the sunrise help urge me past the baseball stadium, in my wool hat and gardening gloves.

Afterward, as I re-read *Lapis Lazuli* in time for Tilden's class, I seemed to hear that trumpet solo behind Yeats' words, to the serenity of his last line: "Their ancient, glittering eyes are gay."

14 September

From the sublime to the ridiculous, of course—from Ravel and Yeats to the realities of a 200-plus lecture class, packed with freshman and sophomore English majors, as well as seniors from science departments desperately rushing to satisfy the school's humanities requirement. (Most of the latter came in thinking that "modern literature" meant jazzy New York stories, full of cocaine abuse and murder.)

The syllabus is like one of those twelve-cities-in-ten-days European tours: half poetry, speed-reading Emily Dickinson, Yeats, and T.S. Eliot, half a romp through just a few novelists—our old friend Joyce plus Woolf, Beckett, Thomas Pynchon.

My job is to see what points Tilden covers and doesn't in the sweep of his lectures. Then in my discussion section, I get to reiterate the points AND fill in the gaps for my little handful of students. If these kids are any evidence, the "Decade of the Brain" has started off rather badly.

Is this what I have to look forward to for thirty years, now that I have followed Will into the halls (hills? hells?) of academia? Though I do always look forward to seeing Barbara Daniels.

To look at her you'd never believe it, to look at her jock boyfriends you'd believe it even less—but there she is, a refugee from the Bible Belt, long blonde hair that streams down her shoulders, and she's hooked on the hard stuff: Eliot, William Carlos Williams, she's never seen language like this. She's me at ten reading to my father, caught up in the unutterable joy of it all.

Only problem is that at nineteen, her brain has already been turned halfway to pudding by TV, bad education, and men (she always has some new jock-type escorting her to class, his hand on her behind as he French kisses her goodbye). Her papers are so badly spelled, let alone constructed, that I've sent her to the writing lab and have spent hours myself trying to show her how to figure out what she thinks and then say it clearly. She takes everything at its face value, just as if it were television. "Do you watch much TV?" I asked her once, when she came to see me.

"No, not a lot. Maybe three hours for a whole day."

Three hours in a day—in addition to classes, work, papers, friends and lovers. Then you ask me to come and pick up the pieces? Yet her eagerness still charms me, just as the model-beautiful body and face charms those jocks. (I forgot to calculate beauty-maintenance in the above, that's at least another hour between blow-drying, shaving, makeup, and taking it all off at night.)

She's also fearless about speaking up in class: "I'm sorry, it's beautiful but he's just whining about the world," she declared the day we zapped through Eliot's *The Waste Land*. In his later years, the poet himself said as much.

But I grow weary, weary of the pre-meds' little watches beeping out the hour change, weary of deciding whether or not it's my job to correct their grammar, weary of their attitude toward Tilden. "He sure is crazy."

Right, sweethearts, and I have a category in my little psychology books for every bleeding one of you. Obsessive-compulsive for the pre-meds, narcissistic personality disorder for the Eliot fan who won't stop talking and wilts when the attention turns to anyone else, and some form of schizoid something or another for the little bohemians in the back of the class. (Barbara is exempt because, in her new thrill for learning, she thinks Tilden is God.)

17 September

My baby sister called this morning, for moral support before her run.

"God, I didn't know it was gonna be so hard, getting out of bed for this," said the former track coach. "I don't know Molly, with the baby and everything . . . I don't know if I have time to seriously train."

"C'mon, Em . . . you of all people can do it." This has always been our special bond, whether it was track team together in high school, all those 5Ks and 10Ks during our college years, or our triumphant New York Marathon, three years ago. So I owe her now: Barry has promised to take care of little Stevie while she trains, and I keep urging her on to a focus other than baby, baby, baby. "Oh Molly, I don't know what I'd do without you."

It must be hard. God knows Margaret offers no support, and Anna has her hands full just trying to keep our mother under control; Shaun is doing the Wall Street routine, and Leo—Leo is lost to us: I doubt he and Emma have spoken since he moved to San Francisco. And I know Emma, unlike me, doesn't have Will's voice inside her, to hold her hand at stressful times.

Of course, until I started studying Joyce I thought I, also, had lost Will forever. When I lost my music to Colin, I let him silence the voice of my best teacher. Now that voice is beginning to murmur again, as I dive into this Joyce-schizophrenia stuff, the teasing erotic pleasures of academic research.

Speaking of which, I'm finally beginning to get a grip here.

I can hear Joyce's echoes in descriptions of schizophrenia's early signs—like a simple hyper-awareness of your body, feeling your heartbeat and the temperature of your skin with the same intensity as the thoughts and emotions that preoccupy most of us. Also trying desperately to screen incoming stimuli, it's all coming at you full force: often schizophrenics can very accurately tell you the names of everyone who came into a room, what they were wearing, their accents and speech patterns, whether there was dust on their shoes. Everything felt so acutely it's an invasion: many of them recoil from being touched. The flood not only sensations but memories and dreams.

So there it is, the connection that tantalizes, that yearns to be touched. In Ulysses, when Leopold Bloom is walking along a street in Dublin and his memories, his feelings about Palestine, his list of errands, and his need to go to the bathroom are all conveyed with equal weight—we may be witnessing more than a brilliant artist uncovering a normal person's inner layers.

That was how Jung saw it, certainly. And yet we've all had those kinds of experiences—at least I have, when memories and body-sensations interfered with something I was trying to do. I remember sitting there in the middle of a Beethoven string quartet feeling the invisible bruise at the base of my scalp, the week Colin first hit me. Not emotion, not even pain, certainly nothing akin to that razorblade-in-the-chest I felt when I finally left him. No, I just remember the slight pressure at the back of my neck, absolutely dominating me when I should have been working on the key-change at the end of the second movement.

Amazing how something is so defined by its context. In Joyce's Paris of the 1920s, Felicia's kind of painting was nonexistent and would have been considered mad—"modern art" itself was shocking the world (Jung also called Picasso a "latent psychotic"), like the music of Stravinsky. Yet I heard Stravinsky's *Rite of Spring* in a TV commercial last week, and Felicia "can't get galleries interested because, oh, I'm not doing anything new—it's like, ho hum, that's fun, next?" (Don't you just love her vivid use of the English language?)

20 September

I don't know if I just had a hallucination, or if that woman standing by the baseball stadium this morning had an uncanny resemblance to Lucia Joyce.

The temperature dropped precipitously yesterday morning, unseasonably cold for this time of year. Twenty-five degrees, and that wind-chill that freezes your face into crusted paper.

I suited up properly—polypropylene long underwear, gloves,

shorts, sweatshirt and a ski mask—and put Prokofiev's Second Piano Concerto in the tape deck to urge me forward, forward, forward with the pianist's frantic fingers. It worked, got me running up Calvert Street in total darkness and crossing Greenmount Avenue as my muscles warmed up.

But I nearly stopped when I saw her motionless on the corner of 33rd and Ellerslie, ignoring the cold and looking as though her heart was about to break.

She looked just like Lucia's photograph in the big Joyce biography, the one by Richard Ellman. Heavy, shining brown hair, cut chin-length with just the slightest flip; slightly crossed eyes with that odd, distant stare, bespeaking secret griefs or inner voices— strong enough to keep her standing in one place. She didn't move the entire time I was approaching her, nor for as long as it took for me to pass beyond sight of her and run toward the reservoir.

If I were as superstitious as my drunken mother, I would say that Lucia was trying to tell me something about my dissertation: something like, *you can't avoid me, no matter how you might try.*

Rachel rejected that notion soon as I got home. "No, I'm starting to see homeless people hanging around Waverly. It's a medium-poor neighborhood to begin with." A half-hour later, as we were getting ready to walk over to campus together, she added: "You know, that woman still could be mentally ill—one of those people dumped out of a mental hospital with nowhere to go." Nowhere but the river, to drown in it instead of diving.

And now, sitting in my library carrel, Joyce and Will's photographs twin icons urging me on, it feels like I am recounting a dream: that instead of running this morning I dreamt a run, haunted by the one figure I don't want near my dissertation. Perhaps tomorrow I will see Nora Joyce in front of the university, wearing a fur coat and eating bon bons, her shoes and hat the height of Parisian fashion.

Will, did this happen to you? Did random people on the street inspire Joycean phrases? Or did you satisfy that urge by the way you named us all, so that Leopold and Molly Bloom, Anna Livia Plurabelle, Emma Cleary and Shaun (brother of Shem) chased each other around your living room?

I have the opposite: my housemates, my siblings, Tilden and Gary dart in among the stuff of my Joyce world, inhabited by all of the above plus Stephen Dedalus, James Joyce, Picasso, Carl Jung, and others—with commentary currently provided by a dozen vaguely anonymous psychiatrists. And bridging the two worlds, Will, is you, standing right beside me as if this were just another cello lesson.

It's a lot to keep in your mind at once, Shem, I know, the gentle voice. But I know you can do it. Then you sit back, and wait.

Now, as then, you occasionally tap my shoulder to the rhythm, touch my hand to offer the correct fingering; but mostly—as you always did—you are waiting, waiting for me to discover it on my own.

The keys to dreamland

"Amazing grace, how sweet the sound That saved a wretch like me. . . ."

The song was good for a sing-along—familiar enough to bring in everyone, including the three or four elderly patients who often found themselves on the sidelines, reluctant and unsure with "Blowin' in the Wind" or "Here Comes the Sun." A volunteer helped a tiny, fragile woman with red fingers turn to the correct page; a tall, patrician man with thick glasses and a bolo tie sang serenely, looking down at the songbook as if it were a love letter. Shana swayed as she must have done in church, her eyes closed.

The Wilkes common room was packed: large contingents from both the closed and open wards, their sound newly graced by the voice of Jim Keene, a brand-new patient still in the overnight unit. Jim's tenor sang out silver, distinct from the breathy sounds of the other patients—as well as from Gail Ryan's guitar and belting, Joan Baez-like delivery. He raised his chin as he sang, a bird-like gesture matched by his sharp features and slender neck.

I once was lost, but now I'm found
Was blind, but now I see. . . .

"Jim," Gail said in a stage whisper between verses, "could you lower your voice a little?" Jim grinned, eager to please, and gentled his tone, although he still couldn't quite blend in.

A gentle tap from behind, and Jim turned. Molly O'Donnell, who had entered the room quiet and shaken, was leaning forward, her eyes bright as she looked at him. Her left arm still rigid in its cast, she held out both arms, her palms up and fingers slightly curved: then she raised them slowly, a conductor asking for a crescendo. Jim shook his head with a grin, nudging a shoulder in Gail's direction. Molly sat back and stopped singing, watching him instead.

When the song ended, Gail asked pointedly, "Is there a problem, Molly?"

Molly pointed to Jim, tilting her head slightly. "James used to sing at home," she said. "He said I had a lovely voice but I did not believe him."

"Molly, we're trying—"

Not responding, the young woman began instead to sing an unfamiliar folk tune, her voice growing louder by the minute. "Oh Molly, I can't say you're honest, sure you've stolen the heart from my breast." What she lacked in voice quality she made up for in determination; Jim turned around, his attention caught, his lips pressed closed so he wouldn't laugh.

Gail put down her guitar, sighing. Her eyes didn't match her mouth, which was still set in a smile. "Molly," she said quietly, "I'm very glad you came to group, and I'm sure Jim is pleased that you like his voice. But Jim also understands that we're trying to sing all together. If you don't feel you can, Steve can take you back to Chatham."

"Yeah Molly, don't you understand?" Shana pleaded. "We

gotta all sing along!" The younger woman's eyes bewildered, a little fearful, as if this truly were a church service gone awry.

Gail bit her lip: then she grinned, picked a songbook off the pile and handed it to Molly. "Why don't you choose our next song, Molly?"

Jim held the greenish cardboard binder for Molly as she flipped through the pages: then she started to sing again. Gail joined her on the guitar as soon as she recognized the song. "Page 63, everyone!"

I'm forever blowing bubbles
Pretty bubbles in the air
They fly so high they reach the sky
Just like my dreams—

The whole room cheered: Gail managed a genuine smile, Jim and Molly agreed on something of a real harmony, and Shana giggled, simulating bubble-blowing by sending air through her circled fingers, her lips puckered in an open-mouthed kiss.

Jim held his songbook out so that he and Molly could share it; Molly moved forward, and Shana came to her other side. For a few minutes the rest of the group fell silent listening to the trio, with Jim offering some conducting of his own. For the first time since her arrival Molly seem childlike, her face nearly as pink as her baggy sweater.

I'm forever blowing bubbles
Pretty bubbles in the air.

The staff conference room's picture window offered a view blurred by humidity, the weeping willows and brick buildings images from a dream or a Monet painting. The room itself, by contrast, was air-conditioned to a subarctic chill, to awaken the staff from Indian-summer languor. Tired vocational nurses and loose-limbed dance therapy interns revived as they entered the room, armed with notebooks and legal pads.

Gail Ryan's thick Irish wool sweater and Peter Pan blouse

formed soft counterpoint to her brisk words. "Record shows ECT in past hospitalizations," she read from a nursing report. "That may explain the cognitive deficits—"

"What cognitive deficits?" Anne-Marie asked.

"Memory loss, mainly."

Anne-Marie's eyes widened as she wrote it down. Gail continued, "Meanwhile she ate 75% of her dinner, but claimed to be sick afterward and vomited. But she's cooperating well in group psychotherapy, and she denies SI."

Anne-Marie bit down from asking yet again: wrote carefully, *denies suicidal ideation.*

Gail turned to the next section in her binder. "Then there's Molly O'Donnell—our former Lucy Doe."

"What a handful!" a young nurse exclaimed. "Kepler took her off lithium, didn't he?"

"Her family is coming this week, thank God. We can fill in the history, and finally get her certified."

Anne-Marie pushed up the sleeves of her Mexican blouse. "Her family? Meaning who? Her mom, the alcoholic?"

"No, it seems there are—" Gail looked down. "Two sisters. Anna O'Donnell and Emma Gahagan. We'll see if we can't get her out of that cast by then: the resident is saying we can do a splint just for the elbow, and sling the rest. . . . It'll be years before that elbow is completely functional."

Anne-Marie was writing furiously, large strokes. Then she looked up and interjected, "By the way, I've also learned a little about Lucia Joyce, if anyone cares: did you know she was hospitalized for almost fifty years?"

Gail's mouth tightened. "Anne-Marie," she said carefully, "thank you for looking into that. I'm sure Dan Kepler will appreciate it." She looked back down at the binder. "Meanwhile you're right, Susie, Molly's lithium level is fairly minimal right now. But we're holding the Prolixin steady, and watching the Prozac carefully. In the meantime, we need to watch what happens—we're moving Shana back into that room with her, to see if Shana can handle being that far away from the nurse's station."

"Molly and Shana, you're kidding!"

"They bonded at sing-along yesterday," said Gail. "Our first encouraging sign. She also seemed to bond with Jim Keene."

"So how did the tests come out?"

Gail shrugged. "About what we expected, no abnormalities from the MRI or evoked potentials. Day after tomorrow she'll take the MMPI."

Anne-Marie watched the circle of obedient pencils note this information, and tried not to laugh. "Oh come on guys, don't you ever get sick of these acronyms?" A few others nodded, the head nurse issuing a dry chuckle: "Next she'll be taking the LAX and BWI."

Gail ignored them all, turning another page. "Jim Keene," she said quietly, "has been certified as a danger to self. He's on a no-harm contract with his doctor, but that won't matter if his Kaposi's gets worse and he starts anticipating a painful death."

The head nurse nodded. "So he stays at Chatham?"

"Yes, of course. The risk of suicide is just too high."

"But he *is* going to die," Anne-Marie said, questioning.

"He's on one of the new anti-viral drugs but it's pretty advanced," said the head nurse. "Barring miracles, I'd guess he'll be gone within a year."

"Yet he's in here on danger to self." Anne-Marie spoke slowly, as if she were trying to pronounce a foreign language.

"That's what 622 is for," Gail said, impatiently. "Jim will be fine, Anne-Marie. His behavior on the ward has been very encouraging." She closed her binder, with a snap. "Any other questions?"

Anne-Marie flushed a little, realizing she might soon acquire a reputation for having a big mouth. "No, no," she said softly, writing in her legal pad. "Makes perfect sense."

. . .

"Oh no you gonna make me look during lunch?"

"What's the matter, you can't take a little blood?"

Jim Keene's sigh of exasperation was big enough to fill the lunchroom. "There's no blood involved, sir," he said to Frank Morrison, who was sitting across the table from him. He pulled up his sleeve, saying softly to Shana, "Don't worry—they just look like freckles . . . Only if you were a doctor or someone who knew AIDS, then you'd realize what they were. But I never had so many before."

Jim sat between Shana and Molly; he wore a large, silky Italian shirt and a set of wooden beads. His arm did indeed look freckled, but for the purplish tinge of the dots and the irregularity of the spaces between them. One clump, near his elbow, swelled slightly, an incipient pimple.

Frank leaned across the table, staring. "How come you're getting so many of them?" Molly, on his other side, reached out with her right hand and traced lightly, not quite touching the arm but noting each lesion, almost as if she were counting them.

"The drug I was on stopped working." Jim rolled his eyes. "Something to do with DNA, it's too complicated and boring to explain. What it comes down to is that I'm likely to die in the most miserable way—and there's nothing in this blessed world they can do about it."

When lunch arrived, Jim rolled down his sleeve and the three of them uncovered their trays. Jim tore apart his roll while Molly did her usual ritual of pushing food around, separating the sugary peach slices from the mandarin oranges in her fruit salad. Only now she kept looking at Jim, fascination mixed with a sort of fear, tinged with anticipation.

"So what are you doing in here?" Frank asked.

"Because I made the mistake of telling my sister I might kill myself!" Jim started to laugh, a laugh that echoed through the lunchroom like his singing or his sighs. After a moment Frank Morrison began to laugh with him, and Shana chimed in with her high-pitched child-giggle.

One of the nurses entered the lunchroom, asking, "Is everything all right?"

Immediately the laughter stopped. Frank Morrison said, in his tired professor voice, "Everything's fine ma'am, just fine. Except, of course, that Jim here is going to die . . . Oh don't look at me like that. I'm not the one threatening him." While Frank was talking Molly was whispering, so softly not even Jim could hear her.

"What?" Jim asked her gently, glad for the distraction.

"Not a proper skin," Molly said, her eyes meeting Jim's as if she were making perfect sense. "The lesions? Internal." Her eyes were bright, and she was touching the lesions at the base of his palm, a curious feathery caress.

Frank nodded. "Yeah," she said, "sometimes what's killing you is harder to see.' He turned to Jim. "You're a lucky man."

The medication nurse entered the room with a small carrying case of transparent plastic, stopping at each table to dispense meds labeled take with meals. Jim threw his Prozac into his mouth as if eating Christmas candy.

Molly ignored the nurse entirely until she heard her own name. "Hey, Molly, I hear your family's coming this week." She then took her eyes off Jim's face with difficulty, let the nurse place the pills on her tongue. She swallowed, looking at Jim again; it was to him as much as the nurse that she said, "My father had blood in his eyes."

"Is he all right?" Jim asked.

Frank shook his head, but it was too late, tears were tumbling down Molly's cheek. "I could not console him," she said, her fingers still lightly on Jim's arm.

Jim turned to Frank. "Is there something I'm missing here?"

Frank wiped his lips with the waxy paper napkin. "I think he's dead. Her father." Stage whispers, amid lunchroom commotion.

"Oh I'm so sorry," Jim said, placing his hand on Molly's shoulder. "Is this recent?"

Molly looked up at him, lifting the shoulder he wasn't touching, a half-shrug. "Ti abbracio," her whisper even quieter.

The dietary aide walked up to their table, gently lifting both Jim's hand and Molly's. "This is a no touching unit," he said. "Didn't your doctor explain that to you, Jim?"

Molly looked at the aide, eyes wide, as if he had torn her arm from its socket. She gestured in Jim's direction. "Love in his eyes and a salt almond voice," she told the aide.

Jim stared. "That's really beautiful, Molly."

Molly stared at Jim, her lip trembling; then she looked down, her shoulders slumped as if he had reprimanded her. She looked down at the table, staring hard, as if reading words in the white-porcelain surface. "First you feel," she whispered, "and then you fall."

Before anyone could respond she was standing up, suddenly, at first unsteadily, leaving her tray behind.

"Molly, where are you going?" Jim asked.

Molly ignored him, moving toward the door. At the last minute she turned, explaining to the dietary aide, "My parents were neither big nor small but they were very young and I never thought they would die so soon." And she was gone.

Jim raised both arms, palms upward, Dali's Jesus. "What a mysterious creature," he said.

Frank smiled mischievously. "I think she has a crush on you."

"Funny way of showing it. . . . Though I confess she intrigues me; sings in tune, cries on cue, speaks in poetry." He shrugged. "I'll catch up with her soon enough."

On the way back to Chatham, staff and patients divided into two distinct contingents, the staff bringing up the rear—a nurse concentrated on the elderly patients, while volunteers surrounded two surly, uncommunicative men. Ahead of them Shana walked with her bouncing step, her playful gestures making Frank laugh. Jim walked alongside Molly, speaking softly to her; as they passed under the weeping willow trees Molly's face was childlike, upturned, her slow movements for once acquiring something resembling grace.

· · ·

"Okay, you mind telling me why she's still hidden away back there, behind lock and key?"

Felicia's tone was clipped; she stood against the wall of Dr. Kepler's office, her hand on her hip, her elbow jutting just above the light switch. "OK, so she's in la-la land . . . though I'm not sure your fucking drugs didn't send her there. But she's not hurting anyone. Even herself."

Kepler sighed. "Ms. Waller, we are all working very hard here, and I'm sorry you felt you had to come all the way here from Baltimore City. We still feel it's safer for all concerned if she remains where she is, until her sisters come."

The late-afternoon sun through the mini-blinds striped Felicia's face, making it even harder to read her expression; she sat back, exasperated. "Didn't I just tell you that I talked to Emma O'Donnell? and that she agrees with me?" Felicia rested her elbow on the arm of her chair and raised her hand to her chin; one long sleeve slid down, revealing a snake tattoo encircling the wrist.

Kepler tried not to stare at the tattoo. "You mean Mrs. Gahagan." He closed the blinds and turned on the fluorescent overhead lights, revealing a slight reddish-brown fuzz on Felicia's otherwise hairless scalp; he finally stopped looking at her entirely, referring instead to the chart on his desk. "Are you aware, Miss Waller, that Molly gets far more attention at Chatham than she would in the open unit? More nurses, more volunteers—in short, we're spending a lot more time and money than we would if we didn't think she needed it. But she obviously does."

"Oh, obviously." Felicia stood up to look at the chart, as if she could read it upside down, from the other side of the desk, and somehow come up with different results.

Kepler gentled his voice and produced a smile. "Please give us some time, Miss Waller. Once her sisters come, we'll have the information we need to really decide on a treatment plan."

As she left the main building, Felicia peeled off her long-sleeved shirt in the heat, revealing a tank top underneath as she headed toward the bus stop near the entrance gate.

"Hey!" Behind her, a crew of dietary aides pushed a heavy cart along the path. "Your doctor know yer leaving?" one of them asked, in a thick Irish accent.

Felicia laughed and extended her arms, with the telltale plastic VISITOR ID. "Hey, I don't live here, I'm just your ordinary bald chick with tattoos. I was visiting Molly O'Donnell, over in Chatham."

The aide smiled, a gentle paternal smile. "Oh sure, sorry miss."

"'S okay." Felicia let herself smile. "I'd rather be mistaken for a patient than a doctor. And Molly is my best friend."

"Hey!" a voice from another direction. "Felicia?"

At first Felicia froze, as if this seemed to negate what she had just told the aides. Then she recognized both the voice and the curvy redhead in white shorts. "Anne-Marie." She stood still, passive, accepting a kiss. "So this is the new job Philip told me about?"

"Gee, I didn't even know he knew about it, it's been so long since we talked."

"How's it going? You like it?"

"Uh . . . I just started." Anne-Marie shrugged. "It's a job. One that *pays*, not easy to come by for brand-new MSWs. So . . . uh—how's the art going?"

"As usual. Too many ideas, not enough time, no space."

They stood there a few moments until Anne-Marie said anxiously, "I gotta go."

"Sure. Nice seeing you."

Felicia used the pay phone at the bus stop to call Rachel. "No, I can't believe it, they haven't fucking moved her yet . . . No, no, I didn't—yeah, Emma asked me too. How would I know? And what fucking business is it of ours? . . . As if the diaries would even mean anything to them, as if they could understand Molly's words . . . Oh listen the bus is coming, I'll see you at home. But guess what—by the way—guess who works here! Anne-Marie, Philip's ex!"

Dr. Kepler stood in the front of the room, a pile of papers in his arms. "Remember, there are no wrong answers."

Molly and about ten others sat in one of the few rooms at Pearlstone that still resembled a classroom: a blackboard lined one wall, and the room was filled with plastic-and-wood chairs, each with a single arm and a plastic desk attached.

Kepler finished his espresso. He had volunteered for this unfamiliar duty—administering a standardized psychological test—in order to watch Molly from a distance. "This will help us figure out how to help you get better," he said as he passed out little booklets labeled MINNESOTA MULTIPHASIC PERSONALITY INVENTORY (Group Booklet).

Molly sat beside Jim Keene, as usual: they had walked in boldly holding hands, singing "Ave, ave verum corpus / Natum de Maria virgine . . ."Molly's arm, now freed of the cast, lay on her breast in a sling, as if she were constantly crossing herself.

When introduced to Kepler, Jim had said "Pleased to meet you, doctor;" then turned to help Molly get herself set up at her desk—like a nurse, or a father, or a lover.

"I know this test," he was the first to declare. "IBM uses it to test applicants."

"It looks like the S.A.T.!" said a nicely dressed woman, who looked terrified to breathe the same air as Molly and Jim. The answer sheets were indeed similar: NAME (Please Print), followed by little circles meant to be filled in with number two pencils. Only two kinds of answers: T (True) or F (False).

"Can I keep the pencil?" Molly asked Kepler.

"No. We collect them at the end."

Test-silence reigned for about five minutes, until Jim spoke again. "There seems to be a lump in my throat much of the time," he read aloud. "No shit, Sherlock, when was the last time you lived in Dupont Circle? Or any gay community?"

"Jim," Kepler said, "this is just a way for you to tell us about yourself. So just say true or false as quickly as you can, and we can take it from there."

"No matter what your freudzay," Molly said. She reached in her jeans pocket and took out a fat pencil stub, with a softer, thicker point; she bent low and began to mark up the answer sheet, without looking at the test.

"Molly?"

Molly ignored him, still humming Mozart under her breath.

"Molly, why aren't you reading the questions?"

Molly was drawing, quick black strokes across the answer sheet. After a moment, Kepler sat back, giving up; he watched the girl's eyes fierce with concentration, her hands delicately sliding, then pressing harder as she made tiny circles to surround her design. She was singing again, what sounded like the echoes of a gospel or blues song, the words too faint to make out.

Jim handed his test back first, rolling his eyes slightly. "I did try to be sincere," he told Kepler, before taking Molly's hand and leading her out.

Molly's eyes dared Kepler to bring up the no-touch policy.

Kepler wrote a little note for the psychologist who was going to score the test: Jim's K scale (for validity) was going to be a bitch.

The others followed soon after, except for one woman in her nineties, who was holding the booklet far enough away from her eyes to see, then filling in the blanks very, very slowly.

Kepler waited for a long time after they had all gone, before he looked at Molly's answer sheet. Traced over the printed oval spaces was a finely detailed, peculiarly shaped letter A, with a striped right side and a paisley left side; little flowers growing from the right, a rose in the center; and the pointed top feathered, a battle helmet or the crown of a bird's head. Instead of Molly's name, at the top of the test sheet: "As we there are where are we are we there. Tea tea too too." Of course, James Joyce, what else had he expected from this? He wrote another note for the scoring psychologist. *Patient did not cooperate with test.*

The tiny Mazda made its way down the curves and loops of I-95, past New Jersey refineries into the heart of Pennsylvania—gentle green hills and the roofs of distant suburbs on either side. The breeze from the car's motion didn't do much to mitigate the stifling heat; nor did the music from the car radio, hypnotic Gregorian chants urging sleep or trance.

"God, Emma, if I'd remembered you didn't have air conditioning, I would definitely have insisted on taking my car."

"I know, I'm about to fall asleep any minute now." The driver— a lithe young woman with long hair nearly as black as her opaque Ray-Ban sunglasses—reached for the radio. Her fingers found hard-driving modern rock, a dance beat competing with angry British voices.

"Oh God, don't!" The woman in the passenger seat sat back and massaged her temples, sinking her fingertips in short graying hair. "That's all I need right now, a headache on top of massive dehydration."

"Listen Anna, I'm not going to be able to keep going unless I either change this music or get some caffeine."

"Then we should stop—it's going to be dark soon. I told you we shouldn't try to drive from Boston to Baltimore in one day." Anna's voice sharp, lecturing.

"I need to get there." The younger woman's voice suddenly tight, her brown eyes closing for a split second. "I need to see her."

"Hey, watch the road! Didn't you see the BMW?"

"Cut me a break. Do you want to drive?"

Anna sighed, as if she had been expecting this. "Yes, Emma, I think you had better get off at the next exit. We'll stop in one of these little shopping malls and get something to eat, and then I'll take the wheel. We'll find somewhere to stay for the night—it's not as if they'd let us see her at two o'clock in the morning." The younger woman kept driving, staring straight ahead, her eyes unreadable behind the sunglasses.

"Emma for God's sake, how many hospital scenes have we been through together? Mam, Poppie, is this one so different?"

Emma pulled over onto the shoulder and stopped the car. "Yes," she said, "it is. And you know why." She pulled the keys out of the ignition and handed them to Anna, a gesture of surrender. When she took off her sunglasses, her eyes were bright; she lowered her head, her shoulders shaking, the long black hair a curtain that hid her face from Anna's view.

"God it's beautiful." Anne-Marie's voice was high-pitched, as Gail passed Molly's MMPI answer sheet around the conference table. "Like the ones Lucia Joyce used to do. Those were called *lettrines*, by the way. Lucia's were even published."

"Interesting as always, Anne-Marie," said Gail. "But right now, this drawing is a sign that Molly's completely delusional."

"James Joyce's daughter—now there's a pretty classy delusion, she couldn't just decide she's Napoleon?" one of the interns asked to general laughter—except for Anne-Marie, who bent her head, and Gail, whose role it was to scowl at such antics.

"Kepler doesn't know," Gail said, "if she actually thinks she's Lucia Joyce or just wants to be. Anyway, a lot should become clearer in the next few days, now that her family's here." She looked at her watch, then turned the page in her binder. "We're nearly out of time—may as well go on to Shana, quickly."

"Speaking of families . . ." said one of the interns, meaningfully.

Gail nodded. "After Shana visits with her mother today, Russell's due to meet with her. He'll try to pursue this question of Shana's relationship with her stepfather—the story she told yesterday in group."

Anne-Marie's head raised suddenly. She closed her teeth against asking what Gail meant—she could guess the answer, well enough to know she really did not want to hear any more.

The long, forested path from the entrance to Pearlstone's main building was a green welcome mat, late-summer sunlight casting highlights through the evergreen branches. "I can't imagine going to school somewhere as lovely as this," Anna O'Donnell said to Dr. Kepler. "We all went to this urban parochial school, nuns and big yellow buses. It must have been so peaceful here."

Emma O'Donnell Gahagan walked behind them, a little more slowly; she murmured something just as Kepler was replying, "The school closed down more than twenty years ago." He stopped, and turned. "Mrs. Gahagan?"

Emma looked startled to have been noticed. "I was just remembering; Moll and I ran past here, when we were training for the Marathon. And we thought it still was a prep school."

"You two ran here? All the way from Baltimore City?"

"Emma and Molly have run many marathons together," Anna asserted, putting a sisterly arm around Emma's waist.

Emma looked down at Anna's hand on her hip. "I wouldn't say many—just the Western Massachusetts, and D.C. one time. Mostly it's been shorter runs. We almost ran New York one year, but Molly —wasn't feeling well." She took a deep breath, her eyes brightening. "This year we were going to make it . . ." She bent her head and waited for Anna to release her arm; then she walked a few feet behind her sister and the doctor, touching each tree as they passed it. She followed them into the main building only after examining the doorway, as if afraid she, too, would not be released.

"This building," said Kepler, "is where everything happens when the patients are away from their units: group therapy, games, arts and crafts." As they entered, a small group was leaving the building, shepherded by attendants jangling keys.

"Where are they going?" Anna asked.

"They don't have any visitors today, so—" Kepler peered over to identify the group. "They're going back to Chatham, the closed unit. Where your sister lives."

"Closed means locked," Emma said, her tone half-that of a question.

"Of course. For her own protection."

"Of course."

They entered a large, sunny room full of sofas and chairs, where family groups sat at discreet distances from one another. A tall, anxious mother in a chiffon dress towered over her tiny daughter; a group of slender men looked around anxiously, holding flowers.

In a circle of folding chairs sat a large family, from matriarchal grandmother to round-eyed toddler. The little one squirmed in the arms of a slight young woman, with the same round eyes, who was crying—saying over and over, "Oh baby dry my tears, oh baby dry my tears."

From behind them, two voices singing in German—one strong, male; the woman's gentler, but still confident. "Oh my sweet, you keep surprising me," the man said. "First bubbles, then Mozart, now Schubert . . . how am I to live without you?"

"Coach me how to tumble, Jame," the woman said, her voice in a full-throated laugh. Emma and Anna turned around, as if in one motion. Dr. Kepler turned more slowly, denied the necessity of an introduction. Anna's brow furrowed, as if she were still trying to identify this ethereal figure in the loose clothing and her arm in a sling, singing in German and kissing a stranger as he went off to join his friends.

"Good afternoon, Molly," Dr. Kepler said. "We've been waiting to see you."

Molly smiled as if she were asleep and in the middle of a

dream. She began to walk slowly toward her sisters. She stopped about a foot away and wrestled out of her sling, wincing, trying to extend both arms: her palms faced Emma.

"Oh, Molly." Emma did the same, extending her hands so that just their fingertips touched.

"Mirror of mirror," Molly said softly. And the phrase was apt: the same long-waisted figures, runner's calf muscles, creamy coloring and strong brow, nearly identical features. But Emma's clear brown eyes, soft shoulders and well-groomed black mane stood sharp contrast to the body angled by anorexia, the veiled blue eyes half-hidden by uncombed hair.

Molly's voice was singsong, elevated. "Well Maggy, I got your castoff devils all right and they fits lovely." She looked over at Dr. Kepler. "You know her? She breaks in my shoes when I've arch trouble and she kisses my white arms for me so gratefully! Apart from that she's terrifically nice really, my sister." Emma reached for her and held her tightly, her own eyes closing. Molly's eyes remained open, her head on her sister's shoulder.

"Where are you, Molly?" Emma whispered. "Can I come there with you?"

"Nyon," Molly murmured.

"Nyon?"

Molly stepped back, gestured to the room. "Dr. Forel's clinic, at Les Rives des Prangins. Or else it's Ivry, I'm not sure, they have not used a camizole du force so I don't know. I like it here very much."

"Molly," Emma said softly, "do you want to come home with me? To Boston?"

At that, Molly's voice raised in alarm. "Sender: Boston, Mass!"

"That's one of her perseverations," Kepler whispered to Anna. "Usually it sounds like an insult."

Molly took Emma's hand and began to lead her across the room, toward Jim and the other patients. "Come, smooth of my slate to the beat of my blosh!" She waved to Jim and he broke away from his friends, took her outstretched other hand. "I was thinking fairly killing times of putting an end to myself and my malody . . ." As she spoke she led her two partners together, until Jim and Emma were looking at one another. "When I remembered all your pupil-teacher's erringnesses in perfection class."

Then Molly began to sing, her voice weak but steady. *"Those are pearls that were his eyes. . . ."*

"Molto bene," Jim said warmly. "Now drop your jaw and open your throat, let me hear that sweet Irish soprano."

Molly nodded, closed her eyes and breathed deeply; after she began, Emma began to sing with her. "Nothing of him doth fade / But doth suffer a sea change / Into something rich and strange . . ."

"Molly and Emma sang that at our father's funeral," Anna said to Kepler, softly. They stayed a few yards away from the trio, as if watching an afternoon concert in someone's garden.

Emma's voice was a scratchy, breathy alto, long-unused, but she still remembered the harmony to Molly's melody; Jim Keene's tenor held them together, Molly boldly reaching over to ruffle the salt-and-pepper curls at the nape of his neck. When the final "alleluia" died out, Jim kissed Molly's hand, walked the prescribed distance away, bowed and returned to his own group.

Kepler turned to Anna and said, "Why don't we go somewhere and talk?"

Anna nodded decisively, as if she'd seen enough. She looked over and called, "Emma?"

Emma's glance was startled, annoyed by the interruption. "You go on," she said. "I'll stay with Molly."

"I think Molly needs to rest," Kepler said. "You can see her later, on the unit. I promise . . . We really need to complete her family history."

Anna paused, then said slowly, "Actually, Em . . . I think it's fine if you want to go back with Molly."

Emma's eyes widened. "You want to do the family history without me?"

Anna shrugged, a restrained, barely perceptible gesture.

"Oh," said Emma.

Two pairs of Irish eyes met, Anna standing with her hands on her hips; the way they stared at each other created a deep silence, even amid the hubbub of the visiting families.

Finally Emma turned to Kepler. "I don't actually have much to contribute, as far as family history goes. I'll stay with my sister." Then she turned, following the student nurse who had arrived to escort patients to Chatham.

The nurse was a tiny young woman in a purple Liz Claiborne jumpsuit: at her waist an enormous key-ring, as if she were the chatelaine of some many-roomed castle. Molly pointed to the key-ring, whispering to Emma, "The keys to dreamland."

Jim rejoined Emma and Molly on the path, the trio leading the group back through the grounds. "He said I had a lovely voice," Molly confided in Emma. "But I did not believe him." At the second sentence she seemed to forget Jim's presence, her eyes filling.

Emma looked from Jim to Molly, eyebrows raised, questioning; Jim winked at her, to clear the confusion. Emma nodded and whispered in her sister's ear, as if she were talking to an infant. "It's all right," she said soothingly. "We love you."

Molly shook her head. "Quand'era bambina nell'ancor diceva," she said haltingly, "mamma pappa essa diceva."

At the word "mamma" Shana, behind them, began to cry again. "Oh baby dry my tears," she said, and then laughed. "Oh baby."

The testing room was full today; the new patients had faces aged beyond their years, eyes scared as trapped minks. A few rows to the right, Anna O'Donnell sat with her back straight, disciplined, as she received the MMPI booklet from the administering psychologist. "There are no wrong answers."

Anna sat as she did at her bookkeeping job: one hand under her chin, the other carefully filling in the circles. Emma started more slowly, bending her head so that her hair spilled onto the desk. Each item was numbered, presumably for the purpose of "scoring" this test with no wrong answers. The list of unrelated items could easily become another of Molly's senseless monologues.

49. It would be better if almost all laws were thrown away.
54. I am liked by most people who know me.
60. I do not read every editorial in the newspaper
every day.
65. I loved my father.

Emma felt Anna's glance and looked across: Anna was looking at her answer sheet. Emma bent her head closer, as if to protect hers behind a screen of black hair.

105. Sometimes when I am not feeling well I am cross.
138. Criticism hurts me terribly.
202. I believe that I am a condemned person.

Anna was finished quickly, handing in her paper with alacrity; she shook the attending psychologist's hand and left the room, leaving Emma to read the questions over and over again, as if consulting an oracle. Anna waited in the rear courtyard, facing the weeping willows that veiled Chatham from their view.

"Now wasn't that special," Emma said as they began to walk. "Number 87, I would like to be a florist. How do you think Molly answered that one? And do you think it mattered?"

"Oh, Emma." Anna put her arm around her sister's shoulders; Emma stiffened but didn't move. "You know there are other, more important questions."

"Of course. *I loved my father.*"

"For example."

Emma laughed. "I didn't answer that one."

Anna stopped walking, forcing Emma to do the same. "You know you're supposed to answer all of them."

"But I didn't know the answer, Anna Livia. Did I love Poppie? Or did I just fear him?" Emma started walking again, reversing the game: Anna had to walk, or else release Emma from her sisterly embrace. "Anna, what did you tell the doctor? About Poppie?"

"Only the truth," Anna said. "That he was a great man, and that he and Molly were very close, and his death was probably the greatest tragedy in her life."

"Maybe I should talk to him separately after all." Emma stopped to run her fingers through the leaves of one of the weeping willows. She began to sing, softly. "*I went down to the river / Down beneath the willow tree . . .*" To Anna's quizzical look she explained, "Molly had a blues tape she played a lot this summer, when I came down to visit—it had this song on it, *and that's the reason why I got those weeping willow blues.* So what else did you tell the doctor?"

Anna relaxed her tone, carefully. "Oh, about school, about her music, about that mad affair with the violinist . . . now look at her, with that AIDS patient."

"What AIDS patient? The tenor?"

"Who else, I can't believe how she acts with him!"

"He's very sweet to her," Emma insisted. "He understands her in some weird way—he lets her love him, maybe she needs it after that professor." Emma bit her lip, as if she'd said something she oughtn't.

Anna's laugh was harsh, unexpected. "Talk about inappropriate behavior—to fall in love with a dying man!"

Emma turned away from the laugh, as if from a blow. "I don't think she's 'in love,' it's more like he reminds her of . . ." her voice trailed off, uncertain.

"The word they use around here," Anna said severely, "is

hypersexual." She blotted her brow with a lace handkerchief. "Something Molly always has been, at least since she was eighteen —another classic symptom." She looked back at the main building, reflectively. "This explains a lot, you know."

"What does?"

Anna gestured toward Chatham. "Think about it, Em . . . Hasn't Molly always seemed—a little more intense than necessary? Even this past year, running across Boston in the snow, living breathing James Joyce worse than Poppie ever did. Playing the blues, for God's sake."

"But does that mean she was always sick?"

"The doctor said sometimes it was called . . . the—um—" She pulled the word out and smiled. "The prodromal phase."

"The prodromal phase?" Emma turned and looked behind them, as a group of patients escorted by volunteers crossed the courtyard. Some were the patients from the testing room: Emma watched as the infant girl with the shaved head tossed a volleyball up and down. "Pro-drome instead of syn-drome, I get it. What's the syndrome?"

Anna's voice turned steely, disciplining a stray student. "Schizophrenia, Em."

"Just like Lucia Joyce. Just for being moody." Emma twirled a weeping willow branch around her wrist, her eyes on the patients.

"It's gone past moody, Emma," Anna declared, as if she were explaining a sacrament to her Sunday-school students. "She's not speaking English anymore."

Emma winced. "I still think I should talk to Kepler myself." She looked up, letting the sun sting her eyes. "Anna, I hurt so much I can barely breathe."

"Oh, Emma." Anna's reached forward and teased Emma's hair out of her eyes. "You care so much—and you want Molly to be happy. Just as we all do." Her voice soothing, the sacrament complete. "And back when we were young, when she had those little crying fits by the window . . . Of course you would try to find reasons, and of course you would blame Poppie. How not, when they were so close?"

Emma's eyes were bright, staring at Anna; she swallowed, hard, and nodded.

"But no one loved Molly more than Poppie, Emma. No one was more hurt when she ran from him so suddenly. And it all makes more sense now that we know she has a disease, one that alters your brain chemistry. And maybe it's hereditary, and maybe Mam has it too, and that's why she's been drinking all these years."

"Maybe that's why Leo ran away from home and never came back?" Emma started to cry finally, leaning against Anna's small, bony frame.

"It's okay, it's okay, let it out, let it out."

Emma shook her head, murmuring "My body hurts."

"Em it's going to be all right—she's safe now . . . And next we'll get Shaun here, get it all straightened out." Anna looked over her sister's head, as the clump of patients went back to Chatham. She nodded to herself and stroked Emma's hair, letting the young woman weep in the shadow of the weeping tree.

The day her sisters left Molly, exhausted, refused dinner; it wasn't until later that she found out Jim Keene was gone.

The night nursing shift had just come on at Chatham, a heady café-smell evoked by rival blends of strong coffee from Styrofoam cups. Most of the patients on the unit were asleep, except for the few curled up in the dayroom, absorbed in a late-night movie. The head nurse kept one eye on the TV while she went over the list of admissions and discharges; she hadn't seen a Bogart film in years.

Molly wandered out into the hallway toward Jim's room, wearing only her lacy underwear, her arm loose from its sling. The night nurse didn't catch up with her until she was just outside the door.

"Molly? Are you looking for Jim?" The nurse stared. "Aren't you . . . cold?"

Molly pointed at the door; her smile sleepy from her night meds. "Be hamlet," she said, her voice low-pitched and throaty. "Be offalia." Then she grinned and began to sing right into the door, making up a tune as she went along.

Tomorrow is Saint Valentine's Day
All in the morning betime,
And I, a maid at your window,
To be your Valentine.

Not knowing what to expect, the nurse signaled with one hand for an aide to stand to one side of her and Clay Worth, the student nurse from Louisiana, on the other. "Jim's not here anymore, Molly. His doctors and his friends agreed that he was ready to go home. Isn't that great news?"

Molly tipped her head to one side, looking at her sideways, as if unwilling to believe her.

"Look, his name is even off the door." The nameplate on each patient's door was just a white peel-off office label: now the only one left read POWERS, K.

Before any of them even saw her reach for the doorknob, Molly had thrown the door open, a theatrical gesture as if in a silent film.

Jim's bed had been stripped. The other bed in the room was filled by a still, sleeping body, gray curly hair peeking above the covers.

Molly turned and moved toward Clay, the others hovering about her uncertainly. She raised herself on tiptoes and put her arm around his neck, as if to kiss him; then she whispered in his ear, "They say he is underground. Do you believe that? You don't realize how sly he is. He's only pretending—actually he's here, watching us all the time!"

Before he could respond, she closed her eyes and slid away

from him down to the floor, precisely as if he had hit an "off" switch somewhere under her left shoulder blade.

Once there, she seemed held there by a great weight: despite her thinness, it took all three of them to lift her and carry her back to her own bed, every muscle in her body held rigid. The student nurse couldn't hide the distress in his face as he covered her with a blanket.

"First time you've seen catatonia?" the night nurse asked.

He nodded.

"Yeah it's not as common as it used to be. I remember when half the patients on my ward at St. Francis were either screaming or just like that. I bet they up her crazy drugs tomorrow."

"Personally," said the aide, "I'm just glad Ken didn't wake up and see her like that. I don't care how many meds they got in him, showing a rapist something like that ain't no way to calm him down."

An unseasonably cool morning brought an unnatural quietness to the briefing room: each murmur of arrival seemed a shout, tossed into the vacuum left by the absence of air conditioning. Gail Ryan's crisp voice calmed the hubbub of greetings.

"Ladies and gentlemen, heavens be praised, Molly O'Donnell has an official diagnosis."

"Schizophrenia, of course." The crisp, no-nonsense efficiency of the head nurse's voice made Anne-Marie wince.

Gail nodded. "With affective and paranoid features. Mother may be too but we knew that already . . . and the sisters' MMPI results should be enlightening."

"Shee-it," said an intern, "if Kepler's diagnosis wasn't enough to increase the dosage on her neuroleptics, the midnight vamp act would be."

Clay, the student nurse Molly had embraced, winced. "Now I really know what you all mean by 'hypersexual.'

Gail smiled. "That, Clay, is a pretty extreme case . . . In any event, we're trying her on a new mix: Mellaril 1200 mg b.i.d. and lithium 40 mg. t.i.d."

Anne-Marie underlined on her legal pad: t.i.d. = 3x a day, b.i.d. = 2x. "No antidepressants?" she asked, keeping her voice coolly professional.

"Same dosage of Prozac as before. Meanwhile, Kepler sees no reason she can't be moved to Wilkes—he even doubts at this point that the car accident was an intentional suicide attempt."

"Yeah," said Anne-Marie, "from what her sister said about the weeks before the accident, it sounds more like she was just tripping out." Under Anne-Marie's voice a mockingbird began set of vocal exercises, apparently prompted by the cooler air. "She even had a delusion that she saw Lucia Joyce, every time she went running."

Gail nodded. "So we're moving her today, but we still can't get her into groups till we stabilize her meds a little." She turned the page. "Ken Powers."

"Wait a minute," said Anne-Marie. She flipped backwards in her legal pad, her voice less tentative than usual. "I went over the full history last night, and there's a few details about her family I think the staff ought to know."

Gail looked startled; Anne-Marie had only been officially assigned to Molly O'Donnell's case the previous morning, after Molly's sisters signed the commitment papers. "That's confidential information, Anne-Marie, and not all of it is appropriate for this meeting. Let's discuss this later."

Anne-Marie nodded, suppressing a half-smile. "Ken Powers, then?" The mockingbird burst into full voice, drowning out the unison sound of everyone flipping to a new page.

The first thing Felicia and Rachel noticed about Wilkes was the carpeting.

In Chatham, the floors were easily cleaned linoleum and the

walls largely bare, except for patients' art and a large schedule of "Weekly Activities." At Wilkes, quiet Renoir prints and soft landscape photographs, beautifully framed, lined the walls above mauve, law-firm carpeting.

"Remind me not to hire their decorator," Felicia whispered to Rachel. Rachel carried a vase of gladiolas, Felicia a box with a smattering of possessions from Molly's room.

"Remember," said the nurse leading them, "she's on some new medications, so she may not be as responsive as you expect."

Rachel nodded. Felicia said, "Expect? What do you think I'm expecting? Last time, she couldn't stop singing Schubert. So what are these new drugs?"

"I'm sorry, you'll have to ask her doctor."

The room itself had no carpeting, not unlike the one Molly had shared with Shana at Chatham; Felicia and Rachel moved in slowly, quietly. Under a green blanket, their former roommate lay still. "Is she asleep?"

But the blue eyes were open; Molly's arms were wrapped around her pillow as she stared at some point above the white-paneled ceiling. Felicia sat on the edge of the bed while Rachel placed the flowers on Molly's night-table.

"Molly? Molly, it's us, we came to see how you were doing."

With a grimace, Molly sat up; she seemed to have trouble moving her limbs. "Thank you for coming," she said slowly.

"How are you?" Rachel pulled up a chair and reached for Molly's hands; the fingers were stiff, and trembled a little.

"I'm . . . I've been better."

An expression of relief crossed Rachel's face, at Molly's coherence. Felicia busied herself tacking things to the wall behind Molly's bed. "Where do you want this Van Gogh, Molly?"

Molly looked over, trying to focus on the print Felicia had brought from her room. "Oh don't put that up," she said, "I don't want to stay here that long. My sisters want me to, though." Her speech had the same jerky quality as her movements. "Blood will suffer blood to die hungry."

"Your sisters just want what's best," Rachel said. "You're being taken care of."

Molly bent her head and started to cry. "I feel so terrible," she said. "My whole body is stiff, my head hurts. Can I please come home to Calvert Street?"

"I'm sorry, Molly, that's not up to us," Rachel said. "Besides, I think you need to get better first . . . Look, we brought you some music."

Felicia went into her shoulder bag and brought out a small, compact sports Walkman, and some tapes. "I couldn't carry them all," she said, trying to manage a smile. "Let me know if you want something else."

"No!" Molly's scream was as unexpected as it was loud. "No music, not anymore." She started crying, lying back on the bed and sobbing into the pillow.

Rachel backed off, trying not to look at the door. "Why, Molly, why?"

Molly sat up then, swallowing hard. As she chanted the color came back in her face, but her body was still, heavy. "He is dead and gone, lady, he is dead and gone; at his head a grass-green turf, at his heels a stone."

"Hamlet," Rachel whispered to Felicia.

"I know." Felicia went sat on the edge of her roommate's bed. "Who, Molly? Who's dead?"

"James the famous Irish writer . . . lesions internal." She closed her eyes and whispered "oh Babbo . . ." Then she placed the earphones directly over her ears, accepting one of the tapes Felicia held out to her; she lay on her side and listened with her eyes closed, her broken arm grieving against her chest.

"Oh I'm so glad you brought music!" Anne-Marie's cheerful, energetic entrance, while a little discordant, did dispel some of the grayness spreading from Molly to her friends. She hugged Felicia,

81

quickly. "You know, I didn't realize when I saw you last week, that it was Molly you had come to see."

Felicia stepped away, creating some distance. "I didn't know you knew her."

"Well—" Anne-Marie shrugged, a little embarrassed. "I've only officially been her social worker since Monday . . . I'd been hoping to talk to her about music."

Rachel gestured to the silent Molly. "Good luck," she said.

"It's okay," Anne-Marie told them. "I know what this is." She turned to Molly and tapped the earphones, until the patient lifted them and looked at her.

"He is dead and gone," Molly said, staring up at Anne-Marie.

Anne-Marie smiled, quieted. "Molly—I told you, Jim is fine. His friends have taken him on a long, long vacation, he always wanted to see the world. I'm sure he'll write to you."

"Words words words," Molly lifted her head. "Young men will do it if they come to it / By Cock! they are to blame."

Anne-Marie swallowed. "Molly I just stopped in to see how you were doing; I don't want to interrupt your visit with your friends. I'll see you later, okay? Maybe just before dinner?"

Molly shrugged her assent; as soon as Anne-Marie left, she put the earphones back on and lay down, ignoring Felicia and Rachel both.

"Anne-Marie's amazing," Rachel said to Felicia as they walked the path from Wilkes to the parking lot, just behind the admissions building. "It's hard to find a person over thirty who's still that wide-eyed—almost childlike."

"I don't know," Felicia said, wiping sweat off her brow with a red bandana. "I never particularly cared for her before—and yet the way Philip talks about her now, even though their relationship didn't work out, you'd think she was some fucking angel." They stopped by the Volkswagen and Felicia leaned on the bumper, waiting for Rachel to take out her car keys. "I'd like to feel like I trusted somebody in this place."

"They're doing the best they can," Rachel said, opening the door and letting out some of the hot-car air.

Felicia slid into the passenger seat. "If that is the best our mental health profession can do," she said, kicking off her sandals, "we are all up fucking shit creek."

"I'm glad to see you so settled in," Dr. Kepler said to Molly the next morning, right after breakfast. "I just came to check on you for a few minutes." He reached down and picked up the Walkman coiled neatly in her lap, extracting the tape. He held the cassette up to the light, to read the titles imprinted on the clear plastic. "Bach cello suites. Do you remember playing the cello, Molly? Your sisters said it was very important to you, once."

Molly's eyes were confused, as though he were speaking about someone else: but her arm moved across her belly in an instinctive bow motion, until she bit her lip from the pain.

"I had a nice talk with both Anna and Emma," Kepler said. "I learned a lot. About your music, about marathons, about Colin—about your mother and father."

Molly's eyes widened, as if he had gotten her attention for the first time. "Mother is putting my secondhand clothes in order," she said softly. She took the cassette out of Kepler's hand and returned it to her Walkman; she placed the headset on her head, but didn't turn it on. "The gloom hath rays," she said, lying down. "Her lump is love." Her words faded out, as though she were falling asleep.

Kepler glanced at his watch, which showed fifteen minutes till the ethics task force meeting. Then, quietly, Molly turned to the Van Gogh print on the wall, painfully enunciating a sentence he had already heard many times before.

"And my father," Molly said to the sunflowers, "had blood in his eyes."

Lucihere!

18 December

I'm furious: I can't believe it. This morning for the first time since November, there she was—Lucia Joyce, haunting the baseball stadium.

I thought I finally took care of this after I called 911. I was sure they'd taken her somewhere safe, where she won't freeze to death or hurt anyone. But this morning she was back at her station, staring her lost Lucia eyes right at Memorial Stadium.

I was working up to just the right pace and didn't have time to stop, but it's definitely the same woman—the same ugly coat, hair a little longer, different sloppy shoes. The same stare: I'm beginning to wonder if she's blind. As blind as Joyce, as blind as Will? But she's not even anyone's father, cries out my eight-year-old self, the child who thought all fathers were blind.

Not even Gary really believes that I thought that: but he was never seven years old in Will's study, looking at photos of James Joyce in books held out to me by a father whose sight was long since gone—Joyce with his white cane and his wife at his elbow, his stiff son and small daughter. (The infamous Lucia, of course.) Nor did Gary hear stories in that blind father's sweet voice, about how half of Paris was seemingly working for Joyce: taking dictation for *Finnegans Wake,* or reading to Joyce or writing his business letters. Including, of course, Lucia.

And just as I'm trying to banish Lucia's messy life from my dissertation, I do my best to contend with her echo at the baseball stadium. I called the police again, just before I called Emma to check times (me: eight miles, 73 minutes. Hers considerably slower, still working off all that new-baby fat).

Emma wants to know exactly when I am coming home for Christmas. To the minute, it seems. "Shaun's getting here on the 22nd, in the afternoon." How can I tell her how I dread coming "home" to Boston?

Everyone else seems devoted to this concept called the "O'Donnell family." It comforts them, they don't question it: even Shaun in New York calls Margaret or Anna at least twice a week. But the concept leaves me cold, a campfire that doesn't tempt me into their circle.

I could absent myself completely, as Leo has done since he was sixteen. I remember his quiet merry comment when I visited him in San Francisco a few Christmases ago, during a Colin concert tour: "There's no law that says one has to go home for Christmas," he said, gathering his hair (longer than mine, behind a receding hairline) into a ponytail. Then he turned it into a joke: "I suppose if I ever did, I'd be a special delivery holiday fruitcake."

But Leo's absence is as expected as my presence, as much a part of the family order. (My absence due to that concert an aberration, tolerated only because of the glamour factor.) So it's left to me to be the black sheep of the family, if I don't come; left to me to break my mother's heart.

I'm the only one leaving the Calvert Street house. Rachel's an observant Jew, "our really important holidays were in October," she'll go to Florida for New Year's at her grandmother's. And Felicia? "I don't do holidays." Of course not, even though these days your Christmas carols could be delivered in screaming rock and roll. (If we survive this year together it will be what she would call "a fucking miracle.")

As for Gary, he's his Italian Catholic self: "Just grin and bear it . . . you'll be back here before you know it." And then he kissed my shoulders, lingering in the hollow of my shoulder blade with his tongue.

This thing is astonishing. The sex keeps getting better and better (I spent every night of last week at his house) and we share our work increasingly, especially now that I might be assisting him in the spring. (Only one other grad student is gunning for the Madness in Shakespeare assistantship, and I happen to know her work's not as good as mine. Even if it is in Renaissance poetry). But now he's off, to his and his wife's matching New York family Christmases. (They were high school sweethearts, that's how a chemist and a Shakespearean get together. "You only get snotty about that stuff later," he said.)

So I'll try to take his advice; we'll all sit around and pretend Margaret isn't drinking too much, and Emma and I will run together through the streets of Cambridge. That part I'm looking forward to—I love it when people mistake us for twins, although I doubt that'll happen in mid-winter unless we buy matching ski masks and gloves.

20 December

Every tellin' has a talin' and that's the he and the she of it . . . between the fight with Felicia and Barbara Daniels' reappearance, I don't know where to begin.

What? The lost sheep of Lit 120, last seen snuggled next to some surfer type at the Senator movie theatre? never to be seen at school again, we thought? yes indeed, my child. Time to tuck up me sleeves and loosen me talktapes.

Barbara first, since she is at this very moment on her way over.

Today was the last day of class, the pre-announced date of a venerable Ross Tilden tradition: instead of a lecture he plays a recording of James Joyces' voice, reciting the *Wake's* "Anna Livia Plurabelle" passage. It's so famous that other faculty show up, grad students from other departments that regard it as theatre; for godsake Tilden even dims the lights. And just as the *Wake* really sends him, the passage sent much of its audience, the prick of the spindle that gives us the keys to dreamland.

From Lit 120 itself we had only a small group, of course, all with that finals-week pallor, a few even lulled to sleep by Joyce's sweet, chant-like voice, an overgrown choirboy or an unsuccessful actor (he was both, of course). I watched as they listened to Anna Livia—both my little group and the others, anonymous faces melted into each Tuesday and Thursday morning for the past four months. Just the right combination of scholarship and frivolity for the final class, to sit and hear Joyce's voice ring out those energetic, maddening words.

Tilden wasn't watching them: he was transported by the words into the realm where he is happiest, he's what Joyce called "abced-minded." He shifted his weight from one foot to another in a little slow dance, the *Wake* feels that erotic to him. Anna Livia certainly is, anyway.

I watched the students bite their lips, trying to make it out as the passage got denser; some laughing out loud at the sexiness of it, perhaps finally getting it—finally getting that underneath Joyce's opaque language, his convoluted Jesuit brain, is the soul of an earthy Irishman who liked his beer cold and his sex dirty. "He had to forget the monk in the man so, rubbing her up and smoothing her down . . ."

And then I saw Barbara, standing in the back of the lecture hall. And crying.

I followed her out when class was over, and she asked to come over this evening. Maybe she wants to try to save her grade after all.

Tilden has already penciled in an F for her. "Your basic no-show—she should have dropped the class if she wasn't going to come."

But I still remember how bright-eyed she was at the beginning, this little Bible Belt sweetie inhaling Yeats and Eliot like newfound oxygen. And I want to give her a chance; there must be some reason for all this.

I can guess what it is, too. Joyce called it the word known to all men, God knows it's known to all women; Barbara wept as Joyce sang, "That was kissahealing with banter for balm!" I remember the jock-types kissing her into Lit 120, until she stopped coming—which one finally persuaded her not to get out of bed? Which one finally broke her?

2:30 a.m.

And Barbara is safely asleep on the couch in my bedroom, having cried herself out: I was right, though she wouldn't (couldn't?) identify the male in question. What I didn't expect was that she is pregnant.

She doesn't know yet what to do, what with her Bible-thumping parents, and she seems to have some qualms herself about abortion. But "if I go home like this," she cried into my towel, "they'll kill me!"

I had no advice for her. The one serious pregnancy scare I ever had did bring on a moment of reflection—of considering the eccentric, musically gifted child I could bring into the world, simply by not acting. Though Colin made it abundantly clear my decision had nothing to do with him: no child was going to interfere with his globe-trotting future. Just as well, the child would now have bruises: probably on the back and neck.

But I wasn't pregnant, and life went on, and what do I say now to this shaking undergraduate, heartbreak mixing with hormones to yield incompletes in all her classes? Her family in Georgia expects her home in three days. I try to imagine eating Christmas dinner and not knowing if you want to be eating for two.

I still want to write about the fight with Felicia, but I'm falling asleep so it will have to wait. Perhaps even for the Amtrak train, on the way up to Boston. (Bringing new meaning to the *Wake's* famous "Letter" and its "Sender: Boston, Mass!")

22 December

Holiday madness in Penn Station (Baltimore): undergraduates with ten suitcases each, whole families with Christmas boxes in their laps, trains delayed for minutes or hours. You have to strain to hear the announcements on the loudspeakers, over the shouting and babies crying and the rap music of some teenager's boom box. The Christmas boxes remind me that I come empty-handed: no gift for Margaret, or Emma, or even little Steve. Looks like a madcap Christmas Eve shopping trip is in order, except that I have about enough money to buy each member of my family a candy bar.

Just as well, I'm carrying as much as I want to—for I have in my pack a syllabus, a Riverside Shakespeare, and a pile of photocopied articles.

What does this mean? Yes, I got the assistantship!

If I have to teach, I hope it's always like this. God what luxury, to shepherd juniors and seniors through a thesis-sized paper! "Madness in Shakespeare" is one of Gary's most popular classes, and we have forty kids signed up.

And no, I didn't sleep my way into the job. It makes all the sense in the world given my dissertation topic—and not just the madness part. Macbeth and Lear are both minor fish in the *Wake*-river, while Hamlet runs through both *Ulysses* and *Finnegans Wake* ("Be hamlet. Be offalia."). Speaking of "offalia," the photocopies are Gary's Ophelia articles, the ones that made his reputation and first birthed this class.

No James Joyce packed, this trip—but several of my notebooks, for I also hope to return from this vacation with some clarity about the dissertation. It all looked so promising in August but I've been treading water for weeks, and am about to drown if human voices don't wake me soon.

All autumn I've been mucking about with pseudo-psychiatric interpretations for both *Portrait* and *Ulysses*: this is obsession, these are hallucinations, blab bola bla. Not only am I straying out of schizophrenia and into just general "mental disorder," it's none of it very original. Every place I stand, someone else has already been, looking farther and often more clearly.

Tilden told me to take the holidays to "think it through," but I already know what he thinks—that I have to abandon my scheme of looking at the work as a whole and go straight into the belly of the beast, into *Finnegans Wake*. "Then perhaps go back," he said to me yesterday, "and touch on the earlier work as support, citing the scholars who have already blazed that trail." How he loves it, scholars holding hands on paper, like scientists building on one another's discoveries.

I don't think I could cite Will, though—he had little truck with "those Freudians." I would, however, probably have to cite or refute the scholars who think mad Lucia was the muse of the *Wake*, a prospect I find even less enticing than this Boston Christmas.

Oh Jesus, my train has just been delayed for two hours, that means 1 a.m.—this is the Amtrak equivalent of a red-eye flight. I need to call Emma, she's supposed to meet me in Back Bay at 7 a.m.

I may as well recount the past 2 days, especially the fight with Felicia—and our house's holiday dinner, a Rachel-midwifed peace ceremony between the other two of us.

I suppose Felicia grew used to my absence from all my nights at Gary's; perhaps that's why she felt free to put her music back up to its former level of cacophony. But night before last I came home late from the library instead, to the sounds of some strange combination of Caribbean drums and New York head-banger rock and roll.

Bone-weary and wanting only to sleep, I climbed the extra flight to her room and knocked, hard. She took her time opening the door: when it opened she was wearing only a huge T-shirt and rubber gloves, her antique (dangerous?) space heater going full blast. Her gloves were covered with paint and her eyes still comatose, my theory about cocaine obviously incorrect. "Oh sorry," she said, "I didn't know you were home. I'll turn it down."

Still angry, I pointed to the space heater. "And how much is that going to escalate our electric bill?"

Felicia shrugged. "We can talk about it when the bill comes. I'll pay extra if you want."

"With what money? You said the tips weren't so great these days." I suddenly saw myself as an unintentional patron of non-arts, losing both sleep and money to this untalented Picasso wannabe.

It was amazing, anger made her eyes go wider than I'd ever seen them. "What the fuck business is it of yours?"

The rest of the argument blurs in my memory. Felicia called me a bitch and a "control freak," whatever that means, while sleeplessness loosened all my inhibitions. I said a lot of what I'd said only to this journal, how disgusted I was by her tattoos, my suspicions of drug abuse.

Already past the point of utter fatigue, I finally walked out at a random pause; she had peeled off her rubber gloves and was staring at the slice of wax-paper on which she had mixed her colors, watching the daubs of paint dry. I stumbled downstairs and fell into bed with my clothes on.

The next day I told Rachel I was moving out, and she said "No, no, I'm sure you guys can work this thing out." As far as I was concerned there was nothing to work out—and furthermore, no one with whom to do so. "I no longer sleep with musicians," I told Rachel, "or traffic with fools."

But Rachel insisted on this sort of family therapy session, and yesterday morning we sat down together over breakfast. Felicia said tightly, her paint-stained fingers clenched, "I don't get it, why do you hate me so much?"

I had to admit I didn't hate her. Reluctantly I told her about Margaret's alcoholism, perhaps inspired by Emma, who blames it for every negative experience in her life. The revelation certainly brightened Rachel's eyes: there's even some truth to it, after all.

For our holiday dinner last night Felicia made a phenomenal spanakopita, one Homer himself would have adored. "My mother is Greek," she said shyly, as if meeting me for the first time.

And it worked; even her tattooed wrists seemed softened by the candlelight. Rachel just sat back and beamed, and Felicia asked me, timidly, how I might feel about switching rooms next semester. She's "thinking of going back to drawing," and covets my light-filled windows. "The attic is huge, you wouldn't be losing space."

"I know," I said, "I grew up in an attic . . . well, half an attic. The other half was my father's study, which was also my rehearsal room." This was the first either had heard of my years playing the cello, so that conversation kept us going till it was time to go to bed.

Now Felicia has the house to herself, and how I envy her; the more the train is delayed the more I dread this eight-hour journey. I hope Emma and I can go for our first run immediately on my arrival —I'll need to after those hours crunched into a train seat, and there's something dreamlike about running half-awake as the muscles protest.

23 December

4:30 a.m. and I actually slept for a few hours, until the train stopped in New York and a flood of noise filled the car. Most astonishing are the businessmen in natty wool coats and paisley ties, obviously on their way to catch a power breakfast in Boston two days before Christmas. I thought that sort of thing went out with the 1980s.

And I dreamt of Will, of course, easily, inevitably—though it was less a dream than a single gentle image, like a Renoir painting.

Will is old, patrician in his big study chair, his hair gone far whiter than it ever did in life. And I am sitting at his feet—impossibly and yet, in the dream wonderfully, I am about eight months pregnant. He speaks slowly, telling me what my child will need to learn, what I must ensure that she reads. "Don't forget Hamlet," he keeps repeating, "She needs to remember Hamlet." No mention of James Joyce, but I knew that was a given. My hand on my belly, I think, "Oh musical child, you'll know Shakespeare, you'll know the violin; you'll know *Ulysses*."

I woke laughing. Of course, the music had to come first, the tiny instrument passed into the hands of the preschooler. Will and I had done music together for six years, I was already ten when he first handed me *Ulysses*, saying "Please read to me, from the top of page 153. The chapter is called 'Lestrygonians.' But it doesn't say that."

In my visual memory of that day, the now-familiar words don't even look like English. I remember disbelieving: "The one that starts 'pineapple rock'?"

"Yes." Will's voice as assured as when he corrected my fingering, his expression calm, inward-looking, as if he were packing for a conference and choosing his clothes (he could match them by the feel of the cloth). "Don't worry about the meaning, just do it. Think of it as a silly poem."

Amazing how soon the confusion went away, how delighted I was (as now!) with the word-plays, with its just plain silliness. I don't need to pull out my book to write down what I read that first day: I still have it memorized as I do the music we played together, memorized from years of reading to him for his book about Judaic imagery. He preferred me to a tape recorder, so I would read the crucial passages over and over again. So there I was at ten: "pineapple rock. Lemon platt, butter scotch. A sugarsticky girl shoveling scoopfuls of creams for a christian brother." God what joy, what juicy sacrilege for a fifth grader still clad in the starched white shirt and plaid skirt of Sacred Heart School.

"Are you saved? All are washed in the blood of the lamb. God wants blood victim. Birth, hymen, martyr, war, foundation of a building, sacrifice, kidney burntoffering, druid's altars, Elijah is coming." I remember laughing as I imagined my religion teacher, Sister Margaret, passing out; and I can still feel Will's hand stroking my hair, gently, in affirmation. (His right hand: with his left he wrote in his huge spiral notebook, notes for some grad student to read back to him later.) It was the same gesture he used when he liked the way I played Bach. His hand came to rest on my neck; I kept reading, no idea that this was particularly hard and certainly none that it bore any relation to those dumb English classes where they were trying to make me write topic sentences.

"Please read," not just a request from my father but a directive from my partner in music. I bet if I ever meet someone who discovered literature the way I did, sort of the Suzuki method, I'll have found the man of my dreams—some Faulkner scholar and former violist who met Mozart and *The Sound and the Fury* the exact same way, through that peremptory, reassuring parental command: "Don't worry that it's hard. Just do it."

Now the train is pulling into New Haven and families squeeze their way on board, shoving huge packages down the aisles (there are no seats left). And I think I'll stand up and let someone sit— maybe that tired young mom just now getting on, arms full with two kids and a stack of packages in Bert-and-Ernie wrapping paper.

2:30 p.m.

In the food court at Fanueil Hall, this tourist trap, to get my shopping done quickly. (Thank God for my small family and my brand-new MasterCard.) I haven't seen any of them yet, except Emma; we meet Anna in about half an hour for the ritual Dance of the Three Sisters, buying groceries for Christmas Eve dinner. So far, all I've done is get here, run, and shop.

And the fatigue is settling in, finally, from the trip. I did stand up for that little family, and the mother soon fell asleep, as soundly as the infant in her front-pack. Her two-year-old daughter looked at me and tapped her ear, asking in wordless syllables what that was on my head. I almost put the speakers on her ears, but it seemed too intrusive.

(And yet I hoped, still dreaming and remembering Will, that somewhere in one of their suitcases was an eighth-size violin; that either this mom or a father somewhere stands by her every day, putting her through the paces of "Twinkle, Twinkle Little Star.")

And there she was: my baby sister. Her front-pack matched that of my little friend's mom, in a sort of Arctic parka with the hood flung back, her hair tangled and sweaty underneath. Little Stevie was looking around with a bleary stare, like a newly awakened kitten: his eyes are turning the same golden brown as Emma's, as Margaret's.

"He's not used to all this noise," Emma said, letting me hug her side. "Remember Aunt Molly, Stevie?"

"Of course he doesn't," I said, "the last time, he didn't even know his hands were attached to his arms." Now, I must confess, he's looking quite a bit more like a person, less an undifferentiated red-faced creature with a nose vaguely like Emma's. He seemed placid enough, not alarmed at the holiday ruckus all around him, and he stayed awake while I dozed, as Emma drove us all back to their house on the border between Cambridge and Somerville.

Today Emma gave me my Christmas present early so we could run together, in matching, new-fangled yuppie running stuff: Olympic-looking spandex, it really does keep you warm and doesn't look quite so much like you're running in your underwear. Even with such equipment, it was far too cold for an extended run, so we settled for a quick slip toward Harvard—I still feel the stab in my stomach, of what might have been had I been able to go there, if I had not had to leave Will behind.

After mild Baltimore I'm not used to these snowdrifts, lining the streets like barricades, gray with car exhaust. In order not to crash into them I had to watch Emma, who breezed past them without even looking.

As we rounded the corner of Mass Ave toward Harvard Yard, I finally asked: "How's Margaret doing, so far?"

"So far so good—she's just so thrilled, she nearly screamed when Shaun came in the door." Of course, her precious son. Nothing more worthless than a daughter, the Chinese say. "And she can't wait to see you, of course," Emma lied hastily.

Harvard Yard was temporarily deserted due to Christmas break, but the paths had been cleared between the snow-covered, winter-bared trees, and the quieting effect of the snow only intensified the Yard's protective embrace. As always, the city felt years away, 300-year-old buildings resting easy in their man-made grove.

Then we emerged into trumpeting Boston traffic and street-vendor smells, leaving by the gate that says ENTER YE TO GATHER WISDOM. Where Shaun, at sixteen, used to drive by with his friends, shouting "I'm not impressed!" So today I bought him a Harvard tie, laughing as I handed over my credit card. I loved the feel of the silk, and it's fun to tease him about his Harvard MBA, after all that shouting.

Otherwise, this shopping trip was my yearly stroke against aliteracy, books and more books. I got little Stevie a beautiful hardcover of Portrait of the Artist as a Young Man, for use in about fourteen years. He'll find out eventually why he's named Stephen, and may as well have his own copy of the book that bears his name.

24 December

Midafternoon scribble, between after-run shower and dressing for Anna's dinner.

All I want to know is, how do I know these people? How do they know me?

What is this disparate group? Certainly not "those O'Donnell kids"—that round-faced clump who dominated the track teams of our respective schools, played music together on Sundays, and showed up in a starched group for Mass, bobbing behind our parents like well-trained dolphins. No these are remote strangers, the more so every time I see them. (Emma, of course, is the exception—either more my friend than my sister, or the only sibling I really have.)

Shaun has gained so much weight—oh, he dresses it and carries it well, a "substantial" businessman, but all the gray pinstripe in the world can't hide the sheer girth. How does he get around the trading floor like that?

I was also shocked by Anna, who seems to have gone gray overnight, or at least in the last six months. I don't know if it's taking care of Margaret, playing aunt to Emma's baby, or too many kids dropping out of Sunday school before they've been nabbed for confirmation. She's taught it for years but she's gotten even more involved lately—yes ma'am, the pope will canonize you any day now.

As for Margaret, she is right now on her best beehiveiour: she's dyed her hair again, a far more outrageous shade of red than it ever was naturally. All dressed up and made up—the only clues to the bottle hidden somewhere are her over-loud laugh and the pink spots at the top of her cheekbones, nearly hidden by all that fat. I almost couldn't stand her greeting, the histrionic "Oh my Molly!," the pillowy embrace as if she really cares. Oh, I suppose she does, but it's love in the abstract: "my Molly" is some three-year-old with black curly hair, no relation to anyone I might be.

Shaun keeps busy as her attendant—*do you want dessert, is it too cold in here for you, no I'll get the sugar bowl.*

Of course, Anna and Margaret will lead the parade to midnight Mass, Margaret's annual attempt to infect us with her love affair with the Church (as if one opiate weren't enough). Perhaps it's her way of bringing Will back, each Christmas, by returning us to the very church where they met—Will a proud and handsome young altar boy, Margaret a red-haired soprano in the choir.

25 December

early, early, early—no one else yet awake. The baby is mercifully too young to be rousing his parents at dawn to check out Santa Claus, so Emma and Barry and I get to sleep off the aftermath of Christmas Eve. God, the minute I stepped into that church I felt my life set out before me, and thought perhaps I was dying.

In fast-forward: Emma and I lining up for First Communion, in mini-bridal outfits complete with tiny white gloves; my own unsuccessful stint in church choir, never quite getting my voice out of mezzo up to soprano; Emma's frosted sugar wedding.

And Will's funeral, of course, Margaret in her most flattering widow's black and most careful tear-proof mascara, weeping royally over the open casket holding his closed face. A wake but not the *Wake* —unlike Finnegan, Will would not rise again from his coffin, no matter how much alcohol you poured into his grave. God knows Margaret tried.

"Look what they've done with the altar," Anna whispered to me last night. To me it looked the same as always, right down to the poinsettias and burning Christmas tapers. I was mostly glad about the music—Dorchester may be a "rough" neighborhood but Sacred Heart still pulls out all the stops for Christmas Eve, the choir helped by a small ensemble with strings and a few brass instruments, giving it all the right sacred feel. And as the families assembled, the choir was singing Mozart's Ave Verum.

Emma and I looked at each other and tried to sing along, though none of us sing anymore. "Ave, ave verum. Co-oo-orpus / Natum de Maria virgine . . ." I am sixteen and standing in the choir, I am nonexistent and Will is an altar boy, I am seven and Will is next to me, fingers twirled in my hair —the first Christmas since his sight left completely, he sends out a rough, sad baritone, so unlike the high pitch of his speaking voice. The mingled smells—flowers, candles, women's Christmas perfume—are exactly the same. Even Father Michael is still with us, though he must be ninety by now, frail and proud in his red and white and gold vestments.

Standing room only: tired children in creased velvet filled the back of the church with their anxious parents. Margaret, Anna and Shaun ignored the Mozart, instead peeping around like everyone else to see who showed up this year, who is missing. Amazing how many families like ours, actually reassemble year after year for this ritual.

I recognized the Dooleys and the McGuires, as well as McNamara's Band with their twelve kids, now taking up three whole rows with spouses and offspring. Emma had Stevie with her, fast asleep; a poor showing indeed, compared with the breeding capacity of our former schoolmates!

And they were checking us out at the same rate—*oh look, the O'Donnell's are here.* Some of the stares friendly, *oh isn't it grand how they still support their poor mother.* Others—perhaps the majority—more critical, distant. Almost no one came over to say hello to any of us, with the exception of Anna's church buddies, other eternal daughters whose divorces are somehow forgiven through devotion to God and family.

I don't know how we got to be such pariahs. Perhaps Will has been gone too long, perhaps it's still the legend of Leo setting fire to the garage and hitch-hiking out of Boston at the age of sixteen. Or maybe some of them have actually visited Margaret, smelled the odor of non-sacramental wine. But I could have sworn a few of the Dooleys were pointing at me—am I still in disgrace for two years of living "in sin" with a British violinist?

Will, did you have Joyce's commentary running in your head when you stood with your parents at these Christmas Eve services? Did you imagine yourself Stephen Dedalus, doing his rosaries eight times a day and dedicating each day of the week to a different saint, before rejecting it all to become an artist? And what would you think now of my footnote, that the intensity of all of Stephen's obsessions could be regarded as the "prodromal phase" of schizophrenia?

When it came time for communion, I took the baby in my lap so Emma could join the line; I sang along with the choir as the aisles swelled, clogged, like Grand Central Station on a winter commuter morning. "Sing, choirs of angels / Sing in exaltation / Sing all ye citizens of Bethlehem."

As they inched toward the altar, Shaun held Margaret's hand exactly as if he were still three years old, ridiculous now that he's pushing forty (not to mention 240 pounds). Emma was close behind, her hand on Margaret's shoulder. Then Stevie woke up, stirred by the noise of people returning to their seats on the pew, and began to fuss a little.

Gingerly I moved him upright to my breast, and let him watch the crowd and the candlelight and the motion. Will you sing someday, little Stephen? *Long lay the world / In sin and error pining / Till he appeared and the soul felt its birth . . .* At *Fall on your knees*, I watched Emma lift her head, her eyes closed as the priest lay the wafer on her tongue. Stevie will you grow up rejecting it all like your namesake did? Will you write in your journal, "Mother is putting my secondhand clothes in order" and leave home, as your Aunt Molly did?

By the time they all returned, Stevie had fallen asleep again. I guess he's what they call a "good" baby, one not easily stirred. Personally, I'd be worried were I his mother: a child that phlegmatic may be far too receptive to TV or Catholic school. After "This mass is ended, go in peace," the choir began *Silent Night*—of course, they haven't changed the end of midnight Mass since 1923. They dimmed the lights in the church, and Emma, Shaun and I looked at one another—for at the organ's opening notes we all become twelve years old again.

There they were, two dozen preteens in well-polished shoes walking down the center aisle with lit candles—their eyes round and serious, a little scared, angels newly pressed into service. "Sleep in heavenly peace."

One year my choir robe was too long and I had to walk extra slow so as not to trip; another, Leo had to drop out because of a black eye. Then there was the famous year Emma, her hair in some sort of curly perm that fell into her eyes, singed it with her candle. We didn't say anything to Will, of course, but his acute nose caught the slight burnt scent. "What have you done?"

Will, what have you done, leaving me here alone with these people? Today Emma is with her in-laws, while I dine with Margaret's family in Waltham and then spend the night "at home," in my old room in Dorchester—right next door to your study, Will.

But first, time for Emma's and Christmas-morning run. Time to swerve past all the overjoyed or disappointed children as they're bundled up by their parents, over the river and through the woods to grandmother's house to go.

1:30 a.m. (26 December, I suppose)

Writing this slung across this undear old single bed of "mine"— Margaret long ago turned my old room into a sewing room, few traces of "my Molly." Just the slanting attic walls the slightly odd angles of my growing up, one still bearing a poster of Yo-Yo Ma; some old clothes of mine are still in a box in the corner, next to the ironing board; and this bed is still right under the skylight, Margaret must have just moved everything else around it. (There are no traces of the attic's original occupant, the notorious Leo. I think Will actually ordered that his things be burned.) And I feel the urge to go next door, to sleep in Will's study chair and try to clear the migraine headache Christmas dinner has given me.

Only the third migraine of my life, each one raising the ghostly threat of the aneurysm that killed my father. And tonight I think I know why the blood vessel burst in his brain so close to Easter, so soon after a

Catholic family dinner choked with smoke, mingled with the stench of alcohol and loud senseless voices. In order to breathe I kept having to walk outside into the snowy, bitter cold of my aunt's suburban lane.

I never remember I have this many relatives, especially after missing two Christmases via Colin's holiday concerts; last year I paid no attention, I was too busy nursing my bruises. This year they expect me to remember and I can't, all these Kellys—my mother's family only, the actual O'Donnells long since melted into their aristocratic Beacon Hill residences.

And I am exhausted by saying over and over again the same words, to family members who don't really give a damn anyway. Baltimore. Teaching. James Joyce, yes, just like Poppie. Running again. No, no music, not any more. Over and over again until it begins to sound like the "perseverations" in the psych books.

All the time conscious of what I'm leaving out: the affair with a married professor, the rock and roll housemate with her nightmare tattoos, the homeless woman with the Lucia Joyce stare. Perhaps I should have put on some other performance entirely—maybe Hamlet, Ophelia's mad scene, scattering flower petals while singing obscene songs. "Young men will do't if they come to it / By Cock, they are to blame." I bet they would have found that more entertaining.

As each group of Kellys arrived Margaret was in her most high decibel, perfumed glory—leaving smears of red lipstick on the cheeks of her sisters and brothers, making sure the smallest cousins noticed the plastic pine cone pinned to her breast. Most of the relatives brought bottles of wine or brandy, the best example I've seen of what Emma calls "denial."

Will, how did you survive this? I see you sitting in the corner, remote, probably planning your next paper or else running the whole event through a Joycean filter in your mind in order to endure it. And I could surely feel the Christmas of *Portrait of the Artist* tonight, as uncles reached into the turkey for "the pope's nose" and my great-grandmother consigned to hell all who didn't attend midnight Mass. "We even saw Molly there, this year," she said, implying with that phrase that she (and the Pope, if not his nose) might now forgive the two years of my unmarried disgrace with Colin.

I missed you most during coffee, Will. I remember your high-pitched voice demanding exactly the right strong brew, the right rich full-bodied cream, your whisper: more cream, Shem—you know my taste. Instead I watched Shaun add a touch of Jameson's to his cup, a possible source for all those excess pounds. Will, what has become of your children?

I don't know, Shem, he answers. *What will become of yours?* By which he means the dissertation—and here I am, no more ready to move forward, still (in Tilden's words) "mucking about having undergraduate fun with Jung and Joyce." What does that child need to read, to flourish? Is it really *Hamlet?*

Perhaps it is. Perhaps Will really has given me the key. Hamlet's "madness" may be Shakespeare's equivalent of Joyce's "schizophrenic" speech, using madness to get at the truth. But then can we ignore Ophelia, the mirror image Gary writes about: a woman driven truly mad when Hamlet rejects her, when he unwittingly kills her father? "Tomorrow is St. Valentine's Day . . ."

Basta, as Gary would say—enough for now. I guess I didn't have a migraine after all, because the aspirin seems to have worked and I finally feel like sleeping. Enough of religion and terror and James Joyce and Shakespeare and the Chinese cellist winking at me from my wall, saying, *You gave up music for undergraduate fun?*

27 December

Back on Amtrak, going home—and my body is sore from shoulders to feet, all along my back, from an extravagant post-Christmas run from Dorchester to Somerville.

After I wrote the above I did, in fact, go crawl into Will's study chair, and fell asleep almost immediately. Then up at 5:30 a.m.

after only three hours of sleep, seized by a sense of nameless, sense-less panic. Perhaps my heart was still speeding from the midnight cappuccino, but I couldn't get back to sleep.

I even wanted immediately to get out of the big easy chair —the one from which he spoke in my dream, telling me that my child should read Hamlet. My favorite place on earth, especially since Margaret keeps the study exactly as it was we could open a Will O'Donnell museum, *that'll be three pence please, mind your head going in.* The same well-waxed smell to his rolltop desk, the same overstuffed bookshelves piled with books and cassette tapes, the same worn plaid carpet (Shaun once joked, it's the plaid that made him go blind). But my eyes wouldn't even close, the heartbeat grew even more rapid.

Only one solution: I ran all the way to Emma's, in Cambridge, escaping the prison-house in one long leisurely move.

It sounds extreme but in fact it was easy. I had been sleeping in my polypropylene long underwear; thus a quick, automatic gesture to tear back into my old clothes and find a pair of running shorts and a T-shirt that said SACRED HEART. And serendipitously enough, for Christmas Shaun had given both Emma and I expen-sive Nike running shoes, the kind with the plastic air-bubble (which cost half my rent). Call it your first real training run, Molly, for the marathon less than a year away.

And it worked, the gods were on my side. It was 27 degrees or so, a perfectly respectable temperature; and every step away from the big wood frame house made my heart lighter, burning Anna's cake and Dottie's potato soup and my uncles' cigar smoke out of my system. Running in new shoes always a fantastic high, toe and heel supports springing each step higher until you feel in mid-flight: and my inner ear conjured up Stravinsky's Violin Concerto in D, frantic double and triple stops exorcising last night's Catholic madness.

The Charles River was as frozen as my face, just now begin-ning to loosen from its cold-stiffness. The commuters chugging across it looked out at me in disbelief: who is this crazy woman crossing the Charles in her underwear the day after Christmas? (I wonder if one of them called the police on me after safe arrival at the office, like me calling the cops after the fake Lucia Joyce.) I was soon completely warmed up, carrying my hat, scarf and gloves in a little ball in my left hand as the violin concerto reached a peak in my head, the marathon-exhilaration the same peak in my blood.

Still it was too far, too fast. I jangled Emma's keys in my right hand and let myself in, then headed for the bathroom. Emma's good-morning from me was thus the festive sound of an overworked runner, throwing up.

New York: I have to cover my nose from the station's commuter sweat, my ears from the racket of luggage being hauled off the overhead racks. Of course, I am thinking of Gary—if I got off the train and looked in a phone book, I could find his parents in Bensonhurst. "Hi, I'm Gary's new teaching assistant, I need to ask about the syllabus." His imagined voice, taking the phone, warms the space between my legs.

But that would break all the rules, unspoken since our first sweaty afternoon together; and I don't truly envy Denise his Christmas, not if their families are anything like mine. I already know I get the better part of Gary—the part spent working, thinking, teaching.

Speaking of which, time to pull out my Joyce notes one more time, before it's too late. I dread meeting Tilden at New Years' without a more defined plan. Will, why is this sheet music so hard to read, why can't I at least figure out what key I'm supposed to be in? Haven't I practiced enough?

29 December

A note from Barbara—stuck in my mail slot the day after I left town, Felicia says:

Thank you for listening, but I can't come back to school.
Talked to my mama for a long-time last night, I know what
I got to do.
I'll miss you.
Keep on reading poems—

So her Christian family managed to hold her, pull her in even from 100 miles away. Probably talked about "bloody babies," all are washed in the blood of the lamb. I find myself even angrier at them than at Mr. Nameless Sperm Donor, because he never threatened to take her away entirely.

She didn't leave an address—or else I would write back, *No, you keep on reading poems.* God, I want to call Gary, he would understand—but he is still behind the Italian curtain, we must wait another week for him to be released. For me to be released.

Meantime I'm writing this atop a pile of boxes—waiting for some of Felicia's artist friends to arrive, helping me move upstairs so that she can have her studio. She thanked me profusely—of course, she already owes me a favor, for I haven't made a fuss upon learning that she's planned a New Year's party at our house. "I thought you'd still be gone," she said, "of course you're invited." Yes, of course, that's what I need, to begin the New Year: to have my hearing completely obliterated by rap music among pseudo-artistes.

Now in my library carrel, anxiety thrumming in my blood. Too much to get done in these next two weeks, speed-reading Hamlet and Lear and Macbeth and the "Dark Lady" sonnets for Gary's class while writing my proposal for the spring's work on the dissertation. Tilden's not actually back yet, but he left me three photocopied articles meant to seduce me back where I began, back toward the *Wake.*

Two articles discuss the ways in which Issy, the daughter-figure, may or may not derive from a true split-personality case from turn-of-the-century Boston, a woman named Christine

Beauchamp. (As if schizophrenia had anything to do with split personality, but what matters is what Joyce thought.)

The third article is about the forty-five notebooks Joyce used as workbooks for the Wake, the links there between his life and his work, pointing inexorably in the direction of Issy's model, Lucia Joyce.

Tilden, you are about as subtle as a sledgehammer. Didn't I tell you I want as little to do with Lucia as I can get away with?

He's suggesting that I cannot get away with much. That if I want to do any original work on this subject, I need to begin with the true psychiatric cases that became part of Joyce's river—the most important being, of course, his daughter. (Maybe I should go back to the cello.)

30 December

Mixed report on my first post-Christmas Baltimore run.

45 degrees so could run bareheaded, letting my hair loose so that it pulled and snarled behind me in the wind, time OK: a stable eight-minute mile, no shortness of breath.

But then at the baseball stadium, there she was: my welcoming committee of one, the last person I either wanted or expected to see. The same place, the same Lucia, the same coat; her sneakers and her hair a little dirtier.

I know the laws, and if it's not too cold they cannot legally detain her. But I was still shocked; I stumbled and nearly fell, as if someone had just turned on all the floodlights of the stadium and pointed them straight into my eyes. Though she was the one squinting, the sun at just the right angle to give her trouble; that made her look even more like Lucia.

I don't want to call the police again; they spend an untoward amount of time looking for the paperwork, and they're starting to sound a little suspicious, as if I bring her on by myself. How can I tell them I could imagine better than that? For the real Lucia, to judge from the Joyce family photos, would never have dressed as shabbily, or let her hair get that dirty.

Instead I feel somehow as if this vagrant is in conspiracy with Tilden, against me.

Now I need to go finish unpacking in my new upstairs room—it feels more like home, actually, echoing the attic I just left, the one I moved into so joyfully at seven years old. But I need to fill my book-shelves and poster the walls, mostly battered art-prints—especially one of James Joyce.

The classic pose, gray-haired and bespectacled, in a battered hat and a striped tie. The expression, from those later years, one of desolation: the grief of World War II? Of his wonderful/horrible book? Or the grief given him by his insane daughter?

Though when I think about it a touch too long, those lost eyes are not so different from those of his daughter, in the few solo photographs of her I've seen. Or, God forbid, of the Lucia girl I will simply avoid from now on—perhaps I'll give my route an urban twist, dashing past the conservatory down to the water and back. It means I have to occasionally enter that whore known as the Inner Harbor, just as I had to go to Faneuil Hall: but then I can shoot straight up Charles into the suburbs again, escaping Baltimore's tourist glitter and other, more ghostly urban ills in the same breath.

1 January

2 a.m., and happy new year—as I lie on Gary's bed, writing this.

He, of course, is still in New York, but I used my key without his permission for the first time, in order to escape Felicia's party. Easing myself off the wagon with his chardonnay, a respectable two-glass dose nursed through 3-4 hours of reading. Chardonnay and Hamlet —thinking about Ophelia, just as Gary has these many years.

Yet I find myself brought closer not to Gary but to Will—and dangerously close to Lucia Joyce.

For if I look too closely at Ophelia, I can see Lucia in her hindmoist.

I envision myself back in Will's study, but he is not there: instead I am in the study chair, the twin daughters standing before me.

Lucia, institutionalized for violent rages later calmed by phenothiazine, holds hands with Ophelia, driven mad by her father's death at the hands of her lover, in an age when people did not speak of diseases of neurotransmitters. "I cannot but choose to weep," she said, "to think that they should lay him in the cold, cold ground." Will, I wish I had thought to say that at your funeral, though I was already singing Shakespeare songs.

Lucia, did you know the line? did you say it in the hospital, when they told you James had died?

Come with us, the daughters are saying. And bring your daughter. And I have to, finally, admit that they are in fact right—that to move forward is to move toward Lucia, my own ambivalences be damned.

For standing off to one side is the white-haired figure himself, lifting his own glass in welcome, as I go to meet the madness turned to the most profound sanity by his words. Looksihere! he says, as he did in the early drafts of the Wake, before purifying it to its inevitable essence: "Lucihere!"

And next to him, the homeless Lucia has replaced the other daughters, standing proudly in her dusty coat. She comes to me with a handful of flower petals, and sings (to Hamlet? to me?):

Tomorrow is Saint Valentine's day
All in the morning betime,
And I, a maid at your window,
To be your Valentine.

Is love worse living?

In late September the Pearlstone grounds, like the rest of Maryland, turned a gentle golden, the weeping willows somehow more fragile, leaves preparing to drop. Jackets and scarves began to appear on the staff and patients as they moved between buildings.

Molly O'Donnell, huddled in her jacket, was a few steps behind the rest of the Wilkes group, Walkman securely in her ears. Her feet slid across the grass with the heaviness of Haldol.

"Please don't wear that during dinner, Molly," a nurse said, dropping behind her. "It's not polite." The nurse was young, with a no-nonsense walk and a New York accent; when Molly didn't respond, she tapped the earphones.

Molly looked at her, startled. She pulled the headset off her head with her good arm, saying softly, "I'm sorry, ma'am, but the trees are far too beautiful for me to listen to you."

"Say what?" The nurse stared.

A smile passed across Molly's like a shadow, replaced by the same earnestness. She looked intent, as if she was really expecting the nurse to understand: then finally she whispered, "Far too lovely a spellbinder for me to listen."

The nurse walked behind Molly, working hard to match her sluggish pace, and lifted one earphone. "I said, please don't wear that Walkman during dinner. It's not fair to everyone else."

After a moment, Molly nodded in agreement, and turned it off. "Music fucks me," she murmured in the nurse's ear. "I'm sure it's bad for me."

"Why is that, Molly?" The nurse backed away a step, to teach Molly proper boundaries.

"Always to imagine something else," Molly said almost inaudibly. Then she turned and looked to the west, where the beginnings of the sunset were transmuted by grey sky to a purplish veil, punctuated by vaguely ominous black rainclouds, as if the sky had been bruised.

The Chatham group had already pumped up the volume in the dining room, the clacking of trays mixed with loud commentary. "You call this curried beef?" Frank Morrison lifted his tray in the air, toward the nose of the dietary aide. "See look at this sheet, I circled 'curried beef' but I swear this never touched either a cow or curry. Maybe curry powder."

"Frank, you never like your food," the aide replied. "Why don't you just quit eating?

"No, it's Lucy who don't eat," Shana piped in. "She don't eat nothing."

"That's true," said Frank, "Molly is quietly fasting for all of us. Christ died for our sins, Molly O'Donnell just cries and fasts for us."

As if on cue, Molly appeared at the end of the Wilkes procession, her eyes focused on the dingy linoleum floor. "Sit with me, my dear?" Frank patted the plastic chair beside him. Molly sat across from him, her Walkman coiled neatly in her lap. "What have you got in there, dear heart?" Molly leaned down and pulled out the tape, handed it to him. "Music fucks me," she repeated.

"Ah, I know what you mean!" Frank took the cassette into one hand, while with the other he plunged into his non-curried non-beef. "Oh, my goodness—Bessie Smith."

"Karen, honey, do you need someone to cut your meat?" asked the aide. Karen Hightower was having trouble with her broiled chicken, holding her utensils high above the food: the new bandages on her arms extended from her wrist to above her elbow, as if she had shattered both her elbows in solidarity with Molly. "Go ahead, if you like," she said, her voice flattened by a high dose of Prozac. "It's all skin anyway."

"Karen, don't you know you're not supposed to hurt yourself?" Shana's attention moved from Molly to Karen, her big eyes teary in sympathy. "Besides—" she pointed, "you gonna end up with *scars!*"

Molly lifted her head, her attention drawn for the first time. "Cover them," she called across the room.

"Oh, of course I will." Karen sat back in her chair, sipping mineral water, as the aide bent over her tray and struggled with the blunt plastic knife and fork. "I may never wear short sleeves again."

"No," Molly said, "blind them with tattoos. . . . My roommate wears her screams on her back."

Interest lit Karen's languid eyes. "You mean that punk girl with the snakes?"

Before Molly could reply, Clay walked into the room, escorting a model-pretty young woman with golden hair and a frantic social smile. "Hi everyone, this is Barb. She's going to be in Wilkes, starting tonight. Shana, can she sit by you?"

The girl looked around the room, nodding nervously. "Good evening," she said, with the slightest hint of a Southern drawl. Then her eyes widened. "Oh my God . . . Molly?" She broke away from the nurse to sit next to Molly. "What are you doing here?"

"I have been lost, angel," Molly whispered into Barbara's ear, before letting the blonde head fall on her shoulder. "I have been lost." The whole room quieted, to hear the murmured words.

While the girl sobbed, Molly put her hand on Barbara's belly, then looked up at Clay. "Tante madonna, tante incinte," she said.

"Hey this is a no touching unit, shouldn't you be separating them?" Frank taunted the nurse. Clay stood still, seemingly as mesmerized as the rest.

After a few minutes, Molly kissed the girl's forehead, tenderly. "Your nerves are bad to-night, Barbara. Yes, bad. Stay with me," she said. "Remember, we are in the rat's alley, where dead men lose their bones."

That made the girl laugh, sitting up. "Yeah right, Molly—we sure are."

"Those are pearls that were his eyes," Molly continued, a serious murmured echo of the song she sang.

Barbara nodded. "That guy Eliot, man he knew what he was talking about," and the two women chanted together: "burning burning burning burning," a liturgy or Vedic mantra.

"What happened to your arm?" Barbara looked at the brace still tight around Molly's elbow; then she pulled back, to get a better view of the still frail figure. "But look," she cried, "what did you do to your beautiful long hair?"

"This one's got two prior hospitalizations," Gail said matter-of-factly to the still air of the conference room. "The first time, in Virginia, she was diagnosed as Major Depression, but meds were contraindicated due to the fact that she was four months pregnant."

"At nineteen, right? Terrific." Anne-Marie had one leg crossed against her lap, her legal pad resting precariously on one leg.

Gail nodded. "She was released to her mother's care after two weeks, only to show up again with an anxiety attack a month later, three days before her scheduled wedding. That was in May; now that the baby's been born, the child's father has apparently gone home to New Jersey. . . . Two weeks ago, while still nursing, patient left the infant with her mother in Virginia and ran away—to her old dormitory, here at the university."

"That sounds delusional," said an intern. "Possible schizoaffective?"

"Right now the diagnosis is a straight BAD, or else severe adjustment disorder."

Anne-Marie wrote on her legal pad, *bipolar affective disorder = BAD!* "Treatment plan? she asked neutrally.

Gail nodded. "Now that she's no longer pregnant, Kepler's going to try her on a mix of Xanax and Elavil. She's rational enough for level A, for the time being."

"Top of the class," said Anne-Marie softly.

"Very good, Anne-Marie!" Gail smiled at the young woman, whose eyes were lowered to her notes. "Group psychotherapy, grounds privileges . . . But the other big news is—she was a student of Molly O'Donnell's this past term. And they bonded the minute they saw one another."

All heads went up, the energy level of the room leaping. "There we are," said Anne-Marie. "Molly's way out of her depression."

Gail sighed. "It's not that simple, Anne-Marie. It could be the opposite. Though God knows we need to do *something*."

"It's hard right now even to give her her meds," said the head nurse, "you can't get her to come out of bed and stop listening to that stupid Walkman. I'm surprised Kepler hasn't let us confiscate it."

Anne-Marie was writing on the bottom of her sheet, *Music = Molly. Take away the music = ???*

"Her status has not been good," Gail agreed, turning to the right section in her binder. "Molly has gained six pounds in the last week; staff noted gait imbalance and muscle rigidity. Yesterday, like every other day this week, she refused food and didn't come to group. Kepler's been considering ECT, to break the cycle."

"Electroshock?" Anne-Marie looked up from her notes, confusion pinching her lip. "I thought we reserved that for emergencies."

"This is serious, Anne-Marie," Gail said. "With Susan and Jim gone, Molly's been isolating more and more . . . and yesterday the nurse reported SI. Perhaps that accident was a suicide attempt."

"Perhaps we're putting the cart before the horse," Anne-Marie said quietly, her eyes wide, intent. "The weight gain and the akinesia are probably from the meds—with those sudden changes, who wouldn't be depressed?"

Gail sighed. "Anne-Marie, have you discussed this with Dan Kepler?"

"Of course I have." In six weeks at Pearlstone the young social worker had changed visibly: much of the schoolgirl cheerfulness was gone, replaced by either puzzlement or a sort of vague defiance. "And I told him, if we tried lowering the Prolixin and dropped the Haldol, the decreased side effects might bring her out."

"And risk another midnight soap opera? Please do wait 'til I go on vacation," said Clay, folding his arms close to his chest as if to guard himself from Molly's embrace.

"Well, now that Barbara is here it's possible we can avoid ECT," Gail said. "We're going to room them together—we already wanted Molly closer to the dayroom, to cut down on her tendency to isolate."

Anne-Marie's head was down, she was writing quickly. ask Felicia and Rachel abt. Barbara. "Meanwhile," she said, "I've got another family visit—both sisters, and this time the brother."

"What about her mother?" the head nurse asked.

"Oh, they want to wait till she's been sober a while longer." Anne-Marie grimaced. "At this rate, we'll have our first full family meeting right after her discharge."

"Actually, speaking of family . . ." Gail looked down at the binder again. "Her sisters' MMPI scores are in. While neither scores particularly high on the schizophrenic scale, the older sister is holding back a great deal of anger and bitterness—she tops the paranoid scale." She looked over at Anne-Marie; the social worker's eyes were downcast, her body slumped.

Gail spoke carefully, in measured, collegial tones. "Isn't that right, Anne-Marie?"

"And the same tests rate Emma as childish and manipulative." Anne-Marie's face and voice now still, closed. "In fact, she tested so high for depression, we may as well admit her next week while we have her down here."

"Well," Gail said, her voice tightening, "now we need to move on." She turned a page in her binder. "I'm sure you have all witnessed the grand return of Karen Hightower."

"And how!" The head nurse whistled. "I've been at this for 25 years, and I don't remember seeing burns that deep on someone who could still stand up. And she was so calm about it too—like oh, it was nothing, all you need is a pack of Parliaments and an evening with nothing better to do."

High noon at the Sikh health-food place on North Charles Street: the usual conglomeration of students, artists, and shy local businesspeople crowded around the salad bar. The frantic lunchtime pace was smoothed out by the gentle reggae pulse of the radio, the air fragrant with curry and cumin and less-recognizable spices. The proprietor stood by a glass case with vitamins and healing crystals, his blue turban surprising the bushy red beard and blue eyes.

"Till I moved here I didn't know there were American Sikhs," Anne-Marie told Rachel as they moved toward the cafe at the rear of the store.

"You're one up on me," the mediaevalist replied, tucking a strand of blond hair back into her neat braid. "I thought he was a Hindu, until you just told me."

"Felicia! Your order's ready," called out one of the cooks, a tall black man with a baseball cap on his head and two rings in his nose.

"He has a ring in his dick, too," Felicia murmured to Rachel and Anne-Marie as she brought the food back to their table. "You remember that opening last summer, Anne-Marie? In Sowebo? Him in gold chains and nothing else?"

"Oh right," said Anne-Marie. "Philip couldn't stop laughing. It was really hot, it was August."

Felicia laughed. "Hey —what would your bosses up at the chemical factory think of him? Have they got a drug to cure it?"

Anne-Marie paused a moment; then she smiled, a small careful smile. "Definitely not Prozac—they might prescribe Valium, but I'm not sure." She looked down at her legal pad, her constant companion full of notes from the morning briefing.

"So let me get this straight," Felicia said, peeking over Anne-Marie's shoulder. "That little baby sophomore who came crying to Molly last year—what is she doing at JPI? Did she kill the baby, or her boyfriend?"

"No, nothing like that—but I'm not supposed to discuss the details of patients' diagnoses," Anne-Marie said uncomfortably. "It's depression, basically."

"Then God help us all! So what else did you want to talk about?"

Anne-Marie looked down at her list. "First, I want to thank the two of you for taking the time to meet with me—my training is in family systems work, and there's not a lot of support for that at Pearlstone. Molly's family is so far away, and so much of what I need to know is in the past." She flipped to a new page and noted the date; then she looked at the two of them with her wide amber eyes. "How much did Molly talk about her family? Her growing up?"

Felicia and Rachel looked at one another. "She can't stand her mother," Felicia said, "but I guess you know that."

"I know the mother's a recovering alcoholic—and Emma did say they didn't have much of a relationship."

"If you talked to Emma," said Rachel, "you probably don't need us."

"I don't know," said Anne-Marie. "I get the feeling that she's . . . being really quiet about things. About the family."

"Unfortunately," Felicia said, "Molly didn't talk much about her family—even all those months she was modeling for me. Certainly not about her growing up. I only knew she was a cellist because of the music she listened to." Felicia spread her arms wide. "Hell, I learned a lot more about the Joyce family."

"Yeah, she had all these pictures stuffed in her notebooks," Rachel added.

Anne-Marie sighed. "About the notebooks—"

"Oh not again." Felicia swallowed the last of her sandwich. "The way you guys keep asking, you'd think they contained the mysteries of the universe. How do you know it's not all just dry literary critique?"

"Speaking of which," said Rachel, "have you talked to her academic adviser? Ross Tilden? From the English Department?"

"Yes, briefly." Anne-Marie smiled. "I'm going over to see him next week . . . Anybody else I should talk to over there?"

"Is there!" Felicia's heat was cut short by Rachel, who touched her arm: as they looked at one another Anne-Marie busied herself with her notes.

"Can you think of anyone else in Baltimore, who was important to her?"

Rachel dabbed at her lips with a napkin, in small delicate motions. "Important how?"

"You know what she's asking, Rae," Felicia rubbed the inside of one wrist in a slow methodical circle; her pulse jumped, as if she were bringing the tiny snake to life.

Rachel bent her head to her soup, seemingly concentrating on the slices of carrot and bay leaf floating on top. "God why do they always do these so bland?" She picked up a container of allspice from a side counter. "Okay," she said, "I guess there's someone else you ought to know about."

"Better yet," Felicia said with some heat, "get him to come to the hospital. He should hear her singing Ophelia songs. If any single person in Baltimore brought her to this, it's that slime bucket." She turned to Rachel. "Goddamn married men, what a bad movie." Rachel's mouth tightened.

Anne-Marie said softly, "I'm not interested in blaming anyone. I only want to help Molly get out of this in one piece."

Rachel sighed, dipping bread in her soup. "When you go to the English Department," she said, "also ask for Gary diCesare."

Felicia leaned across the wood table to write the name on the upper margin of Anne-Marie's legal pad, her handwriting large, spidery. Around them the room was emptying out: the few incongruous business suits had given way to the eternal students lingering over herb tea.

"We're playing dress grownup!" Molly said when Cindy, a new volunteer, arrived to take her to group. "You'll be hypnotized when you see how fetching I am." Her words were slurred, from the medication they'd added to relieve the spasticity in her muscles.

"Very pretty, Molly," Cindy said brightly. Molly had just come from the shower; she was holding a crisp new sweater, her hair still wet. The loose T-shirt she had been wearing for days was on her bed. "And I just know you'll love this group. We're going to draw, and make collages. You too, Barb!"

"You mean I don't have to talk today, if I don't want to?" Barbara toweled her hair, her voice low.

"No, we thought you and Molly might enjoy having a group together."

"Are you really coming, Molly?"

Molly had picked up a comb and was pulling it through her hair, smarting at the tangles. "They won't leave me alone . . . especially since you came, love." She toweled her chest, the place where the weight gain was most evident—she seemed to have sprouted breasts overnight. Before she dressed, she looked in the mirror and held her breath until her ribs became visible. Then she put on the huge red sweater, which extended nearly to her bluejeaned knees.

On the way out of Chatham Barbara reached for, and was given, Molly's hand—they walked together, unbothered by staff despite the no touching rule.

Barbara matched Molly as she lagged a little on the paths, folding her arms against the damp cool air. In five days they had become a pair, the same low arc to their walks, the same contemptuous glances toward the nurses. Frank, upon leaving Jacob Pearlstone Institute for a halfway house, had kissed them both equally, on the lips with just enough tongue to escape staff notice.

Barbara yawned, and rubbed her eyes. "These fucking meds, they make me so sleepy. I almost miss what it was like to stay up all night, even if it's because I was freaking out."

Molly looked off into the distance and began to sing, a meandering, made-up melody. "*Era una piccola bambina che rideva il giorno e non dormiva durante la notte.*" She sang out in the direction of the trees, Cindy nervously shadowing her.

"I never learned Italian, Molly, what does that mean?"

"*Once upon a time, there was a little girl who laughed all day and did not sleep at night.* Soon it's swing low, sweet cheerioot, coming for to carry you home."

Barbara stopped suddenly and put her hands on Molly's shoulders; Molly stood still as the younger girl collapsed against her. "They can't make me go back there, not to my mama's house. I'll stay here, with you."

"No, no dear one," Molly whispered into Barbara's hair. "Hey nonny, nonny no. You'll get them weeping willow blues," she called out to the trees, "just as I have."

In the center of the art therapy room was a ping-pong table, covered in butcher paper and filled with magic markers, pastels and watercolors, as well as hundreds of clippings from magazines. While the patients sorted through it all, Gail walked among them with the energy of a coach.

"That's interesting, Sam, that desert picture. Do you feel like the desert?" Sam, one of the elderly patients, always wore a fishing cap over his bald head. "Today," Gail explained to Cindy and the two latecomers, "we're drawing our initials first, then choosing pictures that fit who we feel we are, right now. Later we'll do a second one, about who we want to be."

"When we grow up?" Molly asked dryly, her lazy tongue losing the "r" in "grow."

Shana laughed. "When we go up, that's good, Lucy."

Barb chose a fat purple magic marker and began very carefully drawing a huge B in block print. Molly reached across the table to the box of square pastels, pulling out two: one nearly as black as her hair, the other a soft gold, like the leaves on the weeping willows. Her arm sling had softened, increasing her range of motion; she still winced as she rolled the pastel between her palms, staring at the piece of blank paper before her.

"I know you can draw beautiful letters, Molly," Gail whispered, her lips close to Molly's ear. "I saw the one on your test paper. Do you remember?"

Molly looked at her, startled. "My *lettrines*," she said. "Have you seen—" she spoke slowly to get every word— "*Pomes Penyeach*? I was paid ten thousand francs for those, I liked that very much." She bent her head toward the blank sheet, intent now.

"Is your "M' going to be square or round?" Gail asked, as if to a nonsense question. "Or were you going to draw an 'L'?"

Molly turned away from Gail, as if she weren't there; she put down the gold pastel and continued rubbing the other between her hands, until the palms were themselves pitch-black. Gail said sharply, "Molly, we're supposed to draw with those. Can I have that please?"

Molly handed the chalk back to her, wordlessly. Then she

quickly bent her head and clasped her face tightly in her cupped hands, scrubbing her face in quick motions. When she took her hands away, her face was streaked with black, a failed minstrel show or Dickensian waif. A smile appeared on her face, a defiant grin that seemed to break the surface of her depression.

"Do you want to go back to Wilkes, Molly?" Cindy asked, working hard to maintain the cheeriness in her voice.

Molly shook her head. "C'est moi qui est l'artiste," she said, so low as to be nearly inaudible. Then her voice rose, and she stood up so that everyone could hear her. "C'est moi qui est l'artiste!" "I think you'd better go," said Gail.

"Then I'm going too," said Barbara loyally, abandoning her BH. She had already surrounded the initials with a purple heart, an early Valentine to herself.

"Barbara, Molly needs to be by herself now," Gail said warningly. "Please, we'd really like you to stay."

Barbara stood up, shaking her head. "I don't feel well. I want to go back."

As they crossed the path toward Wilkes, Molly began her staring act, searching, searching for her lost friend. Barbara's eyes watered.

"Are you okay?" Cindy asked.

"No. I am not okay," Barbara said, "would I be here if I were? And her—" she pointed in Molly's direction— "she's even less okay. What have you done to her?"

Molly lurched forward, Cindy catching quickly up to her as she looked up into the trees. She was trying to sing the blues again, but her voice couldn't fill out the range, so that she ended simply whispering the consonants. "I went down to the river / Down beneath the willow tree / the dew dropped on those willow leaved / An' it rolled right down on me / And that's the reason why I got them weeping willow blues. . . ."

When they got to their rooms, Molly lay back on her bed,

staring at the ceiling. Barbara sat on the edge of the bed, holding her former teacher's hand.

Cindy made it back to the main building just in time for the staff after-group rehash. Gail and the others sat in a semi-circle like a coven or a military command—around a round table, the "patients" binder in its center. Gail looked up at the volunteer. "And?" she asked without preamble.

Cindy shook her head. "I don't know . . . I think Molly is bringing Barbara down."

"I knew it," said Gail, exasperated. "I'll talk to Kepler about moving her again . . . unless he has some miracle up his sleeve."

Two afternoons later Molly was awakened by unfamiliar clatter, opening her eyes to bright lights and the sickly-sweet smell of antiseptic. She looked down at her thin, striped hospital gown, washed so many times it was frayed to bareness in the front.

"Watch out, honey, your nipples are showing."

Molly turned her head, to see Karen Hightower in the adjoining bed. Karen looked ten years older, her usually-careful hair pulled tightly away from the face bare of makeup. She was using one freshly-bandaged arm as her pillow.

Molly tried to sit up, then fell back, sharply, her eyes teared.

"That headache's a son of a bitch, all right." Karen's voice was soft. "Your first time, isn't it."

Molly nodded, rolling on her side to face the other woman.

"It's really not so bad though . . . once you get over the headache you start to feel better, you don't hurt so much inside. It's like a cop movie going on inside your brain, you know? Like depression is some Mafia guy, and the electricity just blew him away." Karen sighed dramatically, staring at the ceiling. "The problem is it doesn't last."

"Ah!" Molly said. "The lethemuse that washes off."

"That's right," Karen said dreamily. "Sometimes I wish I could have ECT every day."

They were the last to be escorted into the anonymous gray

Pearlstone van, joining Sam and Cin-Yuen, two other patients. Cin-Yuen, who looked to be about seventeen, was crying from the headache; Sam, on the other hand, was elated. "I feel wonderful!"

"I don't," said Molly. She was sitting next to the driver, her eyes forward as the van turned north on Loch Raven Boulevard. "I don't feel wonderful," she repeated—but her voice was lighter, and she was no longer singing the blues. "I used to run all this way, you know," she added. When the van turned on Northern Parkway, she started to laugh. "Same turn, too! Am I going home to Calvert Street?" she asked the driver.

"Don't think so, beautiful," the driver said gently.

"Who's beautiful, straight from the electric chair? Doesn't my hair smell burned to you?" She leaned forward and held out a strand of her hair, now long enough to twirl around her finger.

The driver looked sideways at Molly and said softly, "I know you. You used to run through my neighborhood sometimes."

Molly turned to face him, leaning her cheek on the back of the seat. "Tell me," she said. "Every tellin' has a talin' and that's the he and the she of it."

"Always with that fool Walkman," he ignored the knotty speech. "You didn't pay no attention to guys like me. And besides . . ."

"Besides what?" Cin-Yuen was curious. "Last time I saw you, you were too busy singing." He turned back to look at the road. "How's your arm?"

Molly's eyes widened. "Oh! The Dane and his chapter of accidents!" She raised her left arm, to show him the brace.

The driver glanced at it for a split second, then merged smoothly into Interstate 83's midday traffic. "I had a baseball bat," he said. "I thought there might be somebody I should hit—not some car, we don't know what the hell happened. He might not even have known he did it."

"He could not help himself so," Molly agreed, pulling her knees up to her chin.

"George, could you slow down?" Karen called from the back. "I'm getting a little carsick, you know me. Especially since the lithium."

"And maybe we could have some music," Cin-Yuen added. "Like WHFS, how does everybody feel about HFS?"

Molly was lost to the radio station debate, as she looked out at the glass-cube office complexes snuggled in among goldwashed hills. "He could not help himself so," she repeated to herself. "He had to forget, rubbing her up and smoothing her down."

Anne-Marie pulled her hat down against the wind as she and Molly crossed the Pearlstone grounds, leaving the stone paths and cutting through the trees. Steve, the volunteer, stayed at a discreet distance, in case there was any trouble: nurses had reported patient's mood elevated, possibility of mania.

"Look!" Molly gestured to the weeping willows: they seemed to gesture back at her, swaying in the wind. "The trees laugh at the wind's old jokes."

Anne-Marie laughed. "Yeah, but they don't turn red in the cold, the way I do."

"We forgot to do our warm-ups!" and Molly shook each leg, the athlete's intense concentration in her face even as her jerky legs rebelled.

Anne-Marie watched carefully. "You do seem like you're feeling better," she said.

Molly shrugged. "That fat materialistic Swiss man says so." Her words were still a little slurred. "He thinks he can get hold of my soul."

"That fat . . . who?"

"The doctor." Anne-Marie had to swallow to burst out laughing, Dan Kepler's hours in the gym spent to avoid just such a designation. Molly continued, "I much prefer Dr. Oscar Forel. I was rather in love with him."

"Do you love easily, Molly?" Anne-Marie asked, thinking of Jim Keene—and of the man she herself had tried to reach that morning. "Did you love Gary?"

"Gary?" Molly shook her head, spurting ahead of Anne-Marie into the trees. Then she called behind her, "Oh my friend and ah me sweet creature!"

Anne-Marie had to walk quickly, to catch up with Molly; when she did, Molly was sitting down under one of the willows. She began to pull leaves off the lowest branch and pile them in her lap.

"Molly," Anne-Marie said slowly, "you know your family's coming here Wednesday, don't you?"

Molly ignored her, working quickly, furiously until the branch was nearly bare.

"All of your siblings, Molly."

Molly looked up from the soft cushion of leaves in her lap. "Giorgio? With his American wife Helen?"

Anne-Marie swallowed. "No, Molly, Emma and Anna are coming back. With Shaun, this time."

"Shaun Mac Irewick? And who, short of a madhouse, would believe that?" An impish smile crept around the edges of Molly's lips, and she turned her head from side to side, as if just noticing where she was. "Oh."

Anne-Marie laughed. "Very funny, Molly." She waited until they passed another bank of trees. "Since Shaun is coming. we thought maybe we'd give you an eight-hour pass, so you could all go out into Baltimore City together. Would you like that?"

Molly's eyes widened. "Are we going to the seaside?" she asked. "We always have a lovely time there . . . except when there are thunderstorms."

"Well, not the sea, but there's always Harborplace," Anne-Marie said encouragingly. "I'll bet Shaun and Anna have never been there."

Molly shrugged and bent to her lap, lifting a leaf to hold out to Anne-Marie. "My leaves have drifted from me," she said. "But this one clings still." It lingered on her palm, a green benediction. As Anne-Marie took the leaf, Molly added "That they live not is my grief."

"That who live not? The leaves?" Molly closed her eyes, as if talked out.

"I know Moll, I hate winter too." Anne-Marie held the leaf up to the sunlight. "But at least we have spring to look forward to."

"And we'll all dance a jig at Finnegan's Wake!" Molly's laugh was high-pitched, like breaking glass. "Me, Shaun, Anna, and my mirror of mirror, my baby sister Emma." She stood up and they began to walk again; she was crying, just as abruptly as she had laughed.

Anne-Marie looked down at the leaf in her palm just as a gentle breeze passed through it, the veins still green in the afternoon light. It seemed to pulsate in her hands.

When they got to Molly's room, Felicia and Rachel were sitting on Molly's bed, looking through the newspaper. "I'm sorry to have cut into your visiting time," Anne-Marie said quickly. "Molly we're on for four o'clock, right? Just before dinner?"

Molly shrugged. "Hurry up please it's time," she said softly.

As Anne-Marie left, Felicia followed her down the hall. "So what's the scoop—did you reach diCesare, by any chance?"

Anne-Marie walked backwards, so she could face Felicia. "We're playing phone tag—he did return one call, but I wasn't home. What about your end? Have you looked in Molly's room, for the journals?"

"God, is that all you care about?"

"Felicia—" Marie looked at her watch. "Listen. I'm late for my staff meeting." She turned and approached the heavy wooden exit doors.

Felicia followed her. "Wait—"

"I'll call you later. I promise."

Felicia ran and barred the door. "Just—couldn't you have stopped them from electrocuting her?"

Anne-Marie bit her knuckle. "Felicia, they didn't electrocute her. And no, that's Kepler's call, I couldn't have stopped it."

The door opened from the other side, revealing a heavy IV machine pushed by several attendants. Anne-Marie held the door open for them; it closed heavily behind her as she escaped into the cool air, blocking her apologetic wave.

"But would you have stopped it?" Felicia asked the cherry-wood door, which smelled of fresh polish. She ran a long, tanned hand along the grain of the wood, saying softly, "If you want my help, you'll have to do better than that, ma'am."

When she turned the door to Molly's room again, Rachel was saying, "Yeah, Emma said the whole crew is coming this time."

Molly turned to Felicia. saying softly, "She's terrifically nice really, my sister." Her body-stance belied her tone and her words; one fist was clenched, her jaw tight.

"I think they'll be pleased," Rachel said gently. "You're already getting better, even I can see the difference."

"And now they are coming for me," Molly said, her voice faint. "I'm loothing them that's here and all I lothe." She sat back on her bed, her back against the wall. Her emotions seemed lateralized: one side rigid, fist tight, the other limp as a sleeping child.

Felicia looked at her and said, "Can I draw you, Molly? The next time I come?"

"Now," Molly said, and handed her a now-battered notepad. As she flipped to a new page, Felicia tried not to read the words written there, the musical notes and decorated letters and fragments of Joyce spilling over into the corners. She was stopped on one page, momentarily, by the same question written over and over again, in a huge, unfamiliar, almost calligraphic hand.

Is love worse living?
Is love worse living?
Is love worse living?

"I don't know myself, Molly," Felicia whispered, and began to draw.

Shaun O'Donnell was a formidable presence in the boy-sized halls of Jacob Pearlstone Institute; he nearly filled Dr. Kepler's office all by himself, crowding out the doctor, his two sisters and Anne-Marie. "Well, I must admit, I'm impressed." He spread his arms and pointed, gesturing to the window and the carefully groomed grounds beyond. "From what I've seen so far, I'd say Molly's found herself some rather comfortable digs in which to finally go crazy." Anne-Marie winced, sitting behind Shaun with Emma and Anna.

Kepler leaned across his desk toward Shaun, one businessman closing a deal with another. "We're quite satisfied with Molly's progress," he said carefully. "The ECT seems to have broken the cycle of depression, and she's bonding with several of her fellow patients. However, until we can break her speech barrier it'll be impossible to get her into group psychotherapy. We're still trying out different combinations of medications to calm the disorganized thinking."

Shaun sighed. "From the little I just saw, you people have quite a job. I always knew my little sister was smart, but it sounds like she's memorized all of *Finnegans Wake*, then she throws a few curves of her own." He pointed to Molly's chart, which was open on Kepler's desk. *"My father had blood in his eyes?"*

"A reference to your father's blindness," Anne-Marie suggested.

"But Molly was far too young to remember the eye illness. So was I, for that matter: only Leo's actually old enough to remember any bleeding."

"Leo?" Anne-Marie uncapped her pen.

"Our oldest brother—or was, he's been AWOL from the family for years. He ran away from home at sixteen, calls once in a blue moon."

"I've left him at least three messages about Molly," Anna told Anne-Marie, "and he doesn't answer."

Kepler cleared his throat. "Let's talk about this eight-hour pass," he said. "Please make sure Molly doesn't get overexcited. Schizophrenics are acutely sensitive to stimuli, and if she feels overwhelmed, even with her medication she might just break down. The way she did the night Jim Keene left," he explained to Anna. "That was her second episode of catatonia since she's been here."

This time it was Shaun who swallowed, hard. "Maybe she shouldn't go out, I didn't know it had gotten to the point of catatonia."

Anne-Marie looked at Shaun's wide face, as if she could see in his brown eyes all the bad TV-movies and lurid newspaper accounts conjured by the word. "Mr. O'Donnell," she said, "just think of it as a sort of shutdown—if in a rather exaggerated form. . . . I'm sure Molly will be just fine." Slowly, carefully, Anne-Marie began to relax the fist she'd unconsciously clenched, an echo of Molly's own gestures.

"Welcome to Baltimore," Rachel said nervously to the tall, broad man in her front hallway. "Felicia's upstairs—we expected you a few hours ago."

"We drove around for a while," Shaun said absently, never taking his eyes off his navy-blue Cadillac as Anna locked its doors.

The huge, elderly row house on Calvert Street had been the height of gentility in the 1920s, when it had been built. Age and a succession of student tenants had since rendered it one side of shabby; Shaun kept his distance from any surfaces, as if afraid of infection.

Anna, on the other hand, marveled at the hard wood floors and bay windows; the built-in shelves and cabinets; the twelve-foot ceilings; the garden behind the back porch. "This is amazing . . . Do you know how much you would pay for a place like this in Boston?"

"I told you," Emma said. "It's beautiful."

Molly entered gingerly, pulling at the sleeve of her green sweater, which covered her ID bracelet. As she crossed the threshold she shot forward and ran up the stairs. "Love, trees, there is no crime," she called as she climbed exultantly, two steps at a time. Emma and Anna followed swiftly behind, Emma calling "Felicia, I think we're headed to the studio!"

The second-floor room was nearly carpeted with collage material, organized into piles: clippings here, photocopies there, drawings there, with pieces of fabric bordering it all as if the floor itself were a canvas. In the center Felicia knelt among the scraps, wearing black leggings and a long black T-shirt; the collar of the T-shirt was cut off, exposing her the bones of her shoulders. She looked up as Molly entered.

Molly looked down at the collage material and murmured "C'est moi qui est l'artiste!" before moving to the bay window and leaning forward, her fingers clinging to the slightly frosted glass.

Emma leaned down and hugged Felicia; when she moved away, Felicia met the eyes of the man in her doorway. "You must be Shaun." She stood up and reached across her piles of scraps, to shake his hand. "I've been hearing about you."

"And I about you." Shaun looked the young woman over, from shaved head to piercings to tattoos. "I hope you're as anxious to help Molly as the rest of us."

Felicia stared. "Of course," trailing off as she realized the source of the sentence must be Kepler. "Please excuse the state of my studio—I'm in the final stages of a number of pieces for my next show."

Molly pointed at a huge oak, red-gold, whose branches just grazed the window. "Under certain atmospheric conditions," she said in a half whisper, "the human voice can quicken trees into life." She grinned, the color high in her cheeks, and turned to Felicia. "This secret must be told to the Cabinet!"

"What secret, Molly?" Felicia asked.

"One, that trees are alive," and Molly pointed out the window. "Next, that there is no crime. And third, the word known to all men . . . " She raised her right arm in benediction. "Let the raised name of love every person thrill!" When her eyes met Anna's she withdrew, turned back to the window.

"I think that's Virginia Woolf," Felicia said quietly. "It reminds me of something she quoted last summer, when she was teaching Woolf."

Shaun shook his head, professionally sorrowful. "What a tragedy," he said. "My sister had such a fine mind."

"She still does," Felicia said. "And I wouldn't go calling it a tragedy just yet."

Shaun shook his head. "Such a terrible disease," he said *sotto voce*. "She'll need medication for the rest of her life."

Molly turned excitedly and said, "Watch it, Felicia. Watch the watery gold glow and fade," pointing to a swath of late afternoon sunlight. Then Molly reached out and touched Felicia's tattooed shoulder. "So soft this morning, ours," she said.

Felicia swallowed; before she could reply, Emma was speaking from Molly's other side. "It's time to go now, Molly. It's getting late —and remember you wanted to see the water?"

Molly at first didn't seem to hear, until Felicia said softly, "Yes, Molly, you're supposed to go with them. They only come every once in a while. I'll see you tomorrow at the hospital, I promise."

Molly nodded, then turned to Emma and took her hand. "We list, as she bids us, by the waters of babalong." As she started to sing, Anna looked at her watch, tapping her purse. "Take me to the river," Molly sang, "drop me in the water."

The Inner Harbor, Baltimore's tourist centerpiece, was packed with weekend visitors, lightly jacketed for the perfect fall weather. The sunset danced pink and purple highlights on the water—the slices of Chesapeake Bay still visible through the docks and boats and replicas of fighting ships—and gave a gentle glow to the shop-ping-mall buildings at the heart of the complex.

A large crowd near the largest building surrounded a group of street performers—Black teenage girls doing elaborate hip-hop moves, a portable stereo providing the beat and the oldest girl, in skin-tight glittery pants, rapping into a karaoke microphone. Molly began to move to the beat, her behind swaying in small arcs. "I dream the dance," she said to Emma.

"What?" Shaun demanded over the music. "Can we move away from this?"

Molly looked over at him, annoyed. "I didn't say it aloud, Sir. I have something inside of me talking to myself." Then she turned her back on him, moving again to the rappers' pounding beat. When she tried to move forward into the crowd, Emma took her hand; Emma's own body was still, her mouth in a soft, pensive line.

They moved on to one of Harborplace's shopping malls, its booths purveying handicrafts, glass-walled stores with expensive Italian shoes. "Do you need anything, Molly?" Anna asked, but her sister wasn't paying attention: she was searching each face, her eyes moving quickly, deep in concentration.

Shaun took Anna's arm, forming a rear guard behind their two sisters. "Remember what Kepler said about overstimulation," Shaun whispered. "Maybe we should get her out of here." They emerged into the Food Court, right by the foot of the escalator, into smells of fried crab cakes, pizza and Chinese food. "On the other hand . . . " Shaun patted his stomach. "Perhaps we should eat first—eh, Molly?" he called over to his sister.

On the escalator the dull roar of the mall rose to high volume, vendors mixing with families mixing with the rap music still audible from outside. Shaun tried again to be heard. "Molly? Are you hungry? Perhaps we can sit down."

Molly looked back at her brother, distracted; she squinted, as if trying to place his face. Then her eyes widened and she turned to Emma. "My goldfashioned bother near drave me roven mad! I'm dying to keep my linefree!" The unfamiliar words were blotted further by the background noise and the slur in her speech.

Shaun exhaled and said, "Let's find a table, then I'll get us some pizza or something." Then a shout, hardly audible across the food court: "Molly!"

Molly turned. Barbara sat by the long glass window, sandwiched between an elderly couple wearing MARYLAND hats, at a table with empty seats. Molly gestured and led the way, Shaun whispering to Anna, "Is it time for her medication yet?"

"Another hour," Anna whispered back. The sunset was at its peak, blazing through the glass.

Barbara's parents stood up, shaking hands with Anna and Shaun as if they were Molly's parents; they laughed about the coincidence. "Ah came here with Barb when she first came to go to school," Barbara's mother said with a gentle drawl, "and we've always loved it. Right honey?" but her husband was dozing, and she just patted his knee. "Let him be, it's been a long day."

While Shaun went for pizza, Anna and Emma oohed and aahed at the gifts the other family had bought. A pile of lacy baby clothes "for our little Tommy, my grandson," Barbara sitting quietly without comment. "And this," a brightly colored scarf, "for my sister."

"Now that color would be lovely on my mother!" Anna turned to Molly. "Mam would like that for a special present, don't you think so?"

Molly stared at Anna, then reached out and touched the buttery silk. "Is she still at the Klinik?" she asked.

Anna paused, startled by the German roll Molly gave to the word. Then she said, "No, Molly, the doctors say her heart is just fine." To Barbara's mother she explained, "We're a very close family, of course Molly is concerned about our mom. She had a heart attack in the springtime."

Molly laughed. "She was malttreating herself to her health's contempt," she told Barbara. "Right, Emma?"

Emma listened backwards until she thought she understood. "Yes, I guess you could say that, Molly." She picked up a wool sweater that barely covered her hand. "God, I forget sometimes that my son was once this tiny."

"Barb, honey, I think it's time for your pills," her mother said. "Didn't they say six o'clock?"

"No, mama, seven," said Barbara. "It's only 6:30."

Molly moved over to Emma's other side, and put her arm around Barbara. "They're watching you all the time," she whispered.

"I know," a kissing murmur by Molly's ear.

Anna went over to find Shaun, "he probably can't carry all that by himself." Emma was fingering the sweater and saying, "You know, I haven't called home yet . . . I don't even know how my baby's doing. He had a little cold, when I left."

"Our Tommy just keeps getting colds and colds and colds!" Barbara's mother laughed, her brown eyes crinkling at the edges. She reached out and took Emma's hand. "The doctor says get him vitamin C, D, E, X—"

"Vitamins do help," Emma volunteered, looking nervously off into the distance for her sister and brother.

"Well, what I say is, there's nothin' for a little baby's health than his mama's milk. Which is why we gotta get our little girl home as soon as possible—right, hon?" Barbara's father awoke, startled, and said, "yes, of course we do."

"And Barb's all anxious to come home—ain't you, sweetie?" The white-haired woman turned behind her, addressing her daughter. "Barbara?"

But where Barbara and Molly had been there was only the remains of sunset fading into dusk, the mass of tourists pouring out the doors, the smell of cheap Chinese food suddenly powerful, overwhelming.

. . .

135

The small church on 27th and St. Paul Street was filled with sound and motion, decidedly less upscale than that at Harborplace; the smell of cheap beer permeated the smaller fellowship room, while the larger boasted an Afro-Caribbean band and a loud, dancing crowd.

A short redhaired woman in a Guatemalan skirt brought cups of beer to both Barbara and Molly, shaking off Barbara's offer of money. "Don't sweat it . . . So tell me again, why the hell didn't you call me last month, instead of just showing up at the dorm? I wouldn't have turned you in to any fuckin' nuthouse."

Barbara let a long draught of beer trickle down her throat. Then she said, "I was kinda out of my head, Lynn."

Lynn shrugged and finished her beer. "You guys want to go dance?"

Molly lifted her glass in a salute. "Of course. . . . L'Irlandaise!"

Lynn grimaced and whispered to Barbara, "That's French, it means 'the Irish girl.'' What's with her?"

"It's hard to explain . . . it's like she hurts so much she can only talk in poetry." As Barbara spoke they moved into the larger room full of sound and sweat, college kids swaying side by side with aging hippies and tall, elegant-looking men with earrings and headbands.

The sound of conga drums bounced against the high rafters of the church, with bongos, cowbells and tambourines crossing the slender high notes of trumpets and a steady, discreet guitar line. Barbara's friend immediately began to whirl, elbows forward, knees bent; Barbara moved more tentatively, until the sound became pure percussion and she began the multi-muscled moves of a belly dancer, her nipples hardening against her thin blouse. The crowd responded strongly to the drummers, jumping up and down furiously; the band extended its drumming the more they danced, until Barbara stopped, laughing, exhausted, clapping when it all ended in one angular drum roll. She gasped to Molly, "How long has it been since I laughed?"

Molly smiled and closed her eyes; when the music began again she moved in time with the saxophone, her arms raised, slowly including each limb one by one. She was playful with her still-weak left arm, waving it like a child's wobbly toy.

Barbara laughed and clapped but Molly was oblivious: by the end of the song her green sweater was damp, and she pulled it off in one long, effortless motion.

"Molly!" but Molly was wearing a black chemise underneath, so the effect was rather that of a dancer doing a costume change. She took the other women's hands and they danced the next song in a circle, kicking their legs out in synch like a Caribbean chorus line or circular conga line.

A tall, olive-skinned man with curly hair approached Molly, holding out his hand: and before Barbara or her friend could utter a word she had followed him and was dancing with him, first mirroring his twists and trembles, then letting him hold her close.

"Holy shit, what are you guys doing here?" It was Felicia, standing nearby as they watched Molly and the Latino man. "Do you remember me? I'm Molly's roommate."

"Of course I do," Barbara swallowed. "You were there just before I left school."

"Yeah and I heard from unnamable sources that you were locked up same as Molly. You out now?"

"I think I was due back . . ." Barbara looked at the big clock over the band's heads. "About two hours ago. Just like she was."

"So what happened? Where's her family?"

Barbara shrugged. "We got tired of Harborplace, so we left."

When Felicia caught her breath, she started laughing. "Oh man, and you're out in public too!" She looked over at Molly again, and stared.

The three women watched as Molly let her head rest on the man's shoulder, her body in deep relaxation, as if she had found a home. After a moment he was kissing her neck, their hips moving in synch, still holding the conga beat even as their upper bodies were nearly at rest.

"Uh oh . . ." Felicia went over to the couple and tapped the man's shoulder. "Excuse me? I need to talk to my friend." She maneuvered Molly away from the man and said gently, "I can understand the urge, girlfriend, but I think you're a touch fragile just now to be dirty dancing with strangers. Come dance with me, instead."

Molly nodded as she followed Felicia, taking both her hands. She leaned forward and whispered eagerly, "So she said she must go and he asked her why and she said she must, really and he asked but why must she and she said really and truly she must." She grinned, an unusual sight that made Felicia dance, her roommate echoing her in soft motions.

Felicia was wearing a long, loose dress from a used clothing shop, its sleeves cut off and its neckline cut down; long earrings flowed from the bottom hole in each ear, bouncing gently with the rhythm of the drums. She and Molly played mirror-games, their hands reaching for each other as their hips kicked in with the conga beat. Finally, Felicia stopped and applauded. "Well, Moll, I'm glad I taught you somethin'."

The band stopped playing at 1 a.m., Barbara having left with her friend long before. The Calvert Street house was only a block away from the church; Felicia and Molly walked slowly, their steps slowing the closer they came to the house. "I can't protect you from them right now, my friend," Felicia said softly into Molly's ear. "They got the law on me."

It wasn't until the next morning that they came, alerted by Rachel; Molly was sleeping in her attic room, and didn't see the silver-gray Pearlstone van pull up outside. Felicia did, but by the time she was dressed and out of her studio, it was already too late: Emma and Anna were climbing the stairs to the third floor. Molly screamed when she saw them, twisting away even from Emma, and headed for the door. On the landing, she came face to face with Shaun and two orderlies.

Felicia cried as Molly's arms were pulled behind her, the restraints held together with Velcro and buckles. "Oh," Molly said knowingly in exaggerated French, "the *camizole du force.*" She ignored the sleepless row of O'Donnells on the landing and descended the stairs, hugging herself as the orderlies led her into the van.

When they arrived at the hospital Molly tried again to run; an orderly pulled at the restraints, and two more arrived to help escort her back to Chatham. "I know where I am, now," she said softly. Then to Kepler she said "Ivry, near the Bois de Vincennes. Wei?" She lingered on the Parisian *oui*, most of the rest of the French made incomprehensible by her lazy tongue.

Rain was battering the conference room window, in sheets that blurred the trees from view; Gail Ryan had to speak loudly, her makeup made garish by the fluorescent lights pelting them from the ceiling. "We have her back rooming with Shana, since Cin-Yuen's been discharged. Barbara won't be a problem, since her family is taking her home today."

"That was one of the . . . most unhealthy alliances I think I have ever seen," said the head nurse. "To think we had hoped it would be a therapeutic bond!"

Gail nodded. "Meantime Kepler's decided to try Tegretol, 400 milligrams b.i.d. It's had good results with Shana. And we know we can fall back on the ECT, if depression becomes a problem again. After all," Gail said with her bow-shaped smile, "you can't say it didn't bring her out of her shell."

"Out of her shell and into her hell!" Anne-Marie said. Instead of laughing, the group turned to look at her; she leaned back and pulled a strand of red hair around her neck, as if in self-protection.

There were circles under the social worker's eyes; she had been at Pearlstone since Molly's arrival at six.

"Better watch it, Anne-Marie," said Clay, "you're starting to talk like your patient."

That got a laugh; then Gail said to one of the interns, "Katy, would you like to provide the wrap-up on Cin-Yuen?"

The intern brightened. "Gamey and manipulative," she said proudly, reading from the sheet. "Would not cooperate in groups; would not take meds; called 911 immediately upon return from ECT. Her parents are taking her on a trip to China, where, they say, traditional medicine can heal her." Scattered laughter, continuing until the group broke up at 10:30. Anne-Marie stayed at the conference table, taking notes; Gail stood behind her and waited until the others had gone.

"Anne-Marie," Gail said, "there was something to what Clay said. I'd like to schedule a conversation with you . . . about boundaries."

Anne-Marie didn't turn to look at her; instead she lifted her eyes to the ceiling, forcing Gail bend over her. "I know I'm having boundary issues with Molly. I'm working on it. You don't have to lecture me—we got it all the time in school, *proper distance from the client, counter-transference,* the works."

"This isn't school," Gail said quietly. "I know you like Molly. It may be hard to decide what you can and cannot do for her."

Anne-Marie's voice was numb. "I've never had to escort a client into seclusion before."

Gail closed her eyes briefly. "Listen—they're heartbreakers, Anne-Marie. You can't get sucked in like that. I've had it happen to me, more than a few times. Can we talk today? Maybe in half an hour?"

Anne-Marie shook her head. "Kepler and I need to close with the family before they leave," she said. "I could do 2:00 this afternoon."

"I can't—let's try later in the week," and Gail was gone. Anne-Marie sat back with the last of her herbal tea, watching the wind and rain batter the trees outside the window. She massaged the back of her neck, to try to alleviate the morning tiredness; then she rubbed her eyes, as if she could somehow erase Molly's image from the inside of her eyelids. On her arrival, Molly had worn under the straitjacket a long T-shirt with James Joyce's face on it, souvenir of a long-ago conference: even in the drawing's bare outlines the eyes were mournful, matching those of the patient being injected with antipsychotic drugs.

As soon as he entered Kepler's office, Shaun O'Donnell said without preamble, "We'll be back next week—I want to see how this new drug works out. We really would like her closer to home, you know."

"Yes, it would be much simpler," Anna chimed in, behind him. "I'm going to investigate what's available for Molly in Massachusetts—I just wanted you to know, up front."

Kepler sighed, "Every stage of the illness offers valuable information, Mr. O'Donnell," he said, "even this one. We're learning bit by bit what Molly needs, to get her stable. I wouldn't advise moving her at this delicate phase."

Shaun and Kepler compared datebooks, consulting Anne-Marie along the way; but Anne-Marie never took her eyes off Emma. Emma sat behind her siblings, her pallor echoing her sister's.

Anne-Marie walked the family to the parking lot, her small maroon umbrella sheltering under Shaun's majestic black parasol. As Shaun unlocked the car, Anne-Marie embraced Emma briefly. "Listen," she said, "next week . . . can you and I make some time to talk? Just us?"

Emma ducked her head, as if Anne-Marie had sent a gust of rain into her face. "Why?"

"We've never really talked . . . about the two of you, growing up so close. I'm sure there are stories that would help."

Emma shrugged, not looking at Anne-Marie. "I don't know, . . . when I think about it, when I try to remember, it's just a confusing blur." She was speaking so softly Anne-Marie had to stand up on her tiptoes, toward the taller woman's mouth. "The longer this goes on, the less I trust myself—the less I want to do anything but cry and sleep."

"Emma! Over here!" The shout was Shaun's, from behind the wheel; Anna was already ensconced in the front passenger seat.

Anne-Marie watched as Emma got in; before the car had left the parking lot, she was settling in to lie down, and perhaps sleep the sleep of the lost night. The gusts of wind threatened to kill Anne-Marie's umbrella as she hurried across the grounds. The cold rain against her face was either a wake-up call or the tears Molly could no longer cry, immersing the hospital in her grief and buried rage.

Bean bags flew across the music room.

In quick succession and in time to Gail and Cindy's claps, patients and staff tossed brightly colored beanbags to one another, each shouting out the name of the person to whom they were tossing: "Molly! Karen! Cindy! Joyce! Bobby! Gail! Ulrike! Shana! Jennifer!"

Ulrike, the elderly German woman sitting next to Molly, kept dropping the bags, her shoulders slumped and her arms limp. Gail watched closely as Molly assumed exactly the same passive position, their two faces frozen in forced-cheerful smiles as they were pelted with small colorful squares.

Whenever Molly tried to pick up one of the bags at her feet, she stared at her hands and carefully curled her fingertips around the corners, before pitching it across the room, usually to land at someone's feet. This was her first appearance in group, four days after her escape attempt.

"Molly, are you having trouble?" Cindy sat on her other side, her dreamy smile perhaps accounted for by the large diamond ring that had recently appeared on her left hand.

Molly extended her hands forward and grasped Cindy's tightly, one finger pressed against the engagement ring. "I cannot get hold of my hands," she said. "Can you feel them?"

Gail looked over, sharply. "You can't feel them at all?" The rest of the patients stopped throwing. "Or do you mean they feel sort of like pins and needles?" When Molly nodded, Gail made a mental note to find out if the patient had elsewhere reported paresthesia—a not uncommon side effect of Tegretol.

Molly bent down slowly, Ulrike's slight tremble in her movements, and picked up a red bean bag. She held it by one corner and swung it toward Gail. "Gail," she said softly as it skidded across the floor.

Gail grinned hugely at this breakthrough—the first time Molly had called her by her name. She reached forward, in a quick, aggressive motion, and threw it right back. "Molly," she said.

Molly shook her head. "Lucia," she replied, looking down at the red square in her lap. Then she placed the bean bag on her shoulder and rested her head on it, a pillow on which to sleep.

"Well," Gail said brightly, "I think that's probably enough of the bean bag game. I hope you all had fun with that one." Cindy stood up and began to collect the bags, from the floor and patients' hands and laps alike. "Now, we're going to go around the room and say the name of the person next to us, to show that we've gotten to know each other better. Also, one thing we've noticed about that person, if we can. For example, I'm Gail, and you're Shana."

She turned in her seat and faced Shana, her eyes crinkling at the edges as she smiled. "Shana, I've noticed that you've been dressing really nice lately, as if you're feeling better." Shana grinned, her huge, white-toothed smile matching the white silk dress that gleamed against her skin. She turned to Karen. "You're Karen, and you love to eat carrot sticks for dinner."

When it came Ulrike's turn, she turned to Molly and said, "You're . . . Lucia, and you have pretty black hair."

"Actually," Gail said, "that's Molly you're talking to."

"Sometimes," Molly said, querulous. She turned to Cindy and said, "You are Torie, and I see you'll be married soon... And I will be all alone!" Her voice was a low moan of self-pity.

Cindy's eyes widened at this new expression of affection. "I'm not getting married until next year," she said quietly. "And my name is Cindy." When the group had finished, Gail turned behind her, pressing the PLAY button on a small red boom box. "Before group ends, we should all relax," she said. "Let's try those exercises we started with." Accompanied by the tape player's quiet, repetitive synthesizer sounds, Gail demonstrated a simple neck roll, one she'd seen Molly often use as an avoidance tactic. Now Molly seemed to be finding it difficult, as difficult as Ulrike, who could only accomplish the circle in little jerky motions.

Gail watched the two of them as members of the group all reached up to the ceiling, palms facing the air; again, it was as if she were observing two elderly women sitting together, their motions slow and wavelike, their eyes frightened above faint, needy smiles.

A rainy, low-energy Thursday and most of the Chatham patients were clustered around the TV set, watching a videocassette of *Gone with the Wind*. Felicia signed in at the front desk, glancing into the dayroom; as Tara burned, a tall, majestic woman with dyed red hair was sipping tea and crying, tears so delicate they could almost have been staged. The burning South was a fireplace for the gloomy rainy skies, the almost denuded trees visible through Chatham's window.

Molly hadn't turned on the lights in her room; when Felicia

entered, she was sitting on her bed in the dark, writing in her notepad and singing in German with an odd, wobbly vibrato.

"Molly?" At first, her roommate didn't seem to hear her; reluctantly Felicia turned on the overhead lights. "Molly it's me . . . I wanted to give you something, before your family visit on Saturday." She left out the rest—that Shaun had left irrevocable instructions that she was not, under any circumstances, to be allowed to see Molly outside of Chatham's walls.

Molly looked up, and held her hand out to Felicia to be taken. "Thank you for coming to visit," she said, her voice thin, high-pitched. "Often people don't come, and I do not know what became of them. Especially since the war began."

Felicia swallowed, hard, and slung her backpack on a chair. "Look, Moll, I taped the Rhumba Club record for you —I knew you didn't have it already." She pulled the tape out of her pack. "And I could tell last week, they sure do make you boogie!"

Molly nodded, eyes wide. "Samuel Beckett said I danced very well."

Felicia took a deep breath. "When did he say that?"

"When I was just a young girl . . . a long time before I came here." Molly sighed. "He still writes me, though. He has been writing to me for almost forty years. Perhaps someday I will marry him." She giggled, a girlish caricature. "But I still think he is too tall for me."

Felicia sat down next to Molly and took her hands, began to massage her rigid fingers. "My God you're stiff . . . have you told the doctors about your hands?"

Molly sighed. "So hath been, love; 'tis 'tis; and twill be, till wears and tears and ages." She looked down at Felicia's strong painter-fingers, as they pressed and held. "They are very nice to me here."

"Where, Molly?" Felicia looked into Molly's veiled, almost expressionless eyes. "Where are we?"

"St. Andrew's Hospital. They would not have me any more at

Ivry. I like it here very much." She put down her pencil; when Felicia glanced at the notepad the handwriting was in tight cramped swirls, as if Molly's hands had not been able to stop shaking.

Then Molly looked at Felicia directly, for the first time. "My brother Giorgio," she said. "He said he was coming soon."

Felicia winced; she turned and set the cassette she'd brought on Molly's night table, next to a pile of string quartets; the Bessie Smith and other blues tapes had been confiscated. In the formica of the table Felicia could see her face reflected, the shadows under her eyes darker than Molly's after electroshock. Finally she said, "Shaun is coming again on Saturday, did you know that? Also Emma and Anna, they want to see how you're doing." She thought a minute, and then said, "Y'know Molly . . . I remember what you used to tell me, about Giorgio Joyce, how he never used to come see Lucia. At least Shaun does come, I'll say that for him."

"My brother was a very strong swimmer," Molly replied. "But do you know what? Once he was nearly drowned." Felicia looked out at the rain and tried to imagine Shaun swimming in it, drowning in it: but all she could summon was a large young man poised on the edge of the water, afraid to dive in.

By the time Felicia left Chatham, Molly had gone to sleep, curled up under the blanket like an infant; the front dayroom had emptied out, the South long since destroyed and resurrected.

Molly insisted on wearing makeup for her next family visit; since she didn't own any, Shana and Karen Hightower lent theirs. Karen bent over Molly's face with an eyeliner in her hand. "My god, blue eyes and black hair, we need the blackest eyeliner I've got. There! You look marvelous! What clothes are you going to wear?"

"I used to have a velvet dress with wooden buttons," Molly said, her voice thin and breathy. "I liked it very much." She cried until they found her a dress—her closet was full of jeans and shorts, so she ended up wearing one of Shana's, a yellow jersey shift that barely reached her thighs. "My mother," she told the nurse impatiently, "always bought me very nice dresses."

Anne-Marie led the small group from Chatham for their family visits; the rain had stopped temporarily, leaving behind cold damp air. Molly moved very slowly, her singing wobbly but quite in tune. "*O, du, mein holder Abendstern . . .*" Anne-Marie did not try to speak to her, instead listening to her tone, watching the slow clumsy motions of her body.

"Oh, Molly," Karen sighed. "What would Pearlstone be like without you? No one else around here has any culture, now that Frank has gone."

Molly ignored her, walking as if she were frailer and about a hundred pounds heavier; she continued her song, with the same wobbly vibrato, until they passed through the entrance of the main building.

"Molly, I'm so glad to see you!" The moment they arrived, Shaun's voice boomed behind Molly. Molly turned her head, only slowly moving the rest of her body to match. Her eyes widened.

"This man is mountain!" she exclaimed, as she let her brother pull her into a bear hug.

"Thanks Moll," Shaun said, "you always were the soul of tact." He let go and stood back, looking her over. "Though you look lovely. Haven't I been asking for years why you didn't wear makeup?"

Molly ignored the comment and turned to Anne-Marie. "He is a good man," she said, "and very honest."

As Emma moved toward her sister Kepler asked, "Shall we sit down? We might all be more comfortable."

Molly shuffled toward the couch in tiny steps, her eyes and mouth in a cheerful grin. "Thank you for coming," she said to Emma, her voice low, trembling.

"Oh, Molly," Emma said, "of course we would come!" She sat next to Molly and held both her hands. "Barry sends his love, and Stevie would if he could—he does remember you, he calls you 'An-Ma.' That's the closest he can come to 'Aunt Molly.'"

Molly's eyes were sleepy as she looked at Emma, her hands in Emma's shaking a little. "Stephen is a lovely baby," she agreed. "I am sorry I was not allowed to hold him."

"Oh, Molly, that's not true, you play with him all the time! Remember in April, when he smelled your T-shirt and made funny noises?"

Anna, sitting on Molly's other side, kissed her on the forehead. "It's so nice to have you talking to us again," she said. "And Shaun's right, your makeup does look pretty." Anna herself wore light brown mascara and a rust-brown lipstick, matching her hazel eyes and the autumn colors of her blouse and skirt. "I like your hair—who combed it that way?"

Molly's hair now reached her collarbone; it was parted on the side and combed back. She burst into giggles. "Every woman in her turn," she said, confidence in her voice for the first time. She added in a singsong voice that seemed to come from another mouth, "Her tongue, her lipstick. Saviour of the Hair. Redeemer of the Complexion!"

Anne-Marie joined her in her laughter. "You got it, Molly, that's who we worship around here."

Molly looked across the coffee table at Dr. Kepler, her neck motion still slow and stiff, her smile flirty by contrast. "I hope you like my hair too . . . Ash blonde and turf brunette!" She laughed again, a high-pitched caricature of a girl's giggle.

"By the way," Anna said, trying to regain Molly's attention, "Mam sends her love."

Molly's laughter stopped in mid-breath, a singer responding to a conductor's cutoff. She looked down at the floor and said quietly, her voice breaking, "My mother never scolded me. She always wanted me to be happy and have a good time. She was like a sister to me."

Anne-Marie, at the end of the sofa, bent to her notepad and wrote *Reaction formation?* Then, embarrassed at having used such a Freudian term, she wrote *says the opposite of what she feels—or feels the opposite of what she used to feel??????* She knew there was a literary term that could get her out of this, explaining what she had just heard better than either she or Freud could. Molly would know it, she wrote quickly—the Molly she had never known, the one Ross Tilden had said was "quite gifted although perhaps I could already tell she was a little mad."

Tilden had said this to Anne-Marie over long-distance from Paris, where he was on sabbatical "walking in James Joyce's footsteps." Anne-Marie had refrained from saying, *Molly is doing the same thing, with Lucia—and she did not have to cross an ocean to do it.*

The kitchen at Calvert Street still boasted the house's original stove, a black-and-steel creature with a built-in hot plate and an uncertain flame. Rachel stood over it with mittened hands, monitoring a pot of spaghetti sauce.

Emma closed her eyes. "You guys—I'm so glad I'm doing this. It's so peaceful here . . . after that place."

"That place is quiet all right," Felicia said. "Too quiet. It's creepy, they're so doped up, but underneath you can feel all the screams they're not screaming. Anyway, dinner with your family at the fucking Ground Round is certainly no way to rest up." She reached above the refrigerator and pulled down a bottle of brandy, filling three small porcelain teacups. "Listen," she said, "I know about your mom, but—"

"Oh please, oh please," Emma said, accepting the cup gratefully. "These are desperate times."

"Oooh you sound like Molly now," Rachel said. "We are in the rat's alley, she told me. I think she was quoting T. S. Eliot."

"Who can tell? Anyway she's stopped talking literature these days," Emma said.

"No shit," said Felicia, draining her cup in one quick motion. "This week she's one of those scary old ladies on the bus, who wear too much makeup and giggle like they're fifteen years old. Anne-Marie says it's medication side effects."

Felicia reached for the brandy bottle and refilled her cup. "I looked up Tegretol, you know. The book says it's for pain and epilepsy, doesn't say anything about mental illness. But them doctors love it, she's not gonna run away again any time soon."

Emma sipped her brandy, her eyes closed. She murmured, "God grant me the serenity to accept the things I cannot change, the courage to change the things I can—"

"—and the wisdom to know the difference," Rachel finished with her. "Amen to that."

Emma nodded and opened her eyes. "Listen," she asked, "Anne-Marie. What's her job anyway? Does she do therapy with Molly, or what? Or just ask people like me nosy questions?"

"Damned if I can figure out," said Felicia.

Rachel glared at her roommate. "Felicia Waller, there are times to be an anarchist and times when it isn't appropriate."

Felicia shrugged, opening the door to the back porch and lighting a cigarette. "*Appropriate*, that's the kind of words they use, Rae."

Rachel sighed, saying to Emma, "She's supposed to work with Molly's family and friends, to put it all in context and help us become part of her treatment. That's what the nosy questions are about. I mean, she even met with us—remember, Felicia?"

"I don't know, I can't decide if she's a double agent." Felicia stood with her body across the doorway, the arm with the cigarette extended out into the frigid air. "Like, she's nice to us, but really she's just like the rest of them, waiting for the right drugs to kick in."

"Double agent!" Rachel twirled a strand of spaghetti around a fork, and held it out for Felicia to test. "The anarchist again. Are we there yet?"

Felicia bit once, then waved the rest away. "Nowhere near . . . Look, Anne-Marie just goes along, like, *Electroshock? Epilepsy drugs? Whatever you want, doc.* But then I think, but Philip says she's OK, we can trust her."

"Umm . . . " Emma put down her empty teacup and said hesitantly, "When I told her I was coming here, she asked me for something."

"Let me guess," Felicia said sharply. "She wants you to go digging for Molly's notebooks." She took a drag on her cigarette, then returned it to the cool air.

"She and Dr. Kepler seem convinced it would make a difference."

"Kepler, that fascist, the word *privacy* isn't even in his dictionary."

Rachel shut off the stove and turned to face her roommate. "Listen, Felicia, if anybody has a right to look around in Molly's stuff and try to find the notebooks, it's Emma. And who knows what's in them? It might really help."

Felicia shrugged and stepped further out onto the porch. "Rae," she called behind her, "if you want to help her look, I'll watch the spaghetti, but I'll have no part of this. By the time you guys are done, dinner will be ready."

Rachel and Emma looked at one another. "Let's go," Rachel said. "Even if we don't find anything, I bet you'll feel better for having tried."

As they walked out of the kitchen, Felicia stubbed her cigarette under one foot and walked down the back steps into the vegetable garden. As she pulled a few zucchini for a dinner salad, she listened to the evening sounds: a band practicing a few doors down; mothers' raised voices, chasing their kids indoors as the sun set; broken glass crushed under the weight of some toddler's Big Wheel. Before going back up to the spaghetti pot, Felicia found herself looking over toward 27th Street, looking for a thin, sweaty figure. Molly, returning from an evening run, would be juggling a Walkman in one hand and her hat and gloves in the other—face flushed, eyes alive. *I have to start dinner without you,* Felicia said silently. *I'm sorry; but I know you'll be home soon. If I have anything to say about it.*

remembering of a spellbinder

20 February

The runner's legs can finally call themselves that, purring and buzzing after my second ten-mile dash of the year. (My weight down to 117—not quite light enough for true speed, but at least respectable, for five-nine.) Emma's cry over long distance: "I'll never catch up with you!"

It was Bach who took me there, double and triple stops singing out of Yo-Yo Ma's cello until my gloved fingers were tense with frustration—the urge to use the back of the Walkman for a fingerboard, to draw an imaginary bow across my belly. But that would have distracted me from my breathing, the roll of my feet, the burbles and cracks in the pavement waiting to trip me if I don't see them coming.

Still I am so glad to have the music back; no longer does every pressured crescendo evoke Colin's tongue slipping past my earlobe, every crackling pizzicato slam his fist against a wall. Instead, now the music makes me think, much more appropriately, of you, Will. Especially now.

For it's coming up soon, the anniversary of your death—five years ago.

Can it really be five years? Five years since the Sheehan Funeral Home, conveniently across from the John Barleycorn?

If I close my eyes I am back there, my soloist's black dress converted to mourning, stripped of jewelry. I couldn't get them to play the Mozart Requiem you loved so well, Will—or even some gentle Haydn. Instead it was generic funeral-home music, velvet walls and the overwhelming smell of marigolds.

Marigolds seemed to find their way into each of the floral condolences from Joyceans across the globe, as well as from Kellys and O'Donnells trying to outdo each other in how big and ostentatious and horribly ugly a wreath one could find. The smell soaked my skin worse than cigarette smoke. I've hated marigolds ever since; even the color brings bile to my teeth. But their suffocating smell drowned out the formaldehyde that kept Will looking like he was "sleeping," masked the alcohol on familial breaths.

God, it's been years since I remembered so well—I'm only realizing now the numb anesthetic nature of the Colin years (six parts senseless adoration, four Absolut vodka, on ice). Now I can finally observe this anniversary as I ought—Joyce and music helping you emerge, Will, as Bach helps me circle the reservoir at dawn.

As I ran up past Northern Parkway into the wilds of Baltimore County—suburban developments and shopping malls nestling in among older homes, once the proud country refuge of those who had escaped Baltimore proper—I could feel your large hand on my teenage fingers.

The warm voice deep in my ear, quiet imperative. "The fingers are all in the right place, but you're not holding tightly enough. Use that muscle, it's what it's made for!" And indeed, in Will's universe that is what the hand muscles were for: fingering like typing, creating music or words, either way one should press harder, further, more deeply. All as familiar the keys on that Braille typewriter, far more strenuous than any manual typewriter—or the ancient manual typewriter you'd never give up. "If it comes too easily, don't trust it," a Will warning I have ignored far too often.

One can't claim this dissertation is coming too easily, Will. When I have time to squeeze it in among Madness in Shakespeare and other distractions, I am following you into blindness by squinting at Joyce's handwriting in photo-facsimile, churning my way through some of his notebooks for *Finnegans Wake*. Half the time it's about as useful as a Rorschach blot; one can make anything of them.

But certainly I am finding clang formations of the purest kind, nonsense exchanges and passionate Lucia exclamations from Issy, the Wake's daughter / slut / angel girl. Yes, the scholars are right: Lucia makes her voice heard here, her father writing down her words with the assiduous patience of an analyst.

Joyce knew what he was doing: *Jungfraud's Messagebook*, he wrote in his notes, absorbing his own Jungfrau (young girl in German) into analyst names—though by the time you get to the published *Wake* it's "Jungfraud's messagelook."

Then there are the little commentaries, research notes in linguistics or anthropology, other glimpses of family life. "W [Nora] we were too happy, I knew something would happen." Fascinated by anything to do with women, he offers a lovely heroic catalogue of women's cosmetic rituals. *Savior of the hair!* he cries, *redeemer of the complexion!* (The industry that brought us Ultima II wasn't born yesterday.) So Tilden was right, it's worth it to plow through this impossible handwriting, these notebooks with little sigla in place of names.

One simple equation transforms it all: | = Issy = Lucia. It lights up simple turns of phrase, " | whoever thought of this breakfast?" and observations: " | washes hallway with open umbrella." The wry father's humor not yet become the triple puns of the *Wake*, rich and addictive as good chocolate.

This route offers me Lucia's *Wake* contributions without the messy fetishism of her biography. Despite my New Year's dream, I am less interested in the daughter than in her father. Or as I said to Tilden, "I'm interested only insofar as she actually makes her voice heard in the work."

He approved, of course, to him only the works themselves hold any reality. So does Will's voice in my mind: *much better, Shem.*

Meantime I need to gather up my bathroom stuff and head downstairs, hoping for the shower. I already hear a faint thrumming beat from my old room—Felicia is awake! She's taken to rising early a few mornings a week, "for the light—I'm not sure what I'm doing yet, but it's something new." And borrowed? and blue? I've no idea. We may live in peaceful coexistence, but we are hardly friends.

22 February

So this is why people become scholars, addicted to academia as surely as my mom is to alcohol, Colin is to adoration and speed— because sometimes there are evenings like this one: a lovely string from Lucia to | to Issy cluing me keying me in, this is not guesswork, it is not inference, it is not theory!

Watch the phrase blossom, from the notebooks to the first-draft version of *Finnegans Wake* (kindly arranged by its editor so that each revision is set in a different typeface).

From one of the notebooks: " | trees too beautiful for her to listen." and our Lucia absorbed in a summer day, rebelling for once against hearing her father's words or mother's scolding, instead sending her voice into her father's tiny notebook.

Then in the first-draft version of the *Wake*: "Even the remembering of a tree is too beautiful for her to listen."

Next draft: "Even remembering of a tree is too beautiful for her spellbound to listen."

Then back to my dogeared *Wake* paperback, for the final version: "Even recollecting of a tree is far too lovely a spellbinder for her to listen."

Lucia's simple leave-me-alone turned to Joyce's triple-rhythmed music—Bach or a jazz riff, as Gary suggested. "Remember that saxophonist we heard at Bertha's last week, making mincemeat out of Somewhere Over the Rainbow?"

Tilden was at Bertha's the night we were there, by the way, trying not to squint at the smoke in the tiny Fell's Point bar. I suppose Gary and I are common knowledge in the department by now—I've shadowed him more openly since we began working together. They seem to find it all rather unremarkable, and perhaps it is.

We eat lunch together nearly every day, I spend an average of three nights a week in his bed. I phone him when I've discovered something exciting for the dissertation and he calls me (before Denise? after Denise?) when his book gains notice somewhere (*Lear, Ophelia and Lesser Madmen*, finally on the shelves!). Last week he stopped by my library carrel to tell me about the rave review in *Elizabethan Studies*: I kissed him congratulations, the kisses growing deeper and deeper until it was clear we needed to leave and go to his bed.

(Of course, winter has deprived us of our outdoor spaces—a scrap of grassy privacy from the precise angle of a building and its attendant trees. I still get warm remembering that very first night in September, his strong fingers pulling at my skirt in that courtyard by the English Department.)

Meanwhile this morning's run yielded February thaw: a few bold tendrils poking themselves up from the slush, melted snow crying water in the gutters. A far cry from "far too lovely a spellbinder," but that will come—though I would bet Lucia made her comment in autumn. I imagine Paris at that time of year as glorious.

23 February

And with the temporary warming, of course, comes my little vagrant muse, my Baltimore Lucia. Not by the baseball stadium, which somehow surprised me; I guess I had come to think of her as some sort of localized apparition, like those sightings of the Virgin Mary that are said to take place only in some hillside town in Eastern Europe.

No, this time I found her on my new, more urban route, the one that dusts the edges of downtown and touches the corners of our tiny red-light district. At first I didn't recognize her: she's grown thinner, and wore skintight jeans, smoking a cigarette as she leaned against the door of a closed bar.

Her hair was cut short, clinging to her skull in gelled waves. But that squint is unmistakable, and in some ways the resemblance now more acute: now she looks younger, more like the young dancer I've named her for—the flapper who had the gall to whisper in Joyce's ear in the middle of other people's dinner parties. The cloudy day gave her a sort of film-noir quality, her skinny body held rigid in a tough-looking exterior.

Looping up back Perring toward Northern Parkway I felt it, a very gentle rain—I wondered if she had managed to come indoors, or if the rain had turned all that gelled hair to some sort of undifferentiated dark mass. Or perhaps dissolved her entirely, like Issy, like Ophelia.

Gary's class has wedded the two in my mind, the twin daughters. There's Joyce's commandment to Isolde to "be offalia;" there's Ophelia, dragged down into the river "as if a creature native unto that element," echoed by Issy's voice joining with Anna Livia's as they merge with Ireland's great river at the end of the Wake. Or Issy as Nuvoletta, letting the river trip her by and by: "I'se so silly to be flowing but I no canna stay!"

Actually, I'm afraid all the madwomen we're studying (they far outnumber the madmen) are melding into Issy for me. Lady Macbeth says to her husband "What's done cannot be undone. To bed, to bed. Come, come, come!" just as Issy's version of the Letter buried under the dungheap, her telling of the *Wake*'s deepest secret, begins "Come, smooth of my slate to the beat of my blosh!"

The Madness in Shakespeare students are pretty eccentric

themselves: punks attracted by the "madness" theme and Gary groupies, moony long-haired overweight sophomores with suspiciously dreamy eyes. (Come to think of it, my Baltimore Lucia could easily pass for one or the other factions.)

Both groups pay close attention to Gary: still amazing to me that such an acclaimed a scholar is still a winning, charismatic teacher. He's even patient with some of the more stupid questions. "So what did Ophelia mean when she said the flowers all withered when her father died?" While he answered I closed my eyes; my chest filled with the scent of marigolds and the sound of Purcell.

I asked Emma yesterday morning if she remembered the funeral marigolds. "No, I just remember Uncle Frank drinking." She did remember that we are coming up on the five-year mark. Not that we O'Donnells have ever observed the years' passage in any sort of formal way. We never gather to mourn, no Yahrzeit candles as Rachel has taught me about.

I don't know how Shaun and Anna handle it; I know Emma has taken to telling her little Stevie (yes Will, you finally got your Stephen!) stories about Grandpa the Teacher. (Scholar is a hard concept for most grownups, let alone a 2-year-old.) I'm sure even Leo remembers you somehow, though he absented himself from the marigold funeral, perhaps dispersing his sorrow gently in the San Francisco fog.

Margaret, of course, always descends into deeper drinking at this time of year. I did the same during the years of Colin and champagne-soaked roses. This year I can finally recall you clearly, Will, and toast you in Joycean fashion at Felicia's art-gallery reception. With a glass of mineral water in place of James's favorite chardonnay.

25 February

About that reception, Thursday is an opening of Felicia's work at the Bauhaus, that sort of alternative "art space" next to the Charles

Theatre. "This isn't the new stuff," she said, inviting Rachel and me. "It's my big multi-media pieces, from my thesis show."

A group show, so now in our house we see the artists come and go (talking of Michelangelo?). A scruffy bunch in their leather jackets, pants splattered with paint: one of them, a short, bearded fellow, I don't think ever takes a shower—his smell drives me into the bathroom, to wash my face and breathe in the soap until he's gone.

Even though I was hurried out by that smelly sculptor, today's run was a carefully planned first shot at twelve miles; in my Walkman Joshua Bell ready to bestow me with the Tchaikovsky Violin Concerto, urge me on to the new goal.

At first I didn't recognize the couple walking away from campus, ambling toward the Toyota I know so well (I wonder if he ever got my unexpected menstrual blood out of the front seat). They were dressed as if for a concert or a theatre matinee; I've never seen Gary in a suit before, it doesn't become him. And there she was, the photo on his office desk come to life—short and busty, with short frizzy brown hair and big brown eyes.

And it all snapped into focus, as if a projectionist had finally adjusted the picture in some late-night movie theatre. I remembered Gary's subscription to Center Stage—this month they're doing *Antigone* with the action in Central America, something chic and pointless like that.

Between the distance and their absorption in one another, they didn't see or recognize me; from St. Paul Street I watched them laugh as Gary made a show of sweeping the February mud off the sidewalk, Raleigh for his Elizabeth. As I turned up Charles, I stayed across the street, passing right by them as he opened the door, swooping to kiss Denise before she got into the car. His lips forming the words, *I've missed you so much, darling.* At least that's what my eyes saw, and my heart felt.

It all gave power to the rest of the run, a furious pace to try to outrun my furious heart. "Temper, Molly, temper," Anna's voice unwillingly resounding inside me. Up in Mount Washington the tears finally receded; it all melted into Tchaikovsky, the violin's double and triple stops bleeding anguish through the headphones.

It wasn't as if you didn't know the rules, O'Donnell. In fact, you even said in this very journal that Gary was perfect for you at the moment—no thought of a future, just some current sweetness, you were too busy with this dissertation to want anything more complex. Will's voice or my own?

Oh Will, the hormones betray us, the heart betrays us. (Who's us? Women? O'Donnells? Graduate students?) I should have confined it to oral sex: the moment he came inside me I realized it was the wrong idea, I would grow too attached. And I was right: when he kissed her, the most exquisite pain ran through my body.

A car horn as I crossed Northern Parkway, on the way back— Ross Tilden! "My God you look delicious," a brotherly tease instead of a flirt.

"Ross, my nose is running, are you nuts?" I used the moment's stop to bend my knee till it was directly over my sneaker, stretching the hamstrings. "If you want delicious, look at your croissant. Do you live on those things?"

"I do when I'm in Paris," he said.

"Oh, I get it—and your heart is always in Paris."

"I love Paris in the springtime," he sang me a slice of Cole Porter. "How are the notebooks coming along?"

I had to think a minute, Gary having tossed Lucia, Issy and all their Maggie's out of my head. Then I laughed.

"Try this on for size," I said, striking a pose. "Whole, half; no, nay; shot, joot; shriek, screech; edge, egg on; from, fro; leap, loop; mount, meow. . . . The psychiatrists would call that clang formations, but to me it feels playful—maybe Clang Scrabble."

"Lucia and her father conjugating together," Tilden said.

"Something like that; anyway, it's certainly fun. But I'd better get going, Ross, or my marathon hopes will be shot to hell."

"What about those of your doctorate?" he called cheerfully as I sped back, now hearing in my mind this imaginary word-game between James and his daughter, growing faster and faster before dissolving into meaningless joy.

Kind of like those early years with the cello, Will, when the boring scales seemed a big joke and I, all of seven years old, would get silly and collapse into giggles on the carpet. (The music funny enough—the squeaks of an eighth-size cello are a cross between music and mice.) Did Joyce lift Lucia as gently as you, Will? Did he kiss her on the forehead and say, "Fine, fine. Let's start again?"

Time for bed, I have to meet with one of the weepy Shakespeare girls about her paper—as if it will make the difference, as she waits nervously to hear from doctoral programs all over the country. Despite my own presence in one, I find myself wanting to dissuade her from going.

It's true, and somewhat vexing. Seven months in this program, and part of me clenches at the thought of actually joining this fraternity—for that's what it is, a boys' club with women, complete with popularity-contest politics and one-night stands with pretty students. To your average faculty member I'd prefer my Lucia-surrogate, freezing to death in front of Memorial Stadium or smoking in the rain on Baltimore Street. Even if she is, as Gary has since suggested to me, a sex worker, she has probably never tried to stab a colleague in the back for a shot at his Ford Foundation grant, his tenured post or his parking space. (Or out of jealousy, for sleeping with his own wife.)

26 February

It's starting again, Margaret the center of the family drama, Emma crying on the phone. What did I say a few days ago, about Margaret drinking more at this time of year? Yet again it felt like high school scenes, Emma and I leading Will around the halls of the detox ward.

"Anna's finding more bottles," Emma said this morning. "But

she just denies it if you ask, says she's just crying for Poppie. She has all these pictures of him spread around her bed."

I see it so clearly, Margaret holding court—Anna bringing soup, Emma holding Stevie as Margaret cries for her lost love (lost to her, if truth be told, years before his death). Shaun is coming soon, I'm sure. Only Leo and I, the black sheep and the grey sheep, absent from her winesoaked pain.

I closed my jaw against it, swallowed the Joyceanisms rising to the back of my tongue (e.g., she's been "malt-treating herself to her health's contempt"). After Emma hung up, I called Anna, who said "She's getting old, you know, she really shouldn't be living alone." I asked if she meant a nursing home, and she flared, "I will never put my mother in an institution." She sighed dramatically. "Perhaps I should just move in with her."

I know Anna too well to let that martyr-voice pull me. Besides, "Your lease runs up in a few months, doesn't it?" Anna moves from Boston sublet to Boston sublet on a yearly basis, a habit left over from her divorce five years ago. (What's admittedly impressive is how she manages to make each sublet, in its own way, her home.)

I suppose Shaun will call me tonight, and that will complete the circle, the family consult, revolving around this fat perfumed woman we call mother. What's that word Emma uses, "passive-aggressive?" Passive aggressive, dark-light, mother-father, no nay, me meow. All equally leave meaning behind.

Meantime I am further and further absorbed in the James-Lucia duet—the *Wake*'s counterpoint and harmony feeling more of a duo the further I read. Oh Will, do you remember singing with me Mozart's *Ave Verum*? You brought back your little-used baritone to coach my struggling soprano, the voice I never quite inherited from Margaret. Together we wove a duet, now mine alone, the better to mourn you with. "Mozart wept this song into his pen," you said softly to me.

I kept the tears in my voice as I struggled to make the high note in the word "mortis," the word "dead." Why is death always a high note?

27 February

A morning for Carl Jung: the "fat materialistic Swiss man" Lucia hated, who "thought he could get hold of my soul!"

Jung's ideas on schizophrenia are completely out of synch with the Decade of the Brain, but considering that we don't know anyway whether Lucia would today fit the modern definition for schizophrenia, it's useful to read the words of a man who actually met her.

More important, really, is how Jung saw schizophrenics as waking dreamers—which relates directly, do not pass GO do not collect $200, to the dream-river of *Finnegan's Wake*.

The Psychology of Dementia Praecox : so perfect, that schizophrenia was by definition a "disease of young women!" Jung's summation feels uttered by Joyce: to him all madness was a key to the eternal, the archetypal, the intangible in human experience. Joyce's major female figures are so much closer to these impulses, running through their fingers like water, like air.

So to call Joyce a latent psychotic, as Jung did (insulting Joyceans forever after) was only to say that he was closer to the pulse of intangible truths.

Jung was in so many ways a literary critic himself, interpreting the speech and dreams of his "dementia praecox" patients the way scholars dive into a "text." "In dreams," he wrote, "we see how reality is spun out with fantasy creations. . . . Let the dreamer walk about and act like a person awake, and we have the clinical picture of dementia praecox."

We also have the dreamer of the *Wake* running and re-running the same set of archetypal conflicts and resolutions; erotic triangles and deaths and rebirths; a single Irish politician, brought down by a sexual scandal, turned archetypal patriarch subsumed in the female principle.

Do you know where you are? the familiar voice, as I switch positions in time for the triple stop.

Yes, Will, I think I do: for Jung divided schizophrenics into two types, those with an unusually strong unconscious mind and those with a "weak consciousness."

And there's the crucial distinction between James Joyce and his daughter—only he of the strong unconscious and firm post-Jesuit ego/superego could understand the mad speech of his daughter, she of the "weak consciousness." It was for him to listen to her mad speech, take its compressed wildness three steps further and explode the archetypes within it, twisting puns and triple meanings around every word. Lucia's name almost belongs on the *Wake*, a coauthor in clang formations, a neologistic muse.

Perhaps she felt prisoner to this act of creation, and that's why she set fires and threw chairs; perhaps this is why Lucia's father said once to a friend, pointing at his *Wake* manuscript, "Sometimes I tell myself that when I leave this dark night, she too will be cured." Now I am short of breath, nervous—because I know the next step, the one I would nearly give the whole project to avoid.

Yes, I do have to go into Lucia's biography—to understand better exactly who she was, Joyce's partner in crime, the skinny girl who called to me as the old year transformed into the new. The desolate photo in the midst of Joyce's biography, with the fix in her changeable eye.

Will, why am I so afraid of her? but you are silent, your blind eyes turned inward away from me. *Don't lose me now, Will, I couldn't bear it*—it's bad enough that the rest of the family is busy encircling Margaret, as she drinks herself into oblivion to forget you.

1 March

Midnight: and I am almost never awake at this hour. But tonight was Felicia's opening and I found myself in the midst of another group of waking dreamers, the painters I've never met, only seen flowing through the house. I imagined myself both Jung and Joyce, and wished I could take furtive notes on some tiny notepad.

Echoes of concert receptions: plastic glasses of bad red wine, cheap brie with Wheat Thins, young wannabe sophisticates in cocktail dresses and dress-for-success suits. Not many academics—I kept looking for Gary, who had received an invitation and actually said he might come.

Instead of patrons and soloists we had art students from the Maryland Institute in combat boots and hair dyed the blackest of black with cheap dye; instead of Colin in his tuxedo and aloof smile was Felicia, her already-short hair shorter for the occasion, wearing leather pants and a backless leotard that showed off her tattoo. Her eyes widened when she saw me. "Molly!"

"You didn't think I'd show," I teased. "You thought I'd be tucked away in my library carrel."

She shrugged and laughed. Then she introduced me to everyone else, young men I'd seen prowling around our house. "This is John," a small blond child with wide blue eyes and wire-rimmed glasses, "and this is Philip," the one whose smell had driven me to Gary and Denise—a wiry well-built hippie with hair snaking down his back and a beard that just reached the top of his green billowy overalls.

As for Felicia's paintings . . . what can I say? Splashed across those canvases: wraithlike figures with big-lipped faces, blood-red drops the size of quarters issuing from their insides. A towering male figure—father? lover? Satan? Many shared colors with her tattoo, so that when she stood next to one of them with her back turned, one might think each had simply jumped from her body straight to the canvas, full-born, without the smelly oils and loud music I knew full well were involved.

Gary never showed, leaving me to weave in and out among the gray-haired hippies and stockbrokers sipping Beaujolais. At eight o'clock Felicia, in high spirits, invited everyone to a celebratory dinner at an Indian restaurant. I let myself be swept along— perhaps I wanted to summon the ghost of Lucia (who, after all, crossed disciplines, dancing and painting and writing and singing). I felt older than any of them, even the vivacious woman in her sixties who carried a 35millimeter camera on a shoulder strap.

"Hey," Felicia said as we were leaving, "what happened to Anne-Marie?"

Philip, the long-haired one in the overalls, didn't say anything; he just moved on forward. It was one of the others who said quietly, "Anne-Marie's not in the picture any more . . . it happened last Wednesday."

Felicia shrugged. "I could see it coming," she said. "I don't know if artists should ever date non-artists."

I wondered briefly who Anne-Marie was and if she at all resembled Nora Joyce, who after all never read Joyce's work, who thought instead that "Jimmy could have made something of himself if he'd stuck to singing."

Over dinner, one of the artists turned to me and asked, "So what are you studying?" To be honest, I expected them to draw a blank when I mentioned James Joyce, but they all nodded— approaching Joyce from the same vantage point I used for art. "Paris in the 20's, man," Philip said. "What a time to be alive!"

The energy level of the table rose at least 20 degrees. "I'm sick of hearing about Paris in the twenties," Felicia declared. "We need to stop pining after some other time and place."

"I'm not pining," I said, "but sometimes you have to admit a previous era was just qualitatively better than the one we're in." I hooked a thumb toward the street, with its particular mix of yuppies and vagrants.

And we were off: a much more vigorous discussion than I'd expected. Suddenly this was some Paris café, with Joyce and Samuel Beckett arguing whether any age would rival the Greeks. Philip was banging the table just as the tandoori shrimp arrived, declaring "The point is not to always be trying to come up with some new thing—it's to follow the dream inside your head."

"That's what they did," I added, cheering Jung/Joyce's words out of the mouth of the hairy young sculptor.

Then I thought about not about Joyce but about Lucia: did she cling to her father's side at some of these cafés? I doubt she understood, her education hampered by frequent moves (17 addresses in 20 years!). But it seems that she learned too well to follow her own internal dreams—until the dreams were living nightmares and she was screaming nonsense and tearing her clothes and cutting telephone wires, crying out, "C'est moi qui est l'artiste!"

4 March

A little early for April Fool's Day, I feel a fool. There I was clinging around that damn opening looking for Gary's ponytailed head, and he was already on his way to Massachusetts for the weekend. I let myself into his apartment this morning and he had left the phone off the hook; I decided to leave it that way. Let him fret about the empty answering machine, if he was in such a hurry to leave.

Despite my annoyance, I feel I've regained my equilibrium about this relationship. Whatever pangs I may feel about Gary and Denise, they're nothing compared to

5 March

At that moment a student burst into my office in tears, because her entire thesis statement suddenly made no sense to her. "It's all wrong, it's all wrong." (It's not, of course.) But I remember precisely what I was going to say. And I can say it better now, because I've mulled it over in my mind, comparing Gary with Colin in fine detail—even contrasting Gary's absence at the gallery opening with the scenes that took place after many, many receptions. And the bittersweetness of the Gary situation cannot possibly match the hysterical, obsessive nature of the Colin years.

I never again want to adore someone the way I adored Colin.

Love is one thing; I suppose abstractly, somewhere in my mind, is the idea that it would be nice to love someone, and be loved. But what I felt for Colin went beyond love, merging and subsuming it like some sort of *Wake* river, becoming adoration. Adoration is the death word, because you lose your capacity to think.

I remember sitting first chair in the student orchestra and watching the stage lights glint off his blond hair, the sharp angle of his shoulders, the softness with which his blue eyes swept over his violin (a Strad loaned by a wealthy alum, who later sold it to him). And how my center of gravity (so important to a cellist) seemed to drop, as my heart suddenly resided in my mouth and my fingers clenched the bow until the palm of my right hand ached. I stood at the back of the hall as he checked the acoustics, and just watching him made adrenalin shoot through my veins, or perhaps liquid cocaine—something strong, something addictive. I stayed addicted to it for five years, lacing the heady substance with the gentler surcease of wine and champagne.

There I was, giving up the cello—finding whatever talent I had suddenly unworthy, despite seventeen years of hard work. There I was in three-inch heels and a red dress, trying hard to be the proper ornament at receptions, only to learn later that I hadn't glittered enough, hadn't laughed properly, had talked too much or to the wrong people. (Right people: conductors, conductors' wives, PR people, famous musicians with agents. Wrong people: backstand musicians, technical directors, ordinary concertgoers sincerely moved to tears by Beethoven.)

There I was finding a nude baby-girl flautist asleep in our bed one afternoon, and accepting Colin's line that "she lives in New Jersey and needed to nap before rehearsal."

There I was in Columbus, Ohio, the night he cracked my rib, after accusing me of flirting with Nicola Fanzo.

I wish I had kept a journal back then—though I know I would never have dared record the events of that night. I was too ashamed, too confused, anything but angry, anything but thinking or remembering clearly.

Much alcohol, of course, and while Colin romanced a blonde corporate sponsor I exchanged a few words in broken Italian with the guest conductor from Milan. God knows if anyone was flirting, Colin was—I've never known how to flirt, it's been a handicap in my life.

"Don't tell me that" and I am slammed against the bathroom floor of the airport Hilton, my breasts scraped by the tile. "I saw the way he looked at you . . . and he knows our phone number." Do I get up and scream at him?

Do I at least defend myself?

No, I cry, cry against the floor, my cheek clinging to the coolness of the porcelain base of the toilet bowl like a college student after a dorm party. I am also having some trouble breathing, so I concentrate on that—and not on the sounds of the glass breaking, those hotel glasses they give you so you can brush your teeth. Four of them, hitting the wall in turn. One. Two, Three. Four. A shard of glass skids to just below the sole of my foot.

Then to be pulled back up, those slender violinist's hands pulling at the spaghetti straps of my nightgown (I have since burned every one of those lacy nightgowns). "Where I come from," oh here comes the miner's son speech, "you learn to hold on to what you need to survive. You don't lend out your clothes because they're all you have. You don't even share your food, you don't know if there will be food tomorrow."

I have heard this so many times before but when he says it, it still holds me: those blue eyes suddenly those of a child, calling for help, asking for reassurance.

"And you," he says, "you don't know what you are to me. How can I share you?" And he is kissing me, bits of glass crunched under his wing-tip tuxedo shoes. I, dear journal, am kissing him back, letting him lick away my tears, trying to ignore the searing pain in my chest. And the next morning I am the one discreetly whispering to the maid what we need, to clean up, the one packing our bags to go to the airport as he sleeps off his hangover.

(Next stop on the concert tour was San Francisco, and it was Leo who actually took me to a doctor, one who X-rayed my rib without asking too many questions. I told Leo that I had fallen against the edge of the concert stage. Which in a sense, I had.)

Compared with all that, Gary's a walk in the park on a sunny almost-summer day—most of the time I bask in the sunshine, and only now and then does the heat get to the point that I wilt a little. Running the best catharsis, staying firmly in my body with Brahms' Double in my ears and my mind flying, if anything, to Lucia.

Eight miles yesterday in sixty-seven minutes, not too shabby. Though the ghost of my cracked rib was roused by remembering Colin so clearly; I could feel it as I stretched my back after the run.

I alternate between the route that burrows up into Baltimore County and a somewhat more urban route—the one that goes by the hospital, the one where I saw my Lucia girl smoking on Baltimore Street. (I haven't seen her in a while; I don't know if she's left town, or simply perhaps settled into a somewhat normal life, escaping the fate of the name I have given her).

6 March

deep into these Joyce notebooks and wanting to say over and over:

Lucia my girl, your father may be blind half the time, but the other half of the time, he's watching you. He notices:

your tongue across her lips after putting on your lipstick
how you bite your cheek in your sleep
how you cry when you break a plate
your wobbly singing.

For every "W" sigla (Nora) there are maybe ten |, references to Lucia/Issy (I wonder sometimes if he knew the difference).

I brought this all to Tilden, adding Joyce's declaration in his letters (as Lucia was about to be put away for the rest of her life) that she "speaks an exotic language . . . I understand it, or most of it." I told him I needed to do the biography work, to have more of a grasp on whatever half-formed consciousness was wrought on the Joyce genes by schizophrenia.

Tilden sighed in a sort of grandfatherly way. "Just be careful," he said. "Don't stray too far from the text." The text, the text, the Bible, holy of holies. (Or the Torah, generations of scholars arguing and worrying the interpretation of every line.) "Next thing I know, you'll be asking me if you can go traveling to look at Lucia's papers, off to London or Buffalo or bloody Texas."

I assured him that I could do what I need with the more widely available Joyce materials. They describe a dancer/artist who wouldn't be out of place in Felicia's crowd: sharp/alert intelligence haunted by internal demons, less verbal but none the less passionate.

Felicia, by the way, has asked me to sit for her. My first response: "What? I spend most of my time sitting."

She laughed. "No, I mean pose for me. Whenever you come back from running I think, God, Molly has such an amazing back."

Terrific. If I wash up as a Ph.D. the way I did as a musician, I can make the rent as an artist's model. Or perhaps just sell my back. (I guess that's actually slang for prostitution, isn't it? So I may have more in common with Lucia B, as I call her, than I think.)

8 March

And she's doing it, Anna is doing it, she even got out of her sublet three months early. "My landlady was glad, she has a waiting list." She's back in her old room, the big one next to Margaret's—the one we all shared when I was small, until I moved into the attic room that Leo left behind along with the burning garage.

"Are you really sure about this? Do you really think you can do anything about the drinking?" I had to ask.

"If I control the money." Oh my God, Margaret's going on an allowance. Anna's been a co-signatory of that bank account for years, and now my mother has apparently agreed to relinquish her cash card. Ha. I bet they run up a tab for her at the Pakistani liquor store.

"Listen," Anna said impatiently, "it wouldn't all be up to me if the rest of you hadn't decided to leave home."

Home. That word again. Like relatives asking, *So when you get your degree, are you going to move back home?* But I don't know what home is.

Perhaps my home is in Dublin, swimming the river Liffey— merging with it like Anna Livia or Issy, in the manner of Ophelia.

One of Lucia's most famous stunts was to swim naked in the Irish sea, on a two-month visit to Ireland—on the same trip, she also painted all her furniture black, turned on the gas jets with some regularity (the cousins she was staying with turned them off), and was found drugged in a ditch after having put an ad in the paper: "Wanted: Chinese lessons."

That visit, in 1935, ended with the *camizole du force*, as she called a strait jacket. Interesting that so many Joyceans give equal weight to fires, suicide attempts, and such relatively harmless stunts as sleeping in the garden and swimming naked in the sea.

9 March

Rosefrail and fair—yet frailest
A wonder wild
In gentle eyes thou veilest
My blueveined child.

James' poem about his daughter—and the blueveined child is pulling me in, all right, the more mesmerizing the more I read about her.

Lucia, who sang and painted and wrote poems, who danced with professional companies for several years and "cried a month of tears" when she decided to quit for reasons of her health. Who was desperately in love with the young lean Irishman who came to be with her father—Samuel Beckett. Who told a friend of Joyce's who visited her in 1945, "They say he is underground. . . . He's only pretending—actually he's here, believe me, well-hidden and watching you all the time!" So perhaps she knew all along, how many of his notes referred to her.

And surrounding me right now in my carrel are photographic images of this daughter-girl, in propped-open books and photo-copied pages. Watch the madness descend simply by looking at them.

At about ten years old, in a blurry photograph with a huge bow in her hair, her face is still rounded, childlike: she's smiling, nowhere else. A year or so later, in a classroom photo, she's already got that heavy, despairing look, a bored expression surrounding her changeable eye.

What's remarkable about the child-photos is how much she resembles the one childhood photo I have seen of her mother, the then-Nora Barnacle: except the young Nora smiles easily, secure in herself, something entirely missing from the daughter Nora never understood.

By the time we get to a set of posed family photos, she's firmly fixed in despair; although no one seems happy in that era where you had to *wait* for the camera. A cross smirk smears the face of her brother Giorgio while James, of course, is off in another world. Again only Nora smiles, gently, into the camera.

Other photos, of Lucia alone. In one she is maybe fifteen, in what looks like the French countryside but may just be a part of Paris I don't know (my Paris memories are hazy: I was there at fifteen, struggling with my schoolgirl French as I helped Will at the Bloomsday Joyce conference). A shock of Lucia's hair shadows one eye, she looks dreamy but not unhappy. If she was following her dream, it was a relatively pleasant one.

Then the one that haunts me so that I've pasted a copy to this notebook: Lucia at maybe eighteen, her hair cut short (not Felicia-short—blunt-cut to just below her ears), her elbow propped along a wall, leaning on her hand and looking off into the dark and troubled distance of her mind.

Why are you looking at these? Will wants to know. He always hated those who focused on Joyce's personal life, such as the dirty love letters to Nora. *Invasion of privacy, and not a damn thing to do with the work.*

But there is a damn thing to do with the work, Will. What if those lost eyes, the eyes of a waking dreamer, are singing Issy's famous footnote? "I was thinking fairly killing times of putting an end to myself and my malody when I remembered all your pupil-teacher's erringnesses in perfection class." A psychiatrist would surely prescribe phenothiazine for those words.

And obviously did: for the last photo of the lot is Lucia in St. Andrew's Hospital in 1979, a fat white-haired lady with a cheerful grin and lots of eye makeup, the nightmares banished by years of drugs. By then she had been hospitalized for over forty years, first at Ivry (near Paris) and then at St. Andrew's in Northampton, where she roomed with Toria Thursby, another elderly patient—whom she fretted would go off and get married, leaving her all alone. She was also still corresponding with (her sometime lover?) Samuel Beckett, exchanging tales of their digestive woes and confiding in him her great worry—that she did not know where she would be buried, though she hoped it would be near her parents. By then the drugs had erased the lost girl by the wall, and perhaps erased her poetry as well, the voice of the girl who found trees too beautiful for her to listen.

Oh Lucia, were you? Were you weaving *Wake* words there by the wall? Or were you simply immersed in the blackness, the grayness of depression?

That's what I want to ask my Baltimore Lucia, who's come back to the neighborhood, taking up residence in the Waverly branch of the Baltimore Public Library.

It's a small, neighborhood library, about four blocks from Hopkins; I stopped by to return some books and there she was, sitting by the green tinted front window, not paying attention to the copy of USA Today spread before her.

Her hair gone a little ratty today, like the fifteen-year-old Lucia —the eyes angrier than I remembered them, they could burn through the colored glass to watch the people buying vegetables in the market. She didn't see me, and I actually didn't want to disturb her. Surprised at myself, I was pleased to have found her again.

Despite everything, she is a partner in this exploration of mine: perhaps even, if only by contrast, part of my recovery from the Colin years. Perhaps she will run with me one day, and her voice mean as much to my research as all the hours spent reading Joyce's heartbroken letters about his daughter's "malody."

10 March

The real Lucia, of course, would not be surprised at the idea of running to dispel the grayness. At least not at eighteen or twenty, when she was dancing every day, angling her trained body against the darkness.

In yet another photo she wears loose pants and a headdress marked with the same Art Deco boldness: her tall, thin body is curved back at a dramatic angle, her arms forming an O.

Rosefrail and fair, a wonder wild—this photo both frail and wild.

And if I close my eyes, I can see it as they tell it, the frail wild creature dancing in competition, wearing a silver fish costume she'd made herself, one leg exposed, one bare. She lost the competition, despite the enthusiastic audience calling out for "L'Irlandaise!" ("The Irish girl!"), and soon thereafter stopped dancing, leaving the silver costume to languish in the closet next to Nora's furs.

How did it happen? How did the darting silver fish (I can feel her swimming in my hindmost) become the fat woman in the institution, requesting chocolate from her keepers? How did she dissolve, like Issy and Anna Livia Plurabelle, a living Ophelia grieving her father in fractured madness, if not a watery death in a Danish river? I still have a lot to learn.

"That's what's fun about all this," Gary said to me in bed this morning. "You never stop learning." Meanwhile his tongue is learning for the first time how sensitive I am in the hollow of my shoulder, my teeth learning how best to tease the blond curls on his chest.

In that part of my life (Gary) the status quo holds: the same midweek sweetness, good sex and good talk—and the same weekend pain, which I try to ignore. Some pleasures cost money, others exact their cost a different way. *Welcome welcome, that'll just be a little slice of your insides. Liver, you say, I can have some of your liver? Sorry the price has gone up, that'll be one of the ventricles of your heart. Yes, thank you, right this way, right this way.*

12 March

And I am writing this in BWI (I love that name, Baltimore-Washington International Airport: such dreams it bespeaks, planning for a traffic volume that never materialized). All checked in for my flight to Boston, paid for by Shaun. And all I can think of is that old joke—watch out what you ask for, you might get it.

Because I will be in Boston for the anniversary of Will's death. But it is Margaret who brings me there.

Last night, I walked in the door at Calvert Street to Anna's call, tearing through my Lucia ruminations with the long-awaited bad news.

Margaret has finally gone over the edge: Emma left her alone with Stevie for half an hour, and she was so drunk she burned him with hot coffee.

"I'm sure she was trying to sober up," Anna said, "people always tell you coffee will help. But there he was, that little one crawling under her feet."

Amazingly, my mother did the sensible thing—called Anna, who had the situation under control within the half-hour. While Emma and Barry were checking Stevie's burns (slight, it seems—more of a scare than a real injury), Anna put Margaret into her car, along with some clothes and a pile of back issues of the National Enquirer. The four of them then drove off to Peter Bent Brigham—Emma and Barry to the emergency room for their baby, Anna taking Margaret to her favorite resting place, the detox ward.

So why am I going up there? What can I do? I asked Shaun, when he told me he'd already arranged for this plane reservation. He seemed stunned. "It never occurred to me that you wouldn't want to come up." Oh Shaun, this is not news, how many times has Margaret been through detox now? Isn't it bad enough that I lost a recital, that Emma lost her senior prom a year later, that Will lost who knows how many hours of great work to his alcoholic wife?

I called Emma but her phone was busy: I realized my heart was racing, fight-or-flight, I did not want to do this. So I did the unthinkable—I called Leo in San Francisco. His opinion was abrupt: "If you don't want to go, don't. She's an adult, you don't need to feel responsible for her."

"But the family—"

"Oh Molly," he said, "don't let the family screw you up. Margaret will detox just fine without you . . . and besides, you told me it always gets better once the anniversary is over." Which is next week, March fifteenth, the date of your death burnt into my heart, Will. I asked Leo if he remembers it each year, or just tries to forget.

He took a long time answering, finally saying "Molly, I thought we weren't going to talk about Will."

At first I didn't remember, but he prodded gently until I recalled it—when I cried out Will's name in that San Francisco emergency room, after Colin had broken my rib. Leo had gone pale and asked me not to do that again, never again to recall for him the man whose rage still haunted his dreams.

All in all, he did convince me that I needed not go to Boston. I was all set to call Shaun back and tell him to cancel my flight when Emma herself called, in tears. "Oh Molly, I'm so scared."

"But she's safe now. Margaret, I mean. And I thought Stevie didn't really get burned, is that true?"

"Not badly, but—she burned my baby, Molly!" and Emma wept, no words left, just a sort of nameless primal sobbing. And when I tried to ask Will, his voice inside me remained silent, refusing to advise me.

Gary's advice was simple, New York abrupt Italian. "It's your family—do you really have a choice?" And of course, I do not, I am driven to this airplane by my baby sister's helpless tears. And I will be there, Will, tomorrow—in the hospital where you died; I will be there, not playing in some string quartet blissfully ignorant of your bleeding brain.

13 March

Hospitals are black holes painted white.

Sterile halls, unquiet white noise, uniformed guards whose

will is law. I would have nightmares every night if I were here, fearing I would never be allowed to leave that airless, hushed space.

Margaret, of course, is leaving, and in four days. The detox ward is anything but hushed, patients pacing the halls shadowed by aides; a red-haired patient weeping hysterically on a chair by the nurses' station; the volume level in the dayroom impossibly high as patients shouted at the Red Sox game.

(And you are by my side, Lucia. Was it like this at Les Rives de Prangins, the Swiss clinic where you saw Carl Jung? Or Ivry, near the Bois de Vincennes? Could you have been the weeping redhead, or one of the pacing, tight-faced women glancing nervously backward, ashamed of having to be followed?)

Shaun escorted me to Margaret's room, having spent the ride from the airport handing me statistics—blood sugar level, cholesterol level, blood pressure, blood alcohol level. It was 2 p.m. and "Emma and Anna have been here all night, they're getting some sleep." All night pacing the halls. I remember leading Will gently around, guiding his cane to indicate changes of direction.

You asked very few questions, Will, about the wife who had dissolved on the living room floor. Perhaps you were deep inside yourself, busy revising your book, *After Sound, Light and Heat*. (In any event, I actually doubt Will's affection for Margaret then was any greater than mine, now.) Margaret in the hospital: what an odd thing.

There she is, flesh of my flesh (or am I flesh of her flesh?). Her normally ruddy face gray, deprived of makeup and alcohol. Her hair, unwashed, lies flat and greasy against the pillow, and she is wearing one of those paper-thin prison gowns. It is too small on her, of course, and her flesh spills out at her hips, her breasts melding into one huge breast fit to use as a pillow.

And I know what I am supposed to feel. You could see it in Shaun's face as he watched her sleep. *My mother, my Mam, you fed me and put band-aids on my knees, how can you be hurting like this?* What Emma persists in calling "the child within" ought to be bleating, bawling.

But my child is bent over her tiny cello, Will's hand on her shoulder. I can find no pain, and little fear.

Is it true, then, Anna's accusation? Do I really just not love my mother?

I did feel a pang of softness, seeing a vulnerability for once not brought on by a bottle of wine. But that feeling vanished the moment she opened her eyes.

"Shaun! . . ." She picked him out, her golden boy, his red-gold hair shining, a boyish Lacoste shirt stretched tight over his huge chest. And he went to her, holding on tight, his Mister Doctor prattle stopped dead by the sight of her pale skin. (His skin, by contrast, pink bordering on red; I'm sure he'd sought the same solace that brought her here).

"Oh you didn't have to come," she said. "I'm all right."

"I was here last night and this morning," he said softly. "But you were asleep, and I couldn't bear to wake you."

Their eyes met like those of lovers, his wide face mirroring her round one, her forehead damp with exertion or medication. The dayroom noise seemed to have subsided, only a few patients left offering extended commentary on the ballgame, all a pianissimo accompaniment to this Pieta.

After she released him from another hug she saw me, standing quietly on the other side of the bed. A cry of surprise. "Oh, Molly! I never would have thought!"

And I went to her, of course, was received in the embrace. The smell only increased the nausea I already felt. "Of course I'm here, Mam," I said.

"You're so thin," she said. "Good for you, Molly." (Quite a different reaction from Anna's "Christ, Molly, when did they release you from Dachau?")

We couldn't stay long; the ward only allows short visits. Shaun took some of the brochures about their detox program, day-by-day schedules and success stories. I leafed through them in the car, on the way back to Dorchester. "Can I keep these?"

Oddly fascinating, from the simple program (not The Five-Day Weight-Loss but the Five-Day Addiction Loss Plan) to the more academic papers with squiggly lines and trigonometric axes, showing what sort of approaches succeeded or failed with different addictions.

"This is one of the most comprehensive approaches I've ever seen," Shaun said briskly, glancing over as I flipped through the pages. His voice that of a man in charge: this was a business proposition, like a new account or (more appropriately) an unforeseen tax liability. "They even take nutrition into account," he added.

"What a concept," I said. "You think maybe they remember she's diabetic?"

Shaun stopped the car in front of the house. "Molly, let's just be glad we've got Mam into the hands of professionals. Meanwhile we can help Anna finish unpacking and clean the place, so Mam comes home to a nice warm home and a rested daughter to take care of her."

The emotion in his voice, even when reciting businesslike facts, made me conscious again of what I don't feel. I hope abstractly that Margaret recovers, but she has hidden herself so long behind a curtain of alcohol that no-one, let alone me, could claim to really know her: I doubt she knows herself. Shaun is crying for an image, Emma for a feeling of safety. But I never had any illusions that life with Margaret was safe, not with brandy bottles stashed at all corners.

So one of our first tasks was to empty the house of all traces of alcohol.

Bedroom: empty wine bottles hidden under the bed and in the bottom drawer of the bureau. Kitchen: in the refrigerator a whole supply of white zinfandel, she must have cajoled them into delivering cases of the stuff. Empty bottles of cheap brandy slid gently behind the pots and pans, under the sink. Shaun and Anna worked methodically, quietly, a pair of silent convicts working a few years off their sentences. Which, I suppose, is exactly what they saw themselves doing, on their mission of keeping Margaret sober.

Living room: bottles stashed next to cigarette packs, in paper sacks in the closet, hiding behind Will's shoes. *You left your shoes behind, Will, why? Were you hoping I would fill them?*

Until recently I felt I was—now I'm not so sure. It's harder when Lucia also walks beside me.

I left Shaun and Anna to their spy search in the kitchen and climbed the stairs all the way to the third floor, the attic Will's study shares with my former bedroom. If she had the nerve to drink in your study I will never forgive her, Will, no matter how much she sobers up. I would consign her instead to the eternal flame of that detox ward, to compete for oxygen with crack addicts and other quiet alcoholics.

So I pushed open the heavy wooden study door, dark cherry wood with a bevel-cut face, in squares and angles. And of course I was greeted by a soft layer of dust, a sign that she has been drinking more heavily—she stopped dusting in here, losing interest in the Will O'Donnell museum.

Lacking a dishrag, I pulled off my own sweatshirt and knelt by the study chair, began to polish the railings. Then I moved on to his desk: when the glow emerged from rich oak it gleamed my reflection, and it was only then that I realized that I was/am frightened.

Frightened of what? Of Margaret's constant state of non-detox? Or just the basic O'Donnell claustrophobia, as yet unrelieved by a taste of Emma? All I knew was the wide-eyed alarm in the eyes staring back at me from the flat oak surface, now bereft of Will's many papers (always in neat piles, so that he could reach for and identify the exact document he wanted me to read).

Will, I can still find what you need, where are you? but there was instead only the smell of marigolds and the sound of Bach suites. And Purcell again, *Nothing of him doth fade / But doth suffer a sea-change . . .* I continued polishing, even paying attention to the dark-brown frames of the window, looking out on an angle at neighbors' back yards. And I remembered for the first time that I read Lucia to you too, Will. I sang Issy into your ear.

I am fourteen and we are in the study chair, your right arm around my waist. The other hand holds your delicate Waterman fountain pen, taking notes on chapter II, book 2 of the Wake—the one where Issy offers her voice in sometimes sugar sweet, sometimes ribald footnotes. Such a wild chapter, with the main text in its single center column, competing voices speaking from the left and right hand margins (Shem and Shaun, the two brothers angling for a turn) all interacting with Issy's blithe commentary at the bottom of the page.

At fourteen I'm not quite sure how to read it; Will says, "Just jump to wherever your eyes lead you."

Oh Lucia, your voice drew me even then. Sometimes so flirty: "You'll be hapnessized to feel how fetching I can look in clingarounds;" sometimes sighing, "one must sell it to some one, the sacred name of love." I remember asking if Joyce meant selling it the way the whores do in the combat zone (now, of course, I wonder about Lucia B.).

Sometimes angry: "Improper frictions and maledictions and mens uration makes me mad!" and the fourteen-year-old is looking at the ground, embarrassed. Only Will's reassuring kiss helped me go on to Issy's schoolgirl exercise, her attempt at the Letter. "When we will conjugate together . . . verbe de vie and verve to vie, with love ay loved have I on my back spine." Will's hand on my own back spine, urging the right posture as I practiced cello—always a fitting end to these sessions. "First I practice," he would say, "then you practice."

I looked at my face again and it was still scared, as if I felt someone looking over my shoulder with malevolent intent. I put down my discovered T-shirt and started looking behind the books, trying to be as thorough as my sibling pair downstairs in my search for the elusive gin bottle.

Then the closet: filled to bursting with boxes of papers, presumably the ones once spread across Will's desk. I pulled them aside, looking to see if anything was hidden behind the boxes. And jammed back in the corner, next to a full set of outdated encyclopedias, was my tiny cello—the very first one, designed to be held between oft-scraped kindergartener knees. We called it Baby Mamalujo, in preparation for the name Will had already chosen for my full-size instrument (a $10,000 beauty, its neck since broken by Colin).

I took a deep breath and picked it up. Thank you, Will, I acknowledged the gift extended to me from beyond the grave. I looked at my eyes in his desk's mirror and found that they were no longer frightened.

I left Will's study, carrying the little cello into my former room and laying it at the feet of Yo-Yo Ma, life-size cellist still covering the closet door. No liquor bottles in that room either; instead I found myself sitting for a moment on my old bed, an unexpected heaviness in my limbs. Probably simple fatigue—I hadn't stopped since leaving Baltimore.

When Anna called up, "hey, you want some lunch?" it took a moment to rouse myself and come downstairs, to ever-efficient Anna's lunch sandwiches from the local deli. Then they went off to get cleaning supplies, leaving me behind to "watch the house": I did just that, meandering slowly from room to room as if I were there for the first time.

And as if for the first time I found it, my old home: the little window-seat on the second-floor landing, an urban landscape through the square of glass. It was beginning to rain, the first of the eternal spring showers, just a gentle tap-tap-tap ready to lull me to sleep.

I kept looking for Lucia B., she had to be there somewhere amid the grit, perhaps shooting up or smoking crack in a back alley. Lucia Joyce sang into my left ear, That's the lethemuse but it washes off.

Finally I started to cry, water to match the rain, my face against my knee, the sobbing offering familiar comfort. The window-seat always was my crying space, my body relaxing into my tears. I could cry like this for hours and still not feel entirely released.

Yet just as familiar was Anna's voice, her hand shaking at my shoulder. "Molly, we're back. Come on, snap out of it!"

"Hey, be gentle," Emma offered from behind her "She has a right to be upset, too." When did Emma get here? The teasing rain must have put me to sleep after all.

"But we've got work to do," said Anna; over one arm was slung a bright-yellow plastic bag, full of noxious cleansers.

"We've got four more days," Emma said tightly. "And I told you, Molly and I need to go for a run." An urgent, pleading tone in Emma's voice, just this side of hysterical.

Anna nodded, they must have already talked about it. "Why don't you go do it now, before we have to go anywhere?"

I wiped my eyes with the towel Emma handed me, put on a pair of sweats and a windbreaker for the rain. I watched the anxiety drop from Emma's face as we stretched and took off, so I didn't ask immediately about Stevie; instead we concentrated on keeping a good pace, I on checking my form (I've been hunching my back of late, leaning over into the wind). The rain felt cleansing, as if the sky were crying for us so we could stop. (Pathetic fallacy, there's a literary term not listed in the crazy-speech books. Though it describes my life.)

Our first sentences came as we reached Allston and began to turn back: "I knew I needed this," between Emma's harsh (but quite correct) running breaths.

"So overall—how are you holding up, with all this?"

As I'd feared, the question made Emma stop, ostensibly to adjust her shoelace. I saw the tears leaking out from under her eyelashes. "Oh, Molly . . . I'm so glad you're here." She straightened up, took a deep breath and we went on.

Then, as gently as I could, "How's Stevie doing? He's home with Barry, I take it."

"He didn't get hurt that bad," Emma breathed into the rain. "Just one little burned patch on the back of his leg—we need to make sure it doesn't blister, because little ones don't handle blisters well."

"Hell, neither do I." Last year when Colin threw hot coffee at my face, I instantly held up one arm to guard my eyes, yielding a line of blisters from elbow to wrist. I remember rubbing the blisters with butter, cooling them with ice, Colin trying to kiss away the slicing pain every time they were exposed to air. "How about being scared, is he kind of normal again?"

Emma seemed startled by the question. "He's fine, Barry had him laughing when I left."

But I still wonder, made suspicious by my friends the psychologists. Did you hand little Stephen the keys to dreamland, Margaret? We may not know for at least twenty years.

Emma was continuing, "I think I'm worse off than he is. The doctor even prescribed something to calm me down."

"What, Valium?" Or one of the twenty-elven other pills I've been reading about?

The latter, it seems. "Xanax," she said. "I can show you the bottle when I get home. I haven't actually taken any." Thank goodness, little sister. It's a little early for you to grow old and fat and flirty, like your unknown cousin, my new soul sister, Lucia.

The run did calm Emma, far better than Xanax—she took me over to see her wounded child, who seemed far more interested in chewing on the cord of my windbreaker than anything else. Then back to Dorchester to help Anna and Shaun do their industrial-strength cleaning, before another hospital visit to a sleepy and cranky Margaret.

She was nearly obscured by an explosive arrangement of tropical flowers, resting precariously on her side table—the tiny card declaring Get well soon, with love from Leo and Jason. "Where is he?" she exclaimed, angry for the first time. "Where is my Leo? Why isn't he here?" like Lucia at St. Andrew's, begging for word of her brother Giorgio—who visited her only once in thirty years.

Anna condemned Leo on the ride home, "I wish he'd change his last name, so I didn't have to think of someone that awful being related to me." I didn't mention that I had spoken to Leo, or how close I had come to echoing his absence. I just heard his voice in my head, "Don't let the family screw you up."

So here I am back up in my attic, trying not to, not to get lost in those whitewashed black holes. Trying to imagine Lucia stuck behind them for forty years, transmuting slowly from the sultry (albeit sullen and uncontrollable) 27-year-old to the old lady who has been haunting me lately. Those walls alone could reduce me to such weakness, I think—the walls and maybe Thorazine.

15 March

Two lost days: most of my impressions poured out over the phone to Gary, running up Anna and Margaret's phone bill w/ Baltimore calls.

He actually stole time from Denise to talk to me, his colleague in distress—and he's a wonderfully patient listener, keeps offering me reminders of why my presence is important. "Your sister depends on you—and whatever she actually says, it would matter to your mother if you weren't there." Just as she asks for Leo. One would think she were summoning us all to her deathbed.

The house is now clean enough for Margaret's return (the question remaining: is she clean enough?). She is coming back too late for the exact anniversary of Will's death—that comes today, and I am up at 5 a.m. in your honor, Will, so that I can hold your life and death in my heart before Emma awakens. And as usual, when I think of your death I find myself angry.

Not at you for dying. More at Anna, for not telling me you were having unexplained and painful headaches, not calling me the minute she considered getting you to an emergency room—so that I only learned about your aneurysm six hours after the fact. None of this can erase the guilt, of course: I have never been able to forgive myself for not being by your side when you needed me the most.

I suppose it could have been worse, I could have been Lucia learning of James' death weeks later. At the funeral it was left to little Stephen Joyce, the "beautiful baby" she was not allowed to hold, to cry out in her place, "Nonno! Nonno!"

In later years, she'd vary as to whether she believed Joyce was dead: usually she did, even remembering the words "ulcer" and "peritonitis," but occasionally she would let herself forget and cry out to him, or believe him hidden, as in the famous 1945 outburst, "he's watching you all the time!" Of course when alive, he *was* watching her all the time. Unlike Will, whose sight was gone far more completely, who was limited to reaching for my hand or my hair, or leaning his ear close to my lips while I read to him. Love have I on my back spine.

I hear sounds coming from Emma and Barry's bedroom—the kind that indicate that she's not coming out to run any time soon, the kind that make me miss Gary. I think I 'll call him again—they'd be awake by now and his wife will understand, never knowing how his voice makes his colleague go warm inside.

16 March

Dorchester house, getting near midnight. It was only four months ago that we last sat around the long oak table, Anna's roast beef a symbol of Christmas Eve, Shaun generous with the Jameson's. This dinner's quieter, the O'Donnell volume gentled as if with one slow turn of a dial. Anna said grace, as we held hands around the table devoid of wineglasses: "We thank you, Oh Lord, for these thy gifts which we are about to receive, in Thy bounty; and thank you for bringing Mam back happy and healthy, so that we can remain a family for a long time." Anna's voice strong, celebratory, echoing the Mass we all attended immediately upon Margaret's discharge.

Shaun and Anna now more attentive than ever: "would you like some more soup, Mam?" "There's plenty more chicken." Plenty more pity and guilt to pass around.

But Margaret actually managed, with more dignity than I'd expected, to insist that this dinner be an observance—a sort of memorial for Will, albeit a day late.

She passed around old photographs, and told us her favorite Will story (the same one she always tells, but it felt good to hear it). It's about the day they bought this house, she bursting with pregnancy and Will with his junior faculty appointment. "I remember him talking about the wonderful wood floors," she said. "Of course, my Will could still see, back then."

"Only with those incredible thick glasses," Shaun pointed out, holding up one of the photos Margaret was passing around the table. "Do you want some more juice, Mam?"

Will, I looked for you in your photographs, so that I might hear your voice. They were old, cracked, needed to be held like a newborn infant: your glasses are so thick I cannot see through them to your eyes. Only in the wedding photo can I see it, your eyes looking into the camera, shooting warmth into my vein.

Of course, by the time I knew you could no longer make eye contact—most contact, and all warmth, to be obtained by sound. Like Bach, or the music of James Joyce's words. Sound and soft touch.

No wonder you titled your book *"After sound, light and heat, memory, will and understanding,"* a line from Book II usually answered by Issy's whisper. I always thought that "sound" came first because Joyce was nearly blind—and then light, because, like Will, he always could see some light.

Margaret is already looking a little better; of course her hair was "done," Anna having taken her to the hairdresser's before church, but her skin color under the auburn waves was also better, her eyes clearer. She's also been to her first AA meeting, one run by the hospital—we met her "sponsor" last night, a fiftyish Black woman who has been sober for two years. I smiled inwardly; perhaps racism is another bad habit Margaret will have to give up.

While Will's chair gasped its vacancy at the other end of the table, Leo's next to mine was quietly unremarked upon. Margaret no longer missed him, nor mention him. At least the doomed Stephen O'Donnell bore a mention, confusing Emma's alert two-year-old, who was already recovered enough from his burns to recognize his name and bang the table.

As they spoke of future plans I was as invisible as Leo, I am Molly who Moved Away to Baltimore. Then Margaret turned her watery brown eyes on me. "And when are you going, Molly?"

"I'm afraid it's tomorrow, Mam. I have papers to grade." (The first drafts of the Madness papers will be turned in on Friday—and this is where Gary needs me the most, shepherding each student through a rewrite and final draft.)

"Oh that's all right . . . you're so good at your schoolwork," Margaret said, as if I were in third grade. "I'm so glad you came, my dear sweet Molly. You know, your father loved you so much—I still remember the duets, him on the violin, you on the cello. I even kept the cassette tape of Mr. Greenbaum's wedding."

My God, how did I forget that? Did Colin blunt my brain that much? An outdoor June wedding at a Beacon Hill mansion, a blushing grad student marrying the head of the English Department in a green-draped courtyard; the entertainment is Will O'Donnell and his fifteen-year-old prodigy, playing Bartok's Duet in G for violin and cello. After the duet I played a shorter, solo version of Ernst Bloch's *Schelomo*—kind of mournful for a wedding, but the bride had requested it. When I was done, the wedding guests stood up and applauded. Will just stood there, his hand gently brushing the nape of my neck.

Ten years ago and I can still feel it. I bent my head to the dinner table and let my hair flow down to hide my face, breathing deeply so I wouldn't start crying again. Then I sat up and told them all about finding my little cello, and asked if I could borrow the tape.

"We'll make a copy of it," Emma volunteered, her arm outstretched to give Stevie strained peas. (Barry has this state-of-the-art sound system, including CD and digital audiotape; no doubt they'll re-process the whole thing, until Will and I sound like Jascha Heifetz and Yo-Yo Ma.)

Shaun is also leaving tomorrow, "pressing business," so I have no reason to feel guilty. But I volunteered to stay here tonight anyway—to give Emma and Barry some time alone and give me one more opportunity to sit in the alcove by the window seat, to cry a little for the sound of Will's violin.

17 March

11 p.m.

Just crawled into bed, after the short flight home—already awakened twice (the second time from a back-seat nap in Rachel's car, after she came to pick me up at the airport). The plane's arrival in Baltimore had pulled me out of a scary delightful insightful dream —a Will dream, of course.

In this one I was running up North Charles Street as part of a marathon, crowds cheering me on as I led the pack. Then a tall, familiar figure—Will, of course, running right alongside me. He wore his classic teaching outfit, an Arrow shirt covered with a woolly sweater and loose, comfortable slacks; somehow, improbably he was running in loafers. Instead of being delighted that he was joining me, I was frightened: do blind men run marathons? In life I know some have, in the dream it was patently absurd—and meant there was something ominous about his presence. I began to run away from him, not only hard but stupid if I was planning on lasting out the race.

He kept at my heels, tagging along like a small child, or a puppy, or one of those street people you can't shake on the bus. "Do you see her? She's here, she's here," he kept saying. I was sure he meant Margaret, and that made me speed up, I had no desire to see her. His voice wasn't at all his; it was deeper, louder, out of control. "She's here, do you see her?"

The more he followed me the faster I went, and I began to feel sick: I started to feel cramps in my legs and my stomach, and finally ran off the route and over onto a sidewalk, throwing up.

Will disappeared then; holding my head while I vomited was a rail-thin girl, a cross between the Paris and Baltimore Lucias. "I've been looking for you," she said. "I've been terribly worried. I couldn't find you anywhere."

As the flight attendant's voice roused me (warning us all to put on our seatbelts for the descent), I thought: actually Miss Joyce, I'm not sure who has been chasing whom.

"Do you see her?" Will asked. Not yet, I realize now.

I am really only beginning.

Time to give up trying to be an "objective" scholar, to pretend to care only about those details of your life that directly touched the *Wake*. I've been held by the darting silver fish and the elderly patient alike, I am beginning to dream you under my skin.

Time to let go of my toe-hold in your river, the one into which Joyce was diving and you were drowning: time to slide down into the cold water and let it cover me, see what fish I recognize in the process—making sure I get my head above water frequently enough to breathe. Otherwise, I will never finish this particular marathon—and I don't think I mean only my dissertation.

As I write this I've put in the tape of that June wedding where Will and I so improbably sang *Schelomo*, the Hebraic grief piece written in 1916 just as Joyce was beginning to plan another sort of marathon, of his own Jewish hero.

When I first heard *Schelomo* I was twelve, crying in the dark of Boston's huge austere Symphony Hall; Will seemed both proud and startled by my easy tears. But I had just learned about the Holocaust in school, and it didn't much matter to me that Bloch's piece preceded the deathcamps by thirty years—to this day the piece contains for me the cries of the camp victims, perhaps enfolded in memories of pogroms. A hymn to memory and an expiation, simultaneously; the remembering of a spellbinder, nearly too beautiful for me to listen.

Sometimes I feel like a
motherless child

"Such improbable lies!"

Molly's whisper was more of a plea than an insult; she lay on her side, her back against the half-circle of extra pillows on her bed, as if it were a low sofa.

"Cross my heart, Lucy—c'mon, I'll do it first."

The door to their room was closed, unusual for midday; also unusual the quiet, hushed tone in Shana's voice. She stood up, suddenly insistent, in charge; she rooted in her drawer until she found a roll of Life Savers, which she then held out to Molly. "Now put one on my tongue." Her mouth already open wide, her tongue extended, demanding.

Molly sat up, with some difficulty. She wore a loose spring dress, burying her hands in its pockets, while Shana handed her the roll of Life Savers. Molly pulled a circle of candy off the roll very, very slowly, her fingers trembling; the cherry-red of the candy matched Shana's fingernails. "Like this?"

After Molly placed the candy in Shana's mouth, the younger woman closed her lips, a barely perceptible throat motion the only clue to the action of her tongue. Then she swallowed, in a hard, obvious gulp.

Molly's eyes widened. "Shana, pepette!" With practice she had evened out her speech, her tone less trembly, her consonants clear. "You didn't swallow it whole!"

Shana grinned and retrieved the candy from deep in her cheek, barely sucked. "If you can do it with a Life Saver," she said, "it's easy with their pills! Especially the lil' white one."

Molly shook her head. "Tegretol . . . I cannot get hold of my hands."

"I know!" Shana slapped her knee. "And dizzy all the time, too. But not no more!"

"You're so learningful and considerate of yourself!" Molly's voice was touched with wonder. "Pepette, I'm as tickled as can be."

Shana gave forth a burst of giggles, crunching her Life Saver between her teeth. Then she spoke even more softly, her lips by Molly's ear. "Just don' let them give you a blood test," she whispered. "That's how they caught my man Frank Morrison."

The hollow-wood door made a knock echo into the room; the two women pulled apart, as if caught kissing. "Toot and come in," Molly called playfully.

As Kepler entered both women sat up straight, fifth graders honoring the entrance of the school principal. "Hello, ladies," said Kepler, "nice to see you're feeling cheerful this afternoon—especially with this flu that's going around!" He turned to Molly. "How are you today?"

"I'm not the girl I easily might be," Molly replied, pulling another Life Saver off the roll and holding it out to him, resting it on her palm exactly as the medication nurse would hold a double dose of Tegretol.

"No thank you," said Kepler, impatiently. "Molly, I just wanted to let you know—I'm going on vacation next week. It's only for a week, don't worry."

"Bon voyage!" Molly extended her other hand as if he were

supposed to kiss it. "The bark is ready, and the wind at help—To England with you!"

"Not so far as that," said Kepler, trying to smile. "I just wanted to tell you now, so you can get used to the idea."

Molly put the second Life Saver in her mouth and smiled, a distant, beatific smile. "Don't worry, Doctor, I'll be dood."

Kepler made a mental note that Molly's speech, while still dissociative, was much more communicative: the mix of Mellaril and Haldol seemed to be holding the line. "Are you still having problems with dizziness?" he asked.

Molly and Shana exchanged glances. "Not anymore," Molly said softly. "I am borne up out of the medsdreams, like a creature born unto that element." Her voice grew softer with each word, until "element" dropped off the edge into near-silence.

Kepler looked at his watch. "I have to go now, Molly. I'm so glad you're feeling better!" His smile barely reached the edges of his mouth, let alone his eyes.

Once he was gone, Molly turned to Shana, clumsily forcing herself to sit up straight. "Shana," she said, "show me how. Show me all. Show me now."

"It's tricky," Shana warned, "gonna take practice." She leaned forward and pulled gently at Molly's cheek. "Here where you want the pill to end up, so they can't see. Now let's start from the beginning." Finally she stood up, back straight, and placed two round candies onto Molly's palm. "Okay, Molly," she said in her best nurse-voice, "bottoms up."

The owner of the Wayne Gallery had turned October to July with a single turn of the thermostat, echoing his native Martinique; Felicia's arms gleamed with sweat as she and two others carried a huge canvas across the high-ceilinged room.

"Leesh, when'd you get the bright idea to make work the size of Missouri?" one of her friends asked.

"No fair, no one ever asked Jackson Pollock that question."

"Bullshit they didn't!"

The gallery owner hovered, a little map in his hand. He helped guide this final canvas to the place of honor along the back wall.

"Oh Felicia," he said, "this is marvelous—now I wish we did not have to wait two weeks, before our opening. Sometimes I feel I am a slave to the first Thursday of the month."

Felicia wiped her brow with the bottom of her T-shirt, momentarily exposing her breasts as she did so. "I'm perfectly willing to wait until First Thursday," she said. "I'm just glad you were willing to hang early—my studio's so goddamn crowded."

The others wandered among the paintings as if they had never seen them before. "Awesome, Leesh, awesome," said John, betraying his San Diego origins.

Jeff, Felicia's boyfriend, came up behind her and kissed her on the cheek. "I think we're all set, Felizia." His sculptor's arms surrounded Felicia's slim waist from behind; together they looked in silence at the largest canvas, the skeletal nude figure with one arm twisted behind her. Felicia had surrounded her with smoky violet sky, an addition so new that the purple paint was still evident under Felicia's fingernails. "Look at those eyes," she said softly. "Who would want to lock those eyes away forever?"

"Maybe because they're so hard to forget." Jeff let go of Felicia and walked over to the image, until he was so close that Molly's long black hair seemed to brush his face. For a nanosecond Felicia had the irrational fear that he would melt into the canvas, never to return.

How the winds are laughing
They laugh with all their might
Laugh and laugh the whole day through
And half the summer's night. . . .

Gail Ryan pushed the capo on her guitar, changing keys

quickly so that everyone could join in on the folk song. Sing-along was sparsely attended this afternoon; about two-thirds of the Wilkes patients had flu or were on family visits. There was, however, a surprisingly high showing by the wraiths of the hospital —the ghostly figures who spent most of their time either asleep or murmuring incessantly to themselves. The song, chosen by Karen Hightower, fit the gloom of the overcast day, which required the overhead lights to be turned on in mid-afternoon.

Molly sat in the front row with Shana, her face devoid of its old lady makeup; her cheeks flushed, her legs in jeans swinging as if the chair were too high for her.

"On a wagon bound for slaughter / There's a calf with a mournful eye . . ." The tone of the song made Gail a little uneasy, but everyone joined in happily on the chorus: *"Dona dona, dona dona dona dona . . . dona dona dona don."*

Molly was drumming on her knees, swaying from one hip to another in slow, sinuous moves. Finally Gail said calmly, "Molly, it's so nice to see you enjoying yourself. Would you like to suggest the next song?"

Molly shrugged, her gestures loose, free of old-lady tremor. She looked over at Shana, who nodded eagerly. Then she stood up, shaking her head as if to clear it, and walked to the front of the room. Gail put down her guitar.

"Molly?" she asked, but the young woman had already begun to sing. Her voice was newly huge, strengthened by practice in the lunchroom and the seclusion room—the belt-voice of a jazz or gospel singer, driven directly from her pelvis and echoing against the walls.

Sometimes I feel like a motherless child,
A long way from home. . . .

Gail looked through the songbook, knowing she wouldn't find the song. Molly kept singing a cappella, straying off tune now and then, and gestured to the others, her arms in practiced conductor's gestures. Then Shana stood up and proceeded to the front, in slow steps as if receiving communion; she reached for Molly's hand and joined in, her own voice large and round, swaying with her for the long, mournful tones of the aching spiritual.

"So we finally got hold of the stepfather in Florida," said Shana's social worker, a tall woman in her seventies. She spoke in soft undertones, as the conference room filled for the morning briefing —the smooth wood table gradually laden with coffee cups, legal pads and gloves.

"And?" Anne-Marie's voice quiet, intent.

The older woman's mouth pressed into a hard line before she answered. "Oh, the same thing you hear all the time—Shana wanted it, she asked for it, and besides it's none of our damn business."

"Did he admit he's the baby's father?" Gail asked, the question still under cover of the hello-chatter of the staff.

"I couldn't keep him on the phone that long."

"Well ," Gail said briskly, "the way these things work—we'll probably never know." Anne-Marie looked startled, as if someone had just placed a hand over her mouth. Then Gail said in her public voice, "Good morning all, shall we get started?" She opened her blue binder, an effortless, automatic motion. "Now here's a surprise—more trouble with Molly O'Donnell."

Anne-Marie raised one eyebrow. "Really? I've been encouraged by the lessening fatigue."

"Anne-Marie, when you've been here a little longer, you'll recognize mania when you see it." Gail voice was about two degrees short of exasperation. "Right now, Molly's very labile—she's refusing meals, she's smoking all of a sudden—"

"Well, not really smoking," said the head nurse. "Just hanging out on the smoking porch about a dozen times a day, letting cigarettes die in her mouth."

"In any event, Kepler and I agreed that this could be dangerous—her overall mood is now as elevated as before her escape attempt."

"Let me guess," said an intern. "Lithium?"

"She's already on a fairly substantial dose—any more might run the risk of more depression," said Gail. "Kepler thought Xanax would have a somewhat lighter touch."

"Xanax, plus lithium, on top of Haldol." Anne-Marie spoke slowly, as if practicing her consonants. "What dosage, for the Xanax?"

"40 milligrams b.i.d. Kepler has ordered blood draws twice a week, to check her levels for adequate absorption. Then if everything's okay, if we can calm the mania and keep her willing to communicate . . . we might accomplish something."

Accomplish something, written and underlined on Anne-Marie's legal pad. Then underneath, underlined and circled in red:

notebooks

talk to Felicia, Emma!

"Her family's coming again this week," she said aloud. "It looks like the brother is in charge, now—he's paying the bills and has made it clear that any ultimate 'decisions' were up to him."

The head nurse scowled. "Who, that blowhard? Just let him near me."

Anne-Marie bit her lip to avoid laughing. "I know what you mean; her attitude toward him is ambivalent, so we don't really know what's going to happen. The whole visit could muddy the waters even further."

"As if we didn't already have enough mud," said a volunteer, "with these damn monsoons."

Groans all around the table for the joke. "True enough," Gail acknowledged. "Who forgot their hip boots today?"

Anne-Marie joined in by reading from the Employee Handbook, given to her by Gail earlier that morning. "Remember," she said, and read from the first page. "Jacob Pearlstone Institute is located on former marshland."

"Former? Except when it reincarnates," said the older social worker.

Weather details were not the reason Anne-Marie had been given the handbook; she kept it open in her lap, even after the group had begun reviewing other patients.

Grievance Procedures, one sub-head announced, just before *Probation policy*. Anne-Marie's three-month review was coming up; she closed the book, to avoid looking at the third sub-head, *Dismissal*.

"You ever try putting your head in a gas oven?" Molly asked Clay, as he unlocked the door to the seclusion room. Behind him was Steve, the muscular med student who had first brought Molly to Chatham six weeks ago.

Clay kept his smile even. "Sorry hon, can't say that I have."

Molly bent lower on the bare mattress. Her legs were spread in as close to a dancer's split as she could push them; as she leaned forward, her T-shirt slid off her shoulder, ripped and torn in several places.

Steve squatted in front of her. "Are you ready to come out now?" He leaned forward to help her up; at first she didn't react, then sighed and moved her legs together, letting him grasp her hands and pull her up. She still winced just a bit when her elbow locked: the brace was off, and physical therapy was not in her treatment plan.

"Nice stretch," he said. "Are you a dancer? Or is this just from running'?"

As Molly stood up, her clothes slid off her body: first the shorts, then the SACRED HEART T-shirt, both strategically torn to uselessness. She struck a pose, her hands clasped at her waist, arms in a circle brushing her exposed nipples. "I studied with Isadora Duncan. . . . They called me *L'Irlandaise!*"

Clay swallowed hard. "We can't take you out there like that . . . Let me find something for you to wear." He locked the door as he left; after he'd gone, Molly sat down in her BVDs, not looking at Steve. She picked up the T-shirt and ripped it further, one hand forward, the other pulling sharply backward—an archer practicing a perfect shot.

The hall outside the seclusion room was almost as quiet as its interior. Most of the patients were either asleep or in the main building; the quiet had made the nurses and aides tone down their chatter, perhaps grateful for the absence of TV noise.

When Clay arrived at Molly's room, Felicia and Rachel were there—Felicia opening an umbrella to dry it, Rachel squeezing water out of her long blonde hair. Felicia squinted at Clay's nameplate. "Oh," she said to him, "you're Clay. The student nurse, right? The one Molly sassed at midnight that time?"

Clay shifted uncomfortably. "Uhhh . . . yeah."

"So where is she?"

"Well—I gotta find her some clothes before she can come out." He bent to the floor to pick up Molly's sneakers.

"How come?" Rachel turned around, her mouth in a tight anxious line.

"She ripped up the stuff she was wearing," he said reluctantly. "I don't know how, she's got no fingernails left. Can you help me find something?"

Felicia and Rachel went over to the dresser, producing jeans, a sweater and a pair of sneakers. "Can I come with you?" Felicia asked.

Clay shook his head. "Not a good idea," he said. "Thanks for your help."

After he left Rachel went over to the window and Felicia rubbed her hair with a towel she found in the bathroom, looking at the van Gogh posted behind Molly's bed. The sunflowers seemed in shadow, somehow escaping the room's harsh fluorescent light-stand. Then she sat on the bed and unwrapped a package she had brought, unpeeling layers of plastic and paper.

Clay and Steve returned five minutes later on either side of a fully dressed Molly. Her face had the shiny, reddish glow of the newly-washed, and her tangled hair was pulled back with] a rubber band. "I'll leave you girls to your visit," Clay said.

"What girls?" Felicia asked but Steve was already saying, "I'll be in the dayroom—if you stop by the nurse's station on your way out, they'll let me know you're leaving."

"Why?" asked Felicia.

Steve looked over at Molly. "Molly and I are getting' real close," he said, "you could say we're inseparable."

Molly looked at him, levelly. "I'm sure you detest me," she said.

Steve's smile didn't fade one iota. "Bye now," he said.

Rachel turned from the window, blinking away tears, while Felicia busied herself with her package. Molly looked over at Rachel and said softly, "Women will water the world over, Rachel. Leave your little bag of gloom behind!" She began to pace the room, singing under her breath, "Sometimes I feel like a motherless child. . . ."

"Look," said Felicia, "I brought you something else to hang on your wall. Next to old Vince, maybe."

The drawing of Molly was held in a clear plastic frame, the black and white sketch set off by a vibrant, completely inaccurate spurt of color. "Red hair!" Molly exclaimed. "Or auburn, as they say in French."

"It just seemed right," Felicia said.

Molly stared silently as Felicia carefully hung the drawing, which looked even larger on the wall. "The mirror reflects various-ly," she said softly. Then Molly turned to Felicia and smiled again, as if she were about to laugh; she moved forward and put her hands on Felicia's shoulders. "A poem from sister to sister," she said, and held out her arms.

Felicia moved forward into the unexpected hug; she spoke softly into Molly's ponytail, trying to be humorous. "Guess what I'll title it," she said. "L'Irlandaise."

As Felicia and Rachel were about to leave, the medication nurse arrived, five different kinds of pills lined up in her palm. All watched carefully as Molly took each one into her mouth, followed them all with a large glass of orange juice, and swallowed loudly. Felicia bit her lip, as if she were being tattooed all over again.

On their way out they stopped by the nurse's station, as requested.

"So why was she in seclusion this time?" Rachel asked.

"Ummm . . ." The nurse looked embarrassed. "She pulled all our phone cords out of their jacks—it took us about half an hour to figure out why none of the phones on the unit were working. We finally caught her trying to cut one of the phone wires, with her fingernails."

"She couldn't stop laughing," added the other nurse.

Felicia swallowed hard, to suppress her own laugh. "So that's why you've got Steve tailing her?"

"It's an alternative," the nurse shrugged.

"To what?"

"To placing her in restraints."

When Steve came back to her room Molly was still in the bathroom, staring down at the clump of spit-up medications in the toilet. She'd had to hold them for so long in the depths of her cheek that the tablets had nearly dissolved; she watched the green and white lump coalesce in the toilet, the glistening Prozac capsule unscathed in the center. She flushed just as Steve knocked on the bathroom door.

"Hey Moll, you okay?" Steve's baritone voice forced cheerfulness. "Whadya want to do now? You know how to play Trivial Pursuit?"

. . .

205

Felicia and Rachel were silent as they walked the long paved road from Chatham to the parking lot. Felicia was looking over into the trees, watching the sunset set the gloomy clouds on fire. Rachel waited until they were inside the car before she started crying.

All around them nurses and secretaries slammed car doors at the end of the work day, exiting the parking lot without giving a second glance to the two women in the battered Volvo. "They must be used to this," Rachel murmured through her tears. "Families crying in cars."

Felicia reached out a hand to touch Rachel's shoulder, gently; the sleeves of her jacket and sweatshirt slid down, the green snake around her wrist matching Rachel's raincoat. "Hey Rae, it's not that bad—don't you love her energy? It may sound strange but I feel like I saw a little of the old Molly O'Donnell, today. Much as I hate to admit it, this place might be doing her some good."

"The old Molly O'Donnell pulls out phone wires? Rips her clothes to pieces?" Rachel lifted her wet blond braid and shook it, droplets flashing on the dashboard. "Maybe when Anne-Marie comes tonight, she can explain this."

"Don't get your hopes up . . . My guess is, we're gonna hear about Molly's diaries again. Doesn't she understand she should go look somewhere else?" A flash of lightning, the first in hours, passed before the car. "Uh oh we better get started . . . Do you want me to drive?" Rachel nodded. After they shifted positions, Felicia said, "All I can say is, I prefer this Molly to either the zombie or the old lady."

Rachel didn't reply; as they left the hospital grounds and entered the clogged highway, she reached into the glove compartment for a tissue and blew her nose. "That song," she said, "that's how I feel, now." She leaned back on the seat and closed her eyes. *"Sometimes I feel like a motherless child."*

Felicia joined her, her voice completely off-key but much surer of the words to the song. *"Sometimes I feel like a motherless child, a long, long way from home."*

· · ·

The inch-thick stack of paperwork required to transfer Molly O'Donnell from Pearlstone to Park Grove, a Massachusetts state hospital, lay on Dan Kepler's desk like a slab of lead. He lifted it accordingly, slowly and with both hands, carefully handing the pile to Anne-Marie; then he looked across at Shaun, whose Buddha-like stance bespoke a man who has come to an important decision. The two men wore matching blue wool suits, right down to the width of the pinstripes.

Anne-Marie looked down at the transfer papers—mainly authorizations for Kepler to sign, instructing Pearlstone to release all nursing records, therapy notes, medication schedules. The forms were hand-typed onto elderly photocopies, bespeaking an older institution without computer systems; its weight in her lap seemed to lock her in place.

"Their patient-to-staff ratio is fifty to one," Kepler remarked, leaning forward on his desk. "Ours is two to one—and we're *slowly* having some success in stabilizing your sister. Do you really want to risk moving her?"

Shaun sighed, as if bored. "Listen, Dr. Kepler, I have the utmost respect for you and your institution. But you're not claiming you can cure Molly, correct? All you can do is try to make her stable enough to live on the 'outside,' as long as she keeps taking her medication."

Kepler sighed. "It's not as simple as that—but you're right, cures for schizophrenia are few and far between."

"Given that, I'm sure you can appreciate her family's desire to have her closer to home, in an equally professional setting."

"And a less expensive one," Anne-Marie said softly, half to herself.

Shaun turned to her as if he had never seen her before. "Are you accusing me— "

"I'm sorry, Mr. O'Donnell," Anne-Marie said quickly. "I didn't mean to imply anything."

Kepler cleared his throat. "I suppose the question is moot, Mr.

O'Donnell, since you've already filed for the transfer. Have you settled on a date? Most state facilities are quite at capacity, this time of year."

Shaun sighed. "December first is the best they can do—and then only if I can pull a few strings. So Molly will be here for a while longer, anyway."

"In that case," Kepler said, "we'll proceed with our treatment plan, and see what progress we can make with Molly in the interim. In the meantime, I wouldn't suggest telling her yet—she's been improving, but she's somewhat . . . excitable right at the moment."

"Of course," said Shaun. "I'll also tell Emma when she comes tomorrow. I told Anna to stay home, our mother needs her."

Kepler gestured for the transfer papers; when Anne-Marie handed them over, he began to sign each form, one by one. "I'm going to Trinidad for ten days, starting tomorrow," he said. "I'll be back on the twenty-fifth—let's make sure we touch base then, both on her progress and the status with Park Grove."

Shaun nodded, satisfied. When Kepler had finished the last form, he handed the whole stack to Shaun, who bent and put it in his leather briefcase. He then set the briefcase on Kepler's desk, standing up to shake the doctor's hand. "I'm glad we understand each other."

Anne-Marie looked at the blue-suited handshake, two stockbrokers concluding a financial transaction. She bit down hard against the words of rebellion that seemed just under her tongue—instead staring at Shaun's closed briefcase, a brown leather barricade with gold clasps.

Steve, the volunteer, hadn't shaved in three days: his reddish almost-beard glimmered in the noon sunlight as he shadowed Molly in the dayroom. Molly was sitting at the ward's little-used piano, which had been in storage for as long as Steve could remember, now brought out at Molly and Karen's request. Molly was picking carefully, one finger at a time, working her way down the out-of-tune keyboard—her slim fingers pale against the black keys, pink against the stained ivory plates.

"Did you play piano when you were a kid, Molly?" Steve asked, not expecting a reply: he was used to how much Molly ignored him.

But this time Molly answered, from deep in her throat. "Every day we would go to the piano," she said.

"Who's we?"

"My boyfriend Emile. He was very handsome. He taught me Negro spirituals and the blues." She pointed to the world beyond the dayroom window, where slowly drying mud seemed to rise up, coagulating around the dead grass.

Steve checked his watch. "You dressed for lunch, Moll?" he asked the girl in running shorts and an oversized T-shirt. "It'll be time pretty soon."

This time Molly did ignore him; she was trying as hard as she could to place her hand in a correct pianist's position above the keyboard, her wrists parallel with the keys but about four inches above, her fingers curved and fingertips barely touching: her bad elbow against her waist, leverage replacing strength. Her fingernails, cropped extra-short by the nurses, had been painted by Shana: one hand blue for her eyes, the other bright red in honor of their favorite candy.

"Molly, sweetie . . . can you come back in your room for a second?" The head nurse's voice was level, belying her soft words; she was accompanied by a younger nurse who carried a small aluminum briefcase bearing a cross, like a lawyers' first-aid kit.

As Molly turned to face them, the younger nurse's watch issued twelve short beeps: Molly's face brightened. "Big Ben's chimes!" she said. "You can hear them all the way in Galway!" She followed the two nurses with a slow, sashaying pace, humming to herself.

When they'd reached Molly's room, the young nurse piped

up, her voice sweet as a child's cough syrup. "We just need to test your blood, Molly," she said. "It's so we can help you get better." She opened the case, attaching a long test tube to a syringe.

When Molly saw the syringe her eyes widened, and she tried to run for the door. "Go to hell," she said, precisely and carefully. "But not the hell of the damned."

The head nurse gestured to Steve, who put his hands gently on Molly's shoulders, in quiet warning. Molly closed her eyes and began to scream, her new-found lung power as effective for screaming as for singing. As she howled, her body shook so violently that no one even tried the syringe; several aides stopped in, one trailing Shana. Shana started crying, which diverted one of the nurses and two of the aides.

After about half an hour, word came down the hall, a doctor's telephoned orders. "He said let it go for now, he'll check out this resistance before we try again." At this point Molly had collapsed and was sitting on the floor, weeping: when she looked up she said to Steve, "Blood will not suffer blood to be spilt."

Steve looked at his watch again, a motion so automatic one might suspect it for a tic. "Let's find you some clothes to wear out in that wet weather, Moll."

The window of the attic at Calvert Street looked out over back porches, the outlines of the university barely discernible behind trees and other row houses. Emma sat on Molly's futon, running her fingertips along the slanted glass. "From Boston to Baltimore, still living in attics," she said softly. "At first I couldn't believe it . . . then when I saw it, I realized, it probably felt more like coming home."

Anne-Marie nodded. "I can see her now—looking out that window, thinking about James Joyce or Hamlet or something."

"Actually," said Emma, "when she first moved in here she was in that big room, Felicia's studio—they switched rooms in January, because Felicia wanted the morning light downstairs. Also so Molly wouldn't be so bothered by her music."

Anne-Marie laughed. "Artists and their music! Boy I remember that from Philip, that sculptor. . . . He makes these incredible wood masks." As she spoke, she was scanning the books on Molly's shelves, pulling out volumes one by one. "I'd stop by his studio after class and there he was, after midnight, blasting Social Distortion or Nirvana, I couldn't hear myself think!" She sat down, her back against the Shakespeare section of the bookshelf. "But you know? Sometimes I miss it."

"Why'd you break up?"

Anne-Marie shrugged, turning back around to keep searching Molly's shelves. "I don't know—neither of us had any money, I was in therapy and pretty moody . . . Plus he thought what I was learning in school was either common sense or just plain wrong." Suddenly her breath caught, and she squatted to get to the lowest shelf. "What's this?" She pulled out a slender three-ring binder.

"No, we're looking for these big spiral notebooks," Emma cautioned, but Anne-Marie had already discovered her mistake on the title page: *Modernism and Cultural Theory—Austin, Texas.* She showed it to Emma, who said, "Oh yeah, that conference last August."

Emma stood up then and leaned against the slanted wall, leaning against her palms in an instinctive runner's stretch. "I remember Molly and Poppie going out there, to Texas, back when I was still in high school." Her face clouded, her mouth softening: Emma, Anne-Marie noted, was not one to hide her feelings easily.

"Emma," Anne-Marie asked gently, "can we talk, now?"

"What? Oh, you mean really talk. Don't we need a couch for this?" Emma lay down on the futon again, facing the ceiling as if preparing for psychoanalysis. "My Childhood with Molly O'Donnell. She was my sister, I love her. I always looked up to her, I still do even though she's real sick. The End." She sat up. "OK?"

Anne-Marie looked out the window, and swallowed hard. "What's so hard about this? You keep telling me what you remember isn't important, then you have such a hard time saying it I think, it must be important."

Emma sat down on the floor next to the window. "But if this is all some brain disease, what's the point?" Emma crossed her legs in a careful half-lotus, and stared at her feet. Her next words were muffled by her hair. "Is she ever going to get well?"

Anne-Marie sat opposite her, sinking to the floor in a gentle yoga motion. "I think so." she said. "But you have to trust me."

"It's not you I don't trust!" a wail from behind the wall of black hair. Emma pulled her knees up to her chest and hugged herself, in soft unconscious echo of Molly's behavior on the ward. Then her body began to tremble, beginning with her fingertips and traveling up her arms, until she pulled in even tighter. Anne-Marie wrote in her legal pad, waiting.

Finally Emma pulled her hair behind her ears.. "I guess we may as well start with the attic," she said.

Anne-Marie smiled, restrained herself from getting up and hugging Emma; instead she said neutrally, "Was Molly always in the attic bedroom?"

"No but she got it when we were really little—she was seven and I was six. It was after Leo, our oldest brother, ran away—you know about that, right?"

As Anne-Marie nodded, Emma leaned against the wall, settling in to remembrance. "Poppie's study was right next door, so she could read to him and learn cello with him, and then go practice in her room if she wanted." A gentle tapping on the window, another rain shower; she leaned her cheek against the cool glass. "I've never seen two people love each other the way they did." As she spoke the last sentence her hand half-covered her mouth, as if whispering a secret.

Anne-Marie wrote in her legal pad, noting Emma's body language as well as her words. "So he was a cellist too?" she asked softly, ingenuously.

"No, he played the violin, but with the Suzuki method your parents don't even have to play an instrument. They just stand with you while you hold this little baby instrument—like—where did it go?" Emma hoisted herself to her feet and was suddenly on the other side of the room: on the angled wall next to a Seurat print was a vacant space, small pegs making a diagonal, vaguely rectangular pattern. "God, I don't know what happened—she had it on her wall, this beautiful baby cello maybe a yard long." Emma stared at the wall, as if she could summon up the lost instrument; then she sat down, defeated. "Molly was so happy to find it last spring—she was up at the family house for a while, when Mam went into detox this last time."

"And she's been sober since then? Your mom?"

"Seven months now," Emma gave it a soft smile. "I think her recovery is finally happening. Faster than mine, I think I'll be going to ACA meetings my whole life."

"Me too," Anne-Marie admitted. "Sometimes I try to think if I know anyone who *isn't* the child of an alcoholic. But you—what was it like for the two of you, having a mom that was drunk a lot? Did you stick together?"

"Always—except when Molly was with Poppie." Emma looked out the window, at the newest batch of rainclouds massing furiously over the buildings. "I wish the thunderstorm would come and be over with," she said. "I hate these piddly little showers."

"This is unusual, for Baltimore in October," Anne-Marie said. "We usually only get this much rain in the springtime."

"And I still can't believe about the little cello . . . I'm gonna ask Felicia." Emma kept her fingertips on the window glass; her movements were restless, wired, as if she could bolt at any time.

"Emma please sit down . . . Felicia's not even here."

When Emma turned to Anne-Marie her eyes were bright. "Bad

213

enough her real cello got its neck broken, by that evil man in New York. I even hate even the sound of his name."

Anne-Marie swallowed, turned to a new page. *Cello with its neck broken*, she wrote. "Emma please say it anyway . . . I need to know it."

"Actually. I can do more than just tell you his name." Emma rooted in her hip pack until she came up with a glossy brochure, declaring BALTIMORE SYMPHONY. She folded it, exposing one inside photo. Anne-Marie took it, puzzled, until Emma spat the name. "Colin West . . . Fucking drug addict."

Anne-Marie's eyes widened. "Is that why she's so afraid of needles?"

"I don't know, I always thought it was just cocaine."

Anne-Marie looked over at the alarm clock on Molly's dresser. "We should start back," she said. "Molly will be ready to see you, and I have some other clients to see . . . But let's talk in the car—it sounds like we need to. "

Emma shrugged. "Talking about that guy makes me ill . . . the last time Molly and I tried to run the New York Marathon together, he got her so drunk and sick she couldn't even talk straight."

"No kidding." Anne-Marie had to restrain herself from writing on her hand.

"Yeah she kept saying *next year,* crying on the phone *oh please, we'll run it together next year.* . . . Now," she said, halfway down the stairs, "I wonder if we ever will."

Molly's room was wallpapered with colored lettrines.

Fourteen letters of the alphabet, in order, elaborately decorated: some seemed to spout dragons, others immersed in incomprehensible poetry or just wild, extravagant lines. "Molly finally started coming to art group," Steve told Shaun and Emma, "when we promised her we would let her keep it."

"You don't usually?" Emma was sitting at the foot of Molly's bed, where her sister lay with her eyes closed, curled under the blankets in fetal position.

"In general we tend to keep patients' artwork, so that we can go over it when we're doing assessments."

Shaun walked around the room, looking closely at each piece as if he were at an art gallery; Emma watched her sleeping sister for a long minute before she looked up at Steve, questions in her soft brown eyes.

"It's unfortunate," Steve said, practicing his professional-clinician voice. "Her medications can be quite sedative. . . . Though as you can see, they haven't affected her ability to be creative."

"Molly showed me," Emma said softly, "Lucia Joyce did drawings like that."

After Steve left, Emma reached out and touched Molly's sleeping fingers, draped casually over the bedframe. "Shaun?" she asked quietly. "It sounds like they're getting to know Molly really well here. Are you sure we should move her?"

Shaun half-turned, one of his hands pressed flat against one of Molly's drawings. "Look at this nonsense," he said. "No wonder this place costs three times as much, if they're wasting Molly's time and my money on art classes. I find myself wondering what incentive they offer to get well. As far as I'm concerned, the sooner we can get her closer to home, the better."

Emma closed her eyes momentarily, then got up and went over to stand beside her brother. "Please stop leaning on the drawing," she said steadily, all quiver gone from her voice. "Show some measure of respect for my sister."

Shaun moved away, revealing an inscription across the top of the page—*C'est moi qui est l'artiste!*

"It is I who is the artist," Emma said softly. "She knows it even now, Shaun, long after she gave up the cello. I know it, Poppie knew it—I wish you knew it."

Shaun swallowed. "Poppie would never leave her down here," he said. Then his eyes widened and he said, "Wait a minute—did you say anything to that social worker, about Poppie? Like those stories you used to tell me and Anna?"

Emma pressed both hands against her forehead. "Those stories, right. You're gonna keep calling me a liar for another fifteen years?"

Shaun sighed, sitting on the empty bed opposite Molly's. "Emma, when we get home, let's see about getting you a new therapist, one that can help you find out why you still hate Poppie so much. I'm sure there's a perfectly reasonable explanation, one that has nothing to do with Molly." He reached for her hands, held them tightly, a spurned lover or a cop. "Just don't meddle with physicians trying to treat a terrible disease—or have you already?"

Emma pulled her hands away and bent over Molly, running her fingers through her sister's soft black hair. When she finally spoke, her voice was low, tight. "Don't worry, Shaun, I didn't say anything to blemish Poppie's good name." Slowly she stood, made her way to the door. "But what if I did, anyway? What would you do, excommunicate me?" As she fled, Emma's tears were audible down the hall, her exhales full of water in half-sobs.

"Oh, Emma, I didn't mean that the way it sounded!" As Shaun called after her, he didn't notice the open eyes of his other sister, staring at the ceiling behind his back. He followed quickly behind Emma—leaving too soon to see Molly stir and sit up, having lain there awake the whole hour.

Ten-thirty p.m.: the main building was nearly deserted, except for maintenance crews and the occasional psychiatrist finishing up his ward notes. Anne-Marie's office was a partitioned cubicle with no windows, all the way at the end of a corridor. At her left hand a huge bowl of popcorn speckled with soy sauce, at her right a pile of monthly reports, half-complete or untouched. She turned the radio to a loud Latin beat, to fight paperwork's guaranteed sedation.

Taped to the wall in front of her desk a near-collage of photo images, placed so close together they seemed to blend into each other. In the center, an old O'Donnell family portrait—ten-year-old Molly, with a lustrous black braid that curled around her neck and down her chest, standing in a neat line between Emma and the boy Emma had called "Leo." Right behind Molly, a lean, dark-haired figure with soft unseeing eyes, his hands on his daughter's shoulders. Above the latter a photocopy of the family of James Joyce, a small cross-eyed Lucia in a fur coat staring defiantly into the camera. And below them all the Baltimore Symphony's glossy photo of Colin West winked for the camera, violin held up in victory.

Anne-Marie, I'd like to schedule a conversation about boundaries. Gail's voice in her head forced her gaze back to her desk, and to the more matter of-fact words of the head of social work, who would also have a say in Anne-Marie's three-month review. "I mean it—every single case folder up to date and on my desk, by nine a.m. The state doesn't pay us if we don't turn this stuff in. You got it?"

She stared at the sheets of paper, full of small print with blank white squares waiting to be filled with the content of human pain. She preferred the multiple-choice sheets, with boxes to check:

PROBLEM LIST
Altered Fluid Intake
Altered Food Intake
Confusion and Anxiety
Danger to Others
Danger to Self
Excessive Motor and Verbal Behavior
Hostility
Hypersexuality
Inability to Chew
Manipulative Behavior
Poor Self-Esteem and Social Isolation

It could have been one of those tests in women's magazines,

"Does He Really Love You?" Anne-Marie had to keep looking at the names stamped in the upper right-hand corner of the sheets, to remember which patient she was writing about.

Pearlstone's telephones rang a discreet, gentle chirp, easily masked by the Latin rhythms filling the tiny office; Anne-Marie had to look under her papers to find it, turning down the radio with her other hand. "Hello? . . . Oh hi, Felicia, what's all that noise in the background? . . . Oh right, the bar." She turned off the radio and sat back, putting her feet up on the desk.

"You know I don't want them to take her up north. I mean she's finally making some progress—even with the extra meds.They added Xanax, I told you that." She leaned forward and pulled at her toes through their socks, half massage, half nervous gesture. "Yeah, she's entitled to a hearing, but she has to say she wants one— she has to make enough sense to say so! And it helps to have a family member on your side." Anne-Marie's eyes widened as she listened; she put her feet back down on the floor. "Patients' Rights Advocates? Yeah I've heard of them, around here they're The Enemy, you know?" She laughed. "Yeah, just your kind of people. Anyway I don't have the number but–5575, ok."

As she listened, a cleaning man passed through the office and emptied her wastebasket. Anne-Marie automatically lowered her voice, as if even he might report that Anne-Marie Krieger was giving out unauthorized information.

"December 1, or maybe later—so about a month." Anne-Marie reached over and dipped into the popcorn bowl, each swallow followed by a swig from her water bottle. "Where? of course I'll be there. . . . Yeah, I'm hoping against hope that she stays relatively calm till then. . . . okay, talk to you later. Oh wait—about the law firm—we never had that conversation, okay? . . . Thanks, bye."

As she hung up she drained her water bottle, suddenly yearning for caffeine to get her through the night. Instead she turned up the radio, yielding a multi-layered African beat laced with horns.

A half hour later, the maintenance man came back into the room.

"Hey, do you hear that? Cops?"

Anne-Marie turned off the radio and listened. Occasionally a particularly violent patient was brought to Pearlstone by ambulance, but the siren was usually turned off by the time they came to the gate. Instead now came a series of alarms, the siren's howl unlike that of the police, each long steady aria louder than the last. "That's not police, that's fire!"

They hurried to the conference room, where a medical resident and two other maintenance workers were already congregated. Through the window, as if at the movies, they watched two fire trucks speeding along the path toward Chatham. The resident was already in the corner on the interoffice phone, trying to get through to the guards. Anne-Marie's fingers tightened on the back of a chair as she thought of Karen's cigarette burns, of Shana's stepfather's violent threats. But she could see no flames behind the leafless silhouettes of the weeping willows.

"Three trucks—that's a lot to send this far out," said a cleaning woman. "Whatever it is, it must be big."

Anne-Marie watched the resident as he listened to the voice on the other end. When he hung up, his face had cleared; she went over to him, letting the others watch the excitement. "Well, Miss Krieger," he said, "your favorite patient got hold of matches—God knows from where."

"What?"

"Molly O'Donnell," he said. "She just set fire to her room."

Anne-Marie swallowed. "Oh."

"Actually though," he said, "she's okay, everyone's okay, they got most of it with fire extinguishers. The head nurse just overreacted, dialing 911." He shrugged. "But your friend is gonna be in seclusion now for a good long time." He turned to the others. "Okay guys, excitement's over—let's go back to what we were doing.

Everything's under control." He left the room casually, as if crossing a bar after a few drinks.

"Everything's under control—'except his acne," one of the cleaning women muttered after he left. "How old is he, twenty-one? Who he think he is, ordering us back to work?"

Anne-Marie walked slowly down the corridor back to her office, torn between calling Felicia and trying to force her way into the seclusion room. Instead she sat back down to her paperwork, her supervisors' injunctions stuck in her teeth. She looked back down at the problem list:

Hopelessness and Despair
Disrupted Work
Feels Useless and Disengaged

Anne-Marie laughed out loud, checking the name on the sheet again; for she could check all three boxes and send it to her imaginary women's magazine—yes, yes, this is me.

Gail Ryan waited as her afternoon group assembled in a nearly perfect circle, each patient escorted one by one by volunteers. Her small red tape deck played soft Japanese music, wind over soft grasses.

Karen Hightower swept into the room with panache, demoted to this group after being suspended from group psychotherapy. "A roomful of neurotics, bleating about how much they want to die," she declared, towering defiantly over Gail. "I told them yesterday—over at Wilkes, if they really want to die it's easy! Just borrow that blow dryer like you can do there, run the hot water in the sink—plunge it in and there you are! "

"And that's why you're not part of group anymore," Gail said, keeping her voice and face even. "And why you're still in Chatham."

"Where at least people scream!" Karen laughed. "I am so bored with sedation."

Gail suppressed a sigh. Karen's romance with suicide and self-mutilation was a puzzlement to the staff; why mutilate a face that had decorated fashion magazines? The tall, restless ex-model wasn't responding to either medication or counseling, and her husband was unwilling to have her released. Right behind Karen came Molly O'Donnell, who had just been released from seclusion for the third time. She swirled toward the circle with a sort of dusty energy, weightless as she joined the dance. Gail wrote in the notebook of her mind, *Talk to Kepler about withdrawing Prozac.*

When the circle was complete Gail gave out a standard-issue smile. "Good afternoon, everyone. We're going to start with warm-ups and introductions." She modeled a shoulder swivel, arms lifting and lowering in a soft, rotating motion. "Everybody got that? Let's say our names as we do this."

Molly O'Donnell had closed her eyes the moment the stretch was demonstrated; a soft, secret smile accompanied her fluid motions. Gail watched her as she opened her eyes and stretched her palms to the sky; when it was her turn to say her name she sang instead, "Sometimes I feel like a motherless child. . . ." Shana, next to her, didn't look at Molly, instead trying a silent flirt with the just-admitted blushing teenage boy across the room.

When all the intros were done, Gail said "Okay now, let's try something new. Each person take the hand of the person next to them—and of the one right across from them." This took a few minutes, some patients stooping , others standing on tiptoes to reach their required partners; Molly stood almost en pointe, reaching for Karen's hand.

When the process was complete, instead of a circle there was a knot, one person to the north four to the east three to the south. From her position on the sidelines Gail called out, "Now we get to move very slowly, until we have a circle again."

The group began to move, the tortuous process producing

general merriment. "I'm like to break my arm!" Shana cried.

Gail watched Molly, who seemed simultaneously to be paying attention to the game and to some other, inner project; Gail caught her humming to herself, watched as she used dancer-poses to get through the game, at one point squatting and bending herself into a ball to allow a pair to move above her.

As the game played out its slow pace, Gail's mind wandered to the music therapy conference she would be attending the following week. She was therefore startled when the game ended with Molly in the center of the circle, skipping from person to person and planting kisses on all cheeks.

Karen Hightower bent for her kiss, tipping her head graciously.

"What happened here?" Gail asked, keeping her voice bright.

"Lucy let go," Shana explained succinctly.

"Molly? Would you stop for a moment and tell me what's going on?"

Molly instantly stopped skipping and twirled instead, facing Gail when she stopped. "I dream the dance," she said. "L'Irlandaise!"

"The Irish girl, I know, Molly," Gail said reluctantly. "Like Lucia. But here you're supposed to be part of the group."

Molly shook her head. "But you will not have me anymore," she said, her voice breaking. "I like it here very much, but I must move to St. Andrew's." She sighed, an affected faux-French gesture reminiscent of Karen Hightower. "So I am kissing you *au revoir*—and bonne chance, I hope there are no more bombs."

"Bombs?" The teenage boy, Shana's heartthrob, seemed to wake up at the word. "Where?"

Gail sighed, far more deeply. "Not here, Todd. Molly, we can talk about this later, could you rejoin the circle so we can end the group?"

Molly looked confused for a moment, closed her eyes tightly. When she opened them she laughed, low-pitched and brittle. "I cain but are you able?" She marched herself between Karen and

Todd and rejoined the group—closing her eyes as all went back to their silent stretches, the sweet fine Japanese flute music echoing against the room's tall windows.

"So somehow she's figured out about the transfer," Gail told the morning briefing. "This may be why she's been giving our seclusion room such a workout." Her bright eyes reflected today's fluorescent light in the conference room—a stroke against the storm clouds still casting the grounds in gray half-darkness. "What do you think, Anne-Marie?"

Across the conference table the social worker was slumped against the table, her arm propped up on a pile that included her legal pad, an address book, and a brand-new copy of the *Skeleton Key to Finnegans Wake*. Anne-Marie didn't return Gail's glance, instead saying tonelessly, "It's hard to say . . . she certainly has continued manic."

"I'll say," the head nurse interjected. "First the phones, then the fire—and if you confront her, she just laughs, or sings one of her stupid little songs. Thank God Kepler's back."

"Kepler wants to check her blood levels before he decides about her Prozac," said Gail. "That's why we need to overcome her resistance to blood draws."

"But he's letting her go outside, to exercise," said Clay. "I don't get it." Behind his voice a faint rumbling of thunder, the newest gasp of the latest storm—a difficult labor, threatening for days but refusing to come.

"That's the new contract," said Gail. "She'll calm down if he lets her go back on her 'training program.'" Gail grimaced at the last two words. "She still thinks she's going to run the New York Marathon next month."

"Has her family seen her, since the fire?" asked an intern.

"Not yet," said Anne-Marie. "Emma and Shaun are coming on Saturday—and Shaun now insists on completing the transfer to

Park Grove." Her voice was low, throaty, as if she were recovering from a cold.

"You can hardly blame him," said Gail, "since she keeps getting worse." She looked into the distance. "Some people, I think," she said finally, "don't really want to get better. No matter how much we try to help them." She sat back, her shoulders relaxing as she closed the subject with those words. "Now. On to Shana. We may never get around to solving the incest mystery—but I think she's very close to discharge."

Another thunder rumble, behind the word "discharge;" but it seemed fainter than the other, more a discouraged groan than a howl of warning.

Anne-Marie entered Chatham in shorts and a sweatshirt, unsure of where to put her massive keychain. "Is Molly out of group yet?" she asked the nurse at the station.

"Yeah . . . She's all set, wait till you see her." The nurse added impulsively, "She's calmed down a little since Dr. K came back. Though she's still refusing—"

"I know," said Anne-Marie, "I know."

Molly was waiting for her in the corridor, leaning against the wall. "Come on," she said, "calf stretches." She stood in the exact same position her sister had in the attic room, the previous week.

Anne-Marie joined her, reaching out so that her palms were eye level, flat against the wall; each woman had one leg flexed, the other extended behind her, the soles of both feet flat on the floor. "What's the temp?" Molly asked, her tone practiced, professional.

"Not bad," said Anne-Marie. "Forty-five or so, I'd guess. I didn't have to wear my gloves, walking over here just now."

Molly nodded and switched legs, reversing which was flexed and which extended. She sang softly under her breath.

"What are you singing, Molly?"

Molly smiled, turned and sang louder, in her belt-voice, her blues voice. *"T'ain't nobody's business if I do. . . ."*

Anne-Marie tried to remember whether that song was in Gail's songbook or not. "That's beautiful, Molly, did you guys sing it in group last week?"

Molly stood up straight and reached upward into the air, palms flat and upraised, as though she were lifting a heavy object. "No," she said, "my boyfriend taught it to me. He was a good musician, and a very fine pianist."

Anne-Marie's back stiffened, even as she mirrored Molly's stretch. "I didn't know Colin played the piano too, Molly."

A cloud of bewilderment crossed Molly's face; then she smiled and shook her head. "No, it was Emile Fernandez."

As they exited Chatham, Steve followed them, kicking aside a stray leaf or two—the last of the carpet that had covered the grounds all week.

"We need to start slow," Anne-Marie said to Molly, "since it's kind of muddy . . . Also I'm way out of shape."

"You?" Molly grimaced, and gestured wordlessly down her body.

"Actually you look great, Molly, honest." Molly, still not the skeletal figure of her admission, had shed at least five pounds since the fire incident; the bloating was gone from her legs and belly, and her collarbones were visible above the curve of her T-shirt. As they began to run, Steve dropped behind them and kept about ten yards behind, as he'd agreed.

"So who's Emile?" Anne-Marie asked.

"He was in love with me," Molly said between breaths. "He asked me to marry him, but I preferred to stay with my parents." She looked over at Anne-Marie. "Knees up!" she said. "Roll from your heel to the ball of your foot, then bounce off. Like that!"

They ran in companionable silence, weaving in around the trees and underbrush. When they got to the large oak at the edge of the property, they stopped to stretch again, Molly dropping to the ground and bending her head over one knee.

"Hey, Moll," Anne-Marie said, "I hear they came to give you a blood test this morning."

Molly didn't reply, instead massaging her elbow with expert fingers, pressing hard through the thick cloth of her sweater

Anne-Marie swallowed hard. "Look," she said uncertainly, "I know what a pain it is, when they come at you with that needle right before breakfast. But it's just to make sure you're okay."

Molly shook her head. "They want to spill my blood on the floor," she said, looking down at her ankle; then she lifted her head, met Anne-Marie's eyes. "Will all great Neptune's oceans wash the blood clean from my hand?"

She dreams of blood, went into the mental notebook, *she fears it*. A neat answer for Kepler, easily provided tomorrow morning. Anne-Marie relaxed inwardly and said, "We need to turn back now. To be honest, I don't know if I can take much more, anyway. Unlike you, I have never run a marathon."

After a moment Molly joined her in her laugh, returning from Neptune's oceans to the Pearlstone grounds. As the two rose to their feet, Anne-Marie looked up to see Steve gesturing to her, asking if she needed help. She shook her head, and they started back toward Chatham.

On the way back Anne-Marie ran slightly behind Molly, so she could watch the patient's movements. They were graceful, with none of the plodding and shuffling of past weeks. She wondered if she should report her own suspicions, of why Molly was refusing blood draws. Then she wondered if she would.

The 8X10 Club seemed to have sneaked onto its downtown block —tucked in between two art galleries, it was a rock and roll hole— black walls and rough floors, a band wailing from a tiny bandstand and dancers jammed up against one another. Upstairs from the mayhem, Felicia stood with a pay phone at one ear, a finger jammed against the other so that she could hear.

"OK, we're almost done here—yeah, I know it's late, I said I was sorry—just two more minutes, I promise . . . So Greg, the lawyer, he said it's a long shot anyway, but we would have a much better shot with a family member. We need you, Emma. . . . Great, that's all I'm asking right now—I'll get Greg to send up the papers. But keep 'em away from Shaun, okay? . . . The band? They're called the Cyber-Torches, yeah I know they're kinda loud. Can I have your address again?"

Felicia used an eyeliner to write on a scrap of newspaper, leaning it against the small metal phone box. A gentle tap on her shoulder and she turned, looking up to face her boyfriend, his wild curly beard damp above her. He pointed to the six people in line for the telephone, including two young women in combat boots who held a third, rather visibly ill, between them.

Felicia nodded, distracted, and kept talking. "I mean, Park Grove isn't really anywhere near you, is it?" She listened again and finally said, "Look Emma, I got a whole posse here waiting for a phone, including some kid who I think took too much Ecstasy. G'wan back to bed, I'll see you next Thursday." She hung up and looked up again at her sweaty boyfriend. "What's the matter?"

Jeff pointed to his watch. "Carolyn has been ready to go home for over half an hour. Do you realize how long you've been on the phone?" Felicia shrugged, then glanced at Jeff's watch. "Oh shit, is it really two o'clock? No wonder Emma was annoyed."

Jeff sighed heavily, and began to escort Felicia down the stairs. "Leesh, you've hardly danced at all, between phone calls. Can't we ever take a night off from this stuff?"

As they emerged on the dance floor Philip, another friend, waved at her; she broke off from Jeff and began to dance with him.

When the group had finally emerged into the darkness of 3 a.m., Felicia was saying to Philip, "So we're really in a race against time here —they're supposed to ship her up north in a month. . . . You got a light?"

The bearded young sculptor lit Felicia's cigarette. "I don't know, Leesh, I've known folks who really did need their meds."

"But we're talking about Molly!"

Philip shrugged. "You think this sister can help you?"

Felicia tossed her cigarette to the ground almost without smoking it, twisting her boot toe on the sidewalk. "She said she'd think about it—I don't really know what that means."

"What does Anne-Marie say?" The name seemed to linger on Philip's tongue, long after the breakup.

"She's sweet, Philip, but a 'good German' if ever I saw one. She ends up following orders every time."

As she spoke they walked along Mount Royal Street past the art school, a nearly-full moon augmenting the streetlights that lit the old, elegant brownstones. Philip turned and called to Jeff, "You're right—she is making this a full-time job."

"Not that I'm making any money at it," Felicia stood still until Jeff came up behind her, then fell back and relaxed against him. "What do you think, Jeffarino? Do you think I can trust the lawyer, or do I need to go to the law library?"

"I think you're making yourself crazy," Jeff said, as gently as he could manage. "Not to mention the rest of us. Can we give it a break, tonight?"

Felicia nodded, burying her head in Jeff's shoulder as they walked along. "I'm so tired, it's like my nerves are shot," she said. "Like that line from T.S. Eliot, the one Molly used to quote? *My nerves are bad tonight. Yes, bad.*"

They came to a loud three-way intersection, combining three city streets and a highway entrance. Philip and Jeff maneuvered easily among the complicated signals and traffic patterns, while Felicia froze at every car.

"Maybe I'm the next one to go crazy," she said when they had arrived safely at Jeff and Philip's apartment. "I bet if I did get hit by one of those cars, I'd end up at JPI myself—singing the blues and calling for finger paints."

. . .

When the last of the thunderstorms began in earnest, Molly screamed at each thunderclap.

In-between screams, she cried, recalling to those who remembered the crying, singing, bandaged creature admitted six weeks before. Her night meds hadn't seemed to make a difference; the cries only escalated with the frequency of the thunder.

When she wouldn't stop, a nurse, an intern, and the senior resident showed up, surrounding her in a small conclave. After a while she leaned on the aide closest to her, crying wordlessly into his sleeve. Each time the thunder began again she would raise her head and scream again, her eyes passionately afraid. "Molly, it's just a storm," the aide said soothingly. "It'll be over soon."

Molly shook her head, speaking seriously, directly to him. "It's the Germans," she said.

That sent the intern scurrying off to the chart room, to see if there were any references to World War II; he returned, shaking his head at the senior resident.

"There is no bombing going on," the resident said to Molly. "Let's go into the dayroom, you'll see it's just the rain."

As they moved down the hall the resident said to the nurse, "Seconal, 250 mgs."

"Oral or IM?"

"IV push. This girl has spent four out of the last five nights in seclusion, we've got to get her some sleep."

"Yes oh yes oh yes oh yes," Molly affirmed, calling after the nurse. "Bring on the medsdreams, bring them all, bring them now. Sender: Boston, Mass."

As they arrived at the dayroom she cried out again, running over to the window and watching the lightning's delicate dance among the trees and the hills.

An aide stood on either side of her as she leaned against the shatterproof glass. She banged against it with her fists, but weakly, more in protest than in an effort to break it. At one lightning-flash she stopped for a moment, whispering to the aide: "Silver," she said.

"Silver, Molly?"

Molly pointed to the window, though the flash had died down. "I was the silver fish girl, I was a creature unto that element. I was L'Irlandaise."

By the time the nurse returned, the thunder had finally died down.

Molly let the aides lead her back to her room and lay on her bed, exhausted. As the nurse wrapped the rubber strip around her arm to expose the vein, she looked up, directly into the eyes of the senior resident.

"Silver," she said. "A screaming has come across the sky," she said as the needle entered her vein. "It has happened before, but there's nothing we can compare it to, now." Her blue eyes steely, no longer afraid; she helped the nurse hold the gauze to her arm, after the needle was removed. "Molly?" the nurse asked. "Can we try to sleep, now?"

Molly turned on her side, pulling the covers over her like a shroud. The group waited until they saw the Seconal take effect, her hands relaxing, her mouth open and drooling a little, as if she were a nine-year-old child. Then the senior resident said, "Albert, you better stay, just in case the thunder starts again. This one might actually wake up."

But the girl remained asleep, silenced under drugs and blankets —leaving the aide to instead spend the night alone, listening to the screaming cross the sky.

L'Irlandaise!

10 May

And I have been lying awake thinking of Lucia.

Well, maybe half-awake, the rain outside a soft pelting wall that keeps awakening me from one of those spectator-dreams, where I do not exist . . . only the silvery white image as if from a silent film, dancing in her flapper dress, over and over, as if I'd paid 25 cents at some porno palace to see the chaste little dance of the Joyce silver fish.

Just a little wake-up call from my most disquieting of muses.

The facts of her life run together inside me, a wavelike edge surrounding the shiny movie of my dream:

born in Trieste, Italy, 1907 died in England

most of the best worst years of her life spent in Paris

| |my blueveined girl, after moving from city to city, country to country, managed with a thereby broken education to learn four languages, write, sing, dance and paint—and help her father build his masterpiece (though I am stating this more boldly than others

have before, scholars have mostly confined themselves to speculations).

Appropriately enough for the muse of the *Wake*, she comes to me most clearly in a series of remembered nights:

The night of Joyce's fiftieth birthday, when the judge in the United States had just ruled in favor of the publication of *Ulysses*, declaring it "not obscene." The constant ringing of congratulations from all over the world are stopped by Lucia, who cuts the telephone wires, crying out, "C'est moi qui est l'artiste!"

The night Padraic and Mary Colum, friends of the Joyces,' track her down on the streets of Dublin; Mary pins her nightgown to Lucia's, so the girl won't run away. the night of the famous engagement party, most of all.

Still amazing to me that Joyce would think marriage would "cure" his daughter, would hastily arrange an engagement to a friend of Giorgio's. They celebrate at the Restaurant Drouand and half of Paris, it seems, is there amid food and drink and, of course, music. A smaller group goes on to the Léons' house, where the supposed bride-to-be lies on a couch, in a catatonic fit from which she cannot be forcibly awakened.

It must have been too much for her, just like those schizophrenics in the books who find every single sensation—within and without—an assault, an invasion. Too much, from the noise and the people to her own fast-beating heart. Her father calling to her: *wake up, Lucia. There's a party going on.*

My own memory intrudes on the scene: *Molly, what are you doing down here by the stairs? How many times have I told you, the window seat is not a place to sleep?*

Now the sunlight screams into my attic room, informing me that it's after six and I'm not even dressed for my run. I had better go, and follow my sneakers up into the Balto suburbs, sweating off the anxiety of my dreams if not their silver dancing magic.

11 May

Oh, Lucia! I am coming to Texas to hear your voice!

After months of reading what everybody else has to say about you, I finally get to read some of your own words—even if only those written in St. Andrew's Hospital, long after Thorazine had erased the mad silver fish. I'll hear your speech plain, not emblazoned with Joyce's *Wake*-ian flourishes or scribbled in facsimile code.

Yes, the gods be praised, the department released money to send students as well as faculty to Austin for the modernism conference (of course, it's the university that hosted Texas Bloomsday all those years ago!). I'll leave separately, arriving in Texas three days early—three days in the school's rare manuscripts collection, immersed in Lucia.

And of course I can't help thinking about that last Bloomsday with Will. The long plane ride from Boston; the Tex-Mex food I had to arrange carefully so that he could eat what he did not recognize; the airless symposia and hallways heavy with gossip; the sandstone tower of the university. Twelve years ago and I remember it so clearly, even to the stolen moments alone in upstairs classrooms where I held tightly to my little tape deck and listened to my cello scores (trying to prepare my ear, if not my hands, for next week's lesson).

Right now I'm sitting in my library carrel, Shakespeare papers to my right, dissertation notes to my left. So much to do before I go —finish grading the papers, make summer teaching plans, get my own research in order. Not to mention marathon training, especially crucial during this blessed one-month or so of late spring— before Baltimore summer hits in earnest, with the humidity that soaks your lungs. (Oh, and I promised Felicia some hours, she wants to do a painting of me. "Just one, but I have to draw you for a while, to get the feel of it." I wonder what images will end up on canvas, what horror will stare out my eyes.)

Time to run, an emergency meeting at Gary's office—something to do with one of the late papers. "You won't believe this," he said to me on the phone. I thought a minute, about the students who just handed in their work—and I would bet that it's about Jessie Berger. It's hard for me to actually dislike someone I don't see often, but Jessie tests me, with her surly comments and sloppy gestures and loud, New York-accented voice, bringing feminist politics into every damn discussion.

11 p.m.

Well, I get credit for easy guesses. Popular psychology crossed with radical feminism has finally reared its head, just in time to stab Shakespeare in the back. "I've seen this sort of thing before but never so thorough or so vicious!" thus spake Gary.

After talking to him and Jessie in turn I'm wired, totally sleepless on this Tuesday night, a mixture of laughter and rage. How could anyone claim to be an adult and write such trash?

Put simply, crudely: Jessie Berger claims that Ophelia, Lady Macbeth, and the three Lear daughters were all victims of sexual abuse, molested by their fathers. Jessie brings in a lot of psychiatric hoo-ha about "the profile of the incest survivor," and then identifies:

> *Macbeth*: Lady Macbeth's obsession with blood (as if the killing of Duncan weren't enough to accomplish that).
> *Hamlet*: Ophelia's fragile dependency and possible promiscuity (Jessie posits that Laertes, Ophelia's brother, might be an additional culprit).
> *Lear*: the rage of Regan and Goneril, as well as Cordelia's behavior throughout the play.

Her reading of Lear is by far the most audacious. She states that Regan and Goneril are still "in denial" about what their father has done, and that their "revenge" on him is driven by subconscious rage—while Cordelia has "faced the reality of her father's abuse" by refusing in the first act to declare her love for him, and has "passed beyond rage to forgiveness" when she arrives at the end to save her father. "Cordelia's death," Jessie writes, "can thus be seen as evidence that some acts are best not forgiven."

Here we have living proof that you can take anything out of context, twist and turn it to your own uses. To Jessie, when Ophelia sings in her mad scene "And I, a maid at your doorstep, to be your Valentine," she is singing both to Hamlet and to her father, the dead Polonius.

And for her, all these women —even Lear's daughters, who kill their sister, drive their father mad, and nearly destroy his kingdom —are the true victims, almost the heroines of the dramas.

And why Shakespeare would think to write feminist propaganda in the sixteenth century, England still mostly in the grip of Catholicism? "Father-daughter incest, whether actual or fantasized, has been the stuff of tragedy since *Antigone*," she writes. Antigone? Are we talking incest or devotion? Do you know the difference, Jessie?

Well, he can't say I didn't tell him so. I knew that one was going to be trouble the minute she walked into class—one side of her head shaved, the other with black hair flowing to her breast in a zillion tiny braids, plus that little double-bladed ax around her neck (called a labrys, I remember it from the more militant lesbians at Barnard).

I can only feel blessed that Jessie's chosen not to work in Joyce, who did play with some of the issues she identifies, subsuming and transforming them into universal dreams—beginning with *Ulysses*, Bloom meditating on his daughter Milly's puberty: "Soft sweet girl's lips. Prevent. Useless. Can't. Full gluey woman's lips." What would Jessie do with that? Or with the full-blown "insects" of the *Wake*, with Issy turning into Anna Livia and back again over and over, the line between daughter and wife dissolving with every page—could she comprehend that we're talking Jungian archetypes here, not real people?

Though certainly this dissertation has been teaching me—once you take on madness as a subject, you never really know where

2 a.m.

Felicia knocked on the door as I was writing the above—she'd seen my light, and asked if I wanted some tea. We ended up instead finishing half a bottle of wine, left over from some opening; our living room's pretty spooky at midnight and we sipped quietly, like two teenagers babysitting past midnight.

Felicia, of course, thought Jessie's thesis was "pretty funky, but why not? You think incest was invented yesterday? And I always did think something funny was going on between Lear and Cordelia." Then again, what do I expect from a woman whose drawings of me so far resemble heroin addicts and dissipated ballerinas? (Actually in a couple of them I resemble Lucia B, who I've not seen in a long, long time—perhaps they've finally caught up with her, found some shelter or hospital where she can be helped.)

It's fun to watch her work, when I can see from whatever position she's cramped me in. Her sleepy eyes become more focused, her chin moving in quick, startled motions as she looks from me to the paper, me to the paper, back and forth, back and forth; her movements fast and furious, in contrast to the slow sinuous jazz beats on the radio. (We compromised on jazz—I can't really expect her to draw to Bach, not when she's used to that rat-tat rock music). And the tiny green snakes on her wrists seem to come alive, jumping across the page. I keep waiting for the drawing where there are tiny snakes wrapped around my neck.

12 May

Yes oh yes oh yes!

Ten miles for the third day in a row—and another meeting with my flesh-and-blood Lucia, the real-life counterpart to my silvery silent movie.

But first, the run itself. The marathon schedule finally in place: ten miles a day for the next 3 months. Calf muscles firm and loose, hamstrings springing me forward, Molly the jock blots out Molly the wannabe cellist, Molly the aspiring literary lioness.

On Sundays I run past the rowhouses near North Street: people sitting on their tiny little stoops and the sidewalks in front of them, lingering as if they were long, sloping front porches out of *Gone with the Wind*. Broken glass in front of stores, syringes and crack pipes in the gutter, and on Sundays whole families headed to church, little girls dressed absolutely to the nines, complete with patent-leather shoes and white lacey socks against chocolate skin.

And what do they see? A skinny white grad student in shorts and a BARNARD T-shirt, black hair streaming into the sweaty earphones on my tape deck. I wonder what would happen if I asked them to hear the music in my ears.

Then I loop down to the harbor, dodging tourists and students in equal numbers, sliding by the Peabody Conservatory and circling the musicians as they struggle to get their tubas or harps through the tiny stage door of the concert hall.

And it was there, near the front steps of the conservatory, that I finally saw her again—my other Lucia. The sun was shining, dressed-up concertgoers stepping around her as she stared off into nothingness—in startling, unnerving contrast to either the angry prostitute on Baltimore Street or the lost soul of the library.

In earlier days I'd have been calmed, relieved—now I was spooked, saddened, scared. A grayish quality to her whole being: dull eyes, skin so slack it seemed flattened against her bones. Even at her most still, her most distant, like back at Memorial Stadium, there was more life in her than this; she has lost whatever was left to her after the damage done by homelessness or madness.

Could it be one of those drugs I've read about, Prolixin or Trilafon—or Lucia Joyce's drug of non-choice, Thorazine? The name sends me into pale Joyce imitations, Thorazine wipes the brain clean it's so pristine it could be in a magazine.

So of course I rushed back to my library carrel: here I am checking out the elderly Lucia photos, to see what was left there after forty years of drugs, to see again the face that belongs to the Texas notebooks. And what I see is a seventy-year-old child: some energy, some joy, but the smile belongs to a little girl, the one who wrote "My parents were neither big nor small but they looked very young and I never thought they were going to die soon." Schizophrenia or Thorazine, crossed with a bad education? Can I quantify the difference?

Oh Lucia, maybe you can tell me, in Texas.

Will's voice, stern for once: *why absorb yourself in that girl, long after she had played any role in Joyce's work?* Oh Will, don't you understand, don't you know the old woman contains within her the silver fish Joyce grieved so? That perhaps her writings will call out phrases contained in Joyce's work—or sentences from which I can easily imagine him improvising, adding layers until you got to the music of his language. Can't you see that?

Basta! I need to stop journaling and call the youth hostels in Austin. A long list of "Things to Do Before Texas"—in addition to all this teaching and writing, I want to plan an end-of-term picnic for Gary and me. (I've heard people mention Loch Raven Reservoir, where one can picnic and skinny-dip—and if I have to be without him for a whole summer while he lives in Brooklyn with Denise, then I want a long languorous lusty afternoon, I want to see the water sparkle on his freckled skin.)

13 May

Fingers still shaking from the dream, I can hardly read my handwriting even as I write—

When I drank I never dreamed, when I stopped drinking I

would write dreams on scraps of paper and then burn them. Now I can only spill out bits of dreams still caught in my throat:

Harvard Yard, autumn, leaves crackling dry falling / Will and I cross the Yard together / I wear a fat fur coat and long black gloves, he holds my cello / I slip and fall into a thicksoft blanket of leaves/ dark cough can't breathe / crawl out crying, no Will no cello / I hold my bow close crying / Will Will Will / my fur coat covered with leaves / you and my cello small in the distance / my bow grows tall, my walking stick / its string sings out, one huge round note crying / Will Will /

students surround me to stop it / they push me down, the sound is louder / then a hospital room your neck is broken/ tubes everywhere / gliding from your throat to my cello / your open eyes can see me / my arms embrace it / it drinks your fluid as I begin to play / high shrill soprano voice / shaking your IV bottle / my arms exhausted cello singing Lucia's voice / you sleep / the sleep of the dead / Lucia still singing / the book of the dead / Will Will Will

deep breaths, deep breaths.

The sleep of the dead, the book of the dead, my unconscious is so damned literate I've no time for this. And the reversals: it's my cello's neck that was broken, not Will's. I search and think and try to banish the entubed Will from my mind, false yet terrifying memory.

But I can't shake that soprano voice, stolen from my tapes of Lucia di Lammermoor, Lucia Joyce's childhood inspiration! By age fourteen, Lucia was forever carrying around the opera's libretto, her own travel guide for the dark interior. Lucia, was that you singing to me, to Will? Did you want to teach Will the opera? But he knew it, found it "impossible melodrama." It's a Romeo and Juliet story whose Juliet—the Lucia of the title—kills the man she has been forced to marry, descending afterward into insanity and hallucination.

Did Joyce and Nora, such opera lovers, forget that mad Lucia when they named their daughter with that beautiful word, Italian for "light?" Did Joyce ever suspect that by doing so, he was instead planting a wild darkness, one he would harvest for the *Wake*? And how did they feel when their fourteen-year-old rosefrail child held the libretto like a prayer book?

I'll let these questions linger in my mind, as I leave my warm blankets for the cold of bureaucracy—the paperwork needed to teach a summer course with the unsurprising topic, "The Modern Novel." Not that prestigious a gig, not when most of the senior grad students get summer fellowships—but plenty of competition, nonetheless. Followed by a grueling day immersed in Shakespeare papers: every fresh insight into *Lear* a tired retread of *Hamlet*.

And maybe later I'll think again of the fur-clad cellist drowning in Harvard leaves, of my overflowing cello singing Lucia to the man with the broken neck. Too strange too meaningless; perhaps I should give up late-night café latte.

8 p.m.

More on Lucia's life with my research.

Start not with her birth but with 1920: the Joyces' arrival in Paris. Lucia is thirteen and in her third country, her fourth language. The demons that later exploded may yet be quiescent, if Jung and the others are right about dementia praecox. She is growing up in a household completely and utterly centered on the in-house genius, with whatever leftover affection her mother possessed lavished on her charismatic older brother. In earlier years, earlier moves, she and Giorgio have stuck together—stolid children of change, fellow refugees from Trieste, strangers in ever-stranger lands. But the Paris social scene is about to change that forever.

They arrive in Paris just in time for the first in James Joyce's lifelong series of eye operations: Lucia is enlisted as auxiliary nurse-maid, aide-de-camp, guardian of quiet, reader, writer. *I don't know what your father would do without you. He's so lucky to have a daughter like you.* Writing letters trying to see *Ulysses* through to publication—did Lucia learn about Bloom and Milly by reading the galley proofs of Bloom's incestuous thoughts? "Soft sweet girl's lips. Full gluey woman's lips," she pronounces haltingly, the words coming from her soft sweet lips into her father's waiting ear.

By 1923, Joyce "is at another book again," Lucia's mother protests.

This time he is creating a new language, with the help of Lucia, his in-house Issy: diaphanous L and Bab working at c & d, writes the man Lucia called "Babbo. "They all notice it, the Paris literati who come to call on the shy man with the eye patch—the fifteen-year-old girl always underfoot, always by his side. Her parents try sending her to a lycée, but she doesn't last a month. Only piano lessons feel right, she feels the notes in her forearms, the language streaming out of her fingertips. The visitors are gallant: such talent.

She's growing into a beauty (and again her story brings parts of me back to me . . . *Talented and beautiful. Will must be proud. If I wait ten years for you, will you marry me? Flirtation in university corridors, the shy budding cellist just lowers her eyes and counts the tiles on the floor.*)

From 1924 to 1925 the family, between flats again, spends a whole year in a hotel: an eternal rootless vacation. Joyce uses a suitcase for a desktop. The family eats at restaurants for every meal, receives guests in similar fashion. Joyce is in his element, going drinking in the evenings despite Nora's protests. *Jim remember what the doctor told you about your eyes.* Stories of Ernest Hemingway bodily lifting Joyce's wiry frame, carrying him like a babe in arms back to the hotel.

(*Will, Mam can't seem to stop drinking.*

Oh yes, she certainly can. She just doesn't want to.)

In 1925 they move to Square Robiac, their happiest Paris home. There Giorgio meets and falls in love with an American heiress, Helen Kastor Fleischmann, whose photographs show a direct contrast to Lucia: a tiny, extroverted figure with alert dark eyes, so different from Lucia's heavy blue eyes and tall slumped frame. Whatever closeness Giorgio and Lucia ever had now gone forever.

But her father needs her, will always need her. He even refuses to let her visit Trieste to see childhood friends—he wants her close to him during his next eye operation. *Lucia, carissima, it will be possible next year.*

Instead she discovers a use for the tall large-breasted body, the energy that cannot seem to release: the early days of modern dance, its serious, disciplined physical work. In those first years her family supports her completely, paying for lessons and costumes, attending recitals and applauding her success. When she goes to Salzburg to spend a summer at Isadora Duncan's school, they follow her there and stay in a hotel for the summer. Devotion or stranglehold? Or was she, at seventeen, already a little lost, unexpected anger and tears? (| *breaks plate* / *cries*)

(*Molly, this is ridiculous. I cannot keep coming down the stairs to find you! We have a lot of work to do—your recital is coming up and I just received a long letter from Bernard Benstock that I need you to read. . . . Yes, Shem, that's right, dry your tears. It's going to be all right. I love you.*)

At Joyce gatherings at Square Robiac, after Giorgio sings an aria or two, Lucia sings a folk song and then performs a dance she choreographed herself, having made a performance space out of the drawing room. (*She dreams the dance.*) What sort of music did she have? Did Giorgio or one of their guests play the piano, or did she create her dance in silence? I look at the dancing-photo on the wall of my carrel and I cannot see that image in the middle of a party—it must have been something much less abstract, "prettier."

The happiest period in Lucia's life, feel it: working hard at dancing and staying close to her father, unnaturally, impossibly close. Standing close by as he showed his new "Work in Progress" to Paul Leon, to Beckett; bringing him tea while he wrote, whispering in his ear at parties—filling those impossible notebooks with secret speech, later transformed as he dictated to Beckett.

(Reading in Boston's summer heat: *Do you want to hear this letter from Nathan Wilcox right now, Will?*

Yes, I do—is that fan working properly? I am so hot, I feel faint.

I'll get some iced tea then. . . . I'm leaving now but I'll be back in five minutes—all right? And then we can start on the letters.

Very good, Shem. I'll just stay right here.)

From the same period, Lucia as Charlie Chaplin: "I dressed myself in Charly," she wrote about one of their Christmas parties, "we danced and played and sang and I don't know what else." Actually, Lucia's interest in Chaplin went beyond such games—she wrote, and actually published, a short article about him. Her dancer's mind fascinated by the physical brilliance, the rest of her was probably comforted by his persona—the eternal outsider, bewildered by life.

I'm going to stop this now and go home, I promised Felicia a few hours. She wants to do some further work on one of her previous drawings, the one where I am lying across the floor with one knee flexed. (Who knows, perhaps it will end up scissored to bits and placed in the middle of a burning building, or something. If that happens, I will ask her to call it Lucia's Fire.)

14 May

Gary and I just spent an hour and a half trying to convince Jessie Berger to change the slant of her paper. "If you must have this . . . controversial thesis," Gary said, choosing his words carefully, "the least you can do is provide a more balanced view of all the participants in these tragedies, instead of putting black hats on all the men in all the plays."

"Fuck balance," Jessie said. "Besides, I don't put black hats on Horatio, or Banquo, or the Fool. Although I think the Fool is really a woman, anyway." Eventually it came down to a challenge: "If I provide enough textual support," she said, "you can't give me an F just because my thesis scares you."

Gary and I didn't take the bait. "You're not there yet," Gary said. "I wish you luck." Then he tried gently to chat a little, maybe learn a little about why she might be so perpetually angry. While Jessie was unrevealing about her past, she did let slip the completely unsurprising fact that she is writing a novel, and that it's "sort of about father-daughter relationships." Sort of? Then my mother is sort of alcoholic, and Gary is sort of married.

Lucia Joyce, by the way, did begin her own novel, when she was twenty-three or so. I've no idea whether it survived—if it still exists, the Joyce family guards it like the crown jewels. I wonder if it is terrible or beautiful, horrifying or boring, sexual or sentimental. She was trying to write it just as her madness worsened, after the days of dancing at the Joyce parties were over. I wish it were there in Texas, waiting for me.

Further notes from that clear space, the years at Square Robiac: At family gatherings, Giorgio often sings "The Ballad of The Brown and Yellow Ale": "And they asked me was she my daughter / and I said she was my married wife . . ." (Yes you're changing, sonhusband, looking for a daughterwife, cries Anna Livia.) In the meantime, Lucia begins to wonder about her mother's health, and in 1928 her worries prove correct: Nora has an ovarian tumor, and the family is thrown into turmoil. Lucia moves in with Giorgio and Helen while Joyce stays in the hospital beside his wife, from whom he cannot bear to be separated. His daughter cannot comfort him: does that feel like rejection?

Every day, of course, Lucia is at the hospital. It is she who greets Samuel Beckett, the "blond bean-pole with glasses." By now it's a cliché, the one thing most academics know about Lucia: "she was in love with Beckett, right?" At that time, Beckett has taken to dressing like Joyce, walking like him, echoing the man he adores, the man who calls him "Shem" (Will's name for me, in/appropriately enough). Beckett's rejection of Lucia is even more famous, for the breach it created between Joyce and perhaps his closest protégé.

Nora recovers, and the central couple steps back into place as the core of the Joyce household; although at one point later, Nora told her daughter that she enjoyed sex less, after the operation. A once-lively sex life toned down would, no doubt, leave more room for Joyce's suppressed desires for Lucia, the ones exposed in the notebooks before being submerged in the *Wake*:

| *riding afore me*
(*lovely!*)

The next year, 1929, is pivotal. Lucia dances in public for the last time, losing a dance competition—though the audience loves her, calling for encores from "L'Irlandaise!" Convinced she is too frail for a dance career, she cries "a month of tears," four years' hard work down the drain. Was she the one too frail? Or was it her blind father, her mother recovering from her tumor operation, who could not risk her leaving?

Soon after giving up dancing, Lucia begins to complain that she is "sex-starved." The body-energy will out, the need for comfort apparent and overwhelming—until she becomes the easy lay of Paris' bohéme, her body (her heart?) easily accessible. And by now, perhaps, dementia praecox' rush of memories and sensations is beginning to overwhelm her: vertigo no longer curbed by dancing, it is easier to concentrate on other physical sensations. Like Molly Bloom crying out in affirmation of "life" and her marriage and her own growing climax, all at once—the eternal yes yes yes oh yes oh yes.

That feeling I still seek with Gary, even when I know I oughtn't.

This time, after seeing him and Denise on my Saturday run, I went home and promptly threw up. And I know it wasn't just that I was pushing my pace.

Yet I return to him night after night, for the chance to flow my hair around his penis, for his teeth lining my ankle with tiny scars —and for the talk, the talk, the mind-talk almost as important as that mollybloom yes. Last night I asked him, as we sat up in bed and talked about Jessie Berger: "How can you stand this sort of thing year after year?"

He picked up a loose strand of my hair from his shoulder, and delicately lowered it into the trashcan beside his bed, on top of the used condom. "It's a hard lesson, Molly, but you'll get it. I don't get agitated over what doesn't work—I only try to do what I can." And with that he fell asleep.

I lay awake for a long time, thinking, *I only try to do what I cannot. Like get to the heart of Lucia. Reach the schizophrenic who's on the steps of the conservatory in a Thorazine haze. Or love someone who belongs to someone else.*

15 May

Fighting massive fatigue to write this: a week to go before Texas and each day exhausts me further. Every time I turn around something else screams for attention—a meeting with Tilden, a session with Felicia, or one of my last moments with Gary until September. (Time pressures have, alas, turned our picnic into a lunch, at Louie's Bookstore Cafe—then he's up in New York, working on his new book in the summer glow of Brooklyn and Denise's eyes.)

And the heat is enervating, bleeding my days.

As I write this I've escaped to a diner on North Street, just for the air conditioning; I can barely get up the energy for my standard run every day, the Shakespeare papers (not Jessie Berger's: that one's Gary's problem) an attractively untouched pile on my desk, their elegant laser-printed fonts mimicking the books their authors all hope to publish someday. In the evening it's all I can do to make love to Gary, sit for Felicia (laziness crossed with exhibitionism), or do some of my research, coming to the end of what's easily available about Lucia.

This journey to Texas is thus well timed; I depart with my two favorite companions, Lucia and Will, both dancing swimming floating through my clouded, gently lethargic mind. And then there's

16 May

I have absolutely no idea what I was going to say next: I fell asleep in that diner, the journal tight between my knees. Writing now after a nap in my library carrel: narcolepsy or heat stroke? I hope Austin can produce a decent double latte.

I haven't been this sleepy this often since high school, at least without the aid of alcohol. Emma thinks it's academic pressure, reminding me "Moll, you slept through most of senior year, remember?"

God yes, that lazy age of seventeen—coming fully awake only to practice (thank you, Will) and go to my lesson three times a week with Richard Magnusson. (I saw Richard in the Washington Post last month, some Brahms festival in D.C.—I thought to call him but I am far too ashamed. How can I explain how his prize student slept through her career, occasionally awakened by slaps from Colin West?)

The rest of the conversation with Emma revolved around food, how much and when in the training schedule. Both Rachel and Felicia are getting used to my low-cal evenings on regular schedule (my weight finally down to 110), as well as the huge amounts of pasta I consume before a twelve- or thirteen-mile run. Felicia just laughs, she who seems to live on nicotine alone.

Time to get over to campus, for the last Madness class and to find out if I get to teach The Modern Novel this summer. (If I don't, I may be singing Lucia songs while I scoop ice cream or wait tables.)

7 p.m.

I got it!

(and will I be sorry in August, with twenty-some papers to grade . . .)

I've been handed a standard syllabus—beginning with *Portrait*, of course; if anyone created the modern novel in English, Joyce did. (Let's leave aside Kafka for now, shall we? I'd prefer it. Thank you so much, warmly appreciated.) Then Faulkner—*The Sound and the Fury*—before we move on to Virginia Woolf, *Mrs. Dalloway*, a perfect introduction to the post-World War I sensibility. Rounding it off with Beckett's *Watt*, and then I get one optional book. I'm inclined to do something like *Gravity's Rainbow*, have the students end the semester in World War II, watching the screaming cross the sky.

17 May

Saturdays are my special marathon days, reserved for as long a run as I can stand. Over long-distance lines, Emma and I wished each other well and proceeded to have delicious fifteen-mile journeys, companioning each other even across 500 miles. My other companion, of course, Lucia—this time, Lucia and Samuel Beckett. The ground was moist from morning rain, the smell fertile, fruitful, even among the slums of East Baltimore.

In the Walkman the tape was still *Lucia di Lammermoor*, Joan Sutherland as the Lucia singing of her lost love; so the Beckett-Lucia story blurted through my mind, love lost by so many people all at once.

To understand Lucia's urge for him, I see Colin in the lean blond Irishman—light gleaming off translucent hair, delicate bones in his wrists, brilliance evident in the intense dark eyes. To see that every day, when the doorbell rang: *Oh Mr. Beckett, it's you. Babbo, Mr. Beckett is here.* And this was in the midst of her "promiscuous" phase—when, we're told, one poet said to another "I'm going to meet that girl later at a bar," only to hear "But that's Joyce's daughter!" In addition to Beckett, somewhere in these years are Emile Fernandez, a jazz musician; Alexander Ponisovsky, the ill-fated fiancé; and—surprise!—Alexander Calder, the American sculptor.

By his own account, Beckett was, at first, fascinated by Lucia's agile mind and graceful body, but unnerved by the racing non-sequential pattern of her language and terrified by her intensity of emotion. Feeling trapped by her constant attention (or so he told his friends), he took her out to dinner and the theatre, a few times. Famous among his contemporaries for being sexually repressed, he told a friend that he was "dead inside," and therefore incapable of loving her.

At one point, Beckett's biographer merges Lucia and Issy more completely than I will probably ever dare—telling the story of how she felt him avoiding her, and demanded to see him outside of the Joyce flat; how he showed up at a Paris café with a friend in tow, for protection from her declaration of love. She describes Lucia staring off into space, occasionally managing to bring food to her mouth, tears blurring her mascara, "a mannequin left out in the rain." Amazing how even those indifferent to Lucia, like Beckett's biographer, can't help merging her with literary madwomen and Joyce's primal female forces. Ophelia, born unto that element; Nuvoletta letting the river trip her by and by; Anna Livia flowing through all of Ireland.

Perversely, her father made it worse, forbidding Beckett to cross his door again (only years later was the younger man again welcome at the Joyce household, after Lucia was safely put away). No longer could she at least wait to hear him knock, hope his eyes would meet hers even in disgust.

But Beckett was later one of her most faithful correspondents, as she lived out her life behind hospital walls; but the mental patient who constantly spoke of marriage rarely mentioned his name. Instead, she told her attendants at the age of 75, perhaps she would marry Alexander Calder; I will think of her next time I walk past a Calder mobile in some museum, imagine her youthful cries of joy in the arch of steel.

I do wish I knew how promiscuous she really was—did she risk syphilis, did she give over that lean dancer's body to Calder, to the musician Fernandez, even to Beckett? Did her dancing, so abstract in the photographs, betray her desires? And now when I hear Issy's voice, I feel Lucia's erotic energy—Joyce knew his daughter had the same desires as Bloom on the beach, Stephen Dedalus in the brothel.

That's why Issy is such a tease, a flirt, coarse and syrupy by turns. Babbo had a flesh-and-blood example, breathing life into the Isolde stories and his own stereotypes about young girls. He saw clearly his own daughter's sensuality, responded in the only way he knew how: by writing it down. (Words words words.) I wonder if the same erotic energy will smoke through the Texas diaries.

(Speaking of erotic energy, for tomorrow's lunch with Gary I'm borrowing a white cotton dress of Rachel's. The image I want engraved on his summer memory: bare shoulders, timid but insistent cleavage, and the black hair he likes to play with flowing loose around me.)

19 May

And today I am the mannequin in the rain, Issy in her "offalia" mode, Ophelia floating down the river—as fragmented and smashed and drowning. With a touch of Lady Macbeth aching for revenge.

Not a half-hour ago, Gary served notice on me, over grilled salmon and good coffee, that he feels he and I have "learned what there is to learn from having sex together." That "we should leave it in peace, now, and go on to other things." Those words closed my throat, perhaps permanently. How can you breathe when your lungs keep collapsing on you, like the emphysema of some five-pack-a-day smoker? When tears bleed from your chest to your eyes, more vomiting or hemorrhaging than crying?

He said the words with the same grave gaiety with which he says everything: that essential serenity that I found so seductive, that in my own way I have learned to count on. "We both understood from the beginning, that this wasn't forever."

Oh yes. Nothing I knew more clearly, nothing I knew more firmly but that you, my friend, had no real business with me.

I did ask why he didn't take the opportunity of last month's Boston trip to have this conversation with me. "The semester wasn't over yet," he said, vaguely surprised at the question.

That was when I realized: he does this every semester, he'll have another student-mistress in the fall. Sometimes, I imagine, it is one of those moony undergraduates, at other times a grad student like myself. And Denise probably knows, and puts up with it on the understanding that it only lasts a semester each time: it can never burst the confines of its time and place, and is therefore never a threat to her.

That bookstore/cafe pipes classical music, today a taped duet, a pianist and cellist exploring Schumann together. At that moment I hated the genteel sounds, I wanted one of Felicia's British rock and roll tapes, working-class screams against society. The air conditioning was frigid against my skin, unprotected by the thin summer dress. So here I am, dissolving at the edges, and only myself to blame.

I joined this game knowing the ground rules, and have no right to bleat because the timing did not go as I might have wished. So now I try not to think of him while I grade papers for his class; then I'll go for a good, exhausting, cathartic run—dodging baseball fans and undergraduates alike, I will rush red lights whenever possible, daring the traffic to punish my stupidity.

22 May

2:30 a.m. and I never got my run; I kept grading papers, because that's what I would have been doing if Gary had not made the sky fall, so almost forgetting the brunch ever happened. I liked that feeling so much I did the most thorough job of grading ever performed, which took four hours; then I fell into one of my trademark deep sleeps.

Now, of course, I am wide awake; tomorrow (today?) I will shove the papers into Gary's mailbox at the department, unless I decide to set it on fire.

For right now I feel more like Lucia in her twenties. I want to cut telephone wires, I want to set Gary's apartment on fire, I want to damage something or someone. Most of all, my most humiliating desire (hinted at in my last entry): I want to die.

Joyce scribbled in the first of his notebooks, *did you ever put yr. head in a gas oven*—did Lucia ask him that? I wish gas jets were still lethal, although I couldn't endanger everyone else for my own stupid broken heart. Besides it's far too industrial a death; dying, wrote another literary madwoman, is an art, like everything else. Well, so is grieving—I seem born to it so I might as well bear it gracefully.

First Will, then Colin, now Gary, not to mention the cello, not to mention the dissertation that seems more and more elusive every time I turn around. If I cannot do anything with my heart but get it broken over and over again, cannot I do something more sensible with my brain than read semi-meaningless words by a quasi-madman inspired by his truly mad daughter?

4 a.m. After writing the above, I got the bright idea of checking the temperature outside, which was a perfect crisp almost-summer 66. So I got my run after all.

This time I stayed northeast, away from the more dicey neighborhoods—bringing along, of course, my Walkman filled with *Lucia di Lammermoor*. It seemed perfect now to hear yet another faux Lucia, early in the story as she recounted a dream: a ghost appearing to her by a fountain. "*Stette un momento immobile, poi ratta dileguo . . . e l'onda prima si limpida di sangue rossegio.*" The water in the fountain, once so limpid, was suddenly tinged with blood. Will all Neptune's oceans wash the blood from my hands?, she might as well have been asking.

Heading back down Falls Road past the prep schools again. The soprano voice crying out, after agreeing to marry the man she does not love: "*Tu mi togli, eterno Iddio, questa vita disperata, che la morte e un ben per me . . .*" Ah take from me, eternal God, this life of despair . . . I am so wretched that death would be far better for me.

This particular Lucia's madness, like Ophelia's, is "strewn with roses." What is this with madness and flowers, anyway? Or madness and water? Or madness and life? Lucie, in the French version, a purer fusion of Lucia Joyce and Anna Livia Plurabelle: "The song of the sweet warbler echoes through the forest. . . . I am going far from Earth to the dwelling place of light." The dwelling place of light, where all Lucias belong by their very name. Yet they seem to find their way to the other end, the "long dark night" Joyce spent sixteen years exploring.

A ten-mile midnight run! everyone should have one, every once in a while. Of course, now my ankle is complaining—but exhausted enough to sleep, hope to rise in the morning full of Issy's bitter. Improper frictions and maledictions indeed!

23 May

Reason entered the discussion this morning as I limped into Felicia's studio, her matter-of-fact anger cool salve against my self-reproach.

"Fucking male profs," she said scornfully, taking out a green pastel and softening it against her palm. "Half of them do what Gary did, the other half just make like Andre, my adviser at the

Institute, and trade in on a new wife every few years. You know, some nubile grad student to tag along behind them, like some water carrier out of the Bible."

I laughed, though for me "water-carrier" is taken; it's me leading Will around the corridors of the Bloomsday conference, not to mention helping Colin pack his tuxedos and extra rosin for his violin, never forgetting the special secret cache of cocaine and sleeping pills.

To cool the rising heat we had only a single skittery fan; while I was nude, Felicia wore cutoff shorts and a halter top, her snakes and screaming babies exposed. I asked her if people stop her on the street when she's dressed like that.

"Sometimes," she murmured, and I realized she was moving into the state where she no longer feels like talking, only drawing.

When she turned around to change pencils I noticed something odd in the soft-flesh behind her knee: pink and white scar tissue, kind of like the skin on my forearm, almost-healed from Colin's hot coffee. These scars of Felicia's irregular, unplanned, unlike the tattoo's self-imposed scars. "What happened to your knee?"

At first she looked startled, then reached down and rubbed the indicated area. "An old, old burn," she said, in a tone that didn't invite further questioning.

Old, old burns. Like the ones Lucia Joyce inflicted on her cousins' bungalow in Ireland, soon before she was put away forever. Like the ones still remaining in a tiny, blackened corner of the garage back in Dorchester, after Leo's fire. Like the ones in Lucia B's eyes, the burn marks visible even through Thorazine grayness— saying, don't come near me, I hurt too much, you don't want to talk to me.

Lucia di Lammermoor sings, "*Io gelo ad arco! Io manco!*" I am freezing and burning! I feel faint! And I am myself freezing in air conditioning and the chill of my silenced heart, burning in Baltimore heat and my own stupid, stupid hot tears.

Lucia, were you freezing and burning? Did you set fires to melt the ice?

24 May

Leaving tomorrow, and just bought my research supplies: the rare manuscript library there is understandably careful, you can only use legal pads and No. 2 pencils, and you need permission from the Joyce family to photocopy, much less quote. (Permission I will never get, of course.) But I haven't got anything else done, except my run.

The secret of running in Baltimore almost-summer is getting up early; 5 a.m. is ideal. Listened to soothing brainless Vivaldi, I ran thirteen miles toward Owings Mills, up Falls Road across the county line—then along other, less busy roads into prep-school territory, carefully groomed campuses vying for prestige with their upper-class beauty. The McDonough School, of course, where Felicia tells me there is a "very progressive gallery;" St. Mary's and St. Paul's Schools, ecumenically within shouting distance of the Bais Yaakov School for Girls.

Then in the distance, just as I was turning around to head back, the faint outline of the arches of Hillsdale Prep—where Tilden, a Bawlamer native, "learned all the important things: Latin, Greek, classical history, and how to sleep with other boys." I wanted to run right to it but I'd already exceeded my limit, so I promised myself Emma and I will go there when we run the marathon distance together, sometime next month.

Rachel just came and knocked as I was writing the above, asking gently, "Are you okay?"

"Yeah, why?" Just because I'm curled up in my sweaty Radcliffe T-shirt in the middle of the afternoon?

She shrugged. "I'm sorry about Gary."

Then it was my turn to shrug, not an easy trick when you're in fetal position. I sat up. "I seem to learn these things the hard way—I did the physical abuse thing, then the married man thing, now maybe a convent is in order."

Rachel stared. "The physical abuse thing?"

I don't know why I said that, just then: maybe to show my little prim roommate that witches can be burned outside the confines of the Middle Ages. I had her touch my roughened forearm, all I have left from all that pain. "That's why I came to Baltimore," I said, not offering a name or any details. I had already told Felicia quite a bit of the story, during the Gary aftermath—maybe I just didn't want Rachel to feel left out.

She's leaving in a few days for Germany, for a summer's archival work, documenting gruesome tortures of women healers. I wonder if some of those witches, the ones who heard voices, were schizophrenic—or at least would be named so now, and given Thorazine, a blanket, and some milk and cookies at one of our finer state hospitals. (Which is where I fear my dear Lucia B. has ended up.)

25 May

Redeye flight to Austin, Texas: and I am letting myself have a glass of wine, to help me nap after whatever snack they have planned for me. (It has also helped me stop crying, my favorite occupation of the past few days.) I'll be arriving at around 9 p.m. Austin time, just as the sun is setting over the Gulf of Mexico.

And looking out into the soft darkness I can recall Will, and the trip from Boston ten years ago. *Excuse me miss, I'm not trying to cut the line. My father is blind, can you lead him to the bath-room? . . . Yes, some more water please, and another pillow, he needs to sleep.* Actually we both slept, me snuggling against him like a ten-year-old, slinging my legs over his lap. At sixteen I was already taller than most of the flight attendants.

Will, are you with me on this trip? or are you so disapproving of my Lucia project that you will visit me only in nightmares?

For this morning I broke myself from sleep, to short-circuit a nightmare just beginning—Will standing by a fountain, washing his hands over and over. I could remember from Lucia di (Lucia D.?) that the fountain promised no good, so I pulled myself out of sleep and went for a run, sunrise over the reservoir in 70-degree heat.

26 May

8 a.m.

Forget 70-degree heat, try running in 85 degrees with 100 percent humidity!

Austin: oddly reminiscent of Baltimore as I ran down Guadalupe Street at six this morning, under a blanket of wet air. The dome of the city hall like any East Coast city, except that it is partly made of sandstone: and in fact the entire city is like that, desert stone gently supporting buildings that could otherwise be nearly anywhere. Guadalupe Street hasn't changed that much in ten years, still surreal and oddly suburban: a huge superhighway through the center of town, to one side the university, to the other Taco Bells and Seven-Elevens. Will's voice: *"Well, Shem, this is America. Now you see why where we live is called 'New England?'"*

I ran through the campus, which was smaller, more compact than my memory of it: writ large and immaculate, white and pale red stone among incredibly groomed black-green lawns. It has a clock-tower like those at Ivy League schools, though (predictably enough) much larger. Everything here is larger, I am dwarfed.

Writing this now in the chill of air conditioning—the interiors are chilled to sub-zero, at least in this dormitory/youth hostel/co-op where I'm staying ($15 a night including meals!). I'm sitting on a bare mattress, far different from the cordial building where Will and I stayed, renting an entire apartment; there they took our bags and ushered us into rooms with clean linens and soft blankets, a discreet hush laid over the rooms like another soft cloth. *Why Shem, perhaps this is Southern hospitality.*

My adrenalin is up, my sleepiness left behind in Baltimore; good, the library opens at nine, and I want to be there before the doors are unlocked.

6 p.m.

And eight hours later, the first mind-blowing discovery—Lucia used to sing *Sometimes I feel like a motherless child.*

Emile Fernandez taught it to her—and thirty years later it is one of the first things she mentions when first asked to talk about herself and her father. She used to sing, *Sometimes I feel like a motherless child, far, far from home.* It's been bouncing in my head all evening, my first global shock from the Lucia voice. Probably not the last.

I love everyone immediately, from librarians to secretaries to the fresh-faced library page (some freshman no doubt straight out of her own Lit 120 class) who handed me the folder with the three Lucia Joyce manuscripts.

Tiny, tiny, tiny—all three fit in the single manila folder, the first typed on onionskin paper by the ubiquitous Harriet Weaver (what would their lives have been like without her, this patron who provided both money and mothering?). She had to write it in pencil, Lucia said, they'd locked up her pen. I wonder why, what had she attempted with a 1958 ballpoint?

The other two are tiny "Lion Brand" notebooks, their covers green and magenta, dated 1960 and 1961. By this time, Lucia has been in the institution for over twenty years—and on antipsychotic drugs for how long? I don't know that, and don't know who does.

I spent most of today on that first typescript, practically tran-scribing it in my little yellow legal pad. And from the first few sentences of "The Real Life of James Joyce," the psychologists' jargon shouts its claim: these are loose associations, this is clang, this is perseveration, sentences and repeating phrases running together like watercolors in the rain. Again, how much of this is madness, how much drugs?

I find I'm terrified of quoting Lucia directly in this journal, the strictures against photocopying or release of her words feel as punitive as federal laws. The Joyce estate, one librarian told me, "believes Lucia's privacy is being invaded—they wish we didn't even have these notebooks." So I will refrain from copying them over twice: I'll store my legal pads close to the journals, so I have access to them if I use the latter to brainstorm about the dissertation.

So hallucinatory, feeling the pieces of the puzzle join and hold. The long subterranean flow of Lucia's words could be Molly Bloom, let alone Issy/Anna, let alone any of the other endless female non-linear Joyce voices. Women = madness for Joyce? Before or after Lucia?

I almost don't care, right now, her voice is overpowering his in my mind. (Exactly what Tilden had warned me against; and Will in my mind is gently reproachful, *Don't forget the father, don't be overtaken by the daughter*.)

What has me the most wired, my heart already beating overtime, is something none of the biographers seems to have found worth mentioning.

And that is the story of Lucia the musician: how much music still meant to her, thirty years later.

She does mention her dancing, including specific gymnastic moves she loved—even pointing out over and over that this or that teacher danced better than Isadora Duncan herself (the repeats " perseverations," of course). But none of it feels as present in her life as the music—the music her father began teaching her as a small child, the music she carried with her from country to country, from language to language. Lucia, you and I have more in common than I knew.

Every song she sang, every opera they went to, every piano piece etched clearly, directly from her mind and heart to the page.

My notes fast and furious, my journey into Lucia has nothing if not velocity: are you with me, Will? Do you hear her sing to me?

One lovely long run-on paragraph had bits and pieces of the Irish folk tunes her father would sing at home, including some Will sang to me as a small child. *Oh Molly, I can't say you're honest,* he would sing, *sure you've stolen the heart from my breast.*

She mentions how Joyce hated thunderstorms, and would close the windows very carefully against them. Later she mentions that when she was in Ivry, the town were bombarded by the Germans—then says in the same breath that later there was a terrible thunderstorm, and she nearly died of fear. Not from the bombs, but the thunder.

And of all her lovers, the only one mentioned in this piece is Emile Fernandez the jazz musician, who, she says, asked her to marry him—but she preferred to stay at home. She describes evenings at the piano, when he taught her "Negro spirituals."

And I, of course, then take her brief description and inhabit it with the Lucia I know—until it is so clear it nearly has three dimensions, sharper than the wispy silvery film of my dreams.

In my mind's eye Lucia and Emile share a simple dinner of baguettes, cheese and red wine; Emile is olive-skinned, compactly formed. When he kisses her she closes her eyes, when she opens them they are bright.

He takes her hand as they go to the piano; he plays some old blues tunes, perhaps "Go Down Moses," then places her hands on the piano for her to try. They sing a gentle harmony, her voice a tiny but perfect soprano, trained for lieder but light as lace on the notes of the blues. Her favorite, of course, "Sometimes I feel like a motherless child," the song she mentions before her beloved Wagner, before the Irish folk tunes her father sang. I can hear her singing with him, I can feel Emile's eyes on me at the piano: I hear their voices in song and sex.

Lucia ends her "Real Life of James Joyce" on a self-deprecating note, saying that people are probably nice to her now because she is the daughter of a famous writer. No, Lucia, I'm beginning to suspect that you had your own charm, your own winning smile, your own lovely voice, just as everyone kept telling you over and over.

Writing this in the dining hall, trying to ignore the hubbub of the undergraduates and hippies milling all round me: after dinner I will go for a walk in the Austin evening as it cools down (from the 100-degree high to a bearable 87 or so). I know I will sleep well tonight.

And not dream of Will—I cannot, not when my mind is so full of the girl who cried more at thunderstorms than at bombs. Who sang opera and helped her father choose from among his ties, presumably after he went blind. (She marvels at the number of ties.) Who sometimes felt like a motherless child.

27 May

I love you, Lucia.

I wrote that in the top margin of my legal pad this morning—and then felt like repeating it over and over again.

So much to tell—what first? The heartbreaking letter from her beloved Babbo, who thought Tolstoy would be a calm read for her? Her tearful recollection of Joyce's eye illness?

No, let's start clinically, despite the tears that have been in my throat all day. Let's start with the handwriting.

A handful of Lucia's letters in one hand and the "Auto-Biography" notebook in the other, it was hard to stop staring at the elegant script of the one and the tremulous, old-lady squiggle of the other.

Most of the letters are unremarkable, mainly business letters written in French—but from Lucia's visit to Bray in the last year of freedom, two are remarkable indeed. A beautiful letter in Italian from "Babbo," a letter in English from Lucia to Joyce's friend J.F. Byrne, sent to Dublin from the cottage she shared with her cousins.

In the letters Lucia writes, the handwriting is drop-dead beautiful, something one rarely sees in this computer age: long curved slopes, angular Js, I can almost hear the delicate scraping of the fountain pen across the parchment. She tells Byrne that she has been "quiet ill" (she always spells quite "quiet," a poetic misspelling), but that she hopes to come visit him soon.

Such lovely writing, emerging from her most famous "mad" period—when she alternately set her bungalow afire and painted it black; when she would light the gas jets with great regularity; when she would sit in the laps of her cousins' boyfriends and try to undo their trousers. When her Babbo bought her a fur coat, hoping that such a gift would calm her nerves, and wrote her heartbreaking letters in Italian, signed "Ti abbracio"—I embrace you.

When I compare the handwriting of the letter to that of her "AutoBiography" (or of the dream book, which I've not yet read), I am disheartened at the deterioration: in the latter Lucia is only in her mid-fifties, and yet the handwriting is that of some ninety-year-old woman, the kind who take half an hour at the supermarket to write a tiny check for a chicken breast and five cans of cat food. Lucia, did the drugs steal thirty of your years?

But the prose style is quite similar, before and after the hospital —so the drugs only tamed her behavior and ruined her handwriting, did nothing to calm or order her racing, swirling thought patterns. Which are the thoughts of a musician—even more so in the second of the three texts, the "Auto-Biography."

Appropriate to dementia praecox' waking dreamer, she unconsciously uses music as metaphor; everyone important or relevant in her life is characterized as a "very good pianist," even Beckett.

Of all her lovers she sings most frequently of Emile, and quite often of Alexander Ponisovsky, her fiancé—many anecdotes begin with the name "Alec."

As for Beckett, she says that he wanted to marry her, but he was too tall for her. (He complimented her dancing, she says—double entendre?—and also gave her a copy of Dante's *Divine Comedy*. The latter act bespeaks, to me, much more of a substantial relationship than most of the biographers assume. Although it also brings Gary back to me, in a brief unwelcome spate of grief.) Of Sandy Calder, she says that she wanted to be his wife, but that he went away.

She then spins the tale of a tubercular South American youth who kissed her in the moonlight, recalling to any Joycean her father's most famous short story, *The Dead*.

She mentions Giorgio only briefly, but lovingly, and swears that she and her mother were the best of friends—you'd never know from her words that she once threw a chair at Nora, on her father's 50th birthday.

And what of her father? Will asked me not to forget the father —so where is James Joyce the famous Irish writer, in his daughter's self-proclaimed autobiography?

She speaks of his singing voice, of his writing, of how excited she was when *Ulysses* was published and pronounced a masterpiece.

And here I need to take a deep breath.

Because she writes about his eyes.

She speaks of blood in his eyes—perhaps from the time a quack doctor put leeches on his eyes as a failed cure? She could also have just been speaking of the illness itself, some red, puffy inflammation.

And she speaks of a time when he was crying from the pain, and she found no way to console him—a task better left to Nora, I suppose. Still her helplessness obviously caused her great anguish, and I myself finished that passage with tears in my throat.

She was awkward, she says helplessly.

(*Poppie, why can't you see? Is it cause you're so smart?*

No, sweetheart. It's because my eyes got very sick.

Do they hurt?

Not anymore, but they did for a long time.

Poppie, I don't want your eyes to hurt!

Oh, my dear sweet Molly, don't cry. It's been a long time now.

And I can see with my hands and my ears and my mind . . . I know how beautiful you are.)

Of both her parents she says the famous lines, "My parents were neither big nor small and I never thought they were going to die so soon." And throughout the journal she is obsessed with those who die young, from her mother's younger sister to other, more incidental figures along the way.

There's even mention of her nephew, Giorgio's son—the one now appointed as guardian of her memory. In this notebook Lucia moans softly that she was never allowed to hold the lovely little boy. *Did you miss her, Stephen? is that why you look so carefully after her memory?*

Time to go to dinner—thankfully they have a salad bar, so I needn't eat the various forms of chicken they call "food" here. Between that and the heat, I can feel myself dropping weight: I will soon fly away entirely, Lucie de Lammermoor going to the place of light.

And tonight I think I will try a late-night run, for I love running enveloped in darkness, that feeling of serene invincibility. Then up early for a day of solid work: the day after tomorrow the library closes for the weekend and the literary hordes arrive for the conference—and I've not yet finished with the autobiography or read through the dream book, the last of the three manuscripts.

On the inside cover of the dream book Lucia has written in that elderly hand the first verse of that 1920s flapper song, "I'm forever blowing bubbles." A reminder that the fat drugged woman writing all these words was once a radiant flapper, chic in a cloche hat and short dress, staying out till two a.m. with suspicious men—and probably giving her father other reasons to have blood in his eyes.

28 May

Writing this over lunch, students wiping tables to my left . . . I came back here to take a breather, here on my last day alone with diaphanous L. And she tells me stories, the dancer singer artist turning to words.

She tries in her autobiography to provide endings to each person's story: this one married and had children, this one went to America, or else she doesn't know what became of that one and is clearly upset at the fact.

And part of me becomes Virginia Woolf at the sight, her speculations in *A Room of One's Own* about a female Shakespeare: Lucia, what if you had had your father's Jesuit education, his less peripatetic childhood, and the support given him by the Paris literati, your mother, and you yourself—would your stories have changed the face of English literature?

Maybe that will be my first paper, one always wants to write articles on the way to a dissertation.

Except I find that I don't.

I find myself less and less inclined to play the academic game, especially as regards muse and sister musician, Lucia; perhaps I am, after all, more of a musician than a scholar. I suppose the conference will be as good a test of that question as any.

But right now is that the very sight of this university brings on inexplicable emotions. My first response to the sight of the buildings a kind of nameless fear, a little like the panic attack I had in Dorchester last spring, alone in Will's study. Then when I come closer and see the shape of the library that houses Lucia, panic gives way to a kind of fierce adrenalin, my passion for the subject driving me ever closer.

I guess the overall feeling, rather irrationally, is that of danger— at first frightening, then exhilarating. But what danger? of ruined eyesight, from staring at difficult handwriting? of an unpublishable dissertation? I have no idea, but I know I prefer this fear to the lethargy that gripped me in Baltimore even before Gary left me. I fear I would have been Lucia after Beckett, Lucia B. at the conservatory, airless face dull eyes.

Much better this fierce energy, tongue anxious to taste the

nectar of | 's dream book. Before this last day of immersion is out I hope to have reread all three documents, teasing out their tastes and shapes, bathing in | 's scribbled words and the killer air conditioning. I will imagine the little dancing silver fish of my dream, blowing bubbles and taking a bow for Babbo in his spectacles.

Then maybe tonight, before the onslaught of conferees, I'll run toward the Capitol building, with Will and the twin Lucias in my wake. (In my *Wake*? and there we are, the signature of Joyce obsession—certain words we can never use the same way again.)

31 May

My God, conferences still smell the same as they did when I was sixteen.

I don't know if it's the magic marker smell from all the HELLO MY NAME IS badges, the ink from too many pretentious gold fountain pens (the perennial gift to an academic), or the cheap wine from all the intro receptions (on Friday afternoon alone I counted a Foucault-Kristeva reception, a Marxist feminist reception, and a psychoanalytic reception—enough overlap there to get any good little assistant professor completely sloshed). At least at Joyce conferences they always have one sponsored by Bailey's Irish Cream.

And I held my invisible father's hand, remembering how years ago I led him to preferred seating in each session; how I helped work his tape recorder and also took notes; and how I last saw so many of these exact same people in this very spot on the globe.

Many, many scholars who last saw me at sixteen—most of them gone gray or bald, many gone fat. "I thought you'd be playing in the Chicago Symphony," Paul Levitt said, not knowing how insensitive the statement was.

Others had to focus a moment, and place exactly who I was. "I was so sorry to hear about your husband," one extremely emeritus professor (at least 90) mumbled to me. When I corrected him politely—no, it was my father who died five years ago, and yes, I was sorry too—he blushed and said something like oh, of course, Miss O'Donnell, it's a pleasure to have you here.

He wasn't the only one who made that mistake; so did the premier woman at the conference, an extremely fine scholar whose work I must confess I do not wholly understand. When she learned I was Will's daughter and not his wife, she sighed and grinned—"Oh of course, how silly of me," not the slightest hint of apology. (What was that song they sang at Square Robiac? *They asked me was she my daughter, and I said she was my married wife.*) When I mentioned that I was working on "Joyce papers" here in Austin, they all nodded sagely. "Too bad Stephanie isn't here," one of them said, and the others laughed—they were referring to Stephanie Schulman, a radical feminist who is apparently making as much of a mess of Joyce as Jessie Berger did with Shakespeare. (Gary ended up giving Jessie a B, by the way. The coward.) I shudder to think of such crude hands on those delicate little manuscripts.

After registration and the opening address (a droning about the decline of postmodernism), I fled to my little hippie co-op, where no one knows me or thinks they do. I'll go back tomorrow for Tilden's paper, and maybe the session on Virginia Woolf, since I'll soon be teaching Mrs. Dalloway. Maybe.

Will, how did you endure this, was it all worth it as the price of spending your life with Stephen Dedalus? but your voice is silent—perhaps I have left you back at the conference, disappearing into the waiting arms of your former colleagues.

1 June

2 a.m. what a very strange, strange day.

I think I may have caught a flu, perhaps from the combination of stifling heat and subarctic a/c, perhaps from living on carrot sticks, perhaps from some greedy flu-ridden undergraduate who last had Lucia's notebooks. Although I feel better now, so it may have been just the conference food that had me clammy and shaking, cold in Texas blast-heat.

I kept thinking I saw Gary in the hallway, but it was only paranoia. He's safely off in Brooklyn, of course, probably snuggling with Denise or some other proper Saturday afternoon pastime. As for Tilden's paper, "Reader-Response Theory Applied to Metonymy as Metaphor in *Finnegans Wake?*" while not my cup of tea, it was clearly written—and Tilden, when he's excited about a subject, is as entertaining as a dancer, dashing about with overhead projectors and light effects.

Then came lunch with Tilden and a swarm of other Joyceans young and old, including a few University of Texas undergrads who regarded us worshipfully—as if we were attending this conference through some glorious accomplishment, not through some airfare and university $. One of them was my library page, the baby-girl who had brought me the Lucia folder countless times: she asked me, "Did you find what you wanted?" "Oh yes," I said to her, and noticed Tilden watching me.

"And what was that, dear Miss O'Donnell?" Tilden asked.

I swallowed, hard. "Many, many layers." Actually, Ross Tilden, I don't yet know how the bubble-blowing flapper with the scary dreams (I haven't even mentioned them yet in this journal, have I?) will fit into my dissertation. But I know that something essential has happened here.

The Oxford chairman of the conference then fixed his gaze on me, brown eyes filmy, as if veiled by too many years squinting at manuscripts and microfiche. "O'Donnell—why, you're Will O'Donnell's widow!" he exclaimed. "Will and I had many a lively luncheon—and I still find inspiration from his letters."

"I remember your letters, Mister Wilcox," I said politely, quite truthfully. "Will always wanted me to read them as soon as they came." Tilden and I looked at each other; he swallowed his laugh, as minutes passed and he realized I was not going to correct this one on his mistake.

For the afternoon, I decided that I would, after all, attend the Virginia Woolf panel at 2 p.m. Its subtitle was "The Relevance of Biography"—so I thought perhaps I would learn by example, how to synthesize what I have just learned with the magic of the *Wake*.

So I wandered in late and sat in a back corner by myself, a few rows of empty desks separating me from the other attendees. Everyone, including the three presenters, had that after-lunch drowsy look about them.

I knew the moderator from Barnard—Liz Adams, a graceful black woman with salt-and-pepper hair and pale amber eyes. She was trying to shush some agitated member of the audience—"Just keep in mind," she said, "that incest is only one element in Virginia's biography."

"The most important element!" and I snapped to attention, expecting to see Jessie Berger or her evil twin. But the questioner was a reedy young Black man with huge glasses, his voice high-pitched and scratchy.

"That may be," continued Liz, "but I think we do Virginia a disservice if we presume that the transcendent qualities of her work can all be boiled down to the fact that her brother molested her."

Jessie would love this, I thought, and began to drift off. This is always my problem in these sessions—I have a feeling that even if I were on a panel I might have trouble attending to the other panelists. Will, you never seemed to have this problem; your notes were copious as well as neat, and you could quote whole sentences afterward.

I watched Liz and it seemed as if no more sounds were coming from her: yet her mouth kept moving, and so did the raspberry lips of the young man. Then he sat down and so did Liz, and another panelist stood up while Liz dimmed the lights. She turned on an overhead projector so that her illuminated face was the only thing visible.

Perhaps it was that weird light but I began to feel dizzy, dizzy and sick to my stomach. I collected my papers and slid out the back entrance, before the first transparency was off the screen.

I made my way downstairs, to the first floor, intending to get out of the building; by this time my skin was clammy, and it was all I could do to make it to the women's room on the first floor before I started vomiting.

No matter how much I threw up it didn't seem to make me feel less sick, less like a deep gash full of bile needing to force exit. Finally I felt empty, raw inside, in my body the Gary-breakup feeling to the tenth power. Maybe I was just throwing up all of academia, hating it more now than when I was sixteen: how did you stand it, Will? But his voice inside me still silent, drowned out by my dry heaves.

I crawled back to the co-op and slept through dinner, a heavy, pleasant sleep, the first I'd had since my arrival; I might have been at my little window seat in Dorchester, the place where I cried heavy pre-adolescent tears and then slept them off, the lethemuse that washed off upon awakening.

Back in Austin I was up again and running, literally, tracing my sneakered steps of the morning—I sweated more than I had thrown up, and ended up dizzy at the lake at midnight, looking at my reflection and trying to breathe deeply, regain my equilibrium.

I walked the long way back, counting the street lights and eventually stopping at some reggae bar downtown, for water to help me breathe. And suddenly the marathoner clicked into place, cautioning carry water, carry water.

My pulse still racing as I write this, as if the episode were some sort of a long subterranean nap and now I am up, awake. I really want to call Emma and talk about our marathon training, I feel oddly re-focused on it but it's what? three ayem in Boston, she's either asleep or making love with her husband. (Is Molly sexually frustrated? yes oh yes oh yes.)

Now tomorrow (i.e., later today!) I fly back to Bawlamer; I'll call her from there, and see if we can plan a few test runs together, to see how we do.

3 June

And here we are, home again—which seems tiny after Austin, Baltimore's skyline toylike out the window of my stifling little attic.

Emma had a quite intelligent suggestion, about the next step in our training program: to warm up by running that women's half-marathon in New York, the Pepsi Classic or Virginia Slims Lite or some other corporate hoo-ha. There's practically no registration fee and the route is actually modeled on part of the New York Marathon, so we'd get to practice on part of the terrain. The catch: it's in five days.

"Oh we could do it," Emma said. "You've been running thirteen miles, haven't you?"

Yes and more so, to escape nausea under the Texas sky. And besides, in New York it's still spring in June, softer air than the humidity already enveloping Baltimore. So now of course I want to run longer than 13 miles for the next few days, nobody wants to be at the end of the pack even in a recreational run like that one. All in all, a splendid frisson for our training program, one last gasp of vacation before the summer session begins. Speaking of the summer session . . .

Jessie Berger, of all people, has registered for my Modern Novel class.

I can't think what possessed her—if I haven't been openly hostile to her, I was as close as I could come and still maintain some semblance of professionalism. Though perhaps she's simply behind in credits, and "The Modern Novel" certainly sounds more her style than the other summer courses in the department—"Form and Function in the 17th-Century Epic." "Egyptian Myth in English Literature," or "The Mystery Plays: A Cross-cultural Perspective."

Oh and I let Lucia decide the extra book, for my course. Not

"Gravity's Rainbow," after all—that's too much work for one summer, even for me.

No I let | whisper it to me in Texas, her shaky hands writing over and over again her best-remembered addresses, including some of her doctors and hospitals. (Impossible to list them all, dementia praecox or no dementia praecox—all in all, Lucia saw twenty-two doctors in three countries!) She didn't mention Jung, but she did mention the Zurich sanitorium where she met him, Les Rives de Prangins—and that while there, she was in love with Dr. Oscar Forel.

And where in literature is that clinic described, in some detail?

Why, in F. Scott Fitzgerald's *Tender is the Night*, of course. Lucia arrived at Prangins four years after Zelda Fitzgerald spent eighteen months there—under a similar diagnosis of schizophrenia, under the care of the same Dr. Oscar Forel, and under the spell of a similarly grieving writer. While Zelda's own creativity, from her writing to her own ballet career, remains obscured, Scott wrote about Prangins in one of his best books.

So I get to do sneaky work on this dissertation, by learning about Prangins while these kids get a well-deserved break, after the intensities of Joyce and Beckett and Woolf. (As a writer Scott's a relative lightweight, but that's OK, we'll call it our beach book.)

Meantime I'm pretty completely recovered from the Texas illness; and although Tilden says the conference food didn't make him ill, I saw him eat all of the airplane lunch, including the aged non-salad.

Time to sleep, although it feels too early, Texas jet lag pulling at me. I think I may read myself to sleep with the Lucia dream book (well, my transcription thereof)—imagining I can hear my silver fish dancer's rich voice, the voice an Irish painter found charming, "bubbling up as if from a well." (Like a creature born unto that element.) If I sleep, maybe I'll forget that by going to New York, I am going to the city of both Colin and Gary.

2 June

It is already too hot to sit and write in this bleeding journal. I don't know how the famous journal-writers ever got through the summer!

But I want to describe Felicia's painting, the one she kept working on while I was gone. "Adding Felicia to the Molly drawing," she said; I half expected to come back and find not a spark of myself. Instead I see myself all too well.

Except my eyes are not that huge, I know that; and even I can't claim to really have such bony shoulders. In the painting I am lying half-reclined, but no hint of relaxation: I look frightened, as if I have been beaten without bruises. As if Felicia was in Texas with me, saw me as I flared into panic; the girl in the painting could easily have just vomited for hours.

Felicia shrugged at the idea: "I don't really like to analyze my paintings." She does, however, want to do a series. "I know it's a lot to ask . . . but I think this could be a real solid summer's work." She grinned suddenly. "How about if I let you take the fan upstairs at night, it'll keep you cool?"

I pronounced it a fair trade and we were giggling, two children with a secret contract. In truth there is something seductive about someone wanting to draw you over and over; it satisfies the lost performer in me, since now no one ever hears me play the cello.

Today we listened to my Texas blues tape, music Lucia never mentioned but could easily have known. I imagine her by that garden wall, her bubbling voice too low today for soprano arias— instead singing what she heard in last night's club, Emile's surreptitious hand on her knee.

An' if he don't come back to you I'll tell you what to do
Just jump right over board, 'cause he ain't no more to you
I've got those weeping willow blues. . . .

4 June

And today I heard the weeping willow blues in Lucia B's voice.

As the sunrise came complete over the water of the reservoir, there she was, lying on her side and picking at cattails. Her jeans were the kind with flowers all over them: her hair was loose and tangled but clean, and the pain and anger was focused on her reflection, as if she knew the source of her rage lay within.

This time all I felt was relief: for her eyes were clear of the fog that filled her face when I last sighted her, in front of the conservatory. In its place was that resentful, sarcastic stare I know so well, described so well in one of Joyce's notebooks, *Her eyes are blackened by the punch of sleeplessness, she tosses on the couch of separation.* I saw the same purple-blue stains beneath translucent skin, just below the eyes.

Emboldened by my week of madwoman diaries, I spoke to her for the first time. I checked my time and slowed to a walk, squatting behind her; I found myself strangely shy, after all these months. Was it possible that she did not recognize me by now?

"It's lovely that it's so warm," I said.

She twisted her body to look at me—God that tiny squint in her eye is so Lucia, it's too perfect, although the eyes themselves are hazel-brown instead of Lucia's blue. She shrugged at my comment, appropriate for a woman who didn't seem to mind Memorial Stadium in 35 degrees.

"My name is Molly," I said, "what's yours?"

With that she laughed, a laugh deep in her throat. "Wouldn't you love to know that," she said.

Two striking things—the obvious paranoia of the phrase (psych jargon again, *sigh*) and the lovely, deep rasp of her voice. Again like Lucia, the voice bubbling from the well, in both cases the mark of cigarettes as well as sorrow.

I was charmed, even though her manner was somewhere

between indifferent and hostile, her body passive. After a few silent moments I said, "Is it okay if I come talk to you again?"

She looked down at the ground, pinching her mouth as if she were about to spit. Then she said, "Everyone else does."

With that I stood up and put my earphones back on, letting Wagner's overture to *Tannhäuser* carry me the rest of the way back to Calvert Street. "Everyone else does," as if my Lucia were the Cassandra of Baltimore, some oracle consulted on the sly by numerous supplicants.

Who is "everyone else"? My guess is she's actually referring to men—men who've fucked her and left her over the years, men who float in and out of her life like so many tiny fish in the reservoir, Emile Alec Beckett Calder anonymous Parisian glad hand, all of whom said I she danced very well.

And yes, I am beginning to feel the same way, having difficulty separating out Gary's bold blond-furred hands from Colin's long musician's fingers inside me. A half-remembered dream image from last night: both of them pulling at my hair in bed, nearly extracting it from my head—as if the price of having serviced them will be the loss of all my hair, as well as my well-worn heart.

5 June

Dateline Excelsior Hotel, Central Park West, New York City

Here less than 12 hours, and I'm already buzzed: the city's signature adrenalin pumping through my veins, excitement crossed with anxiety, Baltimore revealed again as a small town playing let's-pretend at cityhood. Emma is already asleep, fatigued by travel and motherhood; alone and adrenalined I have already called Lydia, my former quartet partner, and will meet her at midnight at her favorite Third Avenue bar.

But first I want to record the odd argument I had with Emma about an hour ago, over dinner. It was about whether or not I got into Harvard, of all things: you'd think such facts of the past obvious.

I was telling her about my bizarre Will dreams, like the Harvard dream, the one where I lost Will amid autumn leaves; I said "I guess I still haven't forgiven myself for not getting into Harvard."

Emma's head lowered; she was looking at the tablecloth in the Cuban restaurant, concentrating as if the white cloth held a set of legible symbols. She swallowed. "Molly, they did take you, remember? You just wanted to come here, to New York, instead. You . . . you wanted the music scene, don't you remember?"

"What nonsense," I said, astounded she would even question it. "I would never have left home if I had gotten into Harvard and the Conservatory—Emma, I knew where I belonged! . . . Don't you remember how I cried, when the rejection letter came?"

"That was the Conservatory. Harvard you got into."

We went on and on like that, for at least half an hour: Emma offering real-life scenes—remember what you said, the day we packed the car? And me offering concrete reasons why I would have stayed: *Will's eyes were getting even worse, he needed me.*

Finally my little sister gave up. "If you say so," she said, her voice low. "Who knows, maybe I got mixed up who accepted and rejected you. I was sixteen, too busy losing my virginity and stuff like that."

Yet now I find myself searching my memory, wondering if I am, after all, correct. I can't visualize the rejection letter, although I remember crying in the window seat. And I cannot for the life of me remember Will's reaction—did he reassure me that we would always be together, even when I was away?

Instead I have false memories—of dancing in a mist of silver light, of drawing elaborate lettrines for an edition of Chaucer entitled *Pomes Penyeach*; of chainsmoking in an Irish village and writing to my Babbo. L'Irlandaise, my silver fish, what have you done to me?

5 June

5:30 a.m.

Watching the sunrise out the window of the hotel, hours before the run—Emma still asleep, clutching her pillow as if it were her baby. I should be asleep too—but I'm not, and for predictable reasons.

Dreams and dreams and more dreams, Lucia's dream book tossing me into somersaults of Will nightmares. Not one, not two, but three in the course of my foreshortened night: I kept forcing myself awake, and have now seen the park outside this window at every hour. My body feels rigid with heat, like a very bad sunburn, and it's hard to breathe. Tears might release the pressure but I can't find them, can only write the dreaming—

1. a reception for Colin in ruby-red dress and high heels / Will is coming I am nervous I hold a napkin to my face / have you seen my father? I ask the symphony man / Colin is angry and takes away my high heels / screams go home / Then the police come / overturn the big table / fruit rolling all around the floor / they are coming for me / Gary in a police uniform/ he pins me to the floor / shows me your photograph, huge, blown-up / blood covers your face / you stare unseeing/ your eyes stare dead

2. Paris where you showed me the Eiffel Tower / we held hands and drank croissant butter / we carry tiny violins, smaller than our hands / round my neck and my waist / nuns block our path, so many I can't see you anymore / their dress is dark musty faces pale / one has Lucia B's face / she puts her hands on my shoulders and kisses me / whispers ti abbracio / I am condemned

to death / you are gone / you delivered me safely into
Lucia's arms/ to my execution

3. an exotic hotel bathroom / tub Olympic size / you and
   Gary together hold me down / your tenor voice I'm
   forever blowing bubbles / then on campus a violent
   thunderstorm / cannot move / lie still / grassy cove
   where Gary and I played night games / the lightning is
   sure to hit me / scream for help / for you / screaming in
   sex / the thunderstorm making me come / then Gary
   and I at Louie's / Emma is thirteen / short hair freckled
   skin / she hands me one of the tiny violins / says that
   you have died

And now, writing it down, I have finally found the tears—like Anna Livia says, let me rain now, only this time I am raining all over Lucia's dreams.

Lucia dreamed constantly of policemen and nuns (her father hated nuns, and was rather superstitious about them). She dreamed of being condemned to death, in a pool of water. And she dreamed of her father's dying, the one she was not able to witness—over and over and over again.

Lucia, we are more alike than I ever dreamed.

You heard about "peritonitis" long after Babbo was buried; the word "aneurysm" entered my vocabulary about six hours too late. Will, are you reminding me yet again that I abandoned you to a chilly Boston deathbed? Or still angry that I am pursuing my Lucia love affair?

Don't be scared, Shem. Growing up isn't that hard. Why can I only imagine those words, not hear them or remember when you said them first? (God, here I go again—this time I'll close the journal before I cry all over it.)

Actually I didn't cry—the tears rose to my mouth and then dissolved, melting like cocaine into my blood and giving me a blast of energy. I feel cleansed, enough of Will's absence and Lucia's dreams.

Signs of life outside: Friday morning scurrying, businessmen clutching briefcases as they head east to midtown, some fellow-spirit runners catching the morning's reasonable temperatures. Soon it will be time to wake Emma, so we can do the same.

And part of me imagines Gary waking up about now, in whatever sublet he and Denise have found—when he sees runners go past his block, does he perhaps see the occasional Harvard T-shirt to remind him of me?

I also imagine Colin asleep in the apartment on East 55th, no way would he be awake at this hour. But I know for a fact that he's not there—I learned that from Lydia, who played the Trout Quintet with him last summer at Tanglewood. She told me he's touring Asia; his agent lined up gigs in Tokyo, Hong Kong, Manila, and Sydney, "and God knows where else."

(Lydia, by the way, makes me regret less giving up the cello: third year in the Philharmonic and she hates every minute. "You spend all these years studying music interpretation," she said, "and then you're just some fancy key on a super-piano, some asshole conductor will decide how loud or soft or fast or slow, whether Strauss should weep or sing. And these 23- or 24-year-old babies, straight out of Aspen who think they're hot shit—mostly what they are is boring." She stubbed out her third cigarette. "Molly, we're both too smart for this life.")

Meantime the sunrise on the park is quite Homeric, rosy fingers creeping around the trees and softening the debris on the streets, weathered faces of the homeless people rising from their cardboard beds. I have to restrain myself from looking for Lucia B.

Time to wake Emma, so that we can run through Central Park and sing "Negro spirituals." I know she'll remember from high school choir, all those years ago—perhaps we can speak of Margaret and then sing, *Sometimes I feel like a motherless child.*

7 June

Amtrak train: headed safely back to Baltimore, stretching my legs against the seat in front of me, thinking of women's backs.

I hope I dream of them tonight, women's backs and legs and arms moving forward, forward, up toward the Bronx and back, women's nipples hardening in the heat and sweat pouring off their faces.

And by the end of yesterday's run I was crying again, equal parts elation and some deep, deep sadness, the root of which still sticks in my throat: I don't know if it belongs to me or to one of the Lucias, both of whom I could have sworn I saw today.

Amazing variety of women, doing this half-marathon: from stocky athletes with spiked hair to heavy-metal girls with elegantly permed tresses that seemed unaltered by their own sweat. Age range from about thirteen to well over sixty, the older runners glorious with their bright eyes and big smiles. One of the happiest-looking of the older women wore a specially cut tank top, exposing the half of her chest where a breast had been removed. In place of a scar (or one of those implants) was a tattoo on flat skin, the sign for infinity drawn in dusky Southwest hues. I must remember to tell Felicia. And as if she has been purposely following me, there was Jessie Berger, tightening her sneakers at the run's starting point; she waved to me but didn't smile or come near. Neither did I, God knows we will see enough of one another starting next week.

Emma was in high spirits, and I'm amazed at how she's improved—this run obviously made her focus harder on her training, and were we sprinting, she could easily outrun me, just like in the old days. We stayed in the center of the pack, not trying to get to the forefront and reluctant to fall back, so that I felt part of some undifferentiated mass of femaleness urging me down along the river, toward the lower lip of Manhattan.

Over and over again I thought I saw L'Irlandaise, especially in one pubescent track team with signature headbands: Isadora

Duncan's girls dancing together at Salzburg. I felt I saw each of Shakespeare's madwomen, from the wispy Ophelia girl (I hope she's an actor, it's a role she was born to) to the tall, commanding dyke with the blue eyebrows at the water fountain at Battery Park, who seemed, with her commanding presence and huge laugh, to evoke Lady Macbeth at her most powerful.

Will, this is one you never could have run with me, even if you had wanted to.

And perhaps that is why I was crying: after all those terrifying dreams of him, all those dreams about his death, here I am travelling further and further away from him, both in my scholarship and in this women-only run.

But even as I write that, I know that I'm lying—that the tears are like my screams in my dreamed campus thunderstorm, half-pleasure, half pain. Which is after all the experience of every runner, particularly on an overheated June afternoon in New York City, the auto smoke swirling through my lungs, Colin and Gary and Will all taking second place to memories of

| *riding afore me*
(*lovely!*)

good god cry of shame

Chatham, 5:30 a.m.: indistinguishable from midnight in the quiet and dark outside, the soft light of low-watt fluorescent and near-complete silence on the ward—quite as if an army of well-groomed boys were still asleep in the halls of Hillsborough Preparatory Academy. The only distinctive sound was the soft, incessant click! and chatter of the night nurses' poker game.

Clay Richards sat behind the small group, looking at his watch: his training program required a week or two of graveyard shift, but nights taught mainly tedium on this heavily medicated ward. "I think maybe I'll go do the rounds now," he said; he spoke languidly, trying not to stop the game. "If that's okay with y'all."

A whirl of commentary: "Go for it, handsome." "So the six a.m. rounds happen at 5:45, what's the problem?" "Just watch for Shana, if she wakes up she'll be singing' till breakfast."

Richards walked softly, cautiously peering into each room as he came to it. Brian, the newest HIV-positive patient, slept with his heavily muscled arms wrapped around his neck, embracing the thick adhesive bandages darkened with clotted black blood, witness to a careful stab at the carotid artery. Shana, now in a private room, lay on her side like a large cat, in a soft, nearly complete circle.

Toward the end of the hall he heard a tinny buzz: when he opened Molly O'Donnell's door, he saw the tiny speaker attached to Molly's Walkman, the buzz blurring the piano music. Molly stood intently by the bathroom door, letting the notes underline a set of ballet exercises—careful pliés and then relives, up, down, up.

Clay watched her in silence for a moment. In the absence of a barre she used the door handle to the bathroom, stabilized by a heavy black armchair; she wore the temporary elbow brace they still let her wear, so her left arm could hold some of her weight. Her back was perfectly straight, she looked directly ahead and slightly above her, as if paying attention to a teacher. "Un, deux, troi . . ." she counted softly under her breath.

"Hey Molly," Clay said softly. "You're up awful early, don't you think?"

Molly continued her relevés until she had done twenty, then looked over at him. "Welcome to the rue Caumartin!" Her dream-like smile began to fade as she focused on him. "I'm sorry that Madame Preeobjanska is away today—she could tell you, I am making a lot of progress. And she dances better than Isadora Duncan herself!"

Clay stepped in and stood beside her. "I swear, Miss O'Donnell, you are a prize."

Molly's eyebrows lifted, questioning.

Clay grinned. "Between running and dancing, you're the most in shape mental patient I ever did see. You still training for a marathon?"

Molly tilted her head, looking at him as if for the first time. Finally she sank into the armchair, one leg slung straight along the arm. She held her cheek to her knee, her eyes closed. Then she said slowly, carefully, "In my own way."

"What do you mean?" Clay's question was just as slow, measured: Molly's eyes were clear, he noted, without the veil she usually wove from words and song. He ventured a comment: "Well, I guess living at Pearlstone's a marathon, if anything is."

Molly laughed. "Yes oh yes." She switched and began stretching her right leg. She began to sing, softly, "The words of the prophets are written on the subway walls . . . "

"My God, it's a song I remember!" Without conscious intent Clay had lowered his voice to match her hushed tone. "From when I was a little boy, how does it go?" he tried to hum, but the tune wavered wildly, until they were both laughing.

Not wanting to break the mood, Clay circled Molly and helped her clasp her hands behind her back. "I'm glad you're feeling better, Molly. You were pretty sick when you first came here."

"And now?" Molly unclasped her hands, lifted her arms to the ceiling. "How we succeed in courting daylight by saving darkness . . . he who loves shall see."

Clay sighed. "Molly, we all want you to see daylight, everyone here wants that."

Molly moved closer to Clay; while not as tall as he, she could still meet his eyes easily. "Is that so," she said softly, her tone belying the question. Her voice was lower-pitched than Clay knew it, with a bitter reserve of sarcasm. "They want my blood, and we both know why."

Clay shook his head and sat down gingerly on Molly's bed, nodding when she took his cue and sat beside him. "Molly," he said slowly, "those blood tests are for your own good. The sooner we know what meds you need, the better."

At the last sentence Molly's eyes closed, instinctively; she doubled over as if she had been punched in the stomach, but in slow motion. Clay watched as her head rested on her knees; then she opened her eyes and sat up, the color drained from her face.

Clay, spooked, stood up from the bed, taking a few steps toward the door; Molly stared at him, silently. When she finally spoke, her voice had the high pitch and childlike energy familiar to the ward.

"At Ivry they would not have me any more," she said. "I used to set fires and tear my clothes. I like it here very much."

She got up and lay on her bed, her eyes still closed; as Clay began to turn away they opened again, her glance soft, rather sad.

Clay shrugged, embarrassed. "Sorry to interrupt your practice," he said. "Hope you have a good morning." The young woman's gaze followed him out the door, her body completely still until his footsteps faded, swirled in the sounds of the ward waking up: toilets flushing, TV turned to the morning news, medication carts making their heavy-wheeled way along the corridors.

Molly sat up slowly, her eyes half-closed as if she were about to start dreaming. She pulled down one of the *lettrines* sketches that still adorned her wall, turning it over to its blank side. She opened the box of pastel crayons that Anne-Marie had given her, and began to draw.

In black she drew a tremendous M, nearly filling the page, and surrounded it in red swirls; then she turned it upside down and drew a tiny stick figure in the corner, barely visible. She signed the work, holding the red pastel tightly, and held it up next to Felicia's framed drawing.

There were now two signatures on the drawing, below the inverted M which had now become a W. First *Molly*, its long sloping script then crossed out with a thick red line. Then, round printed letters, direct and aggressive: **Shem**. Slowly she began to tear the piece of paper to bits, in long, angular motions.

Finally Molly dropped the scraps of paper and began to cry, silently. She was still crying when Steve came to escort her to breakfast.

"Jessie Berger," Gail Ryan said the name slowly, contemplatively.

"Does that name bring back memories!"

"Yeah, it's amazing how much you remember, even after two

years," said the head nurse. "If I try, I could still tell you some of her other names."

Both women were speaking loudly this morning, Gail's sing-along shout voice in full projection—so as to drown out the leaf-blower lurching across the Pearlstone grounds, blasting aside the muddy leaves. "What were they like, the personalities?" Anne-Marie asked.

The head nurse closed her eyes, as if to better visualize the past. "Some very masculine guy, named Butch or Max or something, you should have seen the way she walked. . . . And one was really young, like an infant—I used to see her lying on the sofa in the hallway, sucking her thumb."

"So they've gone and settled out of court?" Clay Richards asked. He was leaning in the doorway, a late arrival.

"Yes, and apparently Jessie gets a tidy sum."

The head nurse shook her head. "I don't like it. What if every patient who hated electroshock did this?"

"Well," said Anne-Marie, "there is an argument that ECT's not generally appropriate for multiple personality disorder, and besides —" The rest of the sentence was drowned out by the leaf-blower.

"What, Anne-Marie? I can't hear you over that thing."

Anne-Marie shrugged and sat back, twirling a strand of red hair around her little finger. "Just remembering what they taught us in school, about patients' rights."

Gail looked long and hard at the young social worker, who had been placed on a 30-day probation at the time of her review. In response, Anne-Marie bent her head to her notes, scribbling in the margins of her legal pad.

"Listen, sweetie," said the head nurse, "after this lawsuit, who knows? We could end up paying off Karen Hightower, Cin-Yuen Lee, and Molly O'Donnell, just for starters."

"Not Molly," said Clay, easing his long-limbed figure into a seat alongside Anne-Marie's. "I would guess that's the furthest from her mind."

Anne-Marie nodded, looking over at the young Black man as if she were seeing him for the first time. He had spoken softly, without the sarcasm she had come to expect from him.

"Well, pretty soon Miss O'Donnell will no longer be our responsibility," Gail said firmly. "The transfer date of December 15 is firm. Of course, they keep asking for a diagnosis, and Kepler keeps changing his mind."

"No kidding," said Clay. "First you got your schizophrenia. Then you got your multiple personality, Now we got the disease of the week—which is . . ." He ruffled through his notes.

"BAD with delusional features," said Gail, not riffing off Clay's humor.

"Well, places like Park Grove ain't equipped for that sort of thing," said Clay. "I know, I worked there. They need some box they can check off."

"Anne-Marie, what has the family been saying?" Gail asked briskly.

Anne-Marie lifted her head, and read aloud from her pre-prepared notes. "No family visits scheduled for the next few weeks, with the possible exception of Emma, the younger sister." Her voice was empty with exhaustion. "Mostly they all seem prepared to wait till she 'comes home' to Boston."

Behind Anne-Marie, through the window, the leaf-blower changed direction, lumbering beyond the weeping willow trees like some prehistoric animal out to eat Wilkes and all its inhabitants.

Chatham was loud with the sound of *Star Trek*.

One of the younger patients had arranged to rent all the films at once, and the prospect had brought out practically the entire institution: the dayroom was crammed with patients from both Chatham and Wilkes, as well as the youngest of the student nurses, a few aides, and even some visiting family and friends.

"We should have done this in the big building!" complained

one of the visitors from Wilkes. "They got more room over there, not to mention the best TV."

"You are just afraid of being' here, Louie—but these crazy germs are everywhere." That from Shana, who sat down on the floor with a flourish. "Hey Lucy!" she called out into the hall. "Get your ass out here!" After a few minutes Molly emerged and was beside Shana. "Ooze, you're so pretty!"

Molly wore some clothes Felicia had given her the day before —loose baggy pants and a black tank top with Japanese lettering. Her hair was parted on the side, brushing her collarbone. She and Shana stayed near one another, watching spaceships out-maneuver one another in slow elegant war games.

"Hey, look guys—two BMWs on I-83!"

"Too slow for rush hour."

"Hey, can we turn the sound up, if y'all are gonna keep talking?"

Unnoticed in the hubbub was Anne-Marie, unlocking the heavy door and holding it open for a blond, bearded man with a pot belly and the terrified eyes of a newly trapped rabbit. "Welcome to Chatham," Anne-Marie said; but he signed in silently, not looking around him. "Molly's expecting us," Anne-Marie said to the nurse at the station.

"Well she's in there doing Star Trek with the rest of 'em."

When Molly saw the man trailing Anne-Marie into the dayroom, her eyes brightened; she stood up quickly, pulling Shana up with her. "Well, well!" she exclaimed. "Love love to love love!"

Shana laughed. "This your boyfriend?"

Molly shrugged. "Just my all menkind of every deception."

"Sshh!" The assembled Trekkies huddled together against the intruder as Anne-Marie said, "Molly, let's you and me and Gary go back to your room, to talk. What do you think? "Molly turned to Shana, as if the younger woman had the authority to veto Gary's visit.

Shana put her hands on her hips. "He good to you?"

Molly shrugged again, then slid her hand out of Shana's and into Gary's, in one long lazy stroke. "What's done cannot be undone," she explained to Shana; then she turned forward and led the other two out of the dayroom, the beeps and shrieks of imaginary weaponry growing fainter as they walked down the corridor. Steve followed, at a discreet distance.

By the time they got to Molly's room, Gary was able to smile. "It's good to see you, Molly."

"Is it?" Molly sat on her bed, her back against the wall and one leg hanging over the edge. Her black hair contrasted with the red in Felicia's drawing behind her. "Did you come to see what it's like, to be nothing else but mad?"

Standing behind Gary, Anne-Marie could see his shoulders tremble, the barely perceptible nervousness of a hummingbird.

Gary took a deep breath. "I'm sorry that you've been sick, Moll . . . but I know you're in good hands. I've been asking around about this place." He sat near the foot of the bed, his back straight against the heavy armchair—a colleague in consultation. "They say the doctors here are the best, and I've learned a lot from Anne-Marie, here."

Molly looked at Anne-Marie, as if she were trying to get her eyes to focus. "In the darkness of the consulting room," she said, "there are a thousand explanations." Then she turned back to Gary, stepped forward, and took both his hands in hers. "Why did you come here, now?"

Gary looked down at their clasped hands. "Anne-Marie asked me to," he said. "She thought you might want to see me."

Molly closed her eyes and said softly, "I would have liked to be your wife, you know." She opened her eyes. "But you went away."

Gary did not reply; he looked down at the floor, away from the unblinking blue eyes. Finally he said, "Listen, Molly. I brought the Shakespeare Quarterly with the article—the one you helped me with. I thought you'd like to see it, now that it's finally come out." He stood up and put his briefcase on the empty bed; he unlocked it quickly and removed a small scholarly journal, about the size and heft of a paperback book.

Molly took the magazine in both her hands, flipping breezily through the pages. "So tell me, how are things in the department?" she asked, switching to a normal, conversational tone. "Has Ross Tilden found happiness in Paris?"

Gary laughed, a happy, relieved sound. "As far as we can tell from his e-mail, he's mostly drinking café au lait."

Molly got up and sat in a heavy wooden armchair, her hair falling in front of her eyes as she paged through the journal. Gary knelt beside her and pointed to the table of contents. "See—there. Hell, I should have put your name on it."

Anne-Marie stood back, watching the tableau of teacher and student, Molly suddenly younger, softer than she'd seen her. "Oh Gary," Molly said, laughing, "You could at least have let me come up with the title! 'Hamlet, Macbeth, and The Dark Lady—Obsession As an Element of Form?' I could have done better than that."

Gary smiled, his first genuine smile. "I'm sure you could have, Molly."

Molly looked up from the book, and over at him. Their eyes met, and for the first time Gary did not look away; instead Anne-Marie could see the energy between them, could envision the relationship of which Rachel and Felicia had spoken.

"It's true then," Molly said. "You have missed me."

Gary lowered his gaze. "What does your shirt say?" he asked, pointing to the Japanese letters.

"Ask Felicia." Molly reached out and traced his beard with one fingernail, gently. "Where is your wife?" she asked, in nearly a whisper.

Gary gave a careful smile. "She's living in Baltimore now," he said. "We think she might go to med school."

Molly nodded and looked at the floor; her hand lay still on Gary's shoulder. When she looked at Gary again, the water in her eyes made them brilliant, sunlit. "You told me that night you'd teach me to play," she said. "Well, I think love is all there is or should be."

Gary looked at the floor, silenced again.

Molly sighed and stood up, her body stiff, formal. "Mr. Beckett, my father is not here. Isn't it time for you to leave now?" She took Gary's hand and led him out of the chair, toward the door. "You, sir, are too tall for me."

Anne-Marie's eyes widened. "Molly, if you would like Gary to leave, you might just tell him you're tired now."

Molly shook her head, every muscle in her body rigid. Her first gesture was odd: she held her left arm across her belly, as if it held a cello bow; then she walked over to the armchair and leaned on it, looking straight into Anne-Marie's face.

The eyelashes below Molly's eyes were wet as she said, "Often hate on first hearing comes of love by second sight."

Anne-Marie blinked. "What, Molly?"

It was Steve, standing in the doorway, who ran, too late, to stop her: Molly had already turned and picked up the chair with both arms, turning without a pause to swing it in Gary's direction and release. Gary fell when the chair hit his leg, then skidding unchecked to the far wall.

Anne-Marie was stopped dead, unable to speak or call for help. Steve did so instead, shouting into the hallway until two nurses arrived to surround Molly.

"You all right, sir?"

"I don't know," Gary said. "My leg—it hurts like a son of a bitch."

The floor nurse knelt to examine Gary; when she pulled the foot forward to try to straighten the leg, Gary cried out. "I think it's broken," said the nurse.

Anne-Marie went over to Molly, who was staring at her ex-boyfriend, clutching her own arm tightly against her: the wet face was suddenly blank. "Why did you do that, Molly?" she asked, as gently as she could manage.

Molly looked down bleakly at the shorter woman. "To bring him the best from cinder Christinette, my friend." She took a deep breath and then spat: "Sender: Boston, Mass."

Anne-Marie led her gently over to her bed. "What's happening with your arm?" Molly shook her off and whirled back toward Gary, holding onto the bed. "What's done cannot be undone!" she called out. "To bed, to bed!" One set of nurses surrounded Gary's stretcher and another held Molly, whose physical pain was becoming clearer in her body language, even as her face was devoid of expression.

After Steve and Anne-Marie had filled out the correct forms, they led Molly to the medical unit, laying her on a standard hospital bed next to a Wilkes patient with the flu. Molly lay still her body turned limp, boneless, as if the effort of throwing the chair had exhausted all her strength.

When the doctor arrived, Molly looked up at her, soft sleepy eyes. "I am quiet ill," she said, her voice low. "I have been reading the Divina Commedia that Mister Beckett gave me, and I think perhaps that this is purgatory." Then she finally began to sing, not her blues-gospel singer voice but a clear soprano, the song she had been singing when first admitted to Pearlstone. *"Ah, mi togli, eterno Iddio, questa vita disperata—che la morte e un ben per me, si, la morte e un ben per me."*

Shaun O'Donnell strode into Kepler's office, staring at the doctor and the social worker like a football coach impatient with the performance of his team. "We're paying you guys a lot of money," he said without preamble, Emma a silent shadow beside him. "And when I say "we," of course, most of it's my pocket, which is already tapped from caring for my mother. Who, I'm sure you know, suffers from chronic health problems." His loud voice, Boston Irish crossed with the New York Stock Exchange, punctured the second floor's thick silence.

"Yes, Mr. O'Donnell," said Kepler, "we know." Kepler had returned from Trinidad tan a deep bronze—except for the sunglass-shadow around his eyes, which gave him something of the look of a raccoon.

Shaun shifted his substantial weight from one leg to the other. "They won't let me speed up the transfer, I already tried—so I have to trust you for almost two whole months. But how can I, in the face of such irresponsibility?"

"I know it would seem that—"

"Where are the results of your glorious 'treatment plan?'" the large man demanded. "My sister comes here after getting her own arm broken in a car accident, singing a few songs—next thing I hear, she's setting fires and breaking someone's goddamn leg. Isn't she here under a court order, so you can prevent that sort of thing?"

"We determine the level of restraint on a day-by-day basis. And your sister has been much improved." Kepler kept his speech slow, quiet, in contrast to Shaun's bellicosity.

"You may also need to understand, sir," said Anne-Marie, "that some clients act-out bizarre behaviors in the process of recovery."

"Sometimes you gotta get worse to get better," came a soft voice behind Shaun. "That's what my therapist says."

"Very nice, Emma, but I don't buy it," Shaun said. He sat down and opened his briefcase, the one which had held the transfer papers a few weeks before. "If this goes on much further," he said, "we are prepared to sue this institution. I want my sister calm and out of danger—and if that means maximum restraint, so be it."

Kepler's anger flared then, a discreet but pointed businessman's annoyance. "We do not keep our patients on 24-hour lockup at Pearlstone, Mr. O'Donnell," he said tightly. "If that is what you want, we can discharge her into your care now, and that you can take care of her yourself for two months. I will even give you the prescriptions for Molly's current medications, although we still are working on the combination that will keep her stable. Do you want that? Are either of you really interested in tying your sister to her bed for seven weeks?"

"No!" Emma's exclamation came before Shaun's dismissive wave.

"No need for melodrama, Dr. Kepler," Shaun said, quieting down to a mild but still dominant boom. "I'm willing to allow anyone a few miscalculations. Although from my layman's perspective, it would appear that you are not giving my sister *enough* medication."

Kepler opened Molly's chart, a white binder absurdly large for the relatively small volume of papers within. "We have been trying to test her blood for absorption levels," he said. "Our attempts have been stymied by her intense fear of the needle. But I am prepared to conduct the tests ASAP, and up her lithium in the meantime." His brow furrowed as he turned the pages in the chart. "She's quite a difficult patient, you know," he said. "I'll also order that she be closely monitored, even in her calm periods, between now and the transfer. You have my word."

Shaun nodded. "Are you willing to put it in writing?" he asked.

Kepler sighed. "If necessary . . . Can we do it here, or do you want me to wait until Monday, when our lawyer is available?"

Shaun grinned. "Sir, I think a simple letter from you on that thing—" he pointed to Kepler's small laptop computer—"will do just fine. As long as I know that my sister will be given the maximum restraint needed at all times." He turned to his sister. "Isn't that right, Emma?"

Emma did not respond; she was looking down at some papers in her lap.

"Emma?"

The folder Emma held was labeled The New York Marathon and was thick with information from hotel rates to starting times. She had circled the words Excelsior Hotel. "Whatever," she said tonelessly.

"What do you mean, whatever?" Shaun asked.

Emma met Anne-Marie's eyes; the social worker gave a tiny, almost imperceptible nod. "Listen, I haven't seen her in over two weeks," Emma said. "We don't actually know anything beyond what the doctor here has just said. So yes, let's go over there, now—before you ask me to comment about *maximum restraint.*"

At the first floor, Kepler and the O'Donnells moved briskly toward Chatham; Anne-Marie stayed behind, amid a team of staff organizing patients for volleyball. She picked up an inter-office phone.

"Anne-Marie Krieger. I said I was going to call, remember?" She waved at a tiny, doll-like woman in sweatpants, whose turtle-neck covered the scar from her suicide attempt. "So how many of you guys feel like going on a little run, in about half an hour?"

After she hung up, Anne-Marie shrugged into her jacket and started on the same paved path as the O'Donnells, toward Chatham. In the distance she could see Shaun's protective arm around his sister, as if she were a small child. Anne-Marie wished she could see Emma's face.

"She just turned two . . . but she can say her numbers and her alphabet already. I'm so proud!"

Shana had spread photos all over Molly's bed—each one picturing a ruddy toddler with round, laughing brown eyes not unlike her own. In the infant pictures, the child looked wrinkled, somehow elderly; the more recent shots showed a fleshy, inquisitive baby, wielding Legos in her chubby little hands.

Molly lay along the edge of her bed, a mother cat protecting the photos from harm. The cast was back on her elbow: in throwing the chair at Gary, she had re-torn all the ligaments and disrupted a few bone fragments. She maneuvered carefully and picked up a partic-ularly recent photo; then she lay on her back, holding it up above her eyes. "Is she happy you're coming home soon?"

"Oh Lucy, she's only a baby, I'm not telling her yet. . ." Shana's voice trailed off. "Not till I'm good and ready." She knelt by the bed, began to collect the photos.

Molly offered the one she was holding. "Does she look like her daddy?"

Shana closed her mouth, her gleeful grin somehow trapped within. When she finally spoke, it was with a completely uncharacteristic flatness, as if she were some older person. "Not yet—and I pray every night she don't."

Molly sat up for a moment, looking carefully at Shana, who was collecting the photos into a pile.

"Lucy, I pray every night for God to strike him dead, in case he ever wants to come back and marry my mama again."

Molly lay on her back and closed her eyes, the muscles in her body tensing one by one, as if each limb in turn needed to hear Shana's words. She didn't reply.

"Lucy? You okay?"

Molly opened her eyes with great difficulty, and fixed them on Shana. The younger woman sat closer, smiling again.

"Hey look, I learned from you what to do! If he comes back, I just go pooh-CHUNG! with her old armchair, break his fuckin leg!"

Molly finally smiled, and sat up; she began to swing her legs back and forth, as she did in singalong. She whispered darkly, "Improper frictions and maledictions and mens uration makes me mad!" Shana burst into giggles, taking Molly along.

They were still laughing when the door opened; Shaun and Emma entered the room, followed by Anne-Marie and Kepler. Molly pointed to Shaun. "Like him!"

"Hello, ladies," Kepler said. "Mr. O'Donnell, Mrs. Gahagan, this is Shana Bolt, one of our other patients."

"I know Shana," Emma said. "And this is our brother, Shaun."

Molly grinned as she stood taller, striding over to her brother's side with a faux-masculine walk and speaking in in a fair imitation of an Irish accent. "With his broad and hairy face," she told Shana, "to Ireland he's a disgrace."

Shana nodded, pinching a smile close together between her

teeth; "Time to go back to my room," she said to all assembled. Anne-Marie closed the door behind her.

Shaun swallowed. "Hello Molly, you're looking very pretty today." His voice was neutral, no attempt to force sincerity—especially given Molly's masculine stance, her face bare of the makeup he'd complimented on his last visit.

Molly turned to the others and pointed to herself, and then to her brother. "Shem and Shaun," she said. "Nick and Mike and all yore maggies!"

Anne-Marie moved closer, comprehension dawning on her face. "Always fighting," she said. "Mark and Tristan, too, right Molly?"

Molly grinned and put her arm around Anne-Marie's shoulders, a teacher congratulating a star pupil. "I am suggesting to you, again I say, this Shaun Mac Irewick is a sham and a scam." Then she turned to Shaun. "Sure, teasure, a woman do be saying things that make no sense."

Shaun turned to Kepler. "I've seen enough," he said. "Let's go back to your office and conclude our agreement."

"You two go ahead," said Emma. She then said to Molly, "I brought our running stuff. I'm not sure but—I think I might still run the Marathon." Molly's eyes widened; her stance softened as she went over to Emma, and touched her shoulder. "Dear sister in perfect love," she said, almost in a whisper.

Behind her back Kepler was shaking his head. "Absolutely not. You don't have grounds privileges yet, Molly."

"What," said Emma, "do you think she's going to break my leg?"

"You don't understand," Kepler said. "It's just too risky."

"It's all right," said Molly. "We can dance together, here." She pointed to her little fake-barre arrangement, a plastic chair in place of the one she had thrown at Gary. "I used to be good at it . . ." She stepped away from Emma and lowered her gaze to the floor. "I was hoping to be a real artist," she said, "but the newspapers say that I had a breakdown, instead. Or something like that." She sat in the chair and bent her head into her hands, fingers buried in her black hair.

Anne-Marie stepped to face Kepler; with the nine-inch difference in their heights she could have been his daughter coming in late after curfew, right up to her calm, quietly hostile eyes. "You don't get it," she said. "I've already set it up."

"Set what up?"

"This whole thing. I've got two of your hunky psychiatric interns all set, as soon as I page them—all ready to come with us, jogging their lunch breaks away. Plus Steve. What more do we need, a SWAT team?"

Kepler looked at his watch. "Mr. O'Donnell," he said, turning away from Anne-Marie as if the confrontation had not occurred. "I'm late for a meeting—let's meet tomorrow morning, to put our agreement in writing."

Rancho Harbor was the jewel of the Baltimore tourist and singles crowds: a dark-wood-and-brass restaurant bar with a vaguely Mexican motif, it sat at the tip of Harborplace right where the land jutted out into Chesapeake Bay. Most of the waitresses seemed blond and eternally tan, college girls with bouncy ponytails or clingy perms above their perfect smiles and Mexican-flag aprons.

Even Felicia, behind the bar, was toned down; all tattoos covered by her long-sleeved uniform shirt, she wore only one earring in each ear, and her peach-fuzz of brown hair was hidden by the little straw hat and red Tex-Mex scarf.

"This is perfect, right after lunch," she said as she poured two glasses of white wine for Emma and Anne-Marie. "Just enough business so my boss doesn't notice you, but not so busy I'll get in trouble for talking to someone." She saluted them with her own glass of mineral water. "A toast—to diCesare finally getting his! . . . God, Molly should have busted his ass a long time ago. "

"Except we almost lost Molly sooner," Anne-Marie cautioned.

"Oh Christ." Felicia drained her glass. "Em, you been to this Park Grove place, right? So what's it like?"

Emma took a deep breath before answering. "It's clean," she said. "It's pretty crowded—but it's clean." She swallowed. "I keep wondering if Shaun has already given up on her."

"Where's that jerk Kepler about all this?"

Anne-Marie shrugged. "Like me, he'd prefer to keep her at JPI."

"Yeah," said Emma, "but him and Shaun, they speak the same language. They've got that contract now: maximum needed restraint, it says."

"Oh fucking shit. I gotta ask the lawyer about that." Felicia looked over to the other side of the bar; a portly couple, all in white including their hair, was hailing her from the other end. "Hey, I'll be right back," and she was gone.

Emma looked at her watch. "I told Shaun to meet me here at four thirty," she said. "It's a long drive, back to Boston."

Anne-Marie winced. "I thought you and I were going to talk, today. Without Shaun around."

"Wasn't it enough, what I sent you?"

Anne-Marie opened her shoulder bag, extracting a long letter, elegantly laser-printed. "You mean this? When I asked you to write me about you and Molly?"

"Hey, I'm not a writer." Emma closed her eyes and drank half her wine, one long pour down her throat. "What were you looking for?"

"Something more than this." Anne-Marie lay the pages on the bar, and traced a few lines with her fingertip. It was hard to hear her inner voice read, with the mariachi music coming over the loud-speakers. *Sacred Heart was very strict, most of us were always getting in trouble but*

not Molly. All the teachers loved her, especially of course her cello teachers, but also her English teachers because she already

299

knew so much James Joyce and Shakespeare, from helping Poppie. Poppie was very upset when Molly decided to go to New York to go to college, but he knew it was best.

"I thought it would be easier to talk about feelings, if you could just write them down."

Anne-Marie looked down at the bar, speaking to Emma's reflection in the smooth dark wood. "So whose office printer did you use?" She held the glossy document up to the light. "Shaun's?"

Then it was Emma's turn to look down. "Yeah."

Anne-Marie lifted her wine, staring at the tiny air bubbles. "Okay," she said slowly. "I guess I should give up gracefully. I'm sorry to have made you uncomfortable."

"I'm sorry too," Emma said. When Felicia returned, bearing bowls of tortilla chips and salsa, Emma reached gratefully for a handful of chips before continuing. "I'm trying to work this stuff out, with my therapist and my ACA group," she said, each word escaping slowly, as if precious,

"What stuff?" Felicia asked.

Felicia and Anne-Marie had to lean toward Emma to hear her soft words, over the music. "Oh, how I let Shaun boss me around . . . and how little of my own childhood I actually remember."

Anne-Marie and Felicia exchanged wordless glances. "I didn't realize . . . that you were doing that sort of therapy work," Anne-Marie said quietly.

Emma shrugged. "I wasn't, till this all happened with Molly. It's very slow—I spend a lot of time in sessions being completely silent. And as for talking to you about it? " She shook her head. "I just can't."

The three women sipped in silence for a while, letting the plaintive Spanish voices have the empty space. The bar was filling up; on Anne-Marie's other side, a tall blond man in a cowboy hat was telling another man, "I mean the girl was pretty all right, but then I find out she's forty-two and has had her tubes tied. What am I supposed to do with something' like that?"

By the time Shaun arrived, Emma had already finished off all the chips and salsa and a second glass of wine. Felicia was saying, "Anne-Marie, you said you were finally making progress. Can you tell me—"

"Emma! Where are you?" Shaun was pushing his way past the blond waitresses; Anne-Marie sighed and signaled him, an unenthusiastic wave. Emma buttoned her coat, nervously.

"Okay," Shaun said to his sister without preamble, "we're all packed—your stuff too, I just kind of threw it in your overnight bag. C'mon, I'm not even sure I'm parked legally."

Emma accepted a goodbye hug from Anne-Marie, a light kiss from Felicia. "Don't worry," she told Felicia. "I wouldn't miss your opening for anything!"

"I'll call you later this week," Felicia said. "After I've—" She looked over at Shaun. "After I hear from my friend." As they left, Anne-Marie folded Emma's letter and put it back into her shoulder bag.

"I'm sorry it's so busy now" and Felicia was off again, running the big blender for a pitcher of margaritas.

When she came back Anne-Marie said, "Listen, why don't we just talk tomorrow or something?"

"Cause I want to know what I can tell this lawyer, damn it!" The swearword was good-natured, slightly out of breath from racing along the bar.

"Okay, what can I can say quickly before they make me buy another margarita?" Anne-Marie pulled out a small notebook, labeled simply O'DONNELL. "What I meant by 'progress' was, I'm seeing a few signs of self-awareness on Molly's part. Like, she's mostly still immersed in this persona of hers, the one that's got Kepler all unglued cause he can't diagnose her easily—"

"Oh poor baby." Felicia grinned, the way she had when talking about Gary's injury.

301

Anne-Marie's mouth tightened, suppressing a smile. "But every once in a while, just for a second or two, I meet a different Molly. Someone kinda high-strung, sarcastic, a little scared." She finished the last of her wine. "I hope I can get to know her better—sometime before they come to haul her up north." She looked down again at Emma's letter, which was slipped in between pages of the notebook. "In the meantime—I know I asked you about family stuff before . . ." She waited a moment for Felicia to pour a draft beer for the cowboy and then said quickly, "Just think for now, and we'll talk later—please remember everything you can, that Molly might have said about her father."

Felicia nodded, distracted. Anne-Marie kept turning back to watch her, on her way out of the restaurant; Felicia spilled someone's vodka tonic as she was handing the tray to a waitress, then handed over a roll of paper towels to clean it up. Anne-Marie felt similarly clumsy, and had trouble remembering where she had parked her car.

Open art activity in the rear dayroom: often a popular event, it was crowded today due to the upcoming Halloween party. Shana's hands were wrapped in yards and yards of white netting, from some nurse's ex-wedding gown; she and Molly were singing in close harmony.

Molly sat with a spandex unitard of Felicia's, drawing on it with a grease pencil; then she handed it to Steve, wordlessly, pointing at the scissors.

Felicia Waller clapped, from the doorway. "Very nice, ladies!" She went over to Molly and picked up the unitard, frowning: as instructed by Molly, the volunteer had cut one of the legs completely off. "Why did you do that, Moll?"

"It's for my silver fish costume!" Molly held up the other leg, covered now with silver sequins, the sickly-sweet smell of Elmer's Glue matching the antiseptic smell of the ward.

"We're doing Halloween," Shana explained. "And also my go-away party."

Felicia nodded, slowly. "Listen, I didn't know you were busy, do you want me to—"

"No don't go." Molly handed the unitard to Steve like a birthday present. "She's terrifically nice really," she told the group, as she stood up to leave the room.

Felicia followed Molly out of the room and down the hall, the sound of her spike-heeled boots echoing in the silence outside the dayroom. When they got to Molly's room, Felicia volunteered, "Hey that was pretty rich, what you did with Gary. I'd have held him down, if I were here."

Molly took Felicia's hand, shaking her head. "I still didn't hurt him enough," she whispered. She was looking beyond Felicia, to an unseen point, her jaw slack with rage. "I want to *blind* him."

"Oh sweetie," Felicia said gently, "love is always blind."

"No no no no no," Molly insisted. "You don't know."

Felicia slung her backpack off her shoulder onto the bed. "It's gotten so cold, I brought some of your winter clothes," she said. "Remember I kept borrowing these flannel jeans? I finally got a pair myself, I don't even have to roll 'em up."

Molly nodded, holding the clothing bundle close to her chest. "My running shoes?"

"They're kinda trashed, Moll—but yeah, I brought them. Speaking of which—you gonna get to watch the Marathon on TV, maybe you'll see Emma?"

Molly shook her head. "They will not have me here," she said slowly. "They want to send me away."

"Who does?"

"Shaun the Post, of course. That fat materialistic Swiss man, he thinks he can get hold of my soul!"

Felicia laughed. "Molly, sweetheart, I don't think anyone can get hold of your soul." She looked around the room, still festooned with drawings. "Hey, this could be one of our smaller galleries, right here! . . . Listen, I'm gonna try to make them let you come to the opening, get you out on a pass again. I don't care about Gary's fuckin leg, it'll be criminal if you can't."

Molly nodded, without speaking. She sat on her bed with her back against the wall, staring wordlessly into her empty sneakers. Felicia sat beside her, began to rub her shoulders. "I'm also working on getting you out of here, away from Shaun and Kepler and the lot."

Molly looked up and behind her to face Felicia, every muscle tightening at once. "But he put me here," she said quietly, tears behind her words. "Sender: Boston, Mass."

"Honey, if I were you, with your family, I wouldn't accept delivery from anything postmarked Boston. Except maybe from Emma."

Molly nodded. "My brave little sister," she said, and lowered her head again, her face wet. She looked up suddenly. "You haven't given her—"

"No, of course not," Felicia said soothingly.

Molly swallowed her tears and relaxed against Felicia's massage. "How's Jeff?"

"Oh, he's a little moody sometimes, but he's been great with the show and everything—thank God, I am so sick of breaking up with people! . . . Did you know I was gonna be thirty next month? I'm too old for that shit, breaking up, spending six months just crying and eating."

Molly twisted away suddenly, gesturing for Felicia to turn so she could return the massage. She slipped her hand under Felicia's shirt, resting it on her spine. "Are you healing?" she asked. "How is the baby?"

"What? . . . Oh you mean the baby on my back? He's fine and fat, as always. . . . and yeah, he's all healed up. It's been years now, that tattoo."

"But you're not all healed," Molly insisted. She put her hands

304

on Felicia's shoulders, then began to run her thumbs up her neck toward her scalp.

For a moment Felicia didn't reply, listening instead to Shana's giggle echoing down the hall, shouts from the dayroom as patients vied to clean up the crayons. Finally she said "Oh yeah, right there. You sure know how to find it, don't you?"

Molly's face was wet as she began to sing, her throaty blues voice.

Ain't never had a man
But mistreat me in my life
Ain't never had a man
But mistreat me in my life
My father, my brother
The man who wrecked my life . . .

"Man, the blues do hit home sometimes, don't they?" Felicia turned to look at her friend just as Molly's face was hardening, her eyes hooded, suspicious. In the doorway was the reason: the medication nurse, today a large woman with far too many pills on her palm. "C'mon Molly, it's time!"

"HURRY UP PLEASE IT'S TIME," Molly grinned. "When Lil's husband got demobbed . . ." She stopped, pointed to an unfamiliar pill. "Lithium?"

"Yes, dearie, a little more than before. Your doctor decided it was best."

Molly nodded, wide-eyed and docile. "I like it here very much," she told Felicia. She swallowed loudly, as always; the nurse didn't leave until she had drunk the whole glass of orange juice. "Nuee! Nuee!" she called after the nurse; then she trotted off to the bathroom in skipping, adolescent high spirits.

She stayed there for a few minutes, leaving Felicia to contemplate the rage of drawings taped to the walls. Soon Felicia heard

Molly singing softly to herself: "I'm forever blowing bubbles, pretty bubbles in the air."

Felicia walked around the room, until she found the drawing that declared *C'est moi qui est l'artiste!* And then she was crying, for the first time in the entire three months of Molly's hospitalization—trying, with some success, to keep her tears both silent and still.

Anne-Marie pulled her hat tighter over her ears as she and Molly emerged from Chatham into the semi-dark of seven a.m. Anne-Marie was bundled in sweats, Molly in her cold-resistant spandex. "Look at all that frost—and it's not even November yet!"

Molly was busy with one last stretch, her face against her ankle; when she pulled herself upright she replied, "No, but it's novembrance day."

With that they began, their cheeks frosted red by the chill, springing forward in matching, brand-new Avia running shoes (purchased by Anne Marie at a two-for-one sale). Cheers came down from the smoking porch, on the second floor of the main building. "Go for it, girls!" By now both patients and staff at Pearlstone were used to watching the two figures cross the grounds; one of the newer patients at Chatham, a burned-out history professor, made a point on their return of checking their time, with his special watch that showed the time in all the great capitals of the world.

As they rounded past the weeping willows, Anne-Marie said, "Listen Moll, we gotta talk."

"Word words words," said Molly. "Which will fall up?"

Anne-Marie sighed. "Molly, are you aware that Shaun wants to take you to another hospital? What do you want?"

Molly kept turning around, watching the convoy of psychiatric residents comparing watches behind them. *"Go down, Moses! Go down, Moses! Tell old Pharaoh, to let my people go!"*

Anne-Marie smiled, finally. "Okay that was loud and clear. . . .

but you're not making it easy for any of us to get you out. And this Park Grove place, Molly—I don't trust state hospitals, they're kinda like prisons with doctors."

They ran silently, until the residents were far enough behind to be nowhere near earshot. Finally Molly murmured something to the wind, muffled by the hood of her sweatshirt; Anne-Marie came closer, winded by Molly's running pace. "What did you say, Molly?"

"I said, maybe I belong in prison."

"Why, Molly, because of Gary?" Anne-Marie wished for the security of her notepad, hoping to extract some gold and preserve it on the page. But the younger woman just shook her head and ran faster, with far more speed than Anne-Marie would try—and then paid for it about five yards away, retching into a frozen puddle. "Are you all right, Molly?"

The patient nodded, wiping her lips with a tissue. "It happens sometimes."

"Did Poppie ever watch you and Emma run a marathon?" Anne Marie asked, using one of the few gems she'd been able to glean from Emma's benign little essay.

Molly lifted her head and stared at Anne-Marie. "Poppie?"

"Isn't that what you called him?"

Molly shook her head, viciously, and stood up. "Will," she said softly, "Only Will."

"When we go back inside, can we talk about Will?" Anne-Marie spoke slowly, carefully, trying to measure the effect each word had on Molly. "Don't you think it's time?"

Molly's response was to spring forward like a jackrabbit, again outdistancing Anne-Marie. When the social worker caught up with her Molly was already shadowed by the young psychiatrists-in-training, her rage turned to brittle teasing. She looked at the younger of the two of them, who looked like his preferred sport was probably TV.

"Feeling like you is lost in the bush, boy?" Molly asked him.

"Me too." She bent her knee and leaned her left arm on it, the cast an unfamiliar bulge under her sweater: her hand was clenched.

Anne-Marie came over to her other side. "Molly do you want me to forget about Will?"

Molly looked from side to side as she ran again, until the interns stayed still and let Molly and Anne-Marie run past them. Finally she cast a sentence out onto the wind. "You need the book of the dark," she said.

"Oh God, not *Finnegans Wake,* again," Anne-Marie said. "I actually tried, you know, but I can't make head or tail of the thing.

Molly laughed. "Oh, the river has its rewards. Though it may trip you, by and by."

"I feel like it already has," Anne-Marie said. "I might drown."

"One of us diving, the other drowning!" Molly started to laugh, and couldn't seem to stop, giggles choking her breath as they ran. Anne-Marie concentrated on her own breathing, waiting to see if Molly would stop there.

As they reached the oak tree, the younger woman said "No, I mean my nonday diary."

"Your journals, Molly? . . . You mean you didn't destroy them?"

Molly didn't reply, just kept running faster, sweat like melted ice on her forehead. The sky settled into full morning as they ran in silence, approaching the entrance. Then Anne-Marie said, "Molly, do you want me to look at those notebooks? Where are they?"

Molly looked at her sideways. "Kate Strong. . . . She holds the keys, she can make out the bruises in print."

Anne-Marie slowed down; this time, Molly echoed her slower pace. "I'm not wearing my James Joyce decoder ring today, Molly. Who do you mean, when you say Kate Strong?"

Molly paused a moment before she answered. "She lives, breathes and sleeps color," she said, then spurted forward for a final sprint.

The social worker slowed to a walk, watching the athlete emerge in Molly, a focused, intense escape from the exhausting demands of her pain. Sometimes the run would change to a dance, a tiny stop for a little soft-shoe on the frosty dead grass. The sunrise had softened the bitter chill, so that Anne-Marie's sweat was turned to cold water instead of ice.

She lives, breathes and sleeps color, Anne-Marie said softly to herself, remembering a studio daubed with oil paints, a back tattooed in fiery red. The drawing of Molly from her first week in the hospital was still on the wall in Molly's room, Felicia had not taken it for her show next week—an important omission, one Anne-Marie would point out when she called her, that evening.

Shana was a ghost wrapped in white netting, dancing to "The Monster Mash."

The big family visitors' room at Pearlstone had been transformed, black and orange streamers beribboning the light fixtures, walls covered with artwork from both the Level A and Level B groups: wild collages, cutouts of ghosts and goblins, aimless line drawings that curled along the corners. A sheet of heavy black cloth had been hung across the doorway, and the volunteers and interns had conspired with Gail to create a Halloween party tape with appropriate spooky hits. Gail was got up as a gypsy, bright makeup, a full skirt and costume jewelry, her hair in a bright scarf.

The layers of white netting surrounded Shana like a bridal veil, submerging her short white dress as well as the arms, legs and face painted white. She reached out to the history professor in his Robin Hood hat and one of the nurses, a heavy-set woman who laughed as Shana enfolded them both in her net. "C'mon, dance!"

When she approached Clay, he shook his head and pointed to his paper plate, laden with a slice from the enormous orange sheet cake on one of the coffee tables. Then he put the plate down so he could help pull aside the black cloth covering the doorway, as the rest of the Chatham contingent entered—led by Molly, in a bowler hat. "It's Charlie's 30 Year Musical Reminiscence," she explained.

Molly's slender body was now covered with silver, green at the edges; one leg emerged from the sequins and ended in a silver-green ballet slipper. The other leg covered in silver right down to the stirruped foot. The bowler hat sat incongruously, precariously atop her head. Though her mood seemed elevated to Gail, Molly didn't join the others in the rock and roll dancing; instead the girl in the silver fish costume handed a cassette tape to one of the volunteers.

As the volunteer stared at the un-labeled tape Gail said, "Molly, we have Halloween music today! Remember, we're also celebrating for Shana." Gail turned off the tape deck and said, "Okay everyone, listen up! Now that we're all here, I think we need to give Shana a proper sendoff—she's going home tomorrow!"

The patients surrounded the ghost in a vaguely circular clump, Molly moving in a swaying motion to unheard music. Clay started the round of applause and all joined in, a few commenting, "We'll miss you so much!" Molly stepped forward, the male aides rising in alert at the motion. She pulled the layers of veiling away from Shana's face, and kissed her on the lips, quickly. "Ti abbracio," she said softly.

Shana blinked, in seeming comprehension—then said, "Hey, Lucy. Let's dance!"

Molly let Shana enfold her in the netting for a while, while the tape player sang out "Werewolves of London." By the time the tape ended she had moved away, and was sitting by the boom box staring up at the volunteer. "Please," she said, an unusual, pleading note in her voice. "Babbo sang it for me."

Finally Gail nodded, and instead of rock and roll piano, glissandos slipped across the room, as Molly began to dance. She took off the bowler hat and put it down, the rest of the group turning to watch her as she moved slowly through a set of careful, angular motions.

Then a tenor voice, issuing from the boom box:

Oh Danny boy, the pipes, the pipes are calling
From glen to glen and down the mountainside
The summer's gone and all the flowers are dying
It's you, it's you must go and I must bide.

Gail recognized the voice: Jim Keene's, from a mini-recital he had given during his brief stay at JPI. Molly's slow, deliberate motions were curiously abstract, in stark contrast to the melancholy of the song.

But come ye back, when summer's in the meadow
Or when the valley's hushed and white with snow
It's I'll be here, in sunshine or in shadow
Oh Danny boy, oh Danny boy, I love you so.

When the song was over, Molly sank to the floor in a violent, Twyla Tharp motion. "Molly," asked the history professor from under a Robin Hood hat, "who is Babbo?"

Molly looked up from the floor. "He had a lovely voice."

Gail squatted to face the patient. "Did he, Molly?"

"But he had blood in his eyes," Molly whispered in Gail's ear.

With that Molly brought her knees to her chest and pulled her head down, wrapping herself into a ball; after a moment her shoulders began to shake.

"Do you want to go back now, Molly?" Gail asked.

Molly waited a long time before she answered, Clay squatted beside Gail, holding out his hands. "C'mon Moll, remember me? Want me to take you home?"

Finally she raised her head; her face was wet. "He said I danced very well."

"And he was right," said Clay. To Gail he said, "I'll get her back."

"Me too!" Shana was also in tears.

"No," Gail said gently. "Just let them go." She cursed herself for allowing this performance the day before Shana's discharge, and pulled the tape out of the boom box, setting it to one side with the bowler hat. She would give both to Kepler.

The ghost watched as the pair left the room, while others turned away, moving over toward the sheet cake or the box of toys right next to the table. Finally Shana accepted a piece of cake from Cindy and looked curiously into the box, with its little rubber monsters and tiny broomsticks.

Gail stood up straighter, relieved. "Okay, everyone, we have half an hour left—and we still have a whole list of terrific Halloween games."

"God I hate it when the sun sets at fucking four-thirty in the afternoon." Felicia wrapped a shawl around her bare shoulders, above a floor-length black vintage dress. She was staring at the mirror, which flashed a wan reflection. "Emma, are you ready?"

"Just a minute."

"It's beautiful out," Rachel called to Felicia as she walked out their front door, wearing a green velvet dress with an embroidered bodice.

Felicia looked out at the buildings along the street, distracted. Her face was even paler than usual, large circles under her eyes uncovered by makeup. The fancy dress seemed to soften the slow, chilly air inside Rachel's VW Bug: Felicia's thrift-store chic contrasted with Rachel's medieval look, the green dress matching the ribbons in her braided hair. Emma wore a long paisley dress that swept below her knees, her hair permed into long gentle banana curls.

Felicia looked listlessly in the direction of East Baltimore, her eyes belying her defiant words. "I thought we'd get Molly out tonight," she said. "I even invited the lawyer to this thing. Not that he could make it."

"Wasn't he supposed to visit her this week?"

"Yeah but guess where she was, on the day of the appointment." Felicia turned to look at Emma in the back seat, her face grim. "C'mon, say it with me—she was in seclusion!" She turned back, staring almost defiantly out the front windshield, tapping her fingers on the dashboard. She didn't move right away when Rachel pulled up to the front door of the gallery, a few blocks past the Inner Harbor's waterfront tourists.

"C'mon, Felicia, you want to miss your big night?" Rachel leaned over and kissed her roommate on the cheek. "Come on—you two get out, and I'll park."

Felicia got out of the car, then helped Emma squeeze out of the back. "I've got to get my energy up if I'm gonna schmooze all the richies on my mailing list." Her voice still almost toneless, depressed. "Not that I really feel like selling any of Molly. . . . I guess tonight I get to be the stereotype of the 'deeply troubled artist.' Especially once they check out the tattoos." She shook Emma's hand, to demonstrate: the snake on her wrist jumped, seemed to come alive.

As they entered a small group had arrived early, business people making the gallery circuit early on First Thursday before driving home to the suburbs. "These guys might actually buy something," Felicia whispered to Emma; when Rachel came in Felicia assumed her position by the hors d'oeuvres table with a faded smile, answering questions from tourists and stockbrokers. The tone of the evening was then firmly set by the singing notes of a Bach cello suite, coming out of a pair of large speakers in either corner of the gallery.

The sign perched on the pillar by the door read simply, FELICIA WALLER: *Drawings and Mixed Media*—but the face everywhere was Molly's. Molly lying flat on the floor, staring at nothing, her arms positioned above her head as if bound; Molly lying on her side, her ribs clearly showing, eyes fixed on the viewer.

"God they look so different in this place," Rachel said to Emma. Some were bare line drawings, but most were full of color, or overlaid with collage material. To one drawing Felicia had added photo-copies of pages of *Finnegans Wake*; on another she had lined Molly's back with ghostly faces, as if Molly and not herself bore a body full of tattoos. Felicia's own tattoos were in full view this evening, her strapless dress low in the back.

"So will you be able to visit Molly more easily now?" Rachel asked. "Once she's moved, I mean."

Emma had fixed her gaze on a saucy, erotic Molly image, her legs spread and one hand just tracing her pubic hair, Felicia's face in ghostly shadow behind her. She winced at Rachel's question. "Worcester's more than an hour away . . . and their visiting policy is pretty strict, maybe two hours three times a week."

"So how do you feel about it?" Rachel asked, as they moved toward the refreshment table.

"Listen for all its flaws, JPI is—" Emma stopped dead as they came up to Felicia's back; she stared at Siqueiros' raging brown-faced child, its screams mingling with Bach to complete Molly's multiple faces.

Felicia turned to face them. "Thank you for the tape," she said. "Everyone's been asking me who the cellist is . . and when I say it's my model, they freak out."

Emma nodded. "That was the only recital she ever gave, at Juilliard."

"Yeah, before she met Colin West-East Eat-shit-and-die. Listen I gotta mingle but let's talk later, okay? About the lawyer and stuff?" She was gone before Emma could respond.

The gallery was filling up, students and other artists supplanting the suburbanites beginning to wind their way home. Over the speakers Molly guided Bach through some of his most vigorous, rough-hewn sections. "I want to draw her playing the cello someday," Felicia had said when Emma gave her the tape.

Rachel had moved away, toward a series of smaller drawings showing Molly in fast-forward, when the voice came at Emma's shoulder:

"Emma? Emma O'Donnell?" When Emma turned, she saw a young woman in a khaki jumpsuit and leather jacket, with razor-short hair and a nose ring. Her eyes widened, her lips searching for a name. "Julie?" she tried, uncertainly.

The girl smiled triumphantly. "Close. Jessie," she said, extending her hand. "We ran together, last summer—you and Molly and I."

Emma tipped her head to one side. "You've cut your hair," she said.

Jessie grinned. "Just evened it out," she said. "Though it was hard to part with the braids." She gestured around the gallery. "So where's our model?"

Emma bit her lip. "Molly . . . hasn't been feeling well."

"That's too bad. . . . Oh well, I 'm sure she'll get to see it before it closes, anyhow." The softness in the last phrase blotted Jessie's tough mannerisms. "I'm just glad I got to see it—I moved back to New York in September, but I came back for some business."

"Business? Was it successful?" Emma asked.

Jessie grinned. "Wildly. I'll be able to write in peace for at least a year . . . So are you two still planning to run the Marathon?"

"Molly can't," Emma said, "but I think I will. Molly wants me to. I think."

Jessie was already writing on a small Post-it, retrieved from her shoulder bag. "In case you don't want to run alone," she said, "here's my number. I've got a crew of about four." She turned, in response to a shout from across the room. "Hey, I'm sorry I found you so late, I was actually on my way out." She zipped her jacket and wrapped an Arab scarf around her head. "So give me a call, maybe in a couple of weeks—let me know when you're gonna hit New York."

"Sure," Emma said uncertainly.

As Jessie left, her energy was matched by a sea of percussion, one that obliterated Bach in its wake. A scruffy band of bearded and bandanaed young men had entered the gallery—one with a small bongo drum strapped to his waist, others adding gourds and tambourines and bells. The gallery owner rushed over to quiet them, but not before they surrounded Felicia; the two without instruments lifted her above their shoulders, a soccer team congratulating its star player.

After she stopped laughing, Felicia said "Okay guys, cut it, it's the wrong time of year for Carnival!" As she was lowered, Felicia pointed to the man on her right, saying to Emma, "this is my boyfriend Jeff . And this is Philip," kissing the forehead of a short, wiry man with wild curly hair extending halfway down his back. "He knows Anne-Marie."

By the time Anne-Marie herself arrived, most of the crowd had left the gallery, some of Felicia's friends helping the gallery's owner clean up after the hors d'oeuvres. The young redhead rushed in breathlessly, carrying three different kinds of bags—a backpack, a long loose shoulder bag, and a fanny pack slung over one shoulder like a semiautomatic weapon. "I'm glad I made it," she said, running over to Felicia. "I-83 was an absolute nightmare." She then dropped half the bags as Philip caught her from behind, lifting her off her feet: "Hello stranger!"

After the gallery closed, a small group wandered over to the Inner Harbor and walked along the water; they had to maneuver among tourists taking photos of the U.S.S. *Constitution*, a nineteenth-century battleship now permanently harbored for visitor pleasure. Anne-Marie lingered, moving more slowly than the rest; she knelt by the water and stared, as if counting the reflections of the streetlights.

"So you're telling me," Felicia said slowly, her eyes fixed on Emma's face, "that you'd prefer Molly stay at JPI."

Emma nodded. "I don't want her to lose what she's gained."

Felicia turned away and lit a cigarette, looking over at the battleship as her boyfriend came up behind her. "Hey Felizia, did you see how long the guy from BaltimArts stayed? Did he ask you for slides?"

Felicia turned to look at him, distracted. "Um . . . yeah he did."

"And Brian from the D.C. gallery—he didn't stay long but he came all that way!" Jeff's voice was loud, strong; Felicia winced, as if it hurt her ears.

"We can talk shop later, Jeff," she said, "okay?"

Jeff sighed. "You're talking shop." He slowed down and let Felicia, Anne-Marie and Emma walk ahead of him.

Felicia turned back to Emma. "How come Shaun gets to call the shots? Just 'cause he's older?"

Emma shrugged. "I'm outvoted," she said. "Shaun and Anna together make sort of an irresistible force." She turned to Anne-Marie. "Listen, tell me about hearings," Emma said, "you've seen them. Do we go to a courtroom?"

"No it would happen at JPI. Kepler would testify, and me, and members of the family—and Felicia, if she's willing to be responsible for Molly."

Emma stopped, looking over at the battleship. "Let's see if we can do it," she said. "Let a judge decide what Molly really needs."

Anne-Marie cleared her throat. "Emma I was wondering last night," she said, "about your brother Leo. What does he think about all this?"

"Leo?" Emma's eyes widened. "Who the hell knows? He never answers my phone calls. I haven't seen hide nor hair of him in 4 years or so."

"There's another brother?" Felicia turned, carefully, remaining close to the edge of the water. "Shit I thought I knew the whole family by now. Where the fuck has he been?"

"In San Francisco. Anna's been leaving messages on his machine about what's going on, but he never calls back. He doesn't keep in touch, normally. That's probably why you've never heard of him."

"I love San Francisco," Felicia said, in something of a non sequitur. The evening chill was bringing out goosebumps on her shoulders, but when Jeff offered her his down jacket, she shook her head. "I'm also starving."

"So what next?" Jeff was back, pulling his Greek fishing cap more tightly over his ears. "Indian food?"

"If we do Indian food one more time," said Philip, "I'm gonna start talking with an accent."

After the decision was made to move to Thai instead, the scraggly band turned away from the water. Felicia stopped and looked behind her, past the battleship out into the Chesapeake Bay —as if she were looking west instead of east, and could somehow make out the slender skyline of San Francisco if only she looked hard enough.

Ward sounds, 2 a.m.: the wheels of supply trucks, the soft gossip of aides and nurses, early Beatles from the radio at the nurse's station. Few noises penetrated from behind the closed doors of patients' rooms, beyond the occasional low moan of someone crying out his dreams. Behind one closed door, whispers in the dark:

Move over, there's no room.

It's cold in here. Soft rustle of blankets and sheets, wrapping tightly.

Now move up.

But then I can't reach you.

No but I can reach you. . . . Here.

Oh my God, the tight surprised whisper. *Oh yes, oh yes oh yes oh yes . . . Come back to me.*

Wait a minute. Stillness as a laundry cart passed, its wheels creaking, a sweet whistle from the attendant pushing it along the hall.

I think it's okay, now. Movements gentle, imperceptible beyond the door—even the quickening pace, the last groan, the final murmur into the soft flesh of a shoulder: *Ah ah ah ah ah ah—amen.*

. . .

Dan Kepler, smelling of aftershave, led a small convoy of nurses and aides to the seclusion room, with a brisk, no-nonsense morning walk. One of the nurses carried the telltale aluminum briefcase, the one that had provoked Molly into hours of screaming fits. They passed the dayroom, where a few early-rising patients watched *The Price is Right*—a contestant was jumping up and down at the prospect of a new Chevrolet, her excitement echoed by one of the newer patients in tiny, sluggish leaps.

"She's not likely to be violent," Kepler said to the rest, "but I do expect a certain amount of resistance."

Molly lay on the bare mattress in the middle of the room, her hair touching the floor; but she was not asleep. She was singing in German, one hand twined in her hair. When she saw them she sat up and looked at Kepler, and started to laugh. "My! It's Papli! But Papli, how old you've grown!"

Kepler moved closer, slowly. "Are you ready to come out now, Molly?"

"Come out?" She repeated the words slowly, as if it Kepler had spoken in a foreign language. "Excuse me sir and forgive me for trespassing, but it's you who put me in this hell."

"You understand why, Molly."

Molly looked down at the floor again, nodding seriously. "We were too happy," she said. "I knew something would happen when we conjugated together, verbe de vie and verve to vie, love have I on my back spine. . . . Good God, cry of shame!" She drew her knees close, and put her head down.

Kepler knelt by the other edge of the mattress, until Molly lifted her head to look at him. He gestured to the nurse with the metal case.

Molly looked confused, then recognized the nurse from countless other mornings of refusal. "Oh! It's you again, intruding on the only privacy I have in the world."

Kepler sighed. "Molly, this time we're not going away. Unless we test your blood, we can't help you get better. You have to let us do this before we can let you out of seclusion. Do you understand?"

Molly sighed, then gestured past him to the nurse. "Blind me," she said, waving her hand for the nurse to come closer. "Go ahead, spill blood into the Seine. Anna Liffey's already red here."

The nurse looked at Kepler, uncertainly; he nodded and she moved forward. Molly held out her arm for the nurse's rubber strap, which tied with a squeaking noise. Her voice was soft, almost sweet, a singsong chant. "Blind me, beloved enemy of my will."

The three of them watched the syringe fill, splashing red drops against the sides of the plastic container as the blood level rose; then Molly looked up at Kepler. "My father had blood in his eyes," she said.

Kepler nodded to the aides and they pulled Molly up; she rose, unresisting, and let one of them lead her by the hand, like a child. As they left the seclusion room, the nurse turned to leave the building, while Kepler turned the other way, leading Molly in the direction of her room. Molly reached out and touched the nurse's shoulder.

"I could not console him," she said, her eyes bright. "And now here you come, dragging spreads with red blood on them and asking me to fix them. But I can't—don't you understand?"

diaphanous L and Bab working at c & d

13 June dream notes—

Darkness inside a church / *Oh Danny boy, the pipes, the pipes are calling* the coffin heavy above my ten-year-old arms / your smell salty perfume soaks old wood / I am swallowed in the shadow of your coffin / it pitches and sways / I struggle to hold you up / *Oh come ye back, when summer's in the meadow*

Or when the valley's hushed and white with snow my arms about to break/ we carry you through broiling Texas heat / Guadalupe Street, Austin and I am sixteen / the whole conference is singing your death / my clothes slide off from my sweat / I am stronger, a naked teenager carrying you and laughing / we finish the song *oh Danny Boy, oh Danny Boy, I love you so* / heading home to Dorchester, in the rain / cold rain and I am still naked / Bab rushes over with my fur coat, the warm fur makes me sweat again/ it sticks to my body / I am furred feral catlike/ and Lucia B is there / helping me with the coffin, she starts the next song / *Death ain't nothin' but a robber, don't you see, death ain't nothin' but a robber don't you see* / Lucia B is Lucia J and she wants her fur coat back/ she pulls at my fur until I am pink flesh scratched skin / *Death was here, he didn't stay long / looked in the bed an' my daddy was gone / Death ain't nothin' but a robber, don't you see*

My heart still racing, am I dreaming Will's death or my own? Why is Lucia fighting me? Why does Will's real funeral music become Lucia's blues? Or is it just a Baltimore fever-dream, soaked from the humid air of 110 degrees cooled only now, at midnight, to a balmy 93? Did you have nights like this in Paris, Lucia?

Of course! To this day August drives most of France to the seashore for the month. You went along with your family—along with the Gilberts, the Jolases, Paul Léon, Arthur Power. Thirty years later, St. Andrew's would take its favorite crazy old ladies to Bournemouth every summer, those lovely seaside girls. You liked it very much, you wrote.

No seaside for me, only this dripping heat, Felicia's elderly fan barely breathing. I'd forgotten this particular hot liability of living in an attic; back home, at least I could escape into Will's air-conditioned study. In his absence all I can do is take yet another cold shower and peel off the latest layer of sweat, to calm my nerves.

1:30 a.m. and temporarily cooled—and of course, underneath the dream-panic a more mundane anxiety. For I am meeting with Tilden in the morning, the last time before he goes off to Paris (on sabbatical, he'll be gone until next May). I need to announce to him that I am venturing far, far afield from where I started.

For I am finally passionate about a direction: I want to trace, as precisely as I can, the path of diaphanous L & Bab working at c & d.

To seek out evidence of how they created together this wonderful terrible book—watching him drink from her language to create the fragmented, rich madness of the *Wake*.

Jung named her as Joyce's femme *inspiratrice*, blaming their closeness for Joyce's refusal to commit his daughter; when he finally did, Joyce told his patron, Harriet Weaver, "She acts like a fool quite often but her mind is as unsparing as the lightning. She is a fantastic being speaking an abbreviated language of her own. I understand it, or most of it." The language braided through the *Wake*, elaborated and flourished.

What were you feeling , Babbo, the day you scribbled "diaphanous L & Bab working at c&d"? What was diaphanous about L that day? Her dress? Her dancer's body? Her voice bubbling up as if from a well? Like one of Rachel's witches memorizing an incantation, I have been reading over and over again Book II, chapter ii—Issy singing her flirty, crude, hypnotic alternative to the Shem / Shaun debate going on above, whispering from the footnotes below.

"You daredevil donnelly, I love your piercing lots of lies" and I hear Lucia laughing in the face of all those promises in the dark, from men who would treat her as a casual acquaintance in her father's drawing room a few days later. "One must sell it to someone, the sacred name of love."

(And how did it make Joyce feel, when his daughter talked that way? Did he know she meant the men he would later drink with, arguing over Proust or singing Irish folk songs laced with white wine? Did he know that the one who left early might have "Joyce's daughter" waiting for his bed? Questions outside the range of these explorations.)

Fatigue finally kicking in: it's almost four and I meet Tilden at ten, a vague possibility of four hours of sleep before I have to get up and run, the blues tape still in my Walkman pulsing grief into my blood.

14 June

We came, we saw, we triumphed!

It's provisional, however; I get the summer to prove that this can make a dissertation, we won't convene the committee until September. Of course, part of me thinks Tilden would have agreed to anything, his bags packed; as I write this he is aloft, two days to Bloomsday.

Ah, the annual Joyce holiday—the date James Joyce met Nora Barnacle, the day it took 700 pages to recount in *Ulysses*. Thus the date of the annual conference, Will and I together every year in Dublin Vancouver California Texas. (*Will did I leave you in Texas, there to dance happily in conference memories and coded manuscripts? you have left even my dreams.*)

This year the conference is in London again, where the Joyces were married, where Lucia disembarked in 1951, when she was being moved from Ivry to St. Andrew's. So Tilden will stop over on his way to Paris, join the scholars' weeklong party—days crammed with panels no one goes to, nights full of misty Bailey's receptions.

When I sat down in the office he was already high on the giddiness of imminent departure, the weight of the academy lifted from his shoulders. "Well, my dear young lady," he said, "you said on the phone that your peripatetic research has finally found a home." He smiled and sat back, for all the world as if he were about to smoke a pipe. "Well?"

I nodded, hugging the pile of book and papers I had brought as support: my spiral notebook with its outline, my marked-up copy of the *Wake*, Xerox copies of photo-facsimiles and long fat legal pads full of my Texas notes—scraps and highlights of diaphanous L's voice. When I told him what I wanted to do now he leaned across his desk, his eyes bright and his fingers tapping the desk, as if I'd just given him a line of Colin's smoothest cocaine.

"Stephanie Schulman has done some work on this," he said. "Did you see her piece in the *JJ Quarterly*, last April?"

My dear Mr. Tilden, last April I was still recovering from a violinist's blows. "Yes but I don't recall details," I lied, writing the reference down. "Do you mean that—"

"No!" his exclamation a half-laugh. "She just identifies possible Lucia-speech in the *Wake* itself. You may be on to something with these peripheral texts, if you can identify the how." He tipped his head to look at me sideways. "Of course, you could be leading us to another Bloomusalem."

Bloomusalem? Oh right, of course, last year's conference, Bloomsday in Jerusalem—the plane fare alone blowing a lot of department budgets. "I didn't go last year, Ross," I said. "You know that. So what are you talking about?"

"Oh that's right." Tilden stood up, his manic energy barely contained; he couldn't pace without knocking over suitcases. "Stephanie Schulman finally went ahead and did it, said it baldly—the incest allegation." "Incest? Oh lord, I can't get away from it, can I."

Tilden shook his head. "No more than the Joyces could."

The rumors flew through Paris when Lucia was put away, especially among those already offended by the salacious aspects of Joyce's writing . *Of course she would go mad, that crazy Irishman must have done something terrible to her.* I told Tilden about Jessie Berger's Shakespeare paper. "I can't wait to see what she does with Faulkner."

"She's only your first, Molly," he said. Of course, how to escape the obsessions of popular culture? Every week assorted talk show hosts feature allegations of abuse, fathers stepfathers uncles aunts priests cooks, mailmen for all I know. ("Children Abused by Ice Cream Vendors: This Wednesday on Oprah!") "God," I said, "you'd think people never heard the word *sublimation*."

Tilden nodded. "Or wanted to acknowledge," he added, "that these sort of desires exist in all parents, most of whom never act on them. It's just that they don't usually write about it."

I was sitting next to the air conditioner, an instinctive flight from my hot attic; the chill finally made me fold my arms and wriggle away. "Ross how cold did you set that thing? . . . So tell me about Bloomusalem."

Tilden finally settled, finishing his perpetual croissant. "There we are in the King David Hotel. I can see the outlines of the Old City from the window of my room, and every once in a while you can hear the minarets from the Arab quarters—one tended to drift, not concentrate on the panels . . . Then Stephanie, who was very pregnant at the time, declares flat-out that Lucia was a victim of sexual abuse. Not maybe, but *was*. She quotes these psychologists who work with incest survivors, then she tries to squeeze her final proof from the text of the *Wake*." Tilden swallowed. "Soon enough, people were screaming , Stephanie had burst into tears, and we had to restrain Hal Hawkins from phoning Stephen James Joyce."

Stephen James Joyce? The little boy Lucia was not allowed to hold? "Why?"

"Oh, God knows, after Venice." At the Venice conference, Stephen Joyce told the assembled Joyce community that he had burned a pile of Lucia's letters. I made a resolve to begin hiding my notebooks, just in case.

Then it was "Good luck, my dear, happy hunting through the apocrypha!" and Tilden was off, leaving me free to swim in this river at least until September.

I almost don't care what happens in September, I am intoxicated on Lucia wine. I will be allowed this summer romance with L'Irlandaise: if they revoke me when the summer is over I suppose I can always sell shoes, or work as an artist's model.

Which is what I am off to do, now—Felicia's summer series still very much in progress. What will they all look like, I wonder? And will she ever tell me about the "old, old burns" hidden behind her knees?

16 June

Bloomsday! appropriately enough, the first day of my Modern Novel course, starting with *Portrait of the Artist.*

I was, of course, petrified. It's one thing to assist someone else's lectures—but to be the lecturer, the one whose voice rains into students' spiral notebooks, scary for the girl who was always able to hide behind her cello. (If it weren't broken, perhaps I still could talk about Joyce while embracing my cello, the Guarneri instrument Will called Mamalujo.) And to make me even more nervous, there was Jessie Berger's defiant face; I don't know if she hates me, or if she's just so self-involved that any interruption from her private obsessions brings on that New York snarl.

Besides Jessie I recognized several members of Gary's class, and others from Lit 120. Also some Baltimore kids going after extra credits, mostly faculty brats. So I took a deep breath, and wrote on the board:

The novel's spirit is the spirit of complexity. Every novel says to the reader, "Things are not as simple as you think."

—Milan Kundera

Then I handed out the syllabus, explained the 100-Pages-a-Day Plan (response ranged from nods to "Surely you jest!") and took my hits for including all this dense prose in one course. "Joyce and Faulkner and Woolf in one summer? How'm I 'supposed to remember it all?"

Jessie turned to the loudest complainer and said "Get over it! If you don't want to play, go read Tom Clancy or something." *Thanks ma'am*, I warmed to her on the spot.

Somehow on five hours' sleep I managed to give a short lecture on the development of the modern novel, expanding on the Kundera quote with his observation that novels exist to explore life's big questions, without necessarily providing answers. By the end I was beginning to breathe again, to inhabit my body and feel the words coming directly from my throat, if not yet my mind. As I was packing up, I heard Jessie's voice behind me: "So I saw you running up Charles this morning—how far are you going, these days?"

Pretty innocuous question, her tone somehow softer than I

remember it. "Ten miles a day, pretty much. Except on weekends. . . . I'm training for the New York Marathon."

"Me too," Jessie said. "It'll be my third . . . last year was a fucking early frost, it felt like January. I hope this year will be better."

She's still pretty abrasive, demanding to know, "Why only one woman on the reading list?"

"Unless you want to count *Tender is the Night* as being by Zelda Fitzgerald," she said mischievously.

I took the bait, of course. "Oh Jessie, please!" but we spun the subject a little together, writer madwoman ballet dancer, me smiling at the connection to someone Jessie doesn't know.

Then I watched her sprint down the hall, the careless grace in her shoulders echoing all those women in New York, calling forth my imagined Zelda and Lucia as they dance across the grounds of Les Rives de Prangins. Or perhaps run there together, in training for the Madwoman's Marathon.

17 June

And there I was at 5:30 a.m. racing the sunrise through Baltimore County—in my ears Bessie Smith's raspy hurting voice the low-down brung-down done-me-wrong blues.

I've long since gone beyond any specific songs from the Austin material, instead drowning myself in what Lucia might have learned from Emile, could have been singing to her father as she breathed her fragmenting, sensual self into Joyce's work. *Oh lover man, oh where can you be?* Indeed.

Gary-recovery proceeding apace; I even saw a red Toyota without flinching yesterday morning. I am less hurt now, a month after his betrayal, than finally beginning to feel rage. "Improper frictions and maledictions and mens uration makes me mad." So says Issy—so, I suspect, said Lucia.

Who always had to sell it to someone, the sacred name of love.

Good God, the Austin notebooks' heroic catalogue, the Iliad or something: Calder Beckett Alec Emile, not to forget the South American with TB or her favorite of them all, someone named Roger Bichert—a tall dark man who she wanted to marry, but he was too busy (married, perhaps?). I wonder if the lunch with Beckett she wrote about (even naming the café) is the famous encounter of Beckett's biography, Lucia as a mannequin in the rain. It was followed by a terrible thunderstorm, she said.

Is that when she started being afraid of thunderstorms? (Making it up as we goes along, Issy sings.)

And which lover did diaphanous L mean when she told Bab, *He was explaining about Chopin and Schumann but I know he likes me?* Or *he was very continental?* Joyce watched closely, gathering material for his Issy seductress: *She plays with suitors like Penelope.*

Is tryst in flicks as his daughter flirts in the dark theatre; of course Joyce loved the movies despite his blindness, just as Will never lost his fondness for Woody Allen. (No one since, not Colin not Gary, has ever held my hand at the movies. I wouldn't let them, that particular furtive touch belonged to Will, as I pressed his palm whenever the scene changed. "Now they're in Central Park, at night," trying to make my whisper clear against a soundtrack of Rhapsody in Blue.) Did *Charly's* 30 *Year Musical Reminiscence* inspire L's paper on Chaplin, or the other way around?

Later, perhaps after Beckett's rejection, *love is unhappy round |'s neck.* Lucia weeping after the fateful luncheon—did she also say (unrecorded) Oh Babbo, I am sick of it. *I am dying inside, I am so sick of them, all menkind of every deception.* Felicia loved that when I read it to her, "he is my all menkind of every deception." For I have been reading aloud from the *Wake* day by day, as Felicia draws me from behind—lying on my side, my hair spread out across the floor behind me like a flattened Venetian blind. I know she's only half listening, but reading aloud always improves my understanding of Joyce, even if I cannot reproduce his own rich Irish tones.

Of course, II.ii is nearly impossible to read aloud, three columns plus footnotes, but she caught on quickly. When Joyce mourned "Though Wonderlawn's lost us forever. Alis, alas, she broke the glass!" Felicia snorted: "Yeah yeah, leave it to men, grieving some lost innocence. . . . Lewis Carroll was a goddamn pedophile anyway."

Issy's agreement: "Dear and I may trust in all frivolity may I be pardoned for trespassing but I think I may add hell."

I'm glad Felicia is interested enough to listen; I need someone to talk to, about diaphanous L & Bab working at c & d. Now that Tilden is gone, where else can I describe aloud the rosefrail child reading aloud to her father, whispering herself into the daughters upon daughters upon girls upon girls in the Wake? James and Lucia at Gertrude Stein's salon, Joyce ignoring the crowd to lean forward, Lucia's lips close to his ear as he writes in his tiny note-book, | 's blueveined hand still on his arm.

Or Lucia dancing at Joyce parties, James at the piano, perhaps fusing his daughter's observations into the music in his mind, to be laid out later as if on another page of sheet music. Felicia's take: "Sounds like one of those vampire things to me, Rodin and Camille Claudel. Sure, *I love you, use my energy, use my art.* Like you and that violinist."

No. If I had been Colin's inspiratrice he would now be unable to work, not performing in Asia for a cast of thousands. I shook my head.

"Hey, don't move, I'm not done with your neck!" Felicia's voice sharp, almost alarmed. "Just close your eyes and think of Lucia."

Sometimes I feel like a butterfly under glass as she observes me, tracing the whorls of my mind as she slashes the angle of my back across a huge, heavy slice of paper that covers half the floor of her studio. Or else she is the butterfly when I watch her climb the stairs, nude in honor of summer, and wonder about the screaming child on her back, sweat's real tears leaking out of his eyes.

21 June

One of those big moral decisions in the O'Donnell diaspora—which first, my run or my sacred mother? (That priest-phrase, "your sacred mother." Or did they mean the Blessed Virgin, all that time? Words words words.)

The dilemma occasioned, of course, by Emma's pre-run call (she's also running ten miles a day now, it took her a little longer to make it routine.) She reminded me about Margaret's birthday, which also marks our mother's second month clean and sober—as she marches briskly through the twelve steps of Alcoholics Anonymous. "She's been taking inventory all day long," Emma said breezily, as if I knew what that meant. "Anyway I just thought you might want to give her a call. . . . She's awake pretty early," which meant, of course, now.

I still think I'll be more sweet-tempered, more able to deal with her quavery wavery voice, after I've run a mile or six or seven. Right now the thought is making the flesh on my arms crawl a little.

10:30 a.m.

Curiouser and curiouser.

Here I am wondering at Will lost from me—and yet another odd piece of the puzzle emerges, from the words of his wife. I guess it was about time I called my mother, indeed.

I dialed Boston without the slightest idea how to generate sentences my mother would understand. At the other end that gelatinous voice, roused from sleep but apologetic. "Oh of course I want to talk—so sweet of you to call, dear Molly." (Never just Molly, always "dear Molly," as if that were the name on my birth certificate.) Then from that same voice a new kind of sound: "I was awake till five a.m., trying to decide if I loved your father enough."

Or at all, Margaret? but I didn't say that, just answered reflexively, "Oh don't be silly Mam, who else would have put up with a crazy scholar for 30 years?"

Margaret sighed. "That's what you all say—but if I weren't drinking I might have been able to find out why he was so angry, that year before he died. Maybe he wouldn't have even gotten the aneurysm if he was able to talk to me."

"Mam, what anger are you talking about? Poppie—he almost never even raised his voice." What I feared, when I feared, was the glacial silence, the withdrawal, the closed study door.

My mother's voice suddenly, surprisingly sharp: "Sweetheart, it was when you were in New York. . . . Didn't you ever notice how half of our china plates just disappeared, that year?" and I think she was crying, "He even broke my crystal vase, his wedding present to me."

That sounded vaguely familiar; I remember wondering at his funeral what had provoked Will to such rage. "Mam, it was probably faculty politics—I'm sure it had nothing to do with you. Believe you me, the way I see professors behave, it ain't pretty." I suppose self-hatred, mixed with alcohol's silky interior dusk, could converge to make her think it was her fault. But the whole year? Will, why were you angry? Why didn't you tell me?

I took a deep breath. "So what else is new, Mam? What are you doing with yourself all day, when Anna is at work?" How do you do without that constant companion, the bottle? Are you counting the days without it, the way I did when I first came to Baltimore?

"Oh, there's so much to do with the church, and there's always the TV, game shows and news programs. Did you know that women do most of the farming in Africa?"

I was surprised on two counts: that the TV had mentioned such a thing, and that she had been interested enough to retain it. "Yeah I heard that, Mam."

"It makes you think, doesn't it." Not a question, more a firm declaration that had less to do with thinking than with some vague assertion of wronged femaleness. A little knowledge is a dangerous thing.

"Well I gotta go now, Mam. Happy birthday, congrats on spending it dry."

"Oh thank you so much. I love you, sweetie," the phrase as automatic and meaningless as ever. "You'll always be my baby."

To which I replied after I hung up, I was never your baby, Margaret. Shaun was, and Anna, perhaps Emma. But we both know where my loyalties lie—with the blind man with the violin in his hand, even if he does sometimes break your crystal vase.

And I am wondering if Will was angry more often than I ever knew,

If perhaps that's why Leo, off in San Francisco, refuses to speak of him, if Leo's famous fire was just an echo of our father's rage. Perhaps I should call him, find some way to ask gently if it is a wall of anger that separates him from Will, from all of us.

Will is that why your coffin was so heavy in my dream? Why was Lucia fighting with me? Why I was so cold?

22 June

3 a.m.

Woke with a jolt: not a bad dream, not a Will dream, but a memory sparked by Margaret's words. I have seen you angry, Will, frighteningly so.

Madison House, the guesthouse in Austin, Texas where Will and I stayed for Texas Bloomsday: and he is angry at me for leaving him alone at a party, for spending an hour in the corner with a curly-haired graduate student who was telling me of his travels in the Middle East.

I remember quite vividly now—my body warming from the half glass of wine I was allowed at sixteen, not to mention the moist green eyes of the grad student with no idea how young I was. It took a shout across the room to remind me that there was a blind man waiting for me.

And yes, that was the one time I did see Will's rage. He didn't shout the way Colin did, loud and hard: his voice instead full of ice, a long dark deep freeze.

Shem I thought I told you, these men are not to be trusted. . . . And how dare you leave me alone with that insufferable Benstock? Margaret's memory: Will, angry at me for leaving, taking it out on the crockery instead.

Will, I never meant to forget you—and I am not doing it now. You are the one who led me to Lucia.

Speaking of which, this morning I finally found her, my not-so-silent partner in crime, my specter of the 1920s: Lucia B, this time in East Baltimore collecting recycling bottles from the gutter.

Rachel asks me: why do I run down there, subject myself to urban grit with far more wooded routes to be had among the and prep schools of Baltimore County?

Perhaps it's because I have been teaching *Portrait of the Artist as a Young Man*, Stephen Dedalus kicking aside rubbish and "offal" every morning as he leaves his parents' house; perhaps it's simply to remind me where I live. Most likely, I have been looking for her.

She has grown flabbier since I last saw her' she'd wore a thin cotton T-shirt that clung to her breasts; a far cry from the black-clad fellow pallbearer of my dream. I slowed down to a walk when I saw her, right across from the decrepit shopping center's supermarket, cheap shoe store, and Radio Shack. At first, she was too busy to notice me, filling her large black plastic shopping bag with 40-ounce beer bottles and flattening the cans with the soles of her worn sandals.

Then she looked up; she didn't smile, but she didn't spit in my face, either. "Oh, it's you again. . . . Shit, if there are three things I can count on in this world, it's the police, the doctors, and you."

Oh my friend, do you also have nightmares of policemen and nuns and piano teachers? I didn't ask her that: I just said, "Actually, it's been a while—not since that time by the water."

"By the water?" she asked, puzzled.

"The reservoir. . . . You know, Lake Montebello."

She stared a moment, as she bent down to the gutter toward a new row of bottles. Then she started to sing: "Take me to the river, drop me in the water." Just another blues song, even if written too late for Emile to teach his Lucia.

Still singing, she pulled a large Jolt Cola bottle from the gutter; the edge of the dark brown bottle was chipped, and I was suddenly afraid she would cut herself. A sleepiness in her movements, not the sluggish slow-mo of the conservatory but something softer, more graceful somehow. What drugs are they giving you now, Lucia? Or is it drugs you're giving yourself?

I watched her for a while as she squatted. Slow arm motions, gently erotic, dignified despite the stink of summer-heat and urine in the gutter.

We must have been an incongruous sight—she in her flowered jeans and sweaty tank top, her face gritty and hair curling close to her neck; me with my Walkman, my cotton shorts and a bright red headband. Finally I said, "You get enough money doing that?" I pointed to her bag, slowly filling with the detritus of beer and sugar-soda.

She grinned and laughed, low-throated, sweet and salty at the same time. "Keeps me on the streets," she said, and I had to laugh with her—the joke was too good, although bitter, bitter, bitter. I turned away and began to run again, the dampness on my cheeks not only from sweat.

Keeps my blood from clotting inside me, I remembered long after I'd left her murmuring to glass bottles in her raspy voice. Her doctors probably feel she's getting worse, and she does seem to be pulling into her dreams, just as her namesake did. But somehow to me that feels all right, though her namesake did grow exhausted, surrendering gratefully into the *camizole due force*.

But perhaps L learned that only such surrender would make Bab pay attention, get more than letters and copies of Tolstoy. The psych books talk of the "purposeful," goal-oriented nature of psychotic behavior; perhaps she thought she could finally upstage Nora, on whom Joyce was ultimately the more dependent, no matter how much | contributed to it. God it must have felt cruel to Lucia, how much he loved her. Nora, I mean.

Nora never read any of Joyce's books, although she loved hearing the *Wake* read to her; she told everyone that "Jimmy could have made somethin' of himself, if only he'd stuck to singin'." But Joyce adored her, and depended on her to keep up with his personal hygiene needs, his work routine—and his sexual need, the embraces so well-documented in the famous obscene letters. "Is there one who understands me?" he asked in the most famous letter of all, asking her to leave Ireland with him forever.

She did leave Ireland—but did she understand him?

No wonder Lucia screamed when the family tried to move to England in 1932, howling and howling and refusing to get on the boat. In 1932, as war threatened, Lucia resisted as the Joyces tried to establish legal residency in England.

For it was in London, the previous year, that James had finally legally married Nora, making true the lie he had told Paris and Ireland. "No oh no oh no," screamed the girl at the harbor. No need to say: *the last time we went there you chose her, in front of a judge and witnesses.*

For if my thesis is correct, by the time of the wedding diaphanous L and Bab had been working at c & d for nine years. Nine years of her speech and heart poured out to him, the fantastic being's abbreviated language absorbed into his collective unconscious of the human race. Nine years of | becoming Isolde, murmuring the footnotes of a chapter published by itself in a magazine, gilded with Lucia's lettrines. (Some scholars name Issy as the dreamer/narrator of the *Wake*: not the big phlegmatic Irish politician H.C.E., not Anna Livia his motherly Molly Bloomish companion, but little Issy the daughterwife, echo of diaphanous L the Wake-ing dreamer of dementia praecox.)

Nine years—and James was pledging himself to Nora in a judge's chamber, not bothering to ask again: "is there one who understands me?" The one to answer yes oh yes was not the one he married.

He made that question Anna Livia/Issy's final cry, as she becomes a river and flows through Ireland. "A hundred cares and a tithe of troubles and is there one who understands me?" Did Lucia ask that question as she was being bundled off to Ivry? Is that why she set so many fires? Would she, today, be seeking solace in the needle and the crack pipe, or sitting at home with Valium and TV?

Perhaps she would, in fact, be Lucia B—collecting bottles and singing to the Baltimore gutter, *take me to the river, drop me in the water.*

25 June

Awakened by Felicia shaking my shoulder, saying "Molly, Molly, wake up, wake up."

And have never been so glad for intolerable Baltimore summer, suddenly far more tolerable than a Will dream. Even now in the furnace of my attic I am shivering from its cold. The oddest one yet—

Dublin in a blizzard! silent, no city noises no people the cars are big and round like space ships / snow soap like covering automobiles and people / I am five years old, in my pink snowsuit and pink furry hood and my tiny cello case / trying to cry but too cold / my face freezes / stopping to help she wears a long coat and a fur muff, he is tall with round glasses / snowing harder so they are shadow shapes / I sniffle "Number Seven Eccles Street" / where

Bloom lives and you are / he is carrying me like a prayer-book / "Are you Mister Beckett?" "Yes." / takes me to Leo's house, ice-cream pink and old / a long windy path / grab rocks through snow to get to you / the house is Anne Frank's house, tall skinny like in Amsterdam / inside the walls ceiling floors covered in ice / not so little now, I am thirteen and my cello is bigger and made of glass / instead of my snowsuit my concert blouse, no skirt just my under-wear above high heels / they help cut the ice as I climb the stairs / your study door encased in ice / it blocks the top of the stairs / I throw my cello at the door / screaming / the walls are screaming too / my cello shatters the door /

There you are, young as a groom / you are made of glass or ice / a wind blows through the attic / flying glass / you are shadow and outline/ snowflakes tinged with pink and black and you / crystal snowflakes glittering silver / another wind and your shape is gone / I drink the silver snow / I drown in it, laughing / the walls and I do not stop screaming

From your funeral to your disappearance behind a wall of snow: shattering glass courtesy of Margaret's crystal vase story, screaming courtesy of the fat rust-brown babies on Felicia's back.

And now, thank the gods and goddesses, we can leave the ice behind—I am for once actually grateful to have some work to do, especially this work, preparing Monday's lecture on the Southern heat of *The Sound and the Fury*. Perhaps all the heat of Faulkner's fury will help to melt the ice.

June 27

This morning's quotes on the board:

> *History is a nightmare from which I am trying to awaken.*
> —James Joyce

blue: season

What no man can guess and no child can remember to tell.
—William Saroyan

Between grief and nothing, he thought, I will take grief.
—William Faulkner

And with that we began our discussion of *The Sound and the Fury.*

Some of my students are already getting a little winded: I might have switched the order, one of the freshmen pleaded, put Fitzgerald between Joyce and Faulkner. "Give us some room to breathe, and have a little fun." What, this isn't fun? They grew even more glum when I assigned 10-page papers on either Joyce or Faulkner: except for Jessie, whose secret smile I didn't trust.

Then we all took a deep breath and started in on the circular, whirling consciousness of Faulkner's Benjy—the "idiot" full of sound and fury, signifying everything.

God, this Southern whirlwind, Joycean fragmented language in the heart of Mississippi! It even has its own Issy: Caddy, Faulkner's female muse/nature goddess, loving but faithless rebellion against the Southern poison. In the idiot's eternal present she is simultaneously a child, a young woman getting married, an absence sorely missed by Benjy; her brother Quentin an impossibly close companion, her daughter Quentin a promiscuous teenager trying to escape.

The idiot and the madman, waking dreamers. No neologisms, no clang formations, but the same whirling energy to the prose, the same refusal to follow the neat linear paths already violated by Bab and diaphanous L.

I can smell psychiatry running riot over Faulkner's "Passion Week of the Heart," five great novels in a hallucinatory seven years —after *Ulysses* and exactly coinciding with the creation of the *Wake* across the ocean. Would Faulkner have been locked up if he'd been tested for schizophrenia during that time? Did he (like

Joyce?) drink to hold off the flood of the unconscious, to keep from drowning?

Jessie, of course, plays her one-note band. "Just don't try to convince me Caddy's not an incest survivor," she said.

"Hey man, Quentin even says as much" as another student skipped Benjy's chapter to talk of Quentin Compson's long suicide note, his 120-page ill-punctuated stream of remembrance.

"Just keep in mind," I said, "Quentin loves the purity of hellfire —he enjoys the idea of suffering forever! So he might as well indulge in long passionate fantasies of sex with his sister."

"Fantasies, schmantasies," Jessie said. "Wait'll you read my paper, before you go too deeply into denial."

Denial? Jessie, must you always reduce the complexity and subtlety of a great writer to the discourse of the self-help industry? Can't you see that incest is only part of the picture, as Faulkner turns over the stones of Southern society to find the pestilence twisting the souls of its daughters and sons? (Things are not as simple as you think.)

1 July

Cooling-down evening, suiting up for a run: I overslept this morning, ninety-five degrees by 7 a.m. Why risk heat stroke when I can go now, my standard 10-miler into leafy suburb? I'm now regularly running an eight-minute mile, and my weight has finally dropped below 105! In the meantime, I may have had a breakthrough on | — thanks in part to Felicia!

There I was, positioned right next to Felicia's fan, reading II.ii yet again as Felicia worked on "finishing your feet." As an experiment, I started to read Issy's footnotes all together, separate from the text they were annotating (a deconstruction project if there ever was one), as if they were some silly erotic angry poem. Then suddenly from behind me came Felicia's voice: "Who's Laughing Sally?"

For a moment I couldn't remember, where Joyce got the name cited jokingly in the footnotes: then it came back, the famous multiple personality case from the turn of the century. "Her name was Christine Beauchamp," I told Felicia, "and Joyce used her as another important source for Issy." Christine Beauchamp was treated by a Dr. Morton Prince, who actually found four selves—but the primary troublemaker/tormentor was named Sally.

Sally, who cut Christine's hair so she would "look a guy"; who made her stutter and sent her bad dreams; who was openly sexual where Christine was prim and proper and then wrote her taunting letters about it: "Your prayer book is in the salt-box, if you want it. Perhaps you'd better rescue it so you can pray out of it."

The cure, at that time, was to be found by squelching Sally, who ultimately agreed to let the psychiatrist "put her out of existence." Curing the illness by drowning one of Issy's voices—just as Issy herself is transformed and subdued as she flows out to sea, merged with Anna Livia. Then Felicia asked the million-dollar question: "Do you think Lucia was a multiple personality? Did Joyce think she might be?"

Now there's something worth exploration. What is the precise connection (if any) between Lucia and Christine, the quiet young woman from Boston, Mass? After all, Joyce is writing in the 1920s; who really knows what Lucia's current diagnosis would be. If she was, her voice would play even more into the shifting voices and identities of all the Wake figures: Shem and Shaun/Mike and Nick, Issy/Isolde/Isabel/Nuvoletta, Anna Livia/Kate Strong , her illness thus manifesting the multiple nature of all our selves.

Unfortunately, Lucia's medical records are locked away, thanks to the Joyce estate. So I need to return to the med school library where I first learned about dementia praecox, for the literature on multiple personality disorder. Unfortunately, before I can do that I must glance at the short papers from my students.

Even though I assigned them, I have to confess to a sense of shock when the pile appeared in front of me. I had thought I was tormenting them, but who's left with twenty-six papers to grade on a Monday night? I stare at the pile thinking, if I was a multiple personality could I could grade them three times faster?

And did Christine Beauchamp become Sally so that she would not dream about her father turning into snowflakes?

July 7

I want my boys to be more than friends yes Candace and Quentin more than friends Father I have committed what a pity you had no brother or sister No sister no sister had no sister Don't ask Quentin and Mr. Compson both feel a little insulted when I am strong enough to come down to the table I am going on nerve now I'll pay for it when it's all over and you have taken my little daughter away from me My little sister had no. If I could say Mother. Mother

Jessie's Faulkner paper, of course, has that passage lovingly transcribed and cited, to underline the incest theme. She uses the passage to illustrate what she calls the "classic incest constellation": absent or destructive parents, children "denied parenting, having to turn to one another for solace, and violating important psychological boundaries in the process." I recognize from my own research some of the psychologists she cites, family systems therapists on incest and mental disorder.

She even accuses Jason Compson of incest with his daughter, a thought I had never heard expressed before: her textual support again comes from Quentin, who as he prepares to kill himself recounts his father saying "it was men invented virginity not women. Father said it's like death: only a state in which the others are left." *Why couldn't it have been me and not her who was unvirgin and he said, That's why it's so sad too; nothing is even worth the changing of it.*

So when he touched her, Quentin found Caddy to be "unvirgin." And Jason had made her that way, saying virginity is meaningless anyway.

Virginity issues and Joyce? Only Lucia whoring around Paris, her cringes at hearing she was illegitimate ("if I was a bastard," she screamed at Nora, "who made me one?"). Or the mysterious daughter in Ulysses, Milly Bloom, sent off to the seaside perhaps after scandal, *soft sweet girl's lips.*

I think men did invent virginity. When Colin learned I was a virgin at nineteen he was then dreadfully disappointed when there was no blood, running or cycling having burst my hymen at some earlier, un-missed point. Then his disappointment was mitigated when I turned out to be "surprisingly insatiable," in contrast to my prim little cellist appearance.

But Jessie takes out all the grays, all the

2:30 p.m.

Must have fallen asleep right in my library carrel. My body's finally given up trying to remind me gently that now and then one must just stop, both frantic physical and mental activity; instead it just shuts me down. trying to remember what I was going to say . . . I should probably sit down with Jessie and ask, in as even-handed a way as possible: *Ms. Berger, doesn't anything move you outside your own experience? What about the racism and decay of Faulkner's Mississippi?*

For this is the context Jessie is ignoring, the rot of which the incest is only a manifestation, along with Quentin's suicide and his mother's helpless glory—the larger sickness of the American South, its savage history of failure and genocide. The inner and outer sicknesses seen as one, until each individual symptom is almost an inevitability. Jessie why must you drag it all down to feminist psychobabble?

And what would you do with the explicit incest in the *Wake?* With Caddy, the "little daughter," so like Issy in her playful flirty loving changeable self? With Quentin, sharing Stephen Dedalus' obsession with order and his love-hate relationship with his mother, his past, his country (Ireland/the South)?

If Caddy = Issy = Lucia and Quentin = Stephen Dedalus = James Joyce, then Jessie is with the woman at Bloomusalem, the one trying to prove that Joyce and his mad daughter actually did "conjugate together." (Love have I on my back spine, indeed.) I hate to break it to you, Jessie, but better scholars than you or I have wrestled with this for fifty years, and all have come up with the same answer: Joyce confined his desires to the printed page.

I am sick of all printed pages right now: Felicia gets home in a few minutes, and instead of reading to her I will close my eyes and listen to the blues tape we are neither of us sick of yet. *Oh lover man, where can you be?*

July 18

And I was awakened by a sound remarkably like that first Faulkner passage, of Jessie's, the one in the mother's voice. Margaret's voice on the phone.

As she tried this morning to make sense, she managed instead to display just how confused twenty-some years of white wine have left her. "I've been thinking a lot about the past," she said. "That's number nine of the twelve steps, you know—recognizing your past transgressions and making amends."

God, AA was created for (by?) simple-minded Catholics like my mother. "Yes, Mam, I've heard that," I said.

"So I wanted—I wanted to apologize for missing your big recital, that year in New York. . . . The one with the quartet."

Recital, Mam? "Oh you mean sophomore year? Mam that's ancient history, and the concert wasn't that great anyway." My ears still smart at the very mention of that concert, Joan laying back at the crucial moment of the Mozart just when we needed a strong voice to pull us through the Andante cantabile.

"But Emma went, I remember. . . . One of your parents should have been there. And that was when you and your father weren't getting along."

Oh God, now her too? I suddenly felt her and Emma in conspiracy against me, trying to deprive me of the one strong loving relationship I have ever known. "Mam, Will and I never had any falling-out. That's why it was so hard when he died."

Honey entering her voice, softening it nearly the way alcohol used to. "Oh sweetie, it's normal for teenage girls to argue with their dads. You don't need to be ashamed of it . . . I'm sure he still loves you, up in Heaven. He knows you always loved him."

The sweat on my face felt suddenly chilled, I sat down in the old armchair by the phone. "Mam, There's nothing to be ashamed of. Poppie and I were fine."

A long silence, then Margaret said in a placid, singsong voice, "Oh I guess so, honey, I guess so . . . I'm still very sorry I never came to hear you play, when you were in college." *I'm vurry sorry so burry surry so vurry sorry* as if 12-step groups existed for Joyce to parody.

"That's okay, Mam." Give them absolution, that's what they want. "I mean, I forgive you."

Tears replacing the honey in her voice. "Thank you, sweetheart, for understanding."

Understanding? Or tolerating? I called Emma afterward, and she said "Oh, Mam's been calling everyone. With me it was apologizing for not being at the hospital when Stevie was born." (The sight of the hospital where Will died too much for our mother, who found the nearest bar within fifteen minutes of our arrival. (Shaun and I drank coffee and played gin rummy in the waiting room instead—a rare moment of camaraderie with my brother, who now believes, I think, that I have myself gone a little crazy.)

And damn her eyes, Emma did sixteen miles yesterday, while Stevie was with Barry at a baseball game. That's it—tomorrow evening I do the same. I've got a new pair of shoes for the occasion, since the old ones have run at least two hundred miles in two and a half months: I splurged and got the ones with the little plastic air pockets, the kind that inner-city kids quite literally kill for. Does it make me fear to run in the so-called bad neighborhoods of Baltimore? Not really, though I have begun favoring the downtown run again, trying to find my favorite soprano, my own "little daughter."

July 11

Back to the medical library, for those books on multiple personality and, again, schizophrenia, some of the same ones I began with on my abstract "schizophrenic speech" project, not yet knowing that I meant the "strange abbreviated language" of diaphanous L.

And of course now that I have been living and breathing Lucia, certain facts hit more strongly than before.

For example: creative people, given tests for schizophrenia, land in the pathological range, while schizophrenics do very well in tests of creative thinking. Most suggestive is that children of creative people test high for schizophrenia; our own homegrown American poet, Robert Frost, yielded not one but two schizophrenic children.

All various levels of neurotransmitter disruption, as these books would claim? Or do we follow Jung's line, with a line of inner voices more or less in touch with the collective unconscious?

But the books just endlessly cite one another, offer bloodless lists of symptoms. Disordered language. Social isolation. Catatonia —flaccid and rigid. Which did you have, Lucia, the night of your engagement party?

Placing it in context now, it expands, larger than life.

The party took place in 1932, a year after the Joyces' wedding in London, a few months before she threw the chair at Nora and screamed at the Paris harbor. A year after Beckett's rejection—he was no longer in her life, this man who had given her the *Divina Commedia*, who had, with the rest of the family, watched "L'Irlandaise" dance in her silver fish costume. Three years before the famous trip to Ireland when "I have been quiet ill," when she left the land of her fathers in a strait jacket.

And Alexander Ponisovsky holds his bride-to-be's hand (remembered forever with affection, twenty years later he will be inscribed in her journals). Around them at the Restaurant Drouand, the party is buzzing: music and food and Joyce and Nora and all their friends, Paul Léon and Nino Frank and Sylvia Beach. Lucia is growing more and more quiet, pulling into herself, just like her counterpart by the reservoirs and urban streets of Baltimore.

What smells felt invasive, | ? the inevitable cigarettes? The food? The candles? What sounds? Joyce's tenor laugh? competing with those smells and sounds, inside Lucia—*the smell of garlic reminds me of Trieste*

in the dark window I can see the cast in my eye, the tiny scar in my chin from when I had the mumps

Alec looks tall, he said I danced very well

my body is warm, my cunt is wet, but I am growing fat without dancing.

My head aches so.

Lucia's hands are shaking from not screaming.

She waits until the group retires to the Leons' and shuts down, lays on the couch. Catatonia: not sleep, but absence of self.

Babbo sits by her sofa in a back room of the restaurant, holding Lucia's hand. Alec hovers above them, perhaps wondering if even one so lovely and passionate as Lucia is worth this strain. He also notices the tender touch of Joyce's hand on his daughter's brow, the fog of tears on Joyce's thick glasses. *Andiam, carissima, andiam!*

Perhaps when all the guests are gone, Babbo sings to her, a sort of reverse lullaby. *Oh Molly I can't say you're hon-nest, sure you've stolen the heart from my breast.* And Lucia's eyes open, very, very slowly, she allows him to lift her from the sofa, until she is standing tall beside him, her head on his shoulder.

Then Nora comes in, saying abruptly, Let's go home, now. (HURRY UP PLEASE IT'S TIME)

347

Lucia's official diagnosis was "hebephrenic" schizophrenia; the modern term is "disorganized" schizophrenia, which supposedly starts very young and has a poor prognosis, the mind given that much more time to disintegrate. (Is schizophrenia the AIDS of the nervous system, collapsing the brain in upon itself?) The symptoms: "inappropriate emotion, frequently disorganized thinking, extreme social impairment."

Lucia, I am shouting after you in the long dark frozen hallway of number seven Eccles street.

For *I* am full of inappropriate emotion, *I* cry reading the notebooks of a dead madwoman, and then cringe with scorn at my poor mother struggling to recover from alcoholism. What is this journal but a testimonial of my disorganized thinking?

As for extreme social impairment . . . since Gary, I do find myself withdrawing more and more. I see twenty-six students and assorted faculty every day, but at home I am alone for hours with my photos of Lucia and then get up in the morning, run, shower, and creep into Felicia's studio for our morning modeling session.

These damp days she draws wearing only BVDs, her tiny fan entirely devoted to keeping her model (me) as sweat-free as possible. This means that I get to watch her screaming baby weep, every morning; and to stare at the tiny pink scars in the hollows of her knees. (Funny, what we do and do not share—for I am too shy to ask, "So where do those little scars come from, anyway? And why the screaming baby?") Someone should be photographing us, two naked women in a hot Baltimore row house: one drawing, staring into space feeling inappropriate emotions.

22 July

Talk of inappropriate emotions! Remember how proud I was that the sight of a red Toyota no longer unhinged me? Well, it's different when said Toyota is actually recognizable, and so is the person behind the wheel.

I don't have much truck with department gossip, so I'd never learned that Gary was on the interview committee for Tilden's sabbatical replacement. Which I learned the hard way—at the tail end of a fifteen-mile run.

The run itself was fine, I had finally returned from Lucia's music to my own—Mozart's G Major quartet opening with such typical serenity, world enough and time for gentle merriness. The Andante hit when I was up in Towson, north of the city, choking from the stench of country club Chemlawns. The Andante is where Mozart lets himself grieve his father's death, of course, centuries apart from the songs in my funeral dream; his grief soft moans from the cello, a hushed dialogue between violin and viola, God, do we all spend our lives crying out for our fathers?

I was on my way back home, stopping before I crossed Northern Parkway, Mozart's perky Allegretto replacing grief with revived serenity. No Denise, but all it took to slice my gut was the sight of the Toyota, its back fender slightly dented, a bumper sticker saying CHEMISTS MAKE BETTER LOVERS. I fled down a side street, under cover of dappled black-green summer trees.

Ten minutes later I heard his horn: he must have broken several laws to get to that street. As he drove up beside me I slowed to a walk, unwillingly. I couldn't childishly ignore him, but I was inflamed inside, as if that scene at Louie's had taken place yesterday.

"Hey," I shouted to him, "I can't talk now. I'm checking my time."

"You're running the distance already?" The bastard remembered my schedule—I didn't plan to be running the whole twenty-six miles til August.

"No, but it's 15 miles."

"So check your time now, and talk to me a minute. C'mon, whadya got to lose?"

Only my self-respect. "You look good. Where've you been tanning yourself?" The tan made him look sort of exotic, until you

349

got the sunburn just around his collar; he was, as always, a little disheveled. I wanted to hug him, or cut his throat.

He looked me up and down, his face hard to read. Finally he said, "Molly, when did you get so fucking thin?"

"The Total-Weight-Loss-Through-Total-Relationship-Loss-Diet," I sang to him. "Now I really look the part of a marathoner, don't you think?" I lunged forward, stretching my hamstrings, as if posing for a photograph or preparing for a duel.

He changed the subject. "How's the Modern Novel class going?"

"Quite well . . . did you know I have Jessie Berger?"

He laughed. "Of course, our Rebel with No Good Cause. . . . Let me guess, what are you reading now?"

"*Sound and the Fury.*"

"Oh *marón*, she must be a cat in cream, the incest all over that book." God, his laugh, cool water after a long, long drought. (Can it only have been six weeks since he dropped me? It feels simultaneously like yesterday and about ten years ago.) "How's the search for Lucia?"

"Oh Gary—" I suddenly wanted to tell all: Austin, multiple personality tales, the web I am finally beginning to weave between those texts and the Buffalo notebooks and the *Wake* itself. Then I stopped, looked at my watch. "You have to be somewhere, right?" Three-thirty on a Sunday afternoon, I imagined Denise checking movie times.

He was already checking his own watch. "Ohmigod, I suppose I do. I'll call you on—um, you still at the same number?"

"Same number, same house, same life. Almost. It's nice to see you, Gary, you're looking well."

"You look like hell, Molly. I'll talk to you later."

Now there's a sweet thing for your ex-lover to say. The tears stung, as if he'd thrown antiseptic in my face.

L and Bab predicting the fate of any love affair: "For she must walk out. And it must be with who. Teaseforhim. Toesforhim. Tossforhim. Two. Else there is danger of. Solitude." That's why the dance from man to man to man, bed after bed—that desperate fear of being alone. Did he stay up at night waiting for her? No, he would be out drinking himself, occasionally hauled home bodily by one of his friends. Did he look for her at the cafés after midnight, hoping against hope not to see | riding afore him?

Mozart soothed me into finishing the run, even ignoring the ankle pain for the final, simple stretch down Charles Street. As I climbed the back stairs at Calvert Street I was with Lucia again, sneaking up the stairs into one of the innumerable Paris flats at two in the morning, the smell of gin in her hair, semen in her clothes. Nora will scream at me in the morning.

And I think of what Emma said to me, on our way into the hospital last March. "It's our parents who teach us how to love."

What did Lucia's parents teach her? That loving equals chaos? That one day's intimacy could be the next day's separateness? In one of the last, most famous photos of Joyce, he wears a soft fedora and a medium-wide, striped tie. Behind circular glasses his eyes look huge, lost. In other portraits Joyce is dignified, or jolly, or morose, or stiff—but this one is full of too many losses, his father, his country, his daughter.

The same lost darkness in the eyes of Lucia, especially in my favorite portrait—a profile shot with her hair cut short, her strong eyebrows meeting the shock of her front bangs. The resemblance so clear, two strong brows above the exact same expression. Yes, James taught his daughter how to love, while she taught him the speech of madness. *Will, you taught me to love you wisely, others I loved too well, Colin, Gary loved me till it hurts. Did you teach me that too?*

I called Leo last night hoping to learn about the father I never knew, the father he knew. But I got the answering machine, Leo's cheery serene voice admitting matter-of-factly that "we screen all our calls." I hung up, like a guilty solicitor or frustrated bill collector —how could I ask a machine to tell me about my own father? Besides, with the time zones it was only midafternoon in San Francisco; he'd be off hiring a new chef or something, uninterested in rousing Will O'Donnell's ghost.

12 July

Felicia has finished drawing my back and has requested photocopies of II.ii, for collage material—"I'm not sure I'm going to use it, but it's always good to have." Interesting to imagine a drawing decorated with such stuff—I'll try to track down a copy of the literary magazine where it was first published, its very first letter Lucia's *lettrine* A.

She's also bought a tiny air conditioner for her studio, so she's back to working with her clothes on, T-shirts and leggings covering the screaming brown baby and her scarred inner knees. Even with the A/C, sweat still glistens off her delicate collarbone; our sessions grow ever longer since Rancho Harbor has cut down on her hours (which also means I subsidize her meals, she can barely make rent).

Report on today's run: glorious, though still no sign of Lucia B. I went all the way to Patterson Park in search of her, before swinging over toward Dundalk; my ankle firmly in a neoprene brace, I was free to enjoy the pina colada sunrise and the vigorous violence of Bartok's third quartet. I turned back in the midst of that second movement, where the second violin and viola carry on a passionate dialogue—the tone shifting constantly, a schizophrenic's mood or an afternoon rain.

And I thought of James and Nora visiting Lucia at Les Rives des Prangins, the asylum in Switzerland; how she was sunny one moment and turning the next to attack her mother, her father, or both. Speaking of Prangins, I will soon get to wander its grounds, courtesy of my students and F. Scott Fitzgerald: we have finished with Faulkner's Southern madness and are entering Fitzgerald's melancholic Jazz Age. The kids are relieved, after Faulkner, looking forward to Fitzgerald's clear plot and straightforward prose; and Jessie has raised my interest in Zelda. I wish Lucia had known her, this other dancer, singer, writer prowling the hospital grounds.

Lucia also had a lover at Prangins; but the matter was "taken care of and he is going away." Oh lover man, where can you be?

13 July

The clerks at the medical library are beginning to recognize me; instead of searching my bag they simply nod, sleepy even in air conditioning, urban summer scary outside their windows. In the block and a half from the bus stop to the library, I'm asked for money at least five times: hard to read their confused eyes, do they want it for food or drugs or sex.

Once safely here I leave their madness sadness behind, instead reading abstract articles about multiple personality disorder. MPD, as they call it, ranges from a non-specific dissociation of personality styles ("the patient" may simply be cheerful and childlike one day and mean and cussed the next) to the more complex stuff of bad TV-movies, seventeen personalities with separate names and sexes and ages. The etiology (fancy word for "cause") seems to be directly related to two variables—the ability of a child to go into trance and severe abuse.

I grow a little sick just reading the case histories. Children who were held onto electric coils till they burned. Boys raped every day by their older brothers. Little girls held prisoner by mothers who placed foreign objects in their vaginas. Or other, less gruesome-sounding incest experiences, some adult a child trusts violating that trust with a sexual touch, a request, an encounter the child can neither absorb nor fully reject.

So a child who is able to go into trance uses that ability, like the kids in sci-fi movies who use their psychic abilities to protect them-selves. Rather than experience the hurt, they often create another self to feel it; rather than fight the person they love most in the world (i.e., their parents) they create another, aggressive person to do the fighting for them. And the child who first experienced the pain often remains, long after the person has reached adulthood—a primeval "first self," a child crying out in surprise and shock.

So what of Christine Beauchamp, let alone Issy/Lucia?

I have not been able to get hold of the Morton Prince book, c.1906, which described the case of Christine Beauchamp: in those prudish years it is unlikely that any details on child abuse would have been included.

As for Lucia, MPD symptoms would certainly explain her wild mood swings even after she was hospitalized. But then, so would manic depression—or "bipolar affective disorder" (also known as BAD, I love it!). I do think we can say that Lucia had at least some ability to dissociate, if not break apart entirely. I hear her trying out voices, perhaps adopting some of what she heard at the parties and salons they went to, others voicing themselves from her own waking-dreamer mind, "unsparing as the lightning." The sweet Lucia who sat patiently by her father's bed, the tart whoring her way around Paris, the rueful Lucia capable of throwing chairs and setting fires. | 's multiple voices then Issy's, woven through the *Wake* by her father: thick and cloying as she romances her "pepette," crude and angry in the II.ii footnotes, weeping in the famous "win me, woo me, wed me, ah weary me!"

10 p.m.

Back home after leaving the library and straight to class, to stroll through the beaches of the French Riviera with my students. Perfect timing as Baltimore summer grows ever-denser, more oppressive, like a galaxy compressing or an alcoholic gaining weight. But I walked home from class thinking not about Fitzgerald but about Lucia's illness.

If Lucia was dissociating, who made her so?

I wish I had been at Bloomusalem.

I wish I knew how I felt about "the incest controversy."

354

For it seems pointless to speculate about physical abuse or early violence when there is this other possibility—that Joyce was, like the *Wake's* Gracehoper, "always making ungraceful overtures . . . to commence insects with him, there mouthparts to his orifice . . . till she was puce for shame."

That Lucia's illness was a response to the "boundary crossing" cited by Jessie's paper and all these books; that Babbo expressed his desires not only in his notebooks, not only in the *Wake*, but in actions that fragmented his daughter's mind.

The twin Lucia faces in my mind, the Baltimore homeless waif and the Paris flapper, singing together, *Take me to the river, drop me in the water.*

Which is a song about sex, after all.

And now it it's 11 p.m. and time for a run—to sweat Lucia's grief out of me, for now. I hear Felicia stirring upstairs, it's cooling down enough to actually move, and she will go out dancing with her artist friends while I run as far and fast and I can, searching into new neighborhoods in search of Lucia B.

26 July

No Lucia B, not in that run—just sad men clutching beer bottles and sweaty women of the night, none of them as pretty as either of my Lucias.

But meanwhile I have a photocopy of Jessie's paper (to which I gave a reluctant A, she did support her thesis fairly well), so I can cite her as a reference about "incest families." Reading her profile of such families I search for possible Joyce clues, hoping (in truth) not to find them.

The danger signs, as she cites them:

lack of a strong "coalition" between the parents that could leave out the Joyces, that dynamic duo, that inseparable pair.

a disturbed, even hostile relationship between mother and daughter and Lucia hurls the chair in Nora's direction. But then what are we to make of the Austin notebook where she talks about the nice dresses her mother bought her, and says they were the best of friends?

alcoholism all that wine consumed in French cafes late at night—but I've never heard Joyce defined as an alcoholic. A heavy drinker, yes, but unlike, say, Margaret, he did confine his drinking to later hours, spending his days sober and his afternoons working.

Jealousy on the part of the father, suspicion of the daughter's suitor. Joyce did write: "found time for the man of her choice she never cd tell the truth Is—her libido/the Beyond."

Yet he tried so fervently to find Lucia a mate, first Beckett then Ponisovsky; he complained to his friends that all young men seemed "from the point of view of the opposite sex, entirely useless."

the incest itself often precipitated by a physical illness on the part of the mother, leading to sexual estrangement and we are back, inevitably, to Nora's operation for ovarian cancer, after which she enjoyed sex less and told her daughter so. But that was 1928, so Lucia was twenty-one: a little old for such contact to have driven her mad.

Then we finally hit pay dirt—several of the psych texts use the term "seductive" fathers: relationships without overt incest, wherein the daughters often display "the same psychological seque-lae." Now there I feel on firm ground.

Is it "seductive" to claim your daughter's attention at all times? Is it "seductive" to ask her to read salacious passages of *Ulysses* when she is supposedly too young to understand them?

Is it "seductive" to whisper together like lovers at parties of the rich and famous?

Is it "seductive" to watch her so intently, *her tongue her lipstick , that pop walked zigzag*, presumably from his unbearable erection?

Perhaps, then, the question of physical contact is moot. In some ways it makes sense to characterize diaphanous L & Bab as emotionally incestuous only: the relationship is then fraught with ambivalent mystery, just like writing, just like life.

My heart is pounding. I feel like I've just completed a 20-mile run and been doused with celebratory champagne—some of it reaching my throat, the rest splashing down my chest arms legs cunt. I am even wet, sexual arousal from academic discovery, is this the real secret of why people become professors?

Will, return to me now? Now that I have been practicing on my own for so long? I close my eyes but I cannot summon his face, let alone his voice. He is dissolved into crystal snowflakes and there is no way to bring him back.

16 July

Gasping from heatstroke because I broke my own rule, ran at 8 a.m. even though it was far, far too hot. Got home stinking with sweat and my hair was impossible, coming out of the ponytail and plastering itself to every inch of bare skin, I'm going to have to figure out something to do with it.

Felicia advised a French braid, done tightly enough that I could leave it for days, "get all that hair up off your scalp already." She herself has shaved her head completely, finally ridding her scalp of the few over-dyed strands she'd let remain. (After her bleach blond phase, I knew something had to end.)

Today's new drawing even stranger than the last: surrounded by a reggae beat, she had me upright against the wall, moving my arms above my head as if handcuffed. "Just a quick drawing, I won't make you hold it too long—but look straight at me" and for the first time I was in continuous eye contact with diaphanous F, her eyes still veiled in concentration as she works. In this heat we are all losing weight, and I can count her ribs. Only the screaming baby stays fat.

After Felicia, it was off to class, of course, where my damp little group and I relaxed into a discussion of Scott Fitzgerald and the

American leisure class. Pretty soon we were at the heart of the matter, the madness of Nicole Diver—and I let Jessie, our madwoman expert, outline the history of Zelda Fitzgerald, her breakdowns, her stories published under Scott's name, her initial diagnosis of schizophrenia (of course!) later demoted to "feelings of inferiority to her husband."

She studied ballet with Egerova, one of the great Russian ballerinas—which puts her and Lucia at opposite ends of the dance world, in an age where ballet and modern dance were sworn enemies.

No way of knowing, of course, how much Zelda is in Nicole Diver, since Fitzgerald didn't keep the sort of notebooks that help me find Lucia in Issy. Did Zelda's letters accuse her keepers at Prangins of trying to make her forget the past? Did she ever cry out, as Nicole did, about clothes with red blood all over them?

Immediately after class, of course, I was back at the notebooks, to divine the link between my posited "seductive" relationship and Joyce's whirling history of the human race. All linked sideways by Lucia's crucifying illness, which may or may not have been catalyzed by the erotic quality of the bond.

My notes are almost as dizzying as the damn Buffalo notebooks themselves: my handwriting is better than Joyce's but I was writing quickly, trying to cram in the maximum amount of information in the time allotted. Plus when I couldn't understand something I just wrote a sort of scribble, so now I find them in crucial places—to wit:

memb (?) of Is naked is accevable (scribble) my love to procure
But then, without scribbles—
Papa Is goes to bed in silks
"You'll be hapnessized when you see how fetching I can look in clingarounds," Issy taunts in II.ii.
Position of I's legs her moon star in a corner of the sky
Her moon star in a corner of the sky. . . . am I so unrelentingly horny that I read images into that that are not there—moon/mons, remember how in II.ii a geometry lesson draws Anna Livia's cunt?

Wake scholars prefer the subthemes, the Sanskrit puns and Tristan and Isolde tales—to me, those are layers gilding the unassailable truth of a father's desire.

Meanwhile, Gary has remained in town this week, to interview all the eager young faces with brand-new Ph.D.'s, determined to stay a mover and shaker in the department. He's also been calling me but I ignore his messages. He is calling someone he doesn't know any more.

The Molly lying on the floor to a reggae beat, crying over the girl whose father had blood in his eyes, is not the same person who gently nibbled his shoulder, who argued with Jessie Berger in his tiny office, who sat and agreed when he announced our "divorce" at that civilized Louie's brunch.

And I have taken extra precautions to make sure he no longer recognizes me on the street, by cutting off my hair.

What? Actually it just finally got too hot.

This afternoon, I was walking from the classroom over to the library with all this heavy hair plastered to my head, weighing down the back of my neck even in a new, single tight braid. I decided to walk down the harbor, return later to Bab's notes, *Is loves birds/walks in woods . . .*

I went the department office and there they were, slips of paper in my box, matching the plaintive words on the Calvert Street answering machine. *Molly, it's me. Can we talk? I just . . . want to know you're all right. / Molly, I know you're there, will you pick up?"* The last message was one word: *Shit.*

Yes, Gary, I know. If I'd seemed merry, relaxed when you saw me, I'd not hear from you until the fall. But now you're worried, now you're maybe a little guilty—or else I am flattering myself and this is a social worker's concern, like your solicitude about Jessie's childhood. Either way I won't dignify it with a reply.

I passed through to yuppie Mount Vernon and into the gallery district, where I saw a small neon sign: "Studio 338 Hair Design."

Hair design, can you major in hair design at the art school these days?

The heavy braid suddenly burned my skin, it wanted so badly to come off. I walked in and my face frosted from the air conditioning. "Can you do anything about this?"

"We don't take walk-ins," the girl at the front desk demurred, but a tall man inside said "Look, Carolyn just canceled on me. I'll give her a whirl."

When I sat down he unbraided my hair, fingering it admiringly. When I told him I wanted it to be all gone he stared at me. "People die for hair like this."

"Good, so hold onto it and make a wig. I'm sick of it." And really it felt like a scab, a disease, too much twirling around men's bodies or bleeding black onto Felicia's painting. The hairdresser sighed as he washed it, singing under his breath Sarastro's aria from *The Magic Flute*. When I sat up I said delightedly, "Mozart!"

His speaking voice a perfect Sarastro baritone, he said "I'm a failed opera singer, but don't tell anyone." Then he proceeded to cut off my hair.

When it was over my eyes were suddenly huge, my ears long and elfin, with that slight flatness on top where most people's curve —and in the mirror was the face of Lucia Joyce.

I mean, of course, that profile shot I have blown up and on my wall, Lucia with short flapper hair, the bones in her neck in delicate relief. For memory's sake I wrapped a few long strands in a tissue, put it in my pocket; I felt as though I had menstruated, or miscarried, some female act of expulsion of unwanted dark fluid.

I felt lighter the rest of the way home, in tune with the students and tourists eating ice cream. I no longer felt Gary's answering machine voice weighing on me, it had gone with the hair—the hair he loved to play with and Colin to pull, in hard, erotic strokes. Will couldn't see it but he liked to touch it, hold it to his cheek. *My God, it is the softest thing in the world, softer than the cat's back.*

Home now, with extra sunscreen. And I feel ready to go back, bring a caffé latte into the cold-conditioned library and put on my office sweater, to breathe the cooler air of Zurich and Les Rives des Prangins and imagine Lucia meeting Zelda on the clinic grounds— where madwomen do a midnight pagan dance, exchanging the secrets they are keeping even from the artists for whom they serve as muse.

2 August

Mixed reviews on the hair: Felicia loved it, of course, and Jessie Berger actually gave me a tiny round of applause. "Way to go, woman! Summertime, and the living is easy!" Rachel, on the other hand, shook her head sadly. "I would have killed to be able to grow my hair that long."

So go buy it downtown, Rachel, it just can't keep up with me.

Felicia and I sang to her, in our own lightheaded way: "Summertime . . ." I wonder if Emile taught Lucia that one, if Paris humidity glazed her skin as Baltimore's does mine. Time to finish preparing for tomorrow's class: my mind is spinning a little from Nicole Diver's case history.

The diagnosis, written in French at this Swiss asylum: *Schizophrenie. Phase aigue en décroissance. La peur des hommes est un symptôme de la maladie . . .* her first symptom a fear of men (the opposite of Lucia seeking out every mouth tongue penis she could find), slowly addressed by her falling in love with "Captain Diver," the big white cat.

She is brought to Prangins (may as well use its true name) by her widowed father, who speaks of her claiming indecent advances on the part of random strange men—and says "money is no object" in getting her cured. Then he runs away, hoping a cure will be miraculously effected in his absence.

It is the book's Jung-figure who tracks him down, hears the story of their relationship after the death of his wife/her mother. "We used to hold hands. She used to sing to me." (Lucia's father saying that she had a lovely voice, although she says she didn't believe him; the letters to Bray, signed "Ti abbracio"—*my arms surround you*.)

But unlike Lucia's, Nicole's "seductive" relationship with her father crosses over into the physical: "We were just like lovers," her father sobs, "and then all at once we were lovers—and ten minutes later I could have shot myself." (Such a male route of escape, none of the slow dark release of Lucia turning on the gas jets, Virginia Woolf walking into the River Ouse.)

Nicole's first letters from the asylum to "Captain Diver" (her husband-to-be) read like the Austin material, the same looseness of language, streaming from story to story. She calls him a "big white cat," she tells stories of a man on the streets of Paris giving her a flower but then "going away."

In their courtship, Nicole sang flapper songs to Dick Diver, and blues tunes "the cook taught me"—could Zelda and Lucia have sung together, "Sometimes I feel like a motherless child?" *Ti abbracio*, smooth of my slate to the beat of my blosh. Harder and harder to differentiate the fat materialistic Swiss man from the big white cat.

20 July

Last night I felt I was running forever, perhaps twelve miles—then this morning a short run just to Cold Spring Lane and back, immersing myself in green shadow and Lucia Nicole. She used to sing to me. He said I had a lovely voice but I did not believe him.

So of course I was exhausted by the time I showed up for class —giving Jessie a chance to shine. I may need to pay her, this unofficial teaching assistant of mine.

"I'm doing a double major in English and psychology," said our young novelist-wannabe. I sat back and let her hold forth, lecturing the class on "incest constellations," "the cognitive sequelae of incest," and so forth. Her eyes burning through the back of my head, her need to persuade me—Jessie don't worry, I'm with you.

I took it from there, pointing out the poetic nature of schizophrenic speech: "They said you are a doctor, but so long as you are a cat it is different." Or "You told me that night you'd teach me to play. Well, I think love is all there is or should be." *Love have I on my back spine.* How many of Nicole's words were Zelda's, spoken or written, inspiration or plunder?

The voices mingled as I ran last night, blanketed by safe darkness against the manifest perils of Hillen Road. Darkness and Mozart—the hairdresser had inspired me to put in my tape of The Magic Flute, a not-bad English translation that fit perfectly with the blended daughters, by turns satiric and erotic and spiritual. I was just crossing the city line when the Queen of the Night let fly with her hysterical coloratura aria, painfully high cadences weightless under her velvety voice. Mozart knows about women's madness, I thought, the Queen's rage like Lucia di Lammermoor singing in imagined ecstasy.

As I swung up Belair Road I slowed a little, aiming for the steady marathoner's pace, not the hysterical one of the sprinter or the soprano, of Nicole and the twin Lucias.

I had one close call, sort of Mozart's fault: I needed to cross a highway just as the Papegeno/Papagena duet cut in, two earthy comic characters giving the audience a breather from high drama. I was dancing, the liquid baritone sliding out of my little speakers going "pa pa pa pa pa pa" and then

two voices, "papa papa papa papageno papagena."

Suddenly the duet was interrupted by the blat! of a car horn and I realized I had already crossed, completely oblivious to the Jeep Cherokee obviously planning on using the road. The teenager behind the wheel shouted at me as I landed on the other side of the highway; I made I'm-sorry gestures and turned away, back to the lovers' duet, simple joy in being alive.

When I got home, well after midnight, I was hungry—and in

the middle of my sandwich I realized I had not yet eaten, the entire previous day. With this heat I felt no need or desire to eat. Actually food is becoming less and less interesting to me. (Certainly keeps the weight down—102, according to the scale at the gym. I love it, I don't even have to breathe in deeply to see my ribs.) Perhaps I will become one of those Indian swamis, and learn to live on air.

5 August

Kept late hours

   Pop's back home

There is no known record of this scene:

Lucia and her father meeting on the stairs, late some night in the late 1920s, when Joyce has been out carousing with Hemingway and Valery Larbaud. Her face is flushed, she is heavy with exhaustion and smells like sex; he is at the morose stage of drunkenness and holds her in his arms, her glossy hair against his shoulder reminding him of Nora years before. *And they asked me was she my daughter, and I said she was my married wife.*

Did it ever happen? who knows? As I write I'm prowling through all my notes, looking for clues.

Who's the one getting all her kisses that used to belong to me A folk song? Or a father's jealousy, from the same man who follows | *loves fried steak red headed Italian dagodevil, do you mind with whom you did sleep.* And then I find it, the dream-entry, the only one that cites the initials "L.J." He calls it a dream and then after those initials, writes: *Shame gave me light . . . Good god cry of shame (sham?) and horror she only 15*

   Good god cry of shame.

Ashamed of his own desire? Or is he dreaming about something that happened in 1923, the year Bab began his scrutiny of diaphanous L, the year LJ was only fifteen? I am beginning to finally believe it: that Lucia is Nicole Diver.

Without the notebooks you could blame Lucia's madness on

chemistry, without the madness you could speak of Joyce's normal desires, channeled into art.

But 1923 was the year of Joyce's most serious eye illness: great pain, leeches on his eyes, the year he can be said to have gone blind. And I think of the moment Lucia writes of in the Austin notebook, when her father was crying with the pain of his illness and she was too awkward to console him.

Does she mean—as I thought, when I first read it—that she stood helplessly by, while he cried?

Or was it that he was still in pain afterward, after she touched him everywhere he asked, after he touched her in all the warm places, all the right places? That at fifteen she lacked the skill of her mother, to bring James off and help him thus forget his pain?

My head aches so, as Nicole would say. I am frozen at my desk the way you were frozen at Eccles Street, I am staring at your soft lost eyes under the fedora.

You sent her there, James, you sent | to *her place in thadark*. You hoped somehow that it would pass, that once you and she were through creating the book of the Dark, she too would be cured: but you knew what had pushed her over the precipice, the one to which you so delicately clung. "If I never leave till my stave is a bar," you punned in II.ii, "I'd be tempted rigidly to become a passionate father."

And of "The Letter," the truth of the future of the universe and of H.C.E.'s scandal, of which there are so many voicings throughout the Wake—in one of them, the famous II.ii footnote, you allow Issy to admit the truth.

When we will conjugate together toloseher tomaster tomiss while morrow fans amare hour, verbe de vie and verve to vie, with loved ay to love have I on my back spine and does forever. Your are me severe? Then rue.

"Rue, that's for remembrance," Ophelia sang in her mad scene, a confluence already observed by better scholars than I. I am nearly ready to buy Jessie's thesis about Ophelia. What will

Tilden think when I tell him I have reached my own Bloomusalem?

Besides, Fitzgerald knows. Faulkner knows. There was never any secret about this, about incest and madness.

They touched, of that I am sure: and of that touching was born her madness and his pain. And one of the greatest works in the English language bears the mark of both, of the touching and the thought-spirals it produced, of the father's desire and his daughter's lusty agonized speaking, as well as his mortified guilt. *I cd not spare them*, he wrote, perhaps meaning: I could not spare her.

No wonder he looks so sad in those later photographs, he suspects he knows why his daughter is in an asylum in Ivry, one that will soon be bombed by the Germans. And perhaps the thunderstorms they both feared were the ones in their own hearts, and minds.

Lucia I will do it, I will be the one who actually goes beyond a few feeble papers at Bloomsday or the Modern Language Association. I will do it for you for Zelda for the countless un-famous girls represented by Nicole, for the anonymous case history sweethearts spinning off imaginative selves to escape Mother's carving knife or brother's rape-hands.

I will go back to Texas and drown in your words, I will go to London to read your letters to Samuel Beckett, and show them to someone more practiced than I at decoding schizophrenic speech. I will go to the home of Stephen James Joyce and stand in his living room, staring down the man who looks, they say, so much like your Babbo. I will weep until he tells me what he knows. Until he gives me permission to tell the world what I know.

Until he allows me to do what the young James Joyce declared himself ready to do, through the words of Stephen Dedalus. Until I forge in the smithy of my soul the uncreated conscience of my race. Of his race. Of your haunting blue eyes and dancer's body.

23 July

Lucia was too much in my heart and mind to do justice to Fitzgerald this morning in class—we finished him off with dispatch, observing how Nicole Diver must leave her lover/healer, Dick Diver (the one she loved so much they signed letters "Dicole") before her own walls stopped screaming.

And Tilden's note on e-mail this morning (with the time difference he probably left it as I slept) was lighthearted, almost merry: *I had a feeling you would be the one to finally take it on, with all Will O'Donnell's dogged determination and some added ferocity of your own. I'm not sure you can come up with solid, definitive evidence but I cannot imagine a better candidate to try.*

Solid, definitive evidence. As if we literary critics were scientists. We're more like detectives, prowling about for the remains of writers, dancers, artists we've lost to insane asylums, to state hospitals, to private hells. Like Lucia B, I am finally beginning to believe that indeed, "they" have caught up with her.

26 July

Saturday afternoon after a good solid 18-mile push, incorporating parts of all my previous runs. I called Emma first, of course, and she was going to go fifteen again; her training has been quite rigorous of late. Sometimes Barry trails her in the car and clocks her, little Stevie waving from the back seat.

When I told her about my new thesis for the dissertation, all I got was a long, pregnant silence. Finally a soft, almost moaning "oh." God, is she still such a Catholic as all that? I didn't have time to ask—her son started crying for breakfast and I was on a tight schedule myself, before the temperature broke 85 and I would have to cut short the run. When I see her in a few weeks, I can explain to her better what I feel I know, what I am beginning to understand.

"I'm glad you're excited" she finally said: and I do feel like I've just been shot through with adrenalin. I need food even less, as I break mileage records and dig for gold in Joyce's notebooks and go to sleep with diaphanous L's voice in my ears.

Oh Will, why won't you follow me here? Even Tilden says it is your stubbornness that has gotten me this far, but I no longer even dream of you. All that is left is baby Mamalujo, the tiny cello with few ornaments on its blond wood, resting securely between pegs on the wall.

You abandoned me, you answer, and it began in Texas.

And yesterday in Felicia's studio a blues song I'd never heard, a harsh heavy older black woman's voice.

Will, I wonder if I have finally killed you, after all.

In my helpless tears another grief, another loss, one that feels somehow far more permanent: I lost Will long ago but I have finally, definitively lost my Lucia B.

I went everywhere I had ever seen her. I ran up through Waverly, past the baseball stadium: the street was clogged with cars and the sidewalks with families and teenagers, big hulking under-graduates carrying not-very well-concealed cases of beer. Some familiar kids . . . but nowhere in that annoying crowd was my big-breasted, squint-eyed lost soul, my not-very diaphanous L.

She wasn't catching air conditioning in the library.

She wasn't lying by the reservoir.

I thought I saw her in a pack of good-time girls on Baltimore Street, but on closer inspection it was another busty chain smoker in tight jeans. I thought briefly, maybe she was doing nude dancing in one of those GIRLS GIRLS GIRLS places, but on second thought no one would hire her if she talked to them the way she's spoken to me. (And she probably washed out as a prostitute, I'd get nervous if someone I wanted to fuck spoke in code. No wonder Beckett did.)

So they have done it, the "everyone" she spoke of, the police and the nurses—taken her off to the penitentiary, or the hospital, or a shelter. Where, in miserable truth instead of Joycean fancy, she probably belongs. Or else, and this occurred to me at the reservoir, she went and drowned herself in one of our many available bodies of water. Like Ophelia, like Issy, letting the river trip her by and by.

I had Brahms or something in the Walkman, but what I wanted was the blues tape, so I could sing over Lucia B's watery maybe-grave.

Death ain't nothing but a robber, don't you see
Death ain't nothing but a robber, don't you see
Death was here, he didn't stay long I looked in the bed and
my sister she was gone
Death ain't nothing but a robber, don't you see.

After sound, light and heat

"**D**o not leave your baggage unattended," said the voice on the loudspeaker. "All unattended baggage will be confiscated due to the current security threat."

"What's the security threat?" Felicia asked a guard, as she and Rachel wound their way through the caverns of Baltimore-Washington International Airport. The guard shrugged, unable to update them on which war or crime spree was being referenced by the imperious female voice.

Just outside Gate 24 was a video shopping machine, a touch-screen video game offering a universe through telephone and credit card. Rachel chose "Women's Wear" and watched the screen flash to a fair imitation of a Vogue spread. "I can't believe I'm missing class to go shopping."

"That's not why you're missing class." Felicia tapped the screen at some particularly ugly shoes. "You're missing class because a fucking nonstop from San Francisco manages to be forty-five minutes late. What, did the pilot get stoned and get stuck in some really 'awesome' clouds?'"

"Attention passengers! Do not leave your baggage unattended."

Rachel tapped Felicia on the shoulder. "Look, here they come. Did he say what he looks like?"

Flight 9374 from San Francisco came straggling through the gate—mainly businessmen combing their hair for lunch meetings, one large Chinese family with toddler triplets. It wasn't hard to identify the man with shoulder-length hair, a leather jacket, and a beret—he had Emma's large, soft brown eyes.

But when Felicia and Rachel tried to catch his eye he kept looking past them, as if seeking someone taller, or older, or prettier. When Felicia finally called his name he came over to them, mildly startled. "Somehow I thought Molly would be with you," he said softly.

"Are you kidding? Right now they're not letting her out for a walk around the block," said Felicia.

"That's right, you told me that." Leo's brown eyes were alert, different from Emma's in their reserve—a sense of distance, of someone emotionally protected by personal history or years of practice. He yawned, letting his head roll in a neck stretch. "God," he said, "I'm exhausted. Plane flights always do this to me."

"Okay, how about food?" Rachel asked, ever-practical. "You want a cup of coffee?"

"No that's all you get on the plane, over and over, food and coffee."

They walked past the seemingly endless string of airport gates, distinguishable only by the large white numbers posted at each station and the mildly differing airline uniforms.

"What you don't usually get is any sleep," said Felicia. "Feel free to nap when we get back. You have Molly's room, for as long as you're here."

Leo's eyes widened. "You make it sound like that's going to be a long time."

Felicia shrugged. "That's up to you," she said. "But I, at least, was hoping you'd do more than visit."

As they left the terminal for the parking garage, Leo shivered and pulled his leather jacket closer. "Oh right," he said, "I should have brought a scarf. I forgot about November on the East Coast," almost drowned out by "the current security threat."

Leo stretched. "What's that about?"

"Oh, you know how it is, here on the East Coast," said Felicia. "There's always a war going on."

The second floor of Jacob Pearlstone Institute was only minimally heated over the weekend, making for frigid Monday mornings in the conference room. November's first snowfall had just grazed the dead grass; outside the window the few figures hurrying between buildings were wrapped in scarves, gloves, furry hats out of Hans Christian Andersen. Gail Ryan's gloved hands clasped her coffee cup for additional warmth. "The letter arrived on Friday—apparently some of you are familiar with the lawyer, Gregory Cohen."

The head nurse groaned. "How can we forget him? He's the one who brought us *Jessie Berger, Suffering Artiste.*"

In the midst of that sentence Anne-Marie walked in, swathed in white wool gloves and a huge white scarf; as she wound herself out of the scarf, the face that emerged was bright-red cold and exhausted, matching her body language as she slid into the chair. "You're talking about the hearing," she said.

Gail nodded. "A month until her transfer date, now suddenly we have to deal with a hearing—in ten days! Didn't you say her family was unified on Park Grove?"

Anne-Marie bit her lip, choosing her words carefully; her probation had been extended for one more month. "Her roommate still has the legal right to try, with or without the family."

"She just won't succeed," said Gail, "except in wasting our time." She sighed. "What's so ironic, of course, is that no one's even willing to give the new treatment plan a chance—even though for all intents and purposes, she's a brand-new patient. She was cheeking her meds for what, a month?"

"Between three weeks and a month," said the head nurse.

"So a month without any medication, she might as well not have been here—but they all act like we planned it, so we have nothing to offer her now."

"Could you be specific, on the new treatment plan?" asked Steve.

Gail flipped backward in her binder. "Navane, 800 mgs b.i.d. Keeping the Tegretol the same, the lithium the same."

At the name of each medication Anne-Marie's head lowered a half inch further, until her red curls almost obscured her face. She wrote down each name and dosage in large block letters, square contrast to her round handwriting.

"And you're sure she's taking them?" The head nurse's voice skeptical.

Gail paused for effect, before she responded. "Molly is . . . accepting injections."

"You're kidding."

Anne-Marie tried to ignore Gail's careful non-smile. "She regards it all as punishment," she told the head nurse. "For Clay."

"Speaking of which—have you heard anything, about what's happening to him?" Gail asked.

"The scores on his boards came back, he passed with flying colors—it's up to the higher-ups to decide what to do now," said the head nurse. "I have to admit, I'm sorry to lose him."

So is Molly, Anne-Marie wrote on her legal pad, tucking the note away on the last page. *So is the silver fish girl.* Clay had admitted to "inappropriate contact" beginning with the Halloween party, when Molly danced to *Danny Boy.* Finally Gail said, "I'll keep you posted on the hearing as things proceed—we're still trying to contact the family. Is that about it, Anne-Marie?"

Anne-Marie looked up at her supervisor, holding her chain straight, her eyes unrevealing. "Yes," she said, ignoring five pages of notes before her. At the end she had written Emma with a circle and a slash, a small demented traffic sign.

The meeting ended with the slap and shuffle of papers, like the class change at a small, elite college—paper cups drained of coffee and dropped into trash cans with a soft *pop!,* murmurs of gossip among the younger staff. Anne-Marie was still writing in her legal pad when she heard a childlike nurse-voice behind her. "No wonder Clay never complained about the night shift," the girl said, joined in giggles by her friends as they hurried out the door.

Anne-Marie looked out at the desolate grounds, powder-dusted brown punctuated by the bare black branches of the trees. Finally she sighed and stood up; when she turned to leave, Gail was standing there, watching her.

"What do you think?" Gail asked.

Anne-Marie shrugged, her eyes as unreadable as Molly's.

"You're not happy with the injections."

"What do you think? We were finally making some progress—now she's sleepwalking again." Anne-Marie stood up, and put her legal pad in her backpack. "What is Kepler trying to prove?"

From behind them a small tornado of energy, large-bodied secretaries in flowered dresses carrying paper plates and plastic glasses, one loaded down with a huge sheet cake.

Gail murmured something and left; a party descended on the conference table, the women explaining to Anne-Marie "It's Deb's retirement party!" "Can you believe it, forty years in Accounting?" "She used to work at the school!"

Even in her current mood, Anne-Marie smiled at the thought. "So she used to watch little boys running around?"

"Can you imagine?" a young secretary shook her head. "What a difference."

"Right, instead of seclusion they had detention," said Anne-Marie amiably. The women laughed, leaving Anne-Marie to imagine on her own boys lying on cots in the infirmary, flaccid from injections designed to stop them from cutting class or having sex.

. . .

"I married into a very rich and influential family," said Karen Hightower, her speech newly marked by the allegro tempo of Prozac. "They were always going broke, though, that's why they liked me, when I was making $500 an hour." She looked across at Jack, the Star Trek fiend, her head in a magazine-cover tilt. "But then they spent it all. They went broke in 1975, then in 1982, then again in 1987 when the stock market crashed, right around the time I got too old for modeling." She sighed. "And it's starting again. Last year my husband spent $700,000." She picked up the chicken leg on the tray before her. "When will they learn to give me food that I can eat?" Under her silk blouse a bandage lifted one shoulder, the other asymmetrically lower, as if she had lost a shoulder pad.

No one tried to reply to Karen's tirade; only the clacking of plastic forks broke the silence. And very few looked up at the entrance of Molly O'Donnell, who had been in seclusion for three days.

Most of the newer patients were indifferent, still adjusting to their meds; the only ones who showed any curiosity were Jack, the teenage originator of the Star Trek festival, and George, the history professor who'd refused to give up his Robin Hood hat after Halloween, wearing it everywhere except to bed.

Molly slid in on leaden feet, blinking, her greasy hair tucked hastily behind each ear; she had slept through breakfast and lunch, and had had to be forcibly awakened for dinner.

George, in character with his hat, cried out: "But soft! what light in yonder window breaks? It is the east, and Molly is the sun!"

Molly sat down opposite him, carefully, as if she weren't quite sure where all her limbs were. "I have had enough of this day," she said unsteadily. "Everything went off very badly."

"Well it's almost over," said Jack. "After dinner we'll watch TV like any good normal family, until Mommy and Daddy come with our milk and cookies!" He laughed, a low-throated ho-ho-ho out of a horror movie. "Only here, the milk and cookies really put us to sleep. . . . eh, Molly?"

Molly shook her head as the aide placed a tray before her, opened the little plastic silverware pouch, and handed her a fork.

"Try it, Moll. You too, Miss Hightower, I'm not letting either of you get away without eating your dinner." Molly's eyes met Karen's briefly; each began to eat the steamed rice.

When the silence had chilled the room the aide said, "Listen everyone, we're not gonna have Molly with us much longer. She's moving up North very soon."

"Is that true, Molly?" Jack asked, his eyes wide. "You getting out of here?"

Molly's closed her eyes and leaned backward; in a low voice she sang, quiet and unsteady at first, then rising in volume. "Go down Moses! Way down, to Egypt land, Tell old Pharaoh to let my people go!"

"Actually," the aide said uncomfortably but firmly, "Molly's going to another hospital, someplace where she can get better but be closer to her family."

Molly stared at him. "And who, short of a madman, would believe that?" she asked, her words slurred almost to incomprehensibility. Then she answered herself, in what sounded like a drunken spit: "Sender: Boston, Mass."

"Boston is such a beautiful city," Karen Hightower said, deigning to sip her orange juice. "I don't wonder that you'd decide to go there."

Molly shook her head. She worked hard to make her next words more precise. "It is because I have had a lover here," she said. "First he went away, and now they will not have me here anymore." She spoke as if reporting a dream; most of the other patients had lost interest, but Karen Hightower's eyes widened.

"A lover! How exciting, no one tells me anything," Karen said. "But I must confess, my dear, I must tell you that you do not look at your best, remember I helped you with your makeup once? I sincerely hope you looked better when you had a gentleman caller.

Forgive me but your usual allure seems to have dropped off the edge of a waterfall."

Karen's remark, despite its tone, was apt; with her hair clinging to her face and her bleary eyes, Molly did look like someone just pulled up onto shore, still without a place to rest on the edge of the riverbank.

"Anne-Marie's meeting us at the front gate," Felicia said as Rachel steered through the JPI parking lot, looking for a space. "Look Rae, right there!"

"No," Rachel said, "see it says RESERVED, MEDICAL PERSONNEL ONLY."

"So fucking Kepler is out of town," said Felicia. "Can't we take his spot?"

Rachel groaned, finally pulling into a space. "We're fine, she isn't even here yet."

"That's the social worker?" Leo asked. "You've mentioned so many people to me in the last twenty-four hours . . ."

"No, you got it. Her doctor is off at some conference today, thank God," Felicia said. "So we just have Anne-Marie and the nurses to contend with. . . . I don't know what Molly will be like, she might be a zombie again. I'm not even sure these fucking injections are legal . . . Leo, I really want to hear your take on this whole place. I think I've gotten too used to it."

Anne-Marie was late, giving Leo time to looked around him at the grounds, the small brown buildings shaded by leafless trees. His exhales were white clouds, soft as his speech. "I've been to so many hospitals in the last few years, few months," he said, so quietly Felicia and Rachel had to strain to hear him. "None of them anything like this." He gestured to the tops of the trees. "Overgrown prep schools like this—up north, where I grew up, they're everywhere."

As he spoke Rachel was being hugged from behind, Anne-

Marie arriving with the usual breathless apologies. "Don't worry," said Rachel, "we know your standard time. Next time we'll find a warmer place to wait, though."

"Oh and it's so cold . . . and you from California!" she exclaimed to Leo

"Oh yes, poor me," Leo laughed. Leo O'Donnell looked a good ten years younger than his age, except when he smiled: then wrinkles emerged around his eyes and mouth, joy recalling past sorrows. He pointed at the main building. "Why such monstrous windows?"

"For safety," Anne-Marie explained. "Enough glass gets broken around here, as it is." She looked at her watch. "We're meeting up with Molly there, in the family meeting room. You probably won't want to go back to Chatham with her—it's a pretty wild place just now."

"Wilder than usual?" Rachel asked. Felicia was walking ahead of them, barely glancing at Anne-Marie: the social worker kept glancing toward her, anxiety softened by fatigue.

"Lots of new admissions," she said. "And sort of a different population."

"Meaning?" Leo asked.

"Meaning a lot more poor people . . . the kind you usually see panhandling on North Avenue."

Felicia turned around at that, an edge to her voice. "Oh," she said. "You mean more Black people. Like Baltimore." She turned away again, as if to join an unseen partner.

"So let me get this straight," said Leo. "The latest crisis—Molly was having sex with a nurse?"

"Well, we'd—they'd suspected she wasn't taking her meds for a long time." Anne-Marie's tone was carefully neutral. "At least since she set fire to her room."

At the word "fire" Leo gave a small, Mephistophelean smile. "When I left Boston twenty years ago, I set fire to the garage," he said. "Molly couldn't have been more than five—now I wonder if she remembered."

"No shit!" Felicia slowed down, until they were all walking together.

"And how old were you?" asked Anne-Marie.

Sixteen," Leo said with precision, as if he could name the months and days if asked. "Poppie could still see in those days, at least well enough to catch me with a boy in my bedroom. . . . He hit me with a strap, the way he always did, but—worse." Leo shivered, hugging his borrowed coat. "About three hours later I left for good."

The story left an empty space in the air, too hollow to be filled by small talk or information; they entered the main building quietly, hallways still frigid despite the blast-heat coming from floor vents. Felicia winced, "you'd think they'd learn how to heat this place."

Sheets of drawing paper covered the walls, fall scenes mixed with winter; Leo moved along the wall and leaned on one of the sofas, to look more carefully. At the end of a clearly drawn highway was a word in block letters at the end, small in accurate perspective: LOVE. At the bottom of the drawing a larger set of block letters, saying ANGER; then a realistic road sign, even to the typeface used by the highway department. *recovery 38 mi.*

Across the room, just below a winter-scene collage, Molly sat slumped on a sofa, in her spandex running outfit and a bulky cardigan. Her hair was clean but uncombed, the muscles of her face slack as she stared alternately at the coffee table and her sneakered feet.

"Molly?" Molly looked up; when she saw Leo her eyes widened, as if trying to recognize someone from a dream. She blinked hard, breathing deeply; when he moved forward to embrace her, she spoke slowly, painfully trying to enunciate each shy word. "My rib is much better now," she said. "How are you? How is your ice cream house?"

Leo blinked, then leaned forward and kissed her cheek. "I'm glad I was able to help you with your broken rib," he said softly. "Maybe I can help you now, too."

Molly's eyes were bright. "Can you take me home with you?" she asked. "They will not have me here any more." She tried to stand up quickly, to face him, and immediately fainted.

A nearby nurse approached Molly from one side, Anne-Marie from the other. "Nothing to worry about," the nurse explained, "she's just getting used to the Navane." Felicia and Anne-Marie helped her lift Molly from the carpet and lay her on the sofa. Leo retreated to the opposite wall, looking again at the highway to recovery while the nurse took Molly's pulse.

Suddenly a voice behind Felicia: "Excuse me, miss?"

Felicia turned, to see an elegantly turned-out woman in a russet long-sleeved jumpsuit and glossy brown hair, the only clue to her status the telltale white strip of her ID bracelet.

"Hi," Felicia said uncertainly. "Is there something I can do for you?

"Well . . . My name is Karen." The woman's expression was coy, almost flirtatious. "I hate to bother you when Molly isn't feeling well. But . . ."

"Yes?"

Karen took a deep breath and straightened her shoulders, as if about to recite a monologue for the stage. "Molly told me . . . you had covered yours with tattoos. And I thought it might be, oh—" she extended her arms with a theatrical flourish "—an artistic alternative to plastic surgery."

Felicia rolled up her sweater, exposing her tiny green snakes. "These aren't covering anything," she said softly, wanting to be sure she was hearing correctly. "What about your back?"

Felicia closed her eyes. "You've never seen my back," she said. "What did Molly tell you?"

Karen unbuttoned the top of her jumpsuit, pulling the collar down on the left to reveal her shoulder, its padding now reduced to a thin gauze bandage. "I tried to reach my back this time," she said, "but I couldn't do it—not and keep my hand steady. How did you do it?"

Felicia's breath stopped; without thinking, she stepped forward to touch the other woman's hand just below the long glossy fingernails. "Don't bother," she said.

Karen stared, and stepped back. "All I wanted," she said airily, "was the name and phone number of your tattoo artist."

Felicia swallowed. "She costs a lot these days. . . . She was just learning, when she did mine."

"Cost is no object!" Karen declared.

"Karen?" A short, mustached man stood behind them, looking a little ill.

"This is my husband," Karen said in introduction. "We're going for a walk now. . . . Please give Molly the name—when she feels better." She smiled her best supermodel grin. "Thanks so much!" Then she turned away, her husband following her as she walked with featherlight steps.

Felicia turned back to Rachel and Leo. "Whew."

"I know her," Rachel said. "Maybe five years ago, she was in fashion magazines. *Vogue* , at least. I'm not kidding, no wonder she has such nice clothes."

"She needs them, it seems," Felicia said. Leo swallowed; he didn't say anything, just watched as the couple left the meeting room.

In another corner a tall, angry man leaned over his adolescent son; one had to look closely to see that it was the son who wore the white bracelet. Leo kept his hands in his back jeans pockets, his shoulders showing the first signs of visible tension.

When Molly came to, he asked to follow her back to the ward; Rachel excused herself. "I'll meet you guys at the car."

Despite Anne-Marie's warning, Chatham was quiet except for the television; George the professor was watching the news, wars from around the world broadcast into the sunset-filled dayroom. As they entered, the nurse at the station called to Anne-Marie, "Kim's on her way over, for Molly's meds."

"How long?" Anne-Marie asked.

"She's at Wilkes right now . . . maybe ten minutes." Felicia was walking behind the rest; at the nurse's reply she clasped her hands behind her back, pulling in an isometric stretch, as if that would release the tension in her back.

Other than the gunshots on the TV, the ward was quiet. In the back dayroom a tall man was hooking a rug, the word PEACE in rainbow colors; a volunteer helped a group of small, decrepit elderly people with a jigsaw puzzle. "That's just blue, like the sky," the volunteer said helpfully.

"Like heaven," said a weathered man with a Native American cast to his features. "I'm very religious, you know." Leo stopped, momentarily; the man looked up from his puzzle piece and met Leo's eyes. "I pray every day," he said more loudly. Leo nodded and continued down the corridor, toward Molly's room.

Molly hadn't had a roommate since Shana left, and her possessions were scattered around the room—her Walkman and tapes, her clothes and running equipment. Felicia's drawing was pasted carefully above her bed, as always, right beside Van Gogh's sunflowers; the *lettrines* were gone, reclaimed by the staff. Leo began to pick Molly's clothes off the floor, creating a pile on the little lawn chair.

When the medication nurse arrived, Felicia and Anne-Marie retreated to the doorway. Leo sat on the edge of the bed and watched as the nurse checked her syringes for bubbles. "Listen," Anne-Marie said softly to Felicia, "did you get my message?"

Felicia watched the nurse sink the needle into Molly's thigh. "I told you before, Anne-Marie, I don't feel like talking to you anymore."

"But the notebooks—those aren't your property."

"Then what makes you think I have them?" Felicia's voice was so soft that Anne-Marie had to lean closer to hear.

"I told you—Molly told me."

"But how come you believe her? She's crazy, remember?" By now Felicia was whispering. "You're not supposed to trust them if they're not on their meds, and she wasn't when she told you that." Felicia watched Molly's pupils dilate. "She fooled you for a whole month! I'm so proud of her."

"Felicia—" Finally Anne-Marie had to follow Felicia into the hallway. The young artist's full fury was exhaled like smoke, in soft guttural murmurs. "Get the fucking picture, Anne-Marie. Get it. Get. It. Now. . . . This is kind of like the Civil War. You work here, remember? I am fighting to get Molly out of here. "

Anne-Marie closed her eyes. "Felicia, you know I'm on probation—if they fire me, that leaves her in the hands of Kepler, Shaun, and Gail."

Felicia leaned against the doorjamb, looking at Anne-Marie for a long moment; then she reached out and shook the social worker's hand. "What a great 'good cop' you've learned to be," she said. "They teach you in school how to make people trust you, then you come here and get at least thirty thou, plus benefits—"

She stopped as Leo approached: the simultaneous questioning of the two women was like an assault, Anne-Marie asking "How are you?" as Felicia demanded "What do you think?"

Leo rubbed his eyes. "I feel a little like Alice in the looking glass."

"Alis, alas, they broke the glass!" That cry came from Molly, sitting up in bed and calling over to him. "Ours is a mystery of pain, Leo—a mystery of shame."

Anne-Marie closed the door as Leo went back to his sister, so that no disapproving staff would see her arms curl around his neck, see her cry into her brother's shirt. Leo's eyes were closed, his hair coming loose from the ponytail and falling to touch Molly's black hair—the same color, salted with silver strands.

Felicia went over to Molly's other side, not touching either of them; when Leo opened his eyes, he looked only at his sister. He tipped Molly's head up and looked into her face. "I'll be right back, Molly," he said softly. "Just give me five minutes."

As Leo stood up Felicia put her arms around Molly's shoulders to steady her; Molly didn't look up, instead tracing fingertip circles on the floor.

The medication nurse was packing up her little kit, clipping the points off the syringes before discarding them in a bright-red plastic box labeled CAUTION. Leo walked calmly past her to the bathroom, a gentle swing to his walk.

"She really oughtn't have visitors, just now," the nurse said to Anne-Marie as she left, taking the red box with her.

"I know, I know." Anne-Marie closed the door behind the nurse; she moved toward the bed and picked up the Walkman from the pile Leo had made. "I think we need some music," she said, inserting the little external speaker and a random tape. The strong, harsh strokes of a string quartet served their intended purpose—to blot out the sound from the bathroom, Leo vomiting, not violently but steadily, without pausing for breath.

The Holiday Inn in Owings Mills, Maryland, specialized in family visits, both to Pearlstone and the veterans' cemetery a few miles away; on weekends the plant-filled brunch room was full of forlorn parents and children, some come to mourn the dead, others the living.

Saturday morning and the long table near the entrance was full of O'Donnells—Shaun at one end and Anna at the other, with Emma and her husband along one side. Emma kept her eyes fixed on three-year-old Stephen William Gahagan, fast asleep in her lap. "I'm so glad he slept all the way here," she said, her voice betraying only fatigue. "He's been a little rambunctious lately, with me coming down here all the time."

"With you doing what?" Shaun asked. Emma kept her lips

closed, brushing her sleeping toddler's hair. Shaun cleared his throat. "I didn't hear you, Emma."

Emma's husband, Barry, replied in her place. "Don't be a jerk, Shaun. You know this is hard for her. Hell, I even gave you the number of Em's therapist." Stevie began to stir, reaching out to pull a few leaves off the philodendron hanging near the table; Emma began to feed him bits and pieces of her bagel, whispering in his tiny ear.

"It's just absurd," Shaun said, peevish. "Telling someone to stop speaking to her own brother. Who the hell is this shrink to make judgments like that?"

"Judgments like what?"

Shaun jumped, though the voice behind him was calm, a measured question without much emotion. Emma handed her son to Barry, so that she could hug the small, compact man with the ponytail. "It's been so long, Leo, so long!" Emma closed her eyes as she hugged her brother, squeezing them shut as if she were her son's age.

Leo clasped back gently, "Five years, I think. . . . my baby sister's a big girl now." When Emma let go, he shook hands with Shaun and Anna as if they were distant colleagues. "Good to see you both," then he turned back to Emma. "Can I catch a whiff of this young man?"

Leo's hair was a miracle to Stevie, who pulled hard at his uncle's ponytail until Emma said "Be nice, Stevie!"

"Nice!" said the toddler stubbornly, salt-and pepper hair in his fist.

"It's friendly but it hurts," said Leo. "You'd better stop." He looked straight into Stevie's eyes, as if the child were an adult.

When Stevie had had enough breakfast, Barry took him out of the restaurant: "You won't be able to talk now that he's awake." As soon as they were out of earshot, Shaun leaned back against the padded seats of the booth and put his briefcase on the table.

"All right, Leo," he said, "I suppose you'll want to be updated on everything that's gone on so far."

Leo shrugged. He had left on his sunglasses, to block the harsh winter sunlight that streamed through the plate-glass windows of the restaurant. "I've been here for three days," he said. "Between Molly, her social worker, and Felicia, I've had a pretty thorough introduction."

"Who, that—roommate?" Shaun spat the word in place of choicer nouns. "I've already submitted a request, in writing, that Felicia Waller be barred from visiting Molly. I'm sure she taught her how to avoid her medication." He reached into his briefcase and handed Leo a photocopy. "Kepler's meeting with his legal staff, to see what grounds he needs to claim."

"Wait a minute." Leo pulled his chair closer so that a troop of preteen girls could get past him, a stream of Sunday dresses and steaming buffet plates. "I thought you've been planning to transfer her."

"That's at least a month away, maybe more," Shaun said. "It seems that winter is the hardest time to move someone."

"You mean," said Leo, "all the real loony bins are full up." His low gentle voice somehow sharpened the remark.

"Need you be so crude?" Anna's voice carried over the brunch hubbub, at least one waiter turning to look at her. "And please take off those sunglasses."

Leo grinned as he placed the glasses on the table. "Well, Anna, I'm pleased to see you're still in fine form."

Anna stared, waving at the waitress for more coffee. "Leo, I called you months ago about Molly. Why are you coming here now? To insult us all? To take the side of that tattooed anorexic?"

"She cares more about Molly—" Emma stopped and swallowed, her eyes brimming. She opened her purse and placed a postcard on the table: a Felicia drawing of Molly, hair cut short and made vivid by red and purple shading.

Leo picked it up, read the other side. "I haven't seen the show yet," he told Emma; then he turned to Shaun. "Listen, Molly and Felicia are very close," he said. "Whatever you and Kepler have discussed, Molly has rights of her own—and if she wants Felicia to visit, she gets Felicia."

"But those rights are limited," Anna said. "She has the legal status of a minor."

Leo shook his head. "That's not my understanding. . . . And to answer your question, Anna, I came here to learn. That's all."

Shaun leaned forward, his ruddy face close to Leo's. "So am I to believe you're not behind this new legal mess, this hearing I'm now told I have to undergo?"

"I didn't start it," Leo said, "but I'm not at all sure it's a bad idea." Before Shaun could reply, he said, "I thought we were going to see Molly this morning."

"We're waiting for Anne-Marie," Emma said. "She thought she'd talk with all of us together, before we see Molly en masse."

"Oh, that one's always late," Leo said. "I'm going to get some food." He moved toward the buffet table; on the way, he picked up a philodendron leaf Stevie had loosed from its mother. When he came back the leaf was nestled amongst bits of pineapple, a slightly wrinkled garnish.

Emma held the leaf up to the light; its veins showed clearly, signs of recent life. She took a deep breath as she turned it, slowly. "I'm going to keep this," she said. "This fall, we showed Stevie how the leaves die. . . . Now he can start to learn that some things keep growing, even in the middle of winter."

Kepler's office looked like the aftermath of some geographically improbable earthquake. "Two conferences in a row," he explained, embarrassed, "and my secretary's on vacation."

"Your secretary cleans your desk?" Shaun was impressed.

"We don't have much time," said Kepler. "I have some urgent policy matters to attend to. I just wanted to reopen the discussion of

Molly's new situation—we can continue after you've seen her." He opened Molly's chart; recent events had thickened the white binder to biblical size.

"My position has not changed," said Shaun. "This most recent matter only proves she needs stricter supervision."

Anna's back was rigid, agreeing. "This business with the male nurse, I mean really!"

Shaun coughed, as if to suppress a laugh. "Hell, Anna, she practically came on to me, for Christ's sake—you can hardly blame any healthy young male for responding." He shook his head, professionally sorrowful. "More seriously, sir: if I can't be sure that my sister is receiving her medication, how can I possibly entrust you with her overall treatment?"

Behind Shaun's back Leo stood slouched against the wall; he took a fountain pen out of his pocket and wrote on the edges of his newspaper, handing it to Anne-Marie. She read it and nodded, quickly returning her attention to Shaun.

"Just remember," said Kepler, "Park Grove has far fewer staff. . . . Something like what happened with Clay—it may, in fact, be more likely to happen there. Whereas you'll see when you visit Molly, the change is remarkable." He smiled, a Wall Street Pepsodent smile. "She's still delusional, but she's finally cooperating in her treatment."

Shaun, the room's center of gravity in his large armchair, shifted his weight and leaned forward, his shoulders flashing exhaustion in a brief glimpse. "Between my mother and Molly, I must confess I'm sometimes driven to distraction. . . . Listen, my primary concern is the same as before—that you are able to calm her. Don't get me wrong, I always hope for the best."

"I think you'll be impressed," said Kepler. "Once Molly's medication schedule is firmly established we expect her speech to clear—then we can graduate her to insight-oriented psychotherapy, possibly before Thanksgiving. Park Grove may not seem necessary to you, by then."

"That would be wonderful," Shaun said, sarcasm lining his voice. "In the meantime, our agreement still holds." He spread his arms, the gesture theatrical, Catholic. "Dan, for the moment we are at your mercy. We need to be able to trust you—at the very least, to keep my sister on medication and under proper restraint."

"Within legal limits on coercion, of course," Leo added.

"Of course," Kepler said automatically—then he looked over at Leo, startled. Then the Pepsodent smile returned: "Oh! You're Leopold O'Donnell. The long-lost brother." Leo shrugged, silently taking Kepler's outstretched hand. "Well, Mr. O'Donnell," said Kepler, "Molly is cooperating right now—so coercion is not at issue." He looked at Leo for one long moment, his eyes narrowing. "Are you with Patients' Rights Advocates? I had assumed it was all Felicia Waller's doing."

Leo spoke with his usual slow, even pace, toning down the discussion. "No," he said, "but I'm quite interested."

Kepler sighed, and gestured for Leo to look at the chart. "Mr. O'Donnell," he said, "you've seen for yourself how disturbed Molly is. Her hypersexuality, as with Clayton Richards, was only one of the more blatant symptoms." Kepler looked to Shaun and Anna; Emma was in absentia, having opted to go back to Chatham with Molly. "They'll tell you this hearing is hardly necessary."

Leo walked over to Kepler's desk, leaning on one palm at its edge. His long fingers, slightly tanned, brushed the blond wood. "But it won't hurt, will it? You've got her, for now."

Kepler closed his binder with a sigh. "I'm very sorry I didn't meet you when you first came here," he said. "I don't know what sort of ideas you may already have about Pearlstone."

Leo smiled, laugh lines showing at the corners of his eyes. "I reserve judgment in all things," he said, "and that includes this place."

As he spoke, the sun had completely set, shrouding the Pearlstone grounds in darkness except for the lights from Wilkes, visible through the bare tree branches. Kepler leaned over and turned on his office lamp, a high-tech creature with a long arm clamped to his desk; its incandescent light both illuminated and softened his and Leo's faces, leaving the others in shadow.

Lithium, Tegretol and winter snow had slowed Molly's running pace; she also kept stopping every couple of minutes to pick up the snow with her bare hands, burying her face. Each time, Emma, beside her, knelt matter-of-factly and raised her to her feet like a child, to begin to run again. "So here I am, proud new mom, getting ready to write down my little genius' first complete sentence—and it's Why is lunch hot?"

Molly laughed. "Whoever thought of this breakfast?"

Anne-Marie was behind them; forced by the slowness into walking instead of running, she was freezing, even in two layers of sweats. Both Molly and Emma had insisted on this hastily arranged run, the first since Molly had been caught sleeping with Clay. Only one aide trailed them.

"He's really getting the point of Christmas, this year," Emma said between gasps. "Last year he sort of vaguely knew what it was about—now he's already excited, thanks to all those TV Christmas specials!"

While Emma spoke, Anne-Marie watched Molly's heavy legs, her still eyes; under the Xanax-serene responses to the Stevie stories, her facial muscles seemed to sag. As they turned back, Emma signaled to Anne-Marie to move closer.

"Do you want to stay at Pearlstone, Molly?" Emma asked. "You know we've been—Shaun has been trying to get you closer to home."

"Shaun," Molly said, "what a sham." She stopped, hugging herself in a self-protective gesture, and called out into the air, as if bringing forth a spirit. "If I go," she called, "all goes."

Anne-Marie moved so that she was in front of Molly, and reached upward to touch the other woman's shoulder, lightly.

"Molly," she said, "listen to me. People are discussing your future, all around you. Shaun wants to take you to a big hospital near Boston. Felicia wants to take you home to Calvert Street, Dr. Kepler wants you to stay here—and Emma and I want whatever is going to help you the most. But we need to know what you want. If you don't tell anyone, they'll decide for you."

Molly shook off Anne-Marie's hand and spurted forward, her movements still clumsy but quicker; she beat Emma and Anne-Marie to the Chatham entrance by at least 500 yards. When they caught up with her, she said "I'll slip away before they're up. . . . They'll never know, never miss me."

"It doesn't work that way," said Emma.

The blast-heat of Chatham in wintertime was unusually welcome; Anne-Marie was tempted to kneel by a heating vent and soak it in. Molly walked slowly, carefully, as if in a graduation exercise; Anne-Marie found herself wondering how Molly had looked in her Barnard yearbook.

As they entered Molly's room, Shaun and Anna were sitting each to a bed; Leo stood, looking at Felicia's drawing of the red-haired Molly with the aching eyes.

The three runners entered slowly, Molly still at her charm-school pace: she extended her hand, wordlessly. "Well, hello, Molly, how are you?" Shaun forced a grin, not unlike Kepler's bright-toothed smile.

"I've been better," she said with great effort. She then moved over to Anna and shook her hand. "Thank you for coming, Anna," she said. "It is very nice of you, to come see me in this place."

"This place." Shaun smiled. "Do you like it here, Molly?"

Molly's smile was suddenly tinged with humor. "Yes oh yes," she said.

"So they're taking good care of you," Shaun asked slowly, in the tone of a question. Leo stood a few feet behind him, blocked from Molly's view by Shaun and Anna. "And you would like to stay."

"As well here as another!" Molly laughed, dropping to the floor next to her running partners and beginning to stretch. "Yes I will, yes."

"As well here as another? . . . Oh, you Molly Bloom, you." Leo moved away from the wall and sat down next to his sister, who was trying fruitlessly to lower her chin to her knee, despite a stiff back. He watched her for a few moments without speaking further, in his eyes the cat-alertness Anne-Marie had first noticed about him.

When he finally caught Molly's eye, she stopped what she was doing: her jaw went slack and her shoulders rounded, a snake uncoiling or a baby falling asleep. She turned to him as if there were no one else in the room.

"Carry me away," she said, "please carry me away. Save me from those terrible prongs!"

"You mean the needles, Molly?" Anne-Marie asked. "The ones we use for your medicines?"

Ignoring Anne-Marie, Molly leaned forward and touched Leo's face; when he moved a little closer she collapsed against him. "Carry me," she said. "Oh please carry me. . . . Like you did through the toy fair." Her low sobs were unlike any Anne-Marie had heard before.

"It's okay, Molly, it's okay." Leo stroked her hair, flattened by the hood she'd been wearing, and looked up at the others. "You can go now," he said, in a tone that was more than a request. "I'll meet you back at the main building."

Anne-Marie led the remaining O'Donnells out of Chatham, her hat now damp against her red curls. "I'm sorry, I'll have to abandon you at the main building—I have an appointment in Baltimore City."

Shaun and Anna walked ahead of the other two, hurrying against the wind. "What a mess!" Shaun said, drawing closer to Anna. "At least she knows who we are . . . but all that nonsense she's saying to Leo!" He looked behind him, glowering in Chatham's general direction. "What nerve—coming in at this late date and acting like he's in a position to make judgments. How much does he really care about Molly, anyway?" When he saw Anne-Marie's eyes on him, Shaun leaned closer to Anna and began to whisper.

Emma and Anne-Marie lagged a little, to create some distance; Emma sighed, relieved. "This not speaking to Shaun—in Boston it's like being let out of prison, suddenly I can breathe. But here, under this proximity, it's—" her jaw stiffened, as if from a spasm in her neck muscles.

Anne-Marie nodded. "I know . . . but you can't talk to me either, right?" The social worker didn't bother to turn, to see Emma's vigorous nod. "But listen," she said, "Felicia said you're the one who gave her the lawyer's number."

Emma shrugged. "I got it from this girl in New York, a student of Molly's. . . . But I don't see how a judge will actually let Molly out of here. What do you think?"

Anne-Marie hugged her long gray coat, incongruous over sweats. "I think," she said, "that I miss the dancer. The one who had the nerve to have sex on a hospital ward in the middle of the night."

After saying goodbye to all O'Donnells, she pulled her hat tight over her ears, the chill chasing her to the parking lot. Kepler was already there, as if he'd been lying in wait for her; he waved her over as he locked his Jeep.

"How did it go?"

"None of us could run worth a damn," Anne-Marie said, as if that answered his question.

Kepler sighed. "I meant the family visit."

Anne-Marie got out her car keys. "Go see for yourself—Leo's with Molly and the rest are in the main building. Looks like you definitely have Emma, and you may win Shaun over yet."

"Good," Kepler said absently, looking quickly into the distance. Then he focused on Anne-Marie, his eyes widening. "I've got Emma? What about us? You're part of the treatment team too, Anne-Marie." He put a paternal arm around her, his hand on her shoulder. Under his fur-lined leather glove, Kepler didn't seem to feel Anne-Marie flinch.

"And given the rapport you have with Molly," he continued, "we especially need you, if we're going to be able to stabilize her." He gave her shoulder a totally unsolicited squeeze. "Working together, I know we can do it."

"I don't doubt it," Anne-Marie said, with perfect honesty. "I'm sure that in time, we can get Molly cooperating, taking her medications. Maybe even living in a halfway house."

Kepler grinned. "That's the spirit. . . . So when's the next family meeting?"

"Next Sunday," Anne-Marie said. "Give them some time to talk it over."

A thumbs-up signal and Kepler was gone, toward the main building. Anne-Marie got into her ancient Buick and started winding home, wondering if she should start taking whatever kept Kepler smiling.

The Wayne Gallery was medium-full on late weekday afternoons —art students mixing with tourists mixing with suburban shoppers from the malls nearby. One tall blonde woman, wielding a formidable set of GAP and boutique bags, refused to release them to the guard; he finally let her through, there to stroll carelessly among the drawings.

Felicia kept looking u toward the entrance, anxiety framing her brow. "Hey, pay attention," Jeff whispered in her ear. "Sounds like someone's got serious money."

Felicia bent her head over the book; she had begun to let her hair grow in, the faint dust shadow on her scalp a surprising red-gold. She looked over the numbers, blankly. "He wants to buy how many pieces?"

The gallery owner spread his hands. "He was only here a few

minutes," he said. "But grew very excitable, said maybe three or four paintings. Especially the one you called Shem."

Felicia took a deep breath. "That one's not for sale."

"Can we talk, Leesh?" Jeff d'Ambrosio seemed to have gone grayer in the weeks since the show began; he took Felicia's hand and began to draw her away.

Just as she began to turn with him, the gallery door opened and Emma and Leo entered together, a familiar figure between them.

Molly smiled and tossed her hair, another dreamlike, underwater motion. Now that she was back in the category of "good patient," the staff had allowed her to get her hair cut in the city; the hairdresser she had requested, on Charles Street, had cut her bangs and trimmed the rest, so that soft curves brushed her collarbone. Her long-sleeved silk blouse covered the hospital bracelet, and the eight-hour pass from JPI was tucked safely away in her back jeans pocket.

Felicia stepped forward into Molly's spread arms; the two women stood together, Felicia murmuring into Molly's neck, "I hope you love it." Behind Felicia's back, Jeff shook his head; when the two women separated he said to her, "Leesh, let's go for coffee . . . give Molly some time with her family."

Felicia's brow furrowed; then she said to Molly, "I'll be back soon, I promise." Molly nodded as Felicia threw on her coat and scarf, following Jeff out the door.

Molly turned toward one of the canvases; she led Leo along with her and clung to his hand like a child, the effect somewhat lessened by the fact that she was four inches taller than he. "Do you remember, Molly?" Leo asked. "All those months modeling for Felicia?"

"Of course," she said softly, meeting his gaze. She reached out and twirled a long lock of his hair, her fingers lingering under his ear.

Then she withdrew from him and began to move slowly from one canvas to the next, staring at each face as if into a distorting mirror: her own face now softer, rounder than the angles Felicia had accented, her hair neither the long swirls of the early drawings or the short razor-cut of the final, largest pieces. On one canvas, color photographs of all the others were blown up, scissored and collaged together: its title was *Christine Beauchamp*. A small elfin smile crept onto Molly's face; she leaned forward and whispered to the canvas, "Your prayerbook is in the salt-box, if you want it."

Leo and Emma followed a few steps behind, as Molly moved along the walls. Her movements were still slow but less awkward, as she learned to bear the medication with some measure of grace. Others passed between them, students busily taking notes, tourists wielding camera bags.

Molly spoke softly as she arrived at each canvas, faint echoes of an Irish brogue. "How was she handsome! . . . And what is she, the weird haughty one?" She slowed down further, her jaw tightening, one hand in a fist while the other hung loosely at her side. As she grew less self-conscious and her voice louder, the other gallery patrons moved away from her.

Emma looked over at Leo, as if he could tell her how to react; he drew her back so they were both behind their sister, as Molly spoke to herself in Felicia's images.

Her eyes widened at an erotic Molly-figure with her legs spread, clothed with photocopied *Finnegans Wake* quotations. A tiny smile flickered as she whispered, "Hearsay in paradox lust."

She finally stopped at the largest piece, and stared at her own face surrounded with violet, hair cut short and eyes enormous. The title on the card underneath the painting was simple, matching the broad calligraphic writing on the painting itself: *Shem*. Leo and Emma came to a stop behind her, were silent for a moment after Molly's fervent chant. Then Leo pointed to the painting and asked Emma, "Shem?"

"Oh Molly, I had forgotten," Emma said, "I forgot how often Poppie called you that."

Molly shuddered herself into a slight forward crouch. One leg twisted around the other as if in a yoga posture, her left hand gripping her right shoulder; her right hand held tightly to her ribcage, as if she literally needed to hold herself together. "Beloved enemy of my will," she whispered, a chant-like prayer.

"Did Molly name this painting?" Emma asked Felicia.

"Of course," Felicia said softly: her usual angry energy seemed knocked out of her by her heavy coat. "Do you remember, Molly?"

Molly nodded. "Something happened that time I was asleep," she said, very carefully and precisely. "Torn letters, or was there snow?"

"Both, Molly," Felicia said. "Both."

Molly looked at the floor, then turned to Leo. "Come," she said to him, taking his hand and leading him toward the right wall, with its earlier, more realistic sketches. Emma and Felicia watched, not following them.

"God, I need coffee," Felicia said softly. "You want to come up to the office with me?"

The gallery office was a tiny loft-space with a glass wall, through which one could watch the gallery's action as if in box seats at the opera. Felicia slumped in one of the soft chairs near the kitchen-area.

"He didn't come while I was gone, huh? . . . They're always serious when they say they're gonna buy." Felicia's sigh was deeper than intended.

Emma filled two mugs from the coffee maker, handing one to Felicia. "You're exhausted," she said.

"And pissed off." The fatigued words acquired more potency as Felicia drank, tension and dignity returning to her slight frame with each sip. "Here I am doing everything humanly possible to have this come off—contacting Leo, doing my own research, calling the lawyer every day to tell him what I found. And Jeff doesn't give a shit, he thinks I should just care about making money, he *says hey Molly's got her family* . . . He just doesn't get it. Last night he left my house at two a.m."

397

"Why?"

"I wasn't ready to come to bed yet." Felicia closed her eyes. "I was looking at some of the Xeroxes I never used. Molly's pictures of Lucia Joyce."

"Lucia Joyce." Emma sank into a chair next to Felicia. "Sometimes I wish Molly had never heard of her."

"I don't know. . . ." Felicia kept her eyes closed and spoke carefully, deliberately. "If it hadn't been Lucia, it might have been something else." She opened her eyes, extracting a pack of cigarettes from the pocket of her silk jacket. "I think," she said slowly, "it was time, to finally face her childhood shit." She lit the cigarette, shaking the match to put it out. "I know remembering is hard, but look what she's had to do to keep forgetting."

Emma choked on her coffee, spilling some of it on her gray wool skirt; she dashed to wet a paper towel. Felicia got up to help her, providing new paper towels and saying softly, "I'm sorry, I didn't mean to upset you. . . . but it doesn't take a rocket scientist to guess out what she's running away from." She rolled the used paper towels into a ball, held them tightly in her calloused hand. "Emma? What about you?"

Emma had not yet looked at Felicia; she looked up from her skirt to face the young artist, nodding her head very, very slowly. "It's taking a lot of work, just to bring up vague memories . . . it only happened once or twice, not the way it—" She cut off and looked down again, dabbing at her skirt.

"The way it was with Molly," Felicia finished for her, the cigarette smoke curling vampirism around her dark-lined eyes.

Emma stood up finally, tossing her paper towel into the wastebasket.

"Why haven't you said anything? To Dr. Kepler, or at least Anne-Marie?"

Felicia laughed. "And give them another excuse to keep her there longer? I can hear it now, some shit like *Patient's continued denial of childhood trauma.*"

The gallery door opened. The man stood gingerly at the entrance, in an expensive black cloth coat and blue scarf; in one hand he held the invitation postcard, with the reproduction of the Shem painting. In his other hand was a violin case.

The buyer looked around quizzically while Emma, behind Felicia, took a deep breath. By the time they'd had hurried downstairs, the man in question had already found Molly.

"My dearest, where on earth have you been?" Without asking he was hugging her, pulling the young woman to his breast as if she were a child; Leo then separated them, gently. "Hello, Colin," he said. "I don't know if you remember me."

"Molly's brother, of course I do." The Englishman's reserve returned, as he shook Leo's hand vigorously. "Why I couldn't believe it, when my manager brought this card back to our hotel. Then when I came, and saw all this marvelous work—I thought it a grand investment, and hoped perhaps to show Molly that all is forgiven."

"All is forgiven?" Leo raised an eyebrow, until it almost disappeared into his beret.

"Well, you know how it is. About two years ago, quite unexpectedly, our dear girl decided it was time to leave me . . . the best for both of us, I'm sure." He turned to Molly. "And how are you, my dear girl? You look marvelous!"

Molly stood up straight. "I have been quiet ill," she told him. "I was going to be a real artist, but I had a breakdown or something." Her voice was even, flat, her body held so still she might vibrate if touched.

"Well, it seems you've recovered splendidly!" Colin's enthusiastic voice had the tinge of something pre-programmed, as if he had rehearsed this encounter as steadily as any concerto. "And where is the artist, the maker of such haunting work?"

"Right here," said Felicia calmly, extending her hand. "Felicia Waller."

"Colin West," and Colin kissed her hand. "You have captured

399

our Molly so beautifully." He looked over at Molly, who still held her arms close in self-protection; her left arm still stiff, three months after the car accident shattered her elbow.

"My dear, what has happened to your bow arm?" Colin turned to Emma. "Molly left to more fully pursue her career—she's a fine cellist."

Molly leaned against the wall; a tiny impish smile matched her singsong chant. "You daredevil donnelly, I love your pleasing lots of lies."

Colin's laugh atop Molly's was forced, an unexpected improvisation. "You and that James Joyce, your father would be proud. . . . Speaking of bows, I don't think you've seen this violin—yes, I finally got a Strad! Would you like to see?" Before anyone could reply he had opened the violin case; Emma moved closer to Molly, touching her shoulder. Felicia made a gag gesture behind Colin's back, but Leo, Molly and Emma leaned into the case; then Colin let Molly lift the bow, wincing as she tried to hold it in correct cello posture.

Colin touched Molly's hand as she held the bow. "My dear, I see you have had some dreadful injury! I trust you're healing. . . I've come to buy some of these wonderful portraits of you. Which do you suggest?"

The bow still in her hand, Molly led him to a long narrow horizontal piece, the angular nude body washed in blue. "I can feel her," she said, "swimming in me hindmoist. . . . She'll be sweet for you."

Colin's brow furrowed; now he needed to change octaves. "Well then," he said grandly, "I suppose this must be one of my choices."

It was Emma who screamed, even before Colin turned to reclaim his violin: by the time he did Molly had frozen in midgesture, Felicia and Leo turning to hold her at both ends. Molly's fist had closed on the bow at one end, and she had punctured the canvas. She stood with one end of the bow in the air, angled like a dagger—the other still embedded in blue paint.

Felicia broke the silence. "Don't. Do. Anything," she said, slowly, loudly. "If you call the police, I will have every single piece removed from this gallery." She reached out and plucked the bow from the canvas, handing it to Colin and saying, "Before you go looking for damages—don't forget the broken cello."

Colin nodded violently, wordlessly; his flight seemed almost literal, his long legs propelling him from the gallery, the wool coat flaring behind him.

Once he was gone, Molly collapsed; Leo caught her in his arms, notwithstanding that she was four inches taller. He sat on the floor and held her, her head in his lap as if she were asleep.

Felicia squatted next to them, her energy returning. She said gently, "Molly, thank you on collaborating with me on the blue painting . . . I never cut a canvas before." She walked over and lifted the painting from the wall, brought it closer to Molly. "You want to sign it?" The painting's blue-washed Molly was punctured at the center and then torn, so that one eye curled away from the canvas' surface, smudged by the new violation.

Molly looked up: her body was shaking, her voice and face soft. She reached out with her stiff arm and touched the painting gently, with her fingertips. "My cold mad father," she said, "my cold mad feary father." She reached out and touched the painting, then touched her wet face and smeared her tears over the shredded eye. "And those are pearls that were my eyes."

Leo then reached up and took the torn canvas, holding it carefully with both hands. "I'll buy it," he said. "The way it is. I want it exactly like this."

As they left the gallery Emma asked Leo, "How much time do we have left?"

Leo checked his watch. "It's 6:00, we have two more hours." Molly laughed. "Hurry up please it's time," she said.

"What do you want to do now, Molly?" Emma asked.

Molly gestured to the tourist-lit Harborplace, early Christmas lights blending with the sunset to form watercolours on the Chesapeake Bay. "There," she said. "We always go there."

"It's true," Emma confirmed to Leo, "Felicia always hits the harbor after gallery openings. . . . In fact it was down there that I remember first telling Felicia that you existed."

"So you want to go to the harbor, Moll?" Leo shivered. "It's kinda cold."

Molly's smile was relaxed, soft. "Here, weir, island, bridge," she said softly, then singing: "Take me to the river, drop me in the water. . . ."

Leo and Emma looked at each other, Leo raising an eyebrow. After a moment Emma said slowly, "Actually, maybe it's better if we just go back to the house. Rachel wants to spend some time with you—and besides, I'm so tired, I might just fall in and drown."

Molly started laughing again, the loose reckless laugh she'd released at the gallery. "I get it. You're protecting me, so the river doesn't trip me by and by." She followed as they headed toward the parking garage instead.

As Emma drove up Charles Street, Molly turned to Leo and said seriously, "But I am already drowning." She shrugged off her jacket and pulled up her sleeve, resting her forearm in Leo's lap so that he could see the needle marks from the now-daily blood tests.

Leo looked down at the arm in his lap, tracing the red dots lightly before pulling his sister's sleeve back down. Then he had to bend to hear her next sentence, as his sister withdrew her arm and hugged herself. "I am drowning myself in my own defense."

November's early-seeming sunsets were matched by brilliant-early sunrise; the sun blinding the morning briefing was set in a pale-blue sky, the kind that suggests warmth while signifying frigid cold.

"Two days before Thanksgiving, of course," Gail Ryan was saying.

"Why do these hearings always happen at the worst times?"

"Who's the judge?" the head nurse asked. "That'll make a big difference—Bronstein always lets them walk, Kerrey is more inclined to let the treatment go forward."

"Cynthia Maddox," said Gail. "She could go either way."

"We do have winter on our side," said the head nurse. "They're much less likely to let people out on the street when it's getting below freezing on a regular basis." Behind her head, through the picture window the grounds glittered, snow lending a shimmer to the dark brown grounds and black branches.

"I imagine it'll depend a lot on what she actually says to the judge," said Gail, "and how she behaves between now and then." She looked down at the nursing report. "Well, moving her to Wilkes went smoothly enough. Yesterday she was calm, though affect was labile—thoughts less disordered, and she's been eating her meals again. Oh and she's back to oral medication: blood levels confirm she's taking them, so we know she's actually being helped." She looked up from the nursing report with a self-satisfied smile.

Anne-Marie was silent, writing in the margin of her legal pad. Her probation had been suspended, largely because of JPI's crowded winter: new admissions every day had sidetracked the niceties of evaluating, firing and hiring. Now she looked up, brushing her hair away from her eyes. "So now what are we giving her? I can't seem to find it anywhere in my notes."

"Navane, Tegretol, lithium, Xanax and Haldol," Gail said. "With the possibility of Prozac, although it hasn't proved effective with her depression before. There's also the ECT option, although we might have to consult Judge Maddox if it's close to her hearing date." She passed the sheet across the conference table, so that the social worker could copy the dosages.

Anne-Marie glanced at it and passed it back. "Thank you." She wrote down the numbers in the appropriate square on her little form, right under the date.

"So both therapy groups are pretty big," Gail said, looking at the intersecting triangles on her chart. "Fourteen for group psychotherapy, eighteen for art class—if they all show."

The head nurse sighed. "One thing about winter around here, it's never lonely."

"And how," said Gail. "You all know that Ruth Kessler is coming back—this time, a transfer from Shadyside?" General groans from the veteran staff, especially the head nurse.

Anne-Marie hurried to open to a clean page. "Who's Ruth Kessler?" Anne-Marie asked.

"Oh, an old buddy of ours," Gail said. "Thirtyish, drug and alcohol abuser, prostitute. Grossly psychotic—left here against medical advice about eight months ago, said she was headed for California. . . . Looks like she never got out of the state."

"Unless you count her own private Idaho," said a student nurse, provoking laughter bounded by generational lines. Anne-Marie, who fell within the target group, laughed reluctantly as she wrote on a sheet marked NEW PATIENT INFORMATION. "How do you spell the last name?" she asked. "Two s's or one?"

"Two," said Gail. "Two esses, one ell."As Anne-Marie wrote, her shoulders ached, a feeling that ran all along her arms and up into her fingertips, which stung as though she had been burned. She wrote in the margin of her legal pad, *Call the massage school*, even though she knew full well what was stinging—Felicia's voice, the day she first brought Leo to Chatham. *You work for them, remember?*

"Look, Baltimore's a square, did you ever notice? Some planner type just decided one day—everything within this square is a city, everything outside it isn't."

Leo had spread a map across the dining room table at Calvert Street. The mapmaker had filled the square of the city limits with yellow, so that the close-together streets seemed to glow within the larger web of surrounding counties.

"You should see what it does to car insurance," said Rachel. "You can end up paying double what your neighbor pays, across the city line."

On the map Leo traced large, irregular shapes with his black fountain pen, following street paths. "These are the running routes Emma showed me," he explained. "Now show me where it happened. . . . the accident, I mean."

Felicia bent over the map. "Down there, further to the south — Molly got a lot more daring in the summer, about what neighborhoods she'd run in."

"Daring?" Rachel asked. "Or—"

"Anyway it was here," Felicia said, taking Leo's pen and circling an intersection of tiny streets, way below most of Leo's carefully outlined routes. "The police told us, the day we found her at Pearlstone. . . . So what do you think, Leo?"

Leo sat down, staring at the map. One of the lightbulbs in the dining room fixture had burned out; he bent low, his graying hair touching the paper as he looked more closely.

Felicia leaned over next to him. "You know why I called you in the first place, Mr. O'Donnell—I don't have a chance in hell, by myself. But with a family member on my side . . ."

Leo didn't look up. "I don't know if you know what you're asking," he said. "I have obligations of my own. People—people are sick, at home."

She walked around the table, sitting in the chair opposite him. "I know perfectly well it's outrageous," she said. "But I'm still asking. And so did Molly."

"What Molly said," Leo said softly, "was *carry me away*." His normally serene face was stretched tight with tension, as he stood up from the table and stretched his arms out to his sides. "God, all I've done for five days is sit," he said. "Sit and eat and talk. I miss my bicycle—back in San Francisco I bike everywhere, none of this driving stuff."

Rachel walked in from the kitchen, carrying a dishcloth. "Look down in the basement." "What?"

Felicia laughed. "Oh right, Rae's big birthday present from her folks. That poor bike practically never got unwrapped."

"Okay," Rachel handed Felicia the dishcloth, "so I learned my lesson, never start a new exercise plan the same year you write your dissertation."

"Hmmm . . ." Leo's face cleared enough for a faint smile. "You mind if I don't help out with the dinner dishes?"

"Hey, they say a sinkful of dinner dishes is a sure cure for a broken heart," Felicia said. "I guess that means me."

Leo's glance at Felicia was long, level. "You okay?" he asked.

Felicia's smile was sad and sarcastic at the same time. "Jeff's never really understood about Molly," she said. "So fine—he can go be Mr. New York Sculptor, kiss up to every patron no matter how slimy . . . he won't have to worry about me and my damn obsessions. Shit, his little breakup speech even sounded like Kepler."

She reached across and touched the edge of one of the smaller arcs Leo had drawn on the map. "So this is Lake Montebello, the reservoir—it's gorgeous at night, although Molly mostly ran by there in the morning. And just down the street is the old baseball stadium, where Molly kept thinking she saw Lucia Joyce."

Leo brought the map with him, stuffing the first pocket of his leather jacket; he wore his Walkman under a hat and scarf plundered from Molly's closet, with a tape from her shelf marked only "Lucia"—a mad mélange of blues songs and fragments of Italian opera, Bessie Smith and Wagner jammed up against one another.

He shifted the bicycle into third gear as he crossed Charles Street, headed toward the university. The sidewalk near the 29th Street entrance was embedded with bits of colored glass, someone's attempt to transform urban grit into decoration. The surface reflected his face in fragments, as if he were inside one of Felicia's canvases.

Going north, Charles Street bore Baltimore's more affluent face

—punctuated by other universities and religious institutions, including a huge Masonic Temple. The lights were on in many of the large, grand stone homes, and Leo could catch a glimpse here and there of a family eating dinner, an argument going on in front of the TV. He turned at Cold Spring Lane and the neighborhood began to shift, smaller houses, darker faces.

At Loch Raven Boulevard Leo stopped, took off his earphones and pulled out the map, trying to see the tiny marks in the haze of distant street lights. A car pulled up to the corner and a man stuck his head out the window. "Hey man, are you lost?"

Leo looked over at the white-haired black man in a plaid cap, his arm half-out the window of the car. "Kind of . . . I'm not sure."

"Where you trying to get to?"

Leo wheeled carefully over to the car and showed his map, pointing.

The man whistled. "What do you want to go there for?"

"I just have to," Leo said. "But I'll be okay if I go like this, right?"

"Yeah just turn on Perring," the man said. "It becomes Hillen down there, and you just keep on, till you run right into the park. Then you have to zig-zag a little if you want that exact spot."

Baltimore did not lurch from rich to poor neighborhoods as much as follow a gentle slope: first fewer trees, then the distance between homes narrower and narrower, until Leo was on streets with rowhouses much smaller than those in Molly's neighborhood, slim rows of steps instead of front porches. A little like Cambridge to Somerville—and he was thinking about Boston again, the same clammy uncomfortable feeling brushing his skin.

After Felicia's phone call, Jason had told him, "Just stay calm. Don't let your family eat you up." Margaret's detox, Emma's baby had not brought him East—only the sad cellist with the broken rib and broken heart and broken mind.

As the rowhouses grew poorer he kept seeing in the sunset-air other images from Felicia's show, exaggerated by the shadowy light:

407

Molly manacled, Molly weeping Felicia's tears. As he pedaled faster and faster Leo took off his cap, letting his hair flow behind him, propelled forward by the overexcited soprano singing her joy into his ears.

Even after it started to snow, Leo kept going, the music and the darkness twin protectors against the cold, or any attacker, or most automobiles. As he picked up speed he felt accompanied most by Molly's split-personality Christine Beauchamp image, collages of copied photos running crying laughing flying beside him.

The neighborhood where the car had hit her bore broken beer bottles mingled with cigarette packs in the gutters, clumps of newspaper growing sodden with the snowfall. When he got to the street he got off the bicycle, walking by houses with closed faces, closed against the cold and the dark. In the graffiti on the street he almost thought he could see the baby in Felicia's tattoo, the Siqueiros painting on her back screaming music. A faint sound of an ambulance in the distance: Leo stood still, awaiting its approach as if on that August night.

On the way back up to the house he chose one of Emma's marked routes along 33rd Street, where he stopped again, this time to look at the baseball stadium. The proud Roman lines were in half-shadow, without the floodlights that must have once lit it on summer nights.

In the shadows of the stadium, the Molly image that emerged was the three-year-old child he had left behind, with her already sassy intelligence and slender arms. His skin still raw, he hadn't even tried to say goodbye, too busy rushing to set the fire.

Then another image towering above the baby Molly, as tall and arrogant as Colin West but darker-haired, slower movements. Leo stood and stared at the upper bleachers, his legs slung on either side of the bicycle, until his hair grew too wet and his lips chapped from the cold. "My cold mad feary father," Leo whispered.

After a few moments he got back on the bicycle, checking his map in the streetlight. Then he pedaled in the direction of the reservoir, circling the frozen water three and four and five times before he was ready to go inside.

"So first tell me, how did Todd's T-cells come out?" Leo at Calvert Street, the next morning, listened and then grinned. "Hey man, tell him to give some of those bouncing baby cells to Danny, will you?" At the next sentence, Leo sat on the staircase in the front hall, the melting snow like sweat on his worried brow. "Yeah, we kind of expected that. Is the Haldol helping at all? . . . Oh yeah, guess what, Haldol is one of the drugs they've been giving my sister, in this place . . . I'm not sure—and I don't think they are, either."

From behind Leo came Felicia, maneuvering her way to the kitchen. Leo put his leg across the step, blocking her path; she stopped, sitting on the step behind him as he talked to his lover across the continent.

"Next Tuesday—oh and it turns out the lawyer actually helped an ex-student of Molly's sue JPI a few months back, and she got a good-sized settlement. Emma, of all, people, turned that one up. . . . Yeah, the mouths of babes!"

After a while Felicia put her hands on his shoulders, massaging his tense muscles through the damp sweatshirt. The melted snow picked up the cobalt-blue charcoal on her hands; the longer he spoke, the more the shirt looked as if it had been finger-painted.

"So I don't know when I'll be back, or if she's coming with me or what. . . . Oliver can survive without me, all I really do is get in the way. . . . Yeah, you know I will. Just let me know when a crisis starts, if you can. Especially Danny, will you keep track of his Shanti volunteer and make sure he's getting enough vitamin C? . . . What? . . . Oh hell, Jase, 'sfar as I care you can come tomorrow."

After Leo hung up, he looked at his sweatshirt and said lightly, "Hey, now I get to wear a Waller original around the house."

"I almost never say this, especially to men," said Felicia. "But thank you."

Leo pulled off the damp sweatshirt, revealing a slightly less damp T-shirt. dried his face with the part untouched by Felicia's blue fingers. "Okay," he said, "where do we go from here?"

Felicia gestured upstairs. "Up to my studio," she said, "I have something to show you—something Kepler and Anne-Marie have been dying to get their hands on."

"Well, will you look at that!" Jack, the macabre-voiced Star Trek fiend, stood up from his crouch at the pool table in the Wilkes dayroom. "They must be doing the Thanksgiving parade early."

"Sshh! Can't you see Ingrid Bergman is about to kiss him?" Karen Hightower was still providing video hour: today's feature was *Casablanca*.

"She sure is fine, that Ingrid," said Warren, a tall shaggy new patient, nearly bald from the removal of his dreadlocks. "You don' see 'em like that where I been."

"And where's that?" Karen asked absently, drunk on Bogart.

"Shadyside State, the best an' brightest nuthouse in Merlin! What's that? A goddamn army coming in here."

"Man, I love hearing days," Jack said, pointing his pool cue at the group entering Wilkes. "They turn this old folks' home into *L.A. Law*."

They watched the procession signing in at the front nurse's station—a smartly dressed black woman with short graying hair; a tall, curly-haired attorney with a nervous manner and overstuffed briefcase; Dr. Kepler, Gail Ryan, and Anne-Marie; and a neatly arranged phalanx of O'Donnell siblings.

"I hope Molly's dressed up today," said Karen. "The day of my hearing I wore my St. Laurent blouse, my Chanel 19 perfume, and —Oh, there you are." The medication nurse was standing in front of her, and she paused to swallow her pills. "You're late, you know."

"So who's the Black lady?" Jack asked, as the group moved out of their sight, down the corridor.

"That must be the judge," Karen said. "My judge was a man, so my husband was able to get all logical with him, about why I should stay here." She sighed with pronounced, unconvincing sadness.

"And the dude with the curly hair? Not seen him either," asked Warren.

"I know him," said Jack. "He's with some group, he came and interviewed me. Says he's a lawyer, but usually he wears fuckin' blue jeans."

"With all this fun, I haven't seen our young friend today," Karen told the medication nurse, in the tone of a question. "She missed breakfast . . . do you know where she went?"

"ECT," the nurse said casually, handing Jack a glass of orange juice with his meds. "She got back around ten."

"She must look dreadful," said Karen, "they'll never let her out."

"She looks just fine," said the nurse. "Her friends helped her get dressed."

A pair of volunteers came bounding into the room, smiles wide as the Atlantic. "Okay guys," said Steve, "it's time for the winter hike, out to the big house." He pronounced winter like "winner."

"What now?" Karen asked. "I don't want to play Pictionary anymore."

The volunteer consulted his list. "No, you're on for group psychotherapy today," he said.

Karen stood up and let the volunteers lead her to her room, to get her coat. "Oh, how dreadfully tedious," she said. "All these people with their long stories, you'd think some of them"—she pointed to *Casablanca* —"would at least shut up and make films instead."

Molly's room, which had seemed huge ever since Shana left, was suddenly too small to hold the crowd; Gail, Kepler and Anne-Marie sat in a cluster to the judge's right, Felicia and Leo to her left.

411

Molly sat on her bed next to Emma, Shaun and Anna having preferred to remain standing despite the folding chairs hastily brought in for them.

Molly seemed small despite her height, ECT circles under her wide blue eyes and hair still damp from washing out the adhesive. She wore corduroy pants, a button-down shirt and a sweater nearly identical to Felicia's, preppie chic courtesy of the Salvation Army; Felicia wore one of Leo's berets over her peach-fuzz hair, while for Molly, Rachel had added a strand of pearls.

Cynthia Maddox, the judge, was a slender black woman with close-cut hair; she sat in a heavy chair brought in just for her, very like the one that had broken the leg of Gary diCesare. On the portable desk across her lap, Molly's fat chart and a pile of affidavits competed for space with a laptop computer.

"I just want to make sure you understand," Maddox was saying to Leo, "what you say you're willing to take on."

"How can I understand completely," Leo asked, "until I try?" He sat apart from the rest of the O'Donnells, sitting astride an empty bed along with Felicia and Rachel.

"You hear that, Your Honor?" Shaun asked, loud, exasperated. "He doesn't know what the hell he's doing." He shook his finger at the judge, as if he were himself another attorney. "They're out to sabotage everything Dr. Kepler has accomplished—starting with her medications. Isn't that correct, Ms. Waller?" he asked, his voice rising in pitch.

The judge closed her eyes and rubbed her forehead, as if trying to clear her brain from the static in the room. Felicia didn't bother to reply to Shaun's tirade, a speech he had already given in about six other forms.

Molly sat calmly at the eye of the storm; so far she had only nodded when asked questions, and smiled once, when the judge shook her hand. Otherwise she'd merely listened as Kepler went over the treatment plan, as Leo declared his willingness to care for

Molly, as Anna wept about the mother's health problems and declared that Molly belonged closer to home.

She had turned with interest when Anne-Marie, in her most professional slim-skirted suit, had said about Molly's school prospects: "The department seems willing, but . . . the record isn't great, very few ex-patients actually get their doctorates." *I don't know that I want one,* Molly had said. Judge Maddox was looking at her watch. "What about you, Mrs. Gahagan?" she asked. "Where do you stand, in all of this?"

Emma reached for Molly's hand; Molly let her fingers sit limply in her sister's, not clasping back. "I have seen some progress," Emma said slowly. "She seems to recognize me more, now. I would be . . . scared if she were out. . . . but I don't want her in Park Grove, that prison hospital. I think she should stay here." Molly dropped Emma's hand, as if it had burned her. "Does it hurt when she says that, Molly?" the judge asked gently.

"Not as much as my head, from the electricity," Molly said with some humor. Anne-Marie kept her head down, flipping through her legal pad as if it were a script; when Gail Ryan touched her shoulder lightly it was all she could do to remain still, and not shake off the older woman's hand.

"Molly," the judge said, "I need you to talk to me some more. So I can really learn what you want." She looked over at the lawyer from Patients' Rights Advocates. "Mr. Cohen, you have advised your client about this?"

"Of course," he replied. "Please bear in mind that electroconvulsive therapy is quite fatiguing, and can cause memory loss."

"Not at the dosage I ordered," Kepler said sourly. He turned to his patient, his voice switching to an automatic warmth, like a good salesman. "Molly, if you want to leave, you only need to prove to the judge that you're prepared to try to take care of yourself."

"Too late," Molly said. "Everything is sealed and done, that else leans on the affair."

Kepler wrote on a sheet of paper, *Reliance on archaic speech,* and passed it over to the judge as Leo got up, sat next to Molly. "No, Molly," said Leo. "Nothing is sealed, yet. All you need to do is say it."

Molly took a deep breath. "I see. Now it's me who's got to give." She turned to the judge and said with some difficulty, "Yes, Ma'am. I want to go away from here, with my brother. They make me so tired, these people."

The judge nodded, and took notes; her hands on the tiny keyboard jumped a moment when Molly added, "Besides, there are too many thunderstorms here."

On the other side of the closed door, the sharp voice of an elderly patient: "What you mean I can't have another smoke? You full of shit, man!"

"Doctor's orders," the firm voice of an orderly. "You've had enough today." Behind the voices someone had turned the TV up loud, the theme from *The Waltons* a melancholy undertone to the exchange.

"Well if this were up to a vote," Judge Maddox said, "it would be something of a tie—a third of Molly would stay, a third would be discharged, and a third would be moved to Park Grove. Fortunately, these matters are not democratic. You'll learn my decision by Tuesday, after the holiday."

Kepler closed his binder and Shaun his briefcase, with matching exhales of relief; then Anne-Marie said, "Wait, your honor, I need to say something." Her voice shook, her eyes straight ahead, not looking at Kepler and Gail's faces. "This is my personal and professional observation, separate from the rest of the treatment team."

Judge Maddox had begun to take apart her makeshift desk; she reopened her little gray computer. "Yes?"

Before Anne-Marie could speak, a roar from outside the room— as the big wooden door opened to admit a crop of new admissions, the patients on the ward offering loud greetings and sorry laughter.

Jack's horror-movie voice cut through the white noise: "And for our next victims. . . . "

Gail Ryan and Kepler winced; the judge said to Anne-Marie, "You may as well begin. I don't know when they'll quiet down."

"I've followed Molly's clinical progress as carefully as anyone here," said Anne-Marie. "I've watched her in her more and less lucid states. I've seen her come close to insight, to trust, to revealing the heart of what has brought her here." The social worker's voice, at first soft with fear, grew stronger with each word. "And she came the closest, made the most progress, when she was also at her most delusional, her most disruptive—when she was receiving less 'treatment' than we thought."

"Hey look who's here!" a call from the other side of the door. "They're letting everybody out of the big house now!" Warren's yell was answered by a husky female voice, too low to be intelligible inside Molly's room.

Anne-Marie sat up straight, glancing at the door. "Leo and Felicia are right—JPI is only hindering Molly's recovery. Whatever it is that she needs to do to come out the other side of this thing, she can't do it here."

Felicia looked over at Anne-Marie; she leaned forward, as if the social worker were whispering and she had to get every word.

Now Anne-Marie was standing, moving away from Kepler and Gail and looking down at the seated Molly. "I know that what I'm saying flies in the face of every assumption upon which this institution operates, so perhaps I'm way out of line." She turned back to the judge. "But I had to speak in support of Molly's discharge. I think it's the only way she'll ever get out of the river, the one she's drowning in."

At the word "river," Molly looked across to her and said "Yes! Away alone, at last."

Judge Maddox watched Molly's face, her bright-alive eyes as she spoke to Anne-Marie; then she bent and wrote in her notebook again. Felicia looked over at Leo, who nodded.

415

From outside came a burst of applause from the dayroom, as if for Anne-Marie instead of some new arrival. "We should have done this in the conference room," said Shaun.

"We always do it this way," said Gregory Cohen, the patient advocate. "And there's a reason for it."

"I don't believe this," Shaun burst out. "Who are we to believe here? How old are you?" he asked Anne-Marie. "And all this commotion out there—what is this, a goddamn theatre?" He stood up and opened the door, glanced out. "It's a—"

"A madhouse out there?" Leo's smile was very remote, but real.

"And you, Leo." He turned to his brother, towering over the small-boned figure seated on the folding chair. "I am ashamed of you, and I think Poppie would be, too. Molly was the dearest thing in his life, and for you to just take her away on some California voodoo theory—I don't think Will would even acknowledge you as his son."

Leo didn't respond, sitting back in his chair and looking at Judge Maddox, as if his brother didn't exist. In place of his reply came Molly's voice, soft but precise, sure of herself.

"But he is dead and gone," Molly said. "He is dead and gone. And all Neptune's oceans will not wash the blood from my hands."

Judge Maddox stood up and went over to Molly, crouching slightly so that they were face to face. "What did you say, Molly?"

Molly sat back on the bed, her palms facing down behind her, her arms straight. She tipped her head back in deep relaxation, and sang out in a guttural, raspy blues voice, loud and clear enough to cut through the ward's chaos. "*I done killed my good-time daddy / with a sawed-off '44.*" Then she pulled her legs up onto the bed and lay down, her arms around her pillow, her pearl necklace nearly getting caught in the bedframe. Seemingly instantly, she was asleep.

Kepler opened the door, and called for a nurse to take Molly's pulse, and "check for catatonia." While the nursing staff bustled about the still figure, the judge shook hands all around; then Kepler left, along with the judge, Shaun and Anna.

Gregory Cohen stood with Felicia, Emma, and Leo, surrounding Molly's bed. "Now you know," he said to Felicia, "why I was reluctant to take this on in the first place."

"I'm glad you tried," Felicia said, shaking his hand. "Thank you for everything." After more handshakes and a quick exasperated shrug, he was gone.

Felicia turned to the woman in the back of the room, bent over her notebook. "And—thank you, Anne-Marie."

Anne-Marie had taken off her suit jacket and was kneeling by Molly's bed, resting her chin on the edge so that her nose was tickled by soft black hair. "You think I should quit? Or just wait till they fire me?"

"Oh, please don't quit yet," Emma said anxiously. "Molly needs you here." Anne-Marie didn't respond, just reached out and combed Molly's tangled hair with her fingers.

"You better not," said Felicia, "not if the judge comes down on Kepler's side."

Anne-Marie looked up. "What? I work for them, remember?" Then she stood, slowly, her suit jacket on her arm. "Let's go." She waited as first Emma, then Felicia placed soft kisses on the crown of Molly's sleeping head.

As they passed the nurses' station, attendants in unfamiliar uniforms were bent at the front desk, filling in forms as if preparing for a drivers' test. One of them carried a strait jacket over his arm; the soft voice they'd barely heard before came from behind him, saying, "You gonna miss me, ain't you?

"You kidding? Won't even cross my mind, Ruth honey."

"I don't believe it for a minute." Ruth was short and compact, with large breasts, wavy red-brown hair and a slight squint in her left eye. She and Warren exchanged high-fives as the attendants left, just in time for the approach of Anne-Marie, Emma, Felicia, and Leo.

Anne-Marie looked at the jacket on the attendant's arm. "Why the restraints?" she asked him.

He shrugged. "Don't ask me," he said, "doctors' orders. From Shadyside State. . . . I think it's cause she's a troublemaker."

Anne-Marie slowed down, biting her lip, until the men from Shadyside had passed beyond them. Her lips were chapped, and the skin broke easily under the weight of her teeth. "Molly calls that a *camizole due force*," she said.

"That's because Lucia Joyce did," said Leo, pulling his beret down over his ears as they began to cross the grounds.

"Yeah? Where'd you read that?"

"In one of her journals."

Anne-Marie stopped, subjecting them all equally to the cold as she stood in front of Felicia and Leo. "You have them," she said.

Leo nodded, and put his arm around Anne-Marie's waist, urging her forward. "Don't quit," he said. "Not now." Anne-Marie nodded, slowly; they started to walk again in a cluster, ahead over pale frozen grounds.

Anne-Marie's lip was bleeding. She looked at her white wool glove for a moment before she touched it to her mouth, the blood spreading along the cloth until the fingers of the glove were spiked with red liquid. "Well," she said, "where are all great Neptune's oceans when you need them?"

Even before Ruth Kessler was brought to her room, she found an attendant to light her cigarette, and headed out to the chill of the smoking porch.

"Boy, I never thought I'd see you here," said Warren, her fellow transfer. "I thought you was there forever."

Ruth laughed and shook her head. "You fuck the right people," she told Warren, "you can get out of anywhere. I'll do it here too."

When they were through smoking, Warren followed Ruth and her nurse to her new room. Lying on the other bed was a middle-aged German woman with a wide flat face. "Oh man, old home week," Ruth exclaimed. "I know you too. From the dumpster behind the farmers' market."

"The farmers are poisoning us," the older woman said in confirmation, sitting up. She turned to the nurse, "But you protect us from them, I know that. I trust you." She crossed herself.

"Same-o, same-o. Do I get another cig yet?" Ruth sighed, leaning against the doorjamb as the nurse left. "Same people, same doctors, same shit."

"Got a new one you should meet," Warren said. "She can tell you who not to mess around with—about two weeks ago they catch her with one of the student nurses, and they be fucking her up with drugs and shock ever since. She have her hearing today, but I be damned if they let her out."

"This I gotta see," Ruth said. When they crossed over to Molly's room, they were at first blocked by orderlies carrying folding chairs, then four male volunteers hefting the solid black armchair. When they were gone Ruth and Warren entered the room; a nurse was shaking the young woman gently, saying, "Molly, it's lunch time, wake up."

"Holy shit," said Ruth. "That's the bitch followed me all over Baltimore, last summer."

"Hey babe," Warren said, "you know what the doctors say— gotta watch that there paranoia. What you mean, she was following you?"

"I mean she had on her big running sneakers, and her music machine, and everywhere I went she was running, running toward me." Ruth shrugged. "Wouldn't leave me alone, I don't know what she wanted."

When Molly's eyes opened the nurse left, saying softly, "It'll be lunch time pretty soon." Molly stared at the ceiling until the nurse's footsteps had faded; then she rolled on her side and faced the door. When her eyes met Ruth's she stood up quickly, nearly passing out with the suddenness of it.

"You're here," she said, leaning unsteadily on the bedframe.

Ruth laughed. "Yeah," she said to Warren, "that's her all right."

Molly went over to her bureau, still looking at Ruth. "I've been waiting for you," she said, "I even have your nametag." She went digging in a drawer, sifting among underwear until she came out with one of the white Pearlstone bracelets, one that read DOE, LUCY.

She extended the bracelet in a gesture of welcome, smiling. "Lucihere!"

"Say what?" Warren took the bracelet, began looking at it. "Who Lucy Doe?"

Ruth turned to Warren. "Will you look at this . . . and they been locking me up all these years, while they let her do some yuppie college shit all over Baltimore." She pronounced the city's name "BALL-more." "How was your hearing' baby?" Warren asked Molly.

Molly ignored him, her full attention pulled by Ruth's small solid presence. "If only they'd seen you," she said softly, "they might have understood." She spoke as if pulled off balance—more lucid but weaker, lightheaded. "I can't believe it's really you."

"Well what I can't believe," Ruth said with asperity, "is that you chose a student nurse to fuck. How stupid are you, couldn't you figure out that if you want to get out, you gotta get a fuckin' doctor?"

Another end-of-month paperwork deadline and Anne-Marie's music of choice was an African singer, over-produced with soft American synthesizers but still delicious to her, polyrhythms clapping through the night.

Finishing the end-of-month reports, she got to her reward: the three fat spiral notebooks Leo had given her the day before. In two of them the paper crackled as if they had been doused with rain, or tears. Molly's name and the Calvert Street address were written across the top of each one in brisk, no-nonsense handwriting.

The third had a photograph taped to the front cover, photocopied from a book and blown up until it filled the page; the thin, angular female figure, presumably Lucia Joyce, wore a dance outfit reminiscent of early Martha Graham and stood at an odd angle, her arms thrust to her sides and her fingertips meeting to create a circle. Inside the third notebook, the one with the dancer, Molly had scribbled a line from Finnegans Wake: *After sound, light and heat, memory, will and understanding.*

"Oh god Molly," Anne-Marie murmured, "I hope so." She pulled out a fresh legal pad, uncapped a rollerball pen, and opened the first notebook to its opening page.

Those are pearls that were his eyes

3 August

P apa Is goes to bed in silks | tells men = love
go to hell—but not the hell of the damned
Hot weather Sunday afternoon, | and me spread
across my bed. sweltering sweaty work but it's worth it, as Joyce's
Wake notes yield slow clues to the private acts that became such
public speech—until incest is, as one scholar says, a rash blistering
the skin of *Finnegans Wake*.

A vivid Lucia/Issy portrait, probably from one of their family
theatricals:

| *in long trousers my triple vest waistcoat Sunday side out and
woolly side in heart stitched joyous greatly*

And I can see it, Lucia "dressed in Charly" for some afternoon
dance at Square Robiac: in her father's waistcoat the Little Tramp
whose sadness she already shares, making her Babbo "joyous greatly." Incest's real tragedy, when tenderness shares the stage.

A first-draft scrap of II.ii., very little of which got into the published *Wake*: *She glows. She gives a sign. There's time to hear her's, turn her up as turn her down, brat can choose from so many, tween the languour and the weakness of girlhood to* [*the headbeck and heartaches of womanage*]. *And what is more lots heaps and heaps of other things too, yoking apart, from Sis her mystery of pain.*

"Ours is a mistery of pain," Shem declared in II.ii—to which Issy's footnote replied, "Dear sir and I trust I may be pardoned for trespassing but I think I may add hell." No mystery, Babbo. She knows. You know. Not only does he know, he dreams its anguish, as in this 1926 note:

went from god to god till they cried from me is we
met daughter beyond—god and died
nowhenbe
a bad father

Thick lines through the last four words, Bab's routine once he absorbed any notebook snippet into his nonday diary, his book of the dark.

a bad father . . . Lucia was nineteen, the damage already done—by then she is breaking things, crying far too easily, whispering her "strange abbreviated language" into his ear. The touch that turned the blueveined child into a "fantastic creature" must have happened far, far earlier. Perhaps when she was ten or eleven, somewhere around 1918.

In 1918 the Joyces are living out World War I in Zurich. Joyce is struggling with the writing of his new *Odyssey* and the indifferent response to *Portrait*'s publication; Nora is busy trying to run a household in two languages she does not understand; Lucia is lonely without her Trieste friends while Giorgio has an easier time of it, an already sociable child approaching adolescence.

But even in at this refugee stage both Joyce children are learning the piano, learning to sing; wherever it is, the peripatetic Joyce household will always be filled with music.

Lucia, carami, play something for Babbo. I have been writing all day, and my eyes are so tired. . . . No, carissima, no, you are missing the grace notes, I can tell.

His hands on hers, on the keyboard, guiding her young fingers to the right places.

That's better—right there.

His left hand helping her with the bass line, his right hand strays to her collarbone, stroking gently. He kisses the top of her head; then his mouth sinks into her hair, just above the ear. Her breath catches in her throat as his hand moves down and rests lightly on her chest, where no breast has yet begun to form.

A thunderstorm inside her, heart racing; she stops playing and sits very still, unsure.

Immediately he stands up and withdraws both hands. *Time to stop. Perhaps I can sleep, a little. Will you please draw the curtains when you go out?*

And she loses him entirely, Babbo withdraws into his inner world and the pain in his eyes. Lucia goes out into the streets of Zurich and sings to herself, a lullaby Joyce made up for her when she was little. *Era una piccolo bambina,* she sings, *che rideva il giorno e non dormiva durante la notte.* There was once a little girl who laughed all day and did not sleep at night.

My eyes are filling, but that is unsurprising: I cry easily these damp days, as if the humid air were collecting in my eyes and then raining from me. Una piccola bambina, there was a lesson for you that afternoon, one you would soon master—just as you learned to become L'Irlandaise the silver fish, just as you would learn to become Issy-la-Chapelle, the genuine Christine.

Time now to set aside my journals and climb the stairs, Felicia's already turned on the music—more blues, this time a rough mélange of Billie Holliday, Ma Rainey and a dozen others. For the current painting I lie on my stomach with arms extended, like a cat sleeping or a mermaid swimming.

4 p.m.

I ought not to be writing this.

But I have to, because my skin is burning.

I ought to be preparing for tomorrow's class—but how?

How can I think calmly of Joyce Faulkner Fitzgerald Woolf, with Felicia's baby screaming in my ear?

I asked for it, of course.

There she was, mixing colors on a piece of wax paper, while Bessie Smith sang *An' that's the reason why / I got those weeping willow blues* . . . Her back was to me, as I sat against the wall waiting for her; her cutoff T-shirt exposed the bottom of Siqueiros' painting, post-industrial grays and rust reds, the soft pink scars behind her knees just an extension of the same reds.

Pinkish-white, Will as pink snow. Old, old burns.

So I finally let it push its way out, the question held under my tongue for so long. "Felicia, were there other burns?"

She didn't turn away from her wax paper, but her shoulders tensed; she knew what I meant, and wasn't coy about it. "Yes."

"Under all the tattoos?"

She twisted around and extended her hands; the snake seemed to jump with her pulse. "Not these, they were a birthday present from Paula, my tattoo artist."

I stood up and came closer to her; without my asking she peeled off her shirt. "But—your back?"

She reached behind her with a muscular arm, her fingers spread as if in a peace sign; then she ran her hand down her spine, one fingertip tracing each side. Gingerly I reached out and followed her hand's motion, downward.

When I touched her she shuddered, and I withdrew—but not before I felt it, the slight swelled part of the skin, starting just below the larger baby's mouth. "How, Felicia?"

"My brother," her voice toneless as the weather report. "He's ten years older than me. You know, to this day I can't stand the smell of Marlboros?" She turned around to face me. "Okay, time to rock and roll. Ready to assume the position?"

A few minutes to catch the rhythm, my breasts nestled against the cool bedsheet laid over the wood floor, Felicia moving through the music; she paints with her body as well as her fingers and brushes. Then I had to ask the next question, "How old were you?"

"When it started, or when he finally left home?" The matter-of-fact voice came from some other place, unconnected to the swaying narrow hips, the quick-moving hands: her question sliced me into passivity and fear, I almost didn't want to know. "I guess I was maybe five the first time," she continued, "and he joined the army when I was nine."

Four years. Another hard swallow. "What about your mom?"

She shrugged, her voice toneless as the weather report. "The dinner shift ran until midnight, she didn't get home from work until I was asleep. . . . Rob was the one who dressed me in the mornings, it was his job to take care of me. He was so helpful, my mom told everyone."

"She never found out?"

"Not till about five years ago." Felicia wiped her hands and took a swig from her water bottle. "I . . . I was too ashamed to say anything."

I couldn't do it, I broke position and sat up straight, "You were ashamed?" My heart beat double time—like a fifteen-mile run, like the phone call telling me Will had just died, like the day I discovered Babbo's cry of shame.

She met my eyes, her mouth pressed tight. "Rob loved me, he always said so. . . . If he did that, then I deserved it, you know what I mean?" She looked at her watch. "Now c'mon, we only have half an hour left."

When we were done I found one more question. "Where is he now, Felicia? Is there anything you can do to him?"

She was turned away from me, rubbing her hands on a moistened cloth, so it was her baby who responded, arching backward as she bent over. "Home in Buffalo, where else? Get this—he's a fucking doctor. And people wonder why I hate doctors." I hadn't known she did but could only breathe into the hollow, trying not to imagine any more.

After ten minutes of painting, scraping and carving into her multilayered canvas, she added, "Oh, and he's married, house and a dog, the whole thing."

Oh God no. "How many kids?" I asked.

"Three. The oldest, the twins, they're what? sixteen or seventeen now—they seem to be okay." Her teeth bit down hard on the word "seem." Then she shrugged, turning off the air conditioner. "My mom said it was probably just a phase, fucking phases, you remember my painting?" Of course, one of her more violent huge canvases has, its big broad lettering. PHUCKING FACES.

"Like the song says—he was just an excitable boy." She pulled her shirt back on and turned up the air conditioner, beginning to sing, "He's just an excitable boy."

Like Colin. Like Virginia Woolf's brother. Like Babbo, for better or much worse. It's too much for me, right now. I'm just an excitable girl.

I had better go for a run, sweat Felicia Virginia Lucia Nicole Zelda's tears out through my skin. Tonight I want a scummy neighborhood, the sort of place where crime happens in the open—where excitable boys shoot one another, instead of burning their baby sisters with cigarettes.

6 August

and of course the only gunshots last night were inside my head.

I hadn't managed to shake Felicia's burns completely, though I was calmer after the run. But then I was up late with *Mrs. Dalloway*, reading the text and speed-skimming through the Woolf biography: the author blames Woolf's depression and eventual suicide on her sexual abuse by her half-brother, which began when she was seven or eight. Just about the age that Felicia's brother began playing with fire.

Of course, things don't work so neatly as we would like, and *Mrs. Dalloway* lacks the incest undertones in other Woolf works: but it does feature a madman, Septimus Smith, who shot adrenalin through me just the same—for he thinks and talks a lot like Issy.

To Septimus "leaves were alive; trees were alive. And the leaves being connected by millions of fibres with his own body . . . when the branch stretched he, too, made that statement." Even the light streaming from his sitting-room window is mesmerizing, he finds himself "watching the watery gold glow and fade with the astonishing sensibility of some live creature, on the wall-paper." (Gold on the wallpaper, the yellow wallpaper, madmen and madwomen cross the generations.) Trees too beautiful not to listen.

Today in class, one of my students found in Septimus the echo of quite another Joycean figure: Stephen Dedalus, the moody Jesuit of *Portrait of the Artist*, who in the beginning of *Ulysses* watches his comrades dive into the sea, thinking only of his mother's death. Watery grief, like the night I cried imagining a drowned Lucia B.

Standing in the tower, Stephen muses about "the word known to all men"—and in his last incarnation, *Finnegans Wake*'s gentle writer Shem, he cried "Let the raised name of love every person thrill!" (Shem, Issy's brother, we're at Quentin and Caddy again.)

And despite Septimus, we spent much of class on Woolf as an incest survivor (quick flash: June's Austin conference, the session stolen from me by Texas flu). Jessie referred to other Woolf work which shows it more clearly—especially *The Waves*, which even I find difficult reading.

After class I met her girlfriend—a majestic six-foot blonde, whose moist red lipstick defied the heat. (I guess that's what they mean by "lipstick lesbian.") They approached me together, asking if I wanted to do a 20-mile spurt with them, up toward Loch Raven.

"Wait till my sister comes, we can all four go." I can't believe it

—she's actually coming! Emma! Day after tomorrow! I can finally show off my adopted home town, as we run through Baltimore together; all I knew last time she visited were Fells Point and Louie's. (Come to think of it, they still top the list, bless Balmer's unchanging small-town heart. Though can I stand to take her to Louie's again, after the scene with Gary, after the dream where she came there with news of Will's death?)

Time for a gentle run, to take advantage of the cooling effect of the rain—I think I will listen to Lucia's beloved Wagner, yet another excitable boy in his raging religious ecstasy. Ecstasy: ex-stasis , beyond reason; no wonder | loved it as a child, no wonder Lucia declared at fifty-one, "I still like it today!"

August 9

11 p.m.: and Emma is asleep upstairs in my bed, her face soft and childlike amid my covers.

She was waiting in the hallway outside my class, full of energy despite the bumpy overnight train, charged up by coffee and a change of scene: all day I've been watching her slowdown in stages, like one of those toy monkeys in the battery commercials.

"My God, I didn't know you had a twin!" Jessie commented when she saw her. Not so much twin as former self, lean boygirl that I've become; no longer am I that soft body and shoulder-length black hair. Her eyes opened huge when she saw me, and I grinned —I had purposely not told her I'd cut my hair.

"Oh my god, Molly," she said, taking my hand and stepping back so she could get a good look at me. "What have you done to yourself?"

"You don't like it?" I laughed. "I've never felt freer."

She took a finger and ran it along my side, bouncing a little at each rib. "I can count them, all right. Molly how much are you weighing?"

I shrugged. "Depends on the time of day . . . anywhere between ninety-five and a hundred and five, I think I lost at least two pounds when I cut my hair. Although right now I'm hungry, how about Thai food?"

Over pad thai I told her about the class, about modeling for Felicia, about swimming in Joyce fragments. She wasn't listening, instead watching my face, my eyes, my plate. "Aren't you going to finish that?"

("I think Lucia is going mad," Beckett wrote to a friend—was this the same person in whom he confided that the idea of marrying his surrogate-father's daughter felt like incest?)

When Emma first walked into Felicia's studio, she looked back and forth between the drawings and my face, from the first stark line drawing to the newer, erotic canvases. I could tell it disturbed her: Emma's a gentle soul, and even Felicia's most naturalistic portraits carry the faint odor of her brother's Marlboros.

I asked Felicia last night if the pain of the tattooing felt as though she were being burned all over again. "No," she said, "more like I was burning it all away." But Rob is still there, I told her, he fans the flames in her paintings.

She shrugged. "Maybe if I got cured, got therapy or something, I'd lose it all," she said. "That's always the question, right? If Picasso wasn't such an asshole would he still have transformed the fucking art world?" Picasso, it seems, beat many of his wives, a candidate for lithium if the authors of my psych texts had got hold of him. And what then, oh friends, what then?

The million-dollar question. Was the swirling masterpiece of the *Wake* worth a broken Lucia? Are Felicia's paintings, Virginia's masterworks worth the suffering of their eight-year-old selves? The rational answer must be no—but then, we literati aren't famous for rational answers.

Time to sleep. I promised Emma a long run—and that means getting out the door by six at the latest, before the humidity presses down on us like rain.

12 August

So this morning we woke before sunrise, my sister and I, and ran into prep-school territory—dodging malls to reach the older buildings nestled among trees.

I made sure I brought her along the nearly unpaved side road that leads to Tilden's alma mater, Hillsdale Prep. I'd never gotten this close before to its stone arch and weeping willows, the oaks planted along the half-mile stone pathway at the entrance. Emma pointed out an odd building in the distance, a big square fortress shielded with double-paned glass that refracted the sunlight into brilliance: a diamond as big as the Ritz.

We stopped and stretched, watching innumerable staff members drive their cars into the parking lot. "Pretty fancy," I said. "Look at all those guards." The precious Maryland upper class protecting itself—from what?

On the way back I finally told Emma about Gary, which served its intended purpose: to defuse her anxieties about my mental state. A big, relieved hug, right as we were waiting for a light: "Now I get it, the diet, the hair. You'll be okay." She'd found a category for me, Molly of the Broken Heart.

A partial truth, the whole truth more difficult to say simply— that Gary is just the catalyst, one of many bringing me closer to Lucia's angular body, close-cut hair, emotional explosions. She nods absently if I mention | , it's too removed—so this evening we dream our separate worlds. She talks to her baby over long-distance, while I get ready to swim in Clarissa Dalloway's memories—trying, for the moment, to forget the traumas of Clarissa's creator, who felt her stepbrother's hands on her body when she was too young to say a word.

And thirty years later she walked into the river. Just like Lucia turning on the gas jets. (Dying is an art, like everything else.)

14 August

Speaking of suicides, time in class to contend with the one Woolf *wrote*. Septimus Warren Smith, who fought in the "Great War" that catalyzed the "modern era," including the wild idyll we call Paris in the twenties. Much of the work created there thus full of darkness and disorder, as artists and writers and musicians realized life was not so orderly, that nightmares were real. Tangible. A son's death. A generation destroyed. Cities burning. And Septimus, once a man "of great promise," is both torn apart and renewed by the war: he sees his dead compatriot Evans hiding behind trees, hears voices telling him, "The supreme secret must be told to the Cabinet: first that trees are alive; next, there is no crime; next love, universal love . . . " He gasps with what the war has clarified into his very body—sees atrocities behind normal London facades and fears the torments of the damned, finding purity only in the trees and the air.

But when he tries to express these thoughts to his psychiatrist, Dr. Holmes, he is told he needs to go somewhere and "rest" away from his Italian wife, Lucrezia—until he learns to see things "in proportion" and fulfill his "promise" in London's business world.

Instead, Septimus stays at home with her, writing his thoughts and feelings on scraps of paper, "odes to Time; conversations with Shakespeare; do not cut down trees." Lucrezia, at first uncomprehending, begins to share his moments of joy and clarity, to despair less at his moments of confusion and pain and out-and-out delusion.

Until she herself "was a flowering tree to him," their communication nearly as nonverbal and equally transcendent. And Septimus is full of *joi de vivre*, even though he still hears the dead speak behind rhododendron bushes, still sees torments far worse than war.

His suicide is, in a sense, coerced: he is about to be forcibly taken away from Lucrezia—who has become his own Babbo, the only person who can understand at least some of what he says. It is she who barricades the door, against the professionals "who made ten thousand a year and talked of proportion . . . who saw nothing clear, yet ruled, yet inflicted." (Perhaps Virginia felt always in the sway of men like her brothers, who saw nothing clear yet ruled, yet inflicted.) Even as he prepares to jump from the window, "he would wait until the very last moment. He did not want to die. Life was good. The sun hot." (At this passage my throat fills every time.)

Jessie's predictable, yet useful comment: "He had no choice! Psychiatry was the same voodoo shit then as now, and psychiatrists fucking dickheads." And how do you come by these views, Ms. Berger? Though her words echo Felicia's, "he's a fucking doctor."

My Lucia work has me feeling the music in madness like never before, reluctant to chalk it off to sour brain chemicals. Septimus was molested by the war as surely as Virginia by her brothers, neither of them benefiting from doctors' approaches—any more than Lucia did, though she was far less of a "nuisance" once put away. Jessie's voice inside me matching Felicia's, whose brother went from Marlboros to more approved instruments for violating human skin. If he had become a "psychiatrist" the circle would be complete: cigarettes—scalpel—syringe—Thorazine.

How puny by comparison, the poor weak word!

15 August

Words as weapons and Emma has me at gunpoint, her weapon my own words—a letter written in my own hand, written seven years ago. A letter that may have sparked Will O'Donnell's year of rage.

She brought it because Margaret told her about our little dispute, and the letter speaks for itself: I feel sick to my stomach just pasting it in, cutting off the edges where it was ripped from a spiral notebook, wincing at the baby-faced handwriting that was once my own.

15 December

Will—

As you know, I'm not coming home for Christmas this year, partly because of the concert season—our chamber orchestra's doing a Christmas Eve Messiah and the last thing I need is to haul my cello onto Amtrak.

I also think it's better if you and I just not communicate for the rest of this year; I know you understand my reasons. I thought I had made matters clear to you last summer, but your recent actions show that not to be the case.

I've read wonderful reviews of your new book, and wish you all the best this year. From what Emma tells me, your new readers are working out just fine.

—S.

S., Shem, how did I dare use his name for me?

Did blind teenage rage rob me of my last year of Will? "I wish you the best," just like Gary's "we should go on to other things." And the feeling is the same, the helpless hollow Gary-loss feeling; probably when Gary dropped me, he reopened the wound of having divorced my own father.

What did I say back to you in Texas, Will? How did I reply to your rage? I remember crying, I remember being up very late and then swirling coffee down my throat in the morning for the very first time, so I'd be able to help you give your paper. I remember saying, *I do not belong to you,* God how many daughters throw that one out? I don't know what else I said, I only remember those words, over and over, *I do not belong to you.*

But I do, Will. I hope you realize that. Though I no right now to even ask you to come back to me.

Still, I'll try to lure your voice, perhaps by singing myself to sleep with Irish folk songs, the way we used to do. *Oh Danny boy, the pipes, the pipes are calling . . .* or our favorite *Oh Molly I can't say you're honest, sure you've stolen the heart from my breast.* And of course, I could always sing the story of the hod-carrier Finnegan, coming alive in his whisky-soaked his grave. *And we'll all dance a jig at Finnegan's wake!*

17 August

Newsflash from the mad artist front: Molly O'Donnell learning how to dance. (Lucia, I already see why you hated to give it up, the wordless center created by your moving body.)

Felicia's doing, of course; I showed up at her studio a few hours after Emma left and she was playing a record by a local band, an odd combination of salsa and reggae and trumpet, like out of some Club Med tour. (I think she used to date the trumpet player.)

Having finished the silver fish sketch, she wanted a new pose to play with: so she said "OK Molly, here we go. It's time for you to dance for me."

It's a tribute to how much I trust her that I did not walk out that moment. She gave me a long T-shirt to wear, let me copy her as she swiveled her hips in a long, sexy motion. Then the beat picked up and other parts of her body were in motion, her upper body and her arms and even her head, darting from one side to another as if flirting with the walls.

I was mesmerized at first, standing still and looking at her: her dancing had a childlike joy not evident in her drawing or her speech, only hinted at in her laugh. Her dance defied both the screaming baby and the brother who created him.

Then she lifted each shoulder in turn, in synch with the turn of her head: and she made me do it. I was impossibly spastic at first until I began to feel the rhythm, turning with each drumbeat and shaking my hands in agreement with the congas. It felt ridiculous and I couldn't stop laughing, but I had to confess it was also cathartic, almost as good as a good-size run up Charles Street.

At first I kept wondering when we were going to start drawing; then it became clear it wasn't going to be today, today was practice. She changed the music and there it was, that song again, the one Lucia B sings; the one I imagine Lucia J singing to herself, a half-century before it was written. *Take me to the river, drop me in the water.* I watched closely, tried to copy her grinding hips and joyous arm motions; at one point she pulled out the huge mirror she uses for self-portraits and we watched ourselves, flirting with the mirror as well as the walls and each other.

Then Felicia looked at her watch. "Okay that's enough for today," she said, "I have to get to the old' Rancho in an hour. But tomorrow we'll find the pose in your dancing." Of course she wants to draw me dancing.

I could have protested, I could even now tell her it's a ridiculous idea but I find I don't want to. Did you get lost in the music like this, Lucia? Though if reggae existed back then, it was still hidden away in faraway islands. In the summer heat, the dancing feels like sex; I understand even better how after giving up dance L'Irlandaise complained of being "sex-starved." Was it like sex to you too, Babbo? Is that why you made her stop?

20 August

The last week of Modern Novel was sort of genteel, kicked-back as we got to the end of *Mrs. Dalloway*. Clarissa Dalloway's party led easily into our Friday goodbye party, here at Calvert Street with several bottles of wine, cheap cheddar and a few baguettes, along with the stray bag of Doritos.

I don't know if we made any sense but we certainly talked loudly until three in the morning, theories about literature and life. I must confess I'll miss this group. It's been quite a journey for me—perhaps more so than for my students, even though they're the ones who were supposed to learn something this summer. If I could always learn this much by teaching, I would fear the world of academia far less.

Jessie hugged and kissed me goodbye, which surprised me a little; but then she's a Jewish kid from New York, like Rachel, to them it's like breathing. She might be back in the late fall, for "some legal matters" (a speeding ticket?). And perhaps we'll all run the New York Marathon together.

Now I have time undivided here in my library carrel; time to revisit all the bio material, Lucia's life, the Joyces' life—this time seeing the Joyce family's move to Paris in 1920 as part of a continuum, the development of diaphanous L and Bab.

By 1920 thirteen-year-old Lucia has learned her lesson, not to withdraw from her father's secret touches, not if she still wants him to hear her, know her, teach her. The area around her nipples has begun to swell ever so gently, as if teased into life by Joyce's fingers; her smooth thighs, revealed by flapper dresses, used to his casual caress.

(Thus Giorgio's quick withdrawal from Lucia into his new Parisian social life may have been an automatic, unconscious response to an unconscionable thing—what Fitzgerald called "the horror" in *Tender is the Night*, written right around the time of Joyce's "cry of shame / and horror.")

By age fourteen, of course, Lucia is already carrying around the libretto of *Lucia di Lammermoor*, identifying with the legendary madwoman: perhaps she tried in secret to gasp out the mad scene, way beyond the range of her young voice. There is, of course, no record of this—or of whether her speech was already fragmented, whether she was already finding trees too beautiful to listen.

Three years later Joyce begins *Work in Progress*, already secretly titled *Finnegans Wake*: its first written words the story of the children, Shem and Shaun and Issy, even though the book now begins with their parents. | were you there at the beginning, inspiring the Wake's particular whirling narrative poetry? Did you lead Bab to the banks of the river that tripped you by and by?

437

God, I have a headache; for the last half hour, after writing the above, I have been lying here flaccid—tumbling from my bed to the cooler floor, letting the darkness heal my eyelids. Felicia's baby is still imprinted there, an internal tattoo.

Will, this is too hard, I am spinning, I am dizzy, I need you, I don't even care if you come back in nightmares. I do belong to you, Will, I do, I do, I do.

21 August

4 a.m. Can't write, have to stop crying first. Maybe I can run, instead.

8 a.m. Running under cover of darkness, running swirled in the night: God how it cleanses, goddess how it heals. I was still crying when I crawled into my shorts and sneakers—no ankle brace, no Walkman, just me and my dream and the night.

Venturing into neighborhoods that scare my friends even by daylight, I passed old, beautiful synagogues, their Hebrew stone-cut tablets still discernible under the banners proclaiming NEW ZION BAPTIST CHURCH, then slid past boarded-up shops and the sort of liquor stores where even a Pepsi is passed to you over the counter.

Down into the side streets I normally avoid, where syringes and tiny crack vials grow. At first my ankle hurt—then it seemed to swell into comfort, the pain evaporating far faster than the sweat on my neck.

And it worked. By the time I turned around, I could see again, past the blood flowing from my eyes.

While the flash-film of the dream still burns negatives in my brain:

Calvert Street glaring sunlight / you and I by the bay window / your arm around me / I play Bach, my cello against your hip / you hold my notebooks, your eyes glow blue / blue light over the pages / my body is warm/ your left hand turns the pages / photo of dancing Lucia / my bowstring is sharp wire / it scrapes my fingertips / I hold the bow in my fist like a knife / you have the other end / the music keeps on without me / we are pulling and pushing, you want the bow and so do I / my notebook falls / pages and pages spread under our feet / your eyes make the room blue / I release the bow / I am lying down, my legs spread / my notepapers long linen sheets / my handwriting covers the floor / you lean down slowly/ holding the bow / my eyes small moist gemstones, you let them fall through your fingers / they glitter and bleed on the soft sheets / I am going blind / everything in sepia tones / Felicia's baby behind my eyes / from sepia to darkness / blood on my face a hot shower of tears

It was Felicia, appropriately enough, who woke me; apparently I was crying so loudly in my sleep that she could hear it over her music. (Rachel doesn't get back from Germany for another ten days.) I looked up to see her half-naked figure, her hands covered with paint and glue (the "Christine Beauchamp" collage). "Are you okay?" she asked.

The heat on my cheeks was tears, of course, not blood. I wiped my face with the sheet and said, "Just a bad dream, Leesh. Don't worry about it." As much as Felicia knows about my private life I have never described these dreams to her: I haven't even told Emma, even though she slept beside me in New York as I dreamt Will's dying.

She stood uncertainly, paint marks on the T-shirt that hides her double set of burns. "You sure?"

I nodded and turned from her, curling on my side and looking at baby Mamalujo, the tiny cello now suddenly menacing in the half-light.

"Okay . . . g'night," she said, and closed the door.

As soon as she left I started crying again, more quietly; I

couldn't stop seeing Will's hands playing the cello, covered with blood from putting out my eyes. Finally I stood up and reached for the Suzuki cello, at first embracing it as I had when I found it, in Will's study. Now it felt like some sort of voodoo object, carrying out Will's revenge.

I was still crying when I lay it on the floor, put on one of my heavier shoes and stepped on the cello's tiny neck, splintering the wood. An echo of Colin's last gesture, when I told him I was leaving; it actually made me feel worse, not better, did I have to destroy every good memory, in my dreams and my daily life? Nightly life? I put the splintered cello in a plastic Safeway bag and stuffed it in the bottom of my trash can; then I bent down and reached for my running shoes.

Now my eyes are dry, my face is flushed with that lack-of-sleep feeling, but I'm not sleepy; instead my heart is racing , like I'd had that wicked Vietnamese coffee Leo serves in his restaurant.

and yes, my nightmare, my jumpy energy recalls my child's blurry memory, Leo as an overexcited teenager.

By the time I saw him in San Francisco, when he helped me tape the rib Colin broke, Leo had become quieter, slow smile and slower walk. Many years of yoga, he told me: yet I felt a long coil of intensity, something ready for action, prepared to set a fire when called upon. Perhaps I can send him up to Buffalo, tell him to take the revenge Felicia cannot.

17 August

Exhibit C to paste in the journal: the other side of the postcard is a commercial shot of Lincoln Center, a young girl carrying a cello.

> *Molly—*
>   *saw this and thought of you—and of your project. Lucia was an easy lay, you said—do you know the e. e. cummings poem?*

annie died the other day never was there such a lay—who, among her dollies, dad first ("don't tell your mother") had, making annie slightly mad but very wonderful in bed—saints and saviours, go your way; youths and maidens, let us pray

Writing, running going well—and I may see you in October, in Balto! Or else at the Marathon—
    Jessie

Annie! Did cummings know Anna Livia, was he somehow privy to the same currents and eddies I'm swimming in? But I have no doubt that annie was real, that the poem is evidence (just like Nicole Diver) that writers, at least, came in way ahead of all these psychologists with this brand-new hoopla, about the "psychological sequelae of incest." Making annie slightly mad, but very wonderful in bed.

Meanwhile, I have a lot of work to do. I promised Tilden a report by this week, via fax to Paris. I don't know if the progress I've made since he's been gone is the sort he was looking for: should I even mention my wild speculations about Lucia and James? Are they relevant, at least as places to start?

At least I have no course prep to do, at least not yet; unlike Rachel, who is slated this term for History 102, a slice of hell if I ever heard of one.

25 August

While Rachel's away, of course, Felicia and I have been leaving the house something of a wreck, adolescents with parents on vacation. She leaves Diet Coke bottles and sandwich ends by the television set; my Lucia notes remain spread across the dining room table for days on end.

Now that I've become something of a night owl and have no classes to teach, we're starting to work at nine or ten p.m., just as it cools down. The collage sits drying over to the left, she fusses with new colors now and then—now she's begun a huge one simply of my head, eyes staring straight ahead. I watch the snakes dance, impossibly trying to forget the burned baby underneath the T-shirt. I wonder if her twin nieces are shopping for their own tattoos. (Phucking faces, Felicia's private code a distant cousin to diaphanous L's.)

26 August

4 a.m.: Post-run again. Exhilarated this time.

This time I kept beginning to dream, but my body won't let me: it wants no more of my eyes bleeding, no more drowning. Bits and pieces and fragments of dreams vividly interrupted by sudden wakefulness, triggered by the water through the pipes, or a passing car outside my window, or my own supercharged heart.

It's already routine, these post-midnight runs: the time distinguishable from just-before-sunrise only by the depth of darkness and the lack of street traffic, Felicia's music playing when I get home. Only then does she remember to say something like "C'mon, O'Donnell, get with the program. It can't be safe!"

But I feel protected by the blanket of the night, the stars competing with the streetlights, the homes darkened except for a stray light here and there.

This time, I brought along *Lucia di Lammermoor*, in honor of fourteen-year-old Lucia Joyce trying on her namesake's soprano nightmares—the aria where Lucia sings of her bad dream, "la fantasma" at the fountain with her hands dipped in blood (a likely source of this last Will dream).

Matching the music, *Wake* words whispered through my head as I sped along the Alameda, like a mantra leading to ecstatic trance. "Talking of molniacs' manias and missions for mades . . . she who's mind's a jilldaw's nest who tears up letters she never put pen upon when bother her hair's in a queer mood." Ah but Babbo, we know who put her mind in that queer mood.

8 a.m.

So Emma called at six, and I made the mistake of telling her I'd been up most of the night. "I think every time I start to dream, I wake up," I said. (Good thing I didn't tell her about the run, my neighborhood scared her enough already.)

Next thing I know she's quoting some TV program about sleep deprivation and possible side effects—including hallucinations, as the dreams try to push their way through, regardless. Perhaps that has something to do with the extremely vivid visual memories interrupting me lately at random street corners: Emma and I eating popcorn on a snowy day, Gary pacing the front of the classroom, Colin shaking me so hard my neck cramps.

I cannot conjure those images at will, they come to me at stoplights, tossing faces into the midnight-blue sky. Yes, Lucia, I am coming closer to you, to the *Wake*—ing dreamer, the little girl who laughed all day and did not sleep at night.

7 p.m.

And of course other people in the English Department are noticing the same thing.

I realized it when I walked in today, to reserve time on the computer. Even the secretary looks at me oddly, some respect but almost fear: they don't quite know what to make of me, between my legendary father, student gossip about the Mad Modern Novel class, my now-broken ties to Gary DiCesare. I suppose I'm not helped by my haircut and my weight loss (down to 98—yay team!).

O'Donnell's daughter is very odd, they are saying to one another. *Well, wouldn't you be? He was pretty strange.*

Yes, but she gets weirder as she goes along.

I salute them all, draining my water-bottle at stoplights and dashing up Northern Parkway. Of course, now my ankle is finally aching, almost a burn, in sympathy with Felicia's back. (sym + path = hurt together, and who am I, Babbo or diaphanous L, breaking each word apart before weaving it into my strange abbreviated language?)

27 August

And now I am freer than ever to dive back into the vortex—uninterrupted by class or lovers or music or other obligations, deep into James and Lucia. Into 1924, the year of the cry of shame.

By now the touching has become part of how Lucia and James are together, when Nora is off shopping or housecleaning or otherwise leaving "Jimmy" to his work; their warmth together as essential to the work as his pens or his glasses.

She is reading from the final galley proofs of *Ulysses* and his hand is gently stroking her thigh, caressing her back. Her now generous breasts are used to his fingertips, slipped under her chemise, teasing the top above her brassiere.

What caused him consolation in his sitting posture? she asks.

What, Lucia, what. His eyes are closed, drunk on her voice, bubbling from its dark well.

The candour, nudity, pose, tranquillity, grace, sex, counsel of a statue erect in the center of the table. Her short dress leaves room for him to tease the edges of her underwear, though for a long time he never comes close to her center, only hovering.

When they are finished reading they sing together, softly, the Irish ballads they will sing later at Square Robiac. "And they asked me if she was my daughter—and I said she was my married wife . . ." or "Oh Danny boy, the pipes, the pipes are calling . . ."

But then comes the moment Lucia describes in her journal, the one where he was crying with the pain of his eye illness. For 1924 is the year he writes with huge pencils in big strokes, trying to weave the *Wake* without being able to see. He is preparing for one of the most serious of his eye operations, and in great pain.

By 1924 Lucia has truly become diaphanous L—helping him with correspondence, feeding his ears with odd language and sharp observations, curving her body to its own music. Feeling like a motherless child.

The eye operation is scheduled for a week away and Joyce's eyes are covered: he can see nothing, nothing. But Lucia can read to him, and she does: she reads the newest of Pound's Cantos, agreeing with him that they are incomprehensible. He can smell the pomade she uses on her hair, his hand caresses her back's soft skin, she is terrified and aroused.

Lucia, carissima, I cannot listen. It hurts too much, I hurt too much.

She kisses his cheek, which is wet with tears; then she kisses the rest of where the tears are.

He turns his head and meets her mouth: she has never had a tongue in her mouth before, sweet fifteen and never been kissed in France's obscene style. His tongue tastes of coffee, and faintly of the rum he has been using to dull the pain. One arm tightens around her waist; with the other hand he pulls at her underwear, tearing through to do what he has never dared.

It takes a long, long time before he is inside of her—a long and painful time. She can feel herself bleeding down there, she is being torn apart from the inside, all the warmth his touch gave her dissolves at the pain. Now she is also crying but she swallows it, this will help him stop crying, this will make him feel better.

He comes with a gasp and immediately rolls away. When he lifts his head he groans, horrified at what he has just done. He stands up and makes his way to the bathroom, clinging to the walls to get there and choking hard on new, bitter tears. And there she is, alone, crying from above and bleeding from below. After that they touch less but the cord is tighter than before, whirled round and round by a new, bittersweet secret: he is now bound by unwritten contract to listen to her every word.

For eleven more years they weave this dream together, Joyce absorbing his guilt and pain into *Weltschmertz* (worldpain, I love how Germans can make up new words by just adding them together). The guilt and pain of the human race then transmuted into affirmation and joy of life.

But he wrote the final affirmation alone. For by the time Bab wrote the final lines of his book of the dark, diaphanous L was locked away, shattering windows at Ivry and struggling against the *camizole du force*, unable to console her father for the blood in his eyes.

Are the two inevitably linked? If so, could one be possibly worth the price of the other? Now there's a question far beyond my reach.

I am exhausted, I am exhausted. (Who said that? Oh, Sylvia Plath again. It's sort of been a Plath summer, minus the suicide and the kids.)

My whole body is tipping forward sleep, as if I could find soft pillows inside my own sentences; I have to keep startling myself awake, my post-midnight running finally catching up with me. All I really want to do is go home and sleep. If she likes, Felicia can come upstairs and draw me in my bed, or else I'll sleep sprawled out in her studio.

Unfortunately, today is my deadline to fax Tilden, and all I have so far is a heading, Re: Summer progress. Maybe I will nap for a few moments here in my library carrel, pretend it is the window seat back home in Dorchester.

10 p.m.

Four hours on the department computer and I have nothing but a mess, the IBM's green cursor blinking my own failures at me like a bad stoplight.

After an evening of trying I realize I have nothing, nothing to show him, nothing to justify his and the department's faith in me. I have been too busy with my own silver fish dance, drawing lines between Lucia and Caddy and Ophelia, making up things I can't come near proving . . . I suppose my next step is to find textual evidence for my imagined scenes in the *Wake* itself, but that material's been explored before.

So all I can produce, on the basis of my summer's research, is a series of parallel-processing thought experiments, laying psychological data alongside the timeline of Lucia's madness alongside the well-documented incest material in the *Wake*.

Perhaps the hard work to be done now is to return to II.ii, where the *Wake* began, after all. If I really can trace the development of Issy's sarcastic voices, with special attention to 1924 and the cry of shame—then perhaps I will have something substantial to begin with.

I need to choose specific passages and find their origins in the notebooks, connect them to | references and thus to Lucia at different stages of her life—her dancing, her promiscuity, her gas jets and fires in Bray—before her voice left his ear, before he had to work at c & d all alone. Only that will even approach what I want to accomplish, this delicate invigorating dance among scholarship, biography and revolution.

So that is what I will tell Tilden—he'll say I have gone completely backward, weaving wild stories when I should have been immersed in text. I can see him now, sighing over the printout in a Paris café, perhaps the very one where Beckett broke Lucia's heart. (But at Beckett and Lucia's table is a large family of tourists, some tall skinny man with very fat children and two crying babies.) Meanwhile, I'm becoming more careful about my own notes, especially the looser speculations in these journals: I've asked Felicia to keep them if for some reason I can't look after them myself, if I go on a trip or am struck with a raging flu or run off heedlessly on some love affair. Unlikely as any of these scenarios may be, Felicia

447

agreed—she even designated one of her art drawers (in the square steel cabinet, the one that nearly gave Jeff a hernia moving it down from the attic).

Time to massage my ankle, for my evening run; I think I'll avoid urban grit and run up toward the prep schools the way I did with Emma's. Then I can call her afterward and tell her, try to calm that worried voice.

2 a.m.

Okay, so I overdid it, ran fifteen miles up to Hillsdale Academy and back; the guards actually stopped me, asking my name and checking my wrists (for what?). They seemed reassured by, if not completely comfortable with, my little Seiko watch and my fanny pack.

I'm actually not sorry I ran so far: it has comforted me, liberated me, I feel less a failure than a gonzo academic, boldly going where no scholar has dared go. Will, you would approve were you alive, were you not busy blinding me in dreams. (Joyce's poem about the blood in his eyes, *Blind me, beloved enemy of my will.*) I feel comforted about Will, too, less jerky and scared.

The comfort comes from a Purcell tape, what I sang at Will's funeral, the setting from Shakespeare's *The Tempest*:

Full fathom five thy father lies;
Of his bones are coral made;
Those are pearls that were his eyes;
Nothing of him that doth fade
But doth suffer a sea-change
Into something rich and strange, yes,
Into something rich and strange.

Rich as the legend of English departments, the Bach music still in my hands, my teacher of both Joyce and music, the one comfort in my mind after the Colin disaster.

Strange as the news of your shattering rage, as the memory of crying to you in a hotel room, I don't belong to you, as your hands blinding me with my cello bow.

I have spent this year trying to remember one but not the other: perhaps by doing so I have denied your power. For if there is anything that characterizes Will O'Donnell, alive or dead, it is the tremendous intellectual and emotional power residing in that tall slim frame and blind eyes behind dark glasses. Eyes blind, except when they turn my life blue.

Fatigue finally striking me, I think I can sleep; I will put that same tape on, let the small choir and Renaissance songs give me the keys to dreamland.

28 August

10 a.m.

Up since seven, constructing my report for Tilden, a cobbled-together pathetic effort likely to get me canned from the doctoral program.

And when I stopped by the department what did I see but a familiar ponytail, between sunburned shoulders. I tried to ignore him as I went toward the computer, but before I knew it there he was, his beard against my cheek in a casual kiss, "Well, if it isn't Molly O'Donnell!"

I shrugged, didn't turn around. I didn't want him near me, didn't want to smell his stupid Denise-bought cologne or hear about his progress on *Lear*. I just wanted him to sink through the carpet next to me. Or perhaps to do so myself, since the memo was so lame —hoping for some underwater pool under the university that would let me swim out to sea.

Felicia hissed when I told her, like a child at the movies when the villain comes on. She and I are still working on what Felicia calls "the butch piece"—so called because I do look sort of male in it. I've never seen my face writ that large before, about four feet by five feet; a single eye on the canvas is larger than my hand. Felicia's very careful in the initial drawing stages, she mixed colors forever trying to get every gradation of color in my eyes. (There's a fix in my changeable eye.)

I watch her face transform as she works, brow wrinkling in concentration, sleepy eyes alert almost to the point of alarm, as she works to get the angle of the jaw just right. My jaw has been confusing her lately, she says.

Meantime my mind swims to the relaxed reggae beat, through the wreckage of my dissertation—for it already feels like wreckage, even without a reply from Tilden.

And I can feel myself calming, my body detaching from the intensity of my imagined James-Lucia scenarios: as if, having imagined them clearly, I can now step back and begin the truly academic work. I can also swim toward the bigger question, the one that may explain why Joyce scholars have been permanently queasy on the subject of Lucia.

Like Will, like Tilden, like most of us, I have long since fallen in love with James Joyce. How not to love this secular sacred miracle, this tight-assed Jesuit from the slums of Dublin who created spiritual epiphanies from muck and mud, from dance and desire—playing on languages and motifs the way a modern-day rapper dances through an electronic sampling keyboard? When the work thus created is consistently poetic, humane, funny, ribald and spiritual by turns, taking life's tragedies and spinning them into a yes oh yes oh yes?

And the attachment deepens when you read the notebooks, observe the incredible mind at work shaping daubing dappling all his research, personal experiences (including |'s voice), and collective legends into the work one can spend a lifetime reading (and many do).Who can then bear the cry of shame and horror?

How can we live with him? With ourselves for loving him?

Oh I know the litany, Pound the Nazi ,Wagner the anti-Semite, Picasso the batterer. But for those of us who have allowed ourselves to swim deeply in his river, Joyce hits us where we live, becomes father and lover, sonhusband—perhaps that's why so many scholars put the blame on Lucia, as if she were at fault. ("Issy done it. I confesh.") And still they will only acknowledge the desire.

Virginia walked into the Ouse, Lucia turned on the gas jets and ended an incomprehensible old woman singing little songs to her nurses in an asylum, few traces of Rythme et Couleur. How can I let myself write a dissertation celebrating Bab, when diaphanous L was destroyed in the process?

I really ought to be sleepy by now, but I'm not. I think it would be pushing it to go for another run, so perhaps I will clean the kitchen instead—Rachel comes back today, it's time to pretend Felicia and I have been living like grownups.

10 p.m.

And it's finally caught up with me, the fatigue tracing my ankles and up through my shoulders, I am ready for bed.

But I just wanted to record Emma's call—she ran the distance by herself today, something I've not yet done. She was just inspired, she said: she ran across the Charles, skirting both Dorchester and Roxbury (matching white and black dangerous ghettos) to continue to the west, finally calling Barry from some Motel Six to come and get her, after when she'd hit the twenty-six-mile mark. Her time: three hours and forty-eight minutes.

"It was incredible," her voice dreamy with fatigue, high-pitched with the excitement buzzing through phone lines into my tired hand. "Oh Molly, I can't wait till November." Nor can I, though I have been covering less distance at a shot, preferring instead my

451

twice-daily dashes through different sections of Baltimore. I need to make a date to do it, then sit down with a map and plot out a specific distance route, perhaps out beyond Hillsdale Prep and back, sassing those guards who wanted to inspect me as if for drugs.

29 August

3 a.m.

This is the time to do it. The distance, I mean. While I still have Will's blood on my hands.

at the bay window / loud hard rain against the glass / we are together again, me at my cello your arm around me / the rain drowns my music / your hand stroking my shoulder / looking at my baby pictures / in them I am screaming / a screaming infant with red hair and a red face / the clouds darken the room/

your eyes half-closed, no blue light this time / you catch the bow's end / the bow-string sharp, an assassin's piano wire / no music this time as we fight / my baby picture covers one wall / its mouth the size of my head / my shoulders ache from trying to fight you / you are about to blind me again / I bite your ear and your body goes slack with pleasure / you sink to the floor, your eyes open / I drive the bow deep / our face and my arms bloody / your eyes on the floor glisten blue / blue pearls large and pure / smooth as silk or young skin / I cry out to you/ I do not belong to you / I pick them up / they glow in my hands / I do not belong to you

And he is breathing them into me, these dreams, like Bach or jazz or the *Wake*, variations on a theme, the same bloody gyre river cycle of Lucia Nicole Virginia Felicia the goddamn fucking non-mystery of pain, I am not sorry, Will, I am not sorry I am not scared I am joyous greatly.

Now my sneakers and shorts are on; I have marked a route through

My favorite night-neighborhoods and beyond, where I can finally find Lucia B, we will meet in half-dream, we will run together. No Walkman this time, there is only one song I need, your funeral song, the one that melded into my dream.

Those are pearls that were his eyes.

And I could not console him.

And all Neptune's oceans will not wash the blood from my hands.

the opening of the mind to light

Blurred vision casts a veil across the way out.

Coming out of Chatham for the last time, my limbs are heavy with medsdreams; I will never reach the grey stone arch at the end of the path, the Arc de Triomphe dripping with ice.

The nurses from Les Rives des Prangins wear fur coats against the bitter Swiss winter. Nora Joyce's is the best—the others stand in a circle, admiring it, protecting her as I pass by.

Just beyond them Zelda wears only her tutu, snow covering her breasts. She pirouettes, but I cannot dance with her, the days of "L'Irlandaise!" long past. I cannot even find my hands, to reach out and say goodbye. Zelda is Shana in her white ghost dress, she is Emma dressed for a track meet, dashing past me to the Arch of Triumph. I follow her on wooden feet.

Just beyond the grey arch, there you are—round glasses, soft-brimmed hat and striped tie, soft lost eyes. I try to run to you, but Anne-Marie and Leo hold me back.

"Babbo! Babbo!" I cry.

❦

White street through a bay window: Zurich? Paris? Vision still blurred, my arms still ache from the *camizole du force*. The snow clear and cold and laced pale blue—not like you in Dublin, not your crystal silver black snowflakes.

Calvert Street under a white blanket. I am so cold, my nerves are bad to-night. Yes, bad. I lie down next to the heater, craving warmth feeling like a motherless child far, far from home.

❦

Soft voices behind me: *So I broke it to Kepler, it's in the files now, meds discontinued AMA . . . yeah, against medical advice.*

Sure, Felicia's laugh, or *Artists Make Action.*

AMA, Anna Molly Agoniste, Afraid you May be Alive. (Afraid you may kill your father.) As we there are where are we from tomtittot to tootootomtotalitarian. Totalitarian medical advice from the fat materialistic Swiss man.

Zurich out my window but not Les Rives des Prangins. Not the poorhouse we lived in when I was young. Long rows of narrow houses, dappled with light snow, glitter-dust. Not Zurich, nor Paris. Volkswagens parked precariously at the end of the street; a young mother carefully maneuvering a baby stroller, students carrying backpacks.

Baltiskeeamore. I can sleep now.

He did not get hold of my soul.

❦

C'est moi qui et l'artiste!

Felicia and I share her large easel, painting side by side like matching angels.

My arms are still heavy, what's bled in the bone crops out in your flesh. If I'm very careful I can draw long blunt lines with the tip of my cello bow. I work slowly so it does not cut me, the paint is red-black, clotted blood.

I am working hard to make one of my *lettrines*, but it's hard to see through the smoke rising from Felicia's back. Underneath her T-shirt, the rust-brown baby will not stop screaming.

My fingers slip, one of my fingertips is sliced by the cello bow. Felicia's soft brushes hit the floor quietly, fin fin, kissing noises against the hard wood. Leo leaves the room, choking from the smoke.

Days of burning.

I am the one screaming. I only stop when Leo comes back with a sweater for Felicia and tea for me, and opens the window: I reach out, plunge my hands into the snowy air. When the smoke clears Felicia closes the window again.

And you are there again, in the glass. They say you are underground, but they do not realize how sly you are, well hidden and watching me all the time.

Emma is my mirror of mirror, cinder Christinette to my Laughing Sally.

She is crying, but I have no words to comfort her. I sing to her, *I'm forever blowing bubbles*. Now strong enough. I hold her hands and try to make her dance with me, Zelda still at Prangins surrounded by fur coats.

Anne-Marie's face is wet from melted snow—her skin so pale she could be made of rain, I must be raining now. Were you chaste me child? All Neptune's oceans will not bleach the stain of our lives.

We try to run up North Charles Street together, dressed in winter spandex; but after three blocks my legs refuse, they drag under me even without the medsdreams. (It wasn't so far, then, from Chatham to the weeping willows. It only felt like miles away.)

And you are at every streetcorner, with your white cane. Sometimes you wear the fedora and the round glasses, other times you carry a violin and your glasses are dark.

The cold burns my throat, so I cannot sing.

It freezes my fingertips, so I cannot kill you again.

(A bit of warning about the tenderloined passion hinted at.)

Baltimore wears Christmas lights like a diamond necklace. The ice on the sidewalk makes us walk slowly toward the harbor, Anne-Marie holding my hand as we walk toward the malltitudes. Walking slow steadies me (though I wish I had my cello, to pierce the ice). Huge Christmas boxes move toward us, casting big square shadows in the night light; behind them squat jacketed bodies.

We walk down to the bay and Anne-Marie squats next to me by the water's edge—dark ripples under the layer of ice. My profile is half in shadow, half flashing in and out of Christmas lightning. I look like you, like Shem, that insufficiently malestimated notes-natcher. Even Samuel Beckett would not be able to tell the difference.

Then your reflection is beside mine, a boy-reflection, the young altar boy at Sacred Heart. In the water's darkness you put your arms around my shoulders, you cover my eyes. Blinded I feel your warm body, your lips against my neck.

Together we lean forward, closer to the water. I open my eyes and the reflection has changed: you are alone, streaks of blood remaining on your cheeks from my cello bow. My cold mad feary father.

And I rush, my only, into your arms—pulling against Anne-Marie, she is next to me, holding me back. I want to wash the last of the blood off your cheeks, with my tongue.

I'se so silly to be flowing but I no canna stay.

～

St. Louis woman don't wear no diamond ring All the men around pull her apron strings

I sleep on the floor of the studio these days, next to the heater. Felicia has moved her paints up to my old room; she still draws me down here, almost every day. Leo sleeps in the bed, behind the partition.

My nonday diary is fat, Jungfraud's messagebook: Anne-Marie holds it out to me, while from behind Felicia combs my hair. Her low, sultry voice bubbles up from the well, blending with the music. "It's really growing now, maybe I should braid it." The notebook is full of pictures of my face—looking over a Paris wall, dancing in *Ballets Rythme et Couleur*. But the scars are not there: no darkness under my eyes, no punch of sleeplessness, no headache from the ECT lethemuse. Would the lethemuse have eased you? Better than leeches or operations in Switzerland?

Aneurysm, a blood vessel bursting in the brain. Flickering squares, long scratchy drawings of the blood in your eyes. Would the tiny electrodes have somehow lessened the pressure, the scream of the cry of horror?

But it washes off, Babbo. I told you that after Prangins. And I cannot console you. I told you that in Texas.

Outside a snowfilled night, inside the pages are brittle with words, words, words: odes to Time, conversations with Shakespeare, do not cut down trees. And over and over again the word known to all men, the verbe de vie, bled all over the notebooks and sliding out of the tape deck. *The man I love wouldn't go nowhere.* . . .

"God Molly, your hair is so soft." then Felicia's hands on my hair are yours, her voice your boy soprano, oh Shem bring it closer to me, it is softer than anything in the wide world.

I drop the notebook and pull my head away, Felicia still holding a lock to braid—the pulled hair a sharp pain, bracing as the cold. And I am looking out at the street, snow soaking my hair—drowning the verve to vie and verbe de vie, melting the adhesive they use for the lethemuse. Felicia calls to Leo, who comes upstairs and brings me back inside.

"I am so, so sorry," he says. "I didn't mean to leave you."

No crime, I tell him. Only love, universal love. This secret must be told to the Cabinet, let the raised name of love every person thrill!

Snow is different from thunderstorms, it makes me sleepy. Leo helps Felicia lift my hair off my neck, they wrap it in soft cloth. I lie down next to the heater.

The medsdreams have ruined my stomach. I retch at the sight of food, any food. Leo keeps trying, he broils fish delicately, cajun spices to tease my tongue, California salads with French named cheeses. "You're getting our whole menu here" and Felicia grins, she and Rachel eat gladly. I try but it doesn't stay down.

Felicia has gained a little weight, smooth skin over curves. She and Anne-Marie are making me draw, huge shapeless faces.

Anne-Marie asks me to draw your face: I look at the bay window but all I see are bare-bone trees and snow. I shake my head, I cannot explain that she must wait until darkness falls; that only then will I be able to see you.

Shana wears a blue dress when she comes to see me. She lies down with me and holds me like her baby, she kisses me as if I were a crucifix. I touch her freckled shoulders, there is no snow on them. I love you, I hate you, I love your chuckly neck.

Oh lover man, where can you be?

∾

Come, smooth of my slate to the beat of my blosh! I dress myself in Charly and wait for you.

∾

Trying again, to run: my legs a little lighter. they listen to me now.

Anne-Marie and I speed along Charles Street, sometimes running sometimes walking. Christmastime and the university is deserted; melted snow and ice and the buildings are dripping with water, quiet rainstorms under awnings and staircases. *Let me rain now*, the walls ask quietly, weeping to welcome the Christ child.

My sneakers are new and I close my eyes into the curve of each footfall, from the heel to the ball and then a spring forward. A stitch begins in my side and I breathe deeply against it.

"So I talked to Emma," Anne-Marie says. "About Christmas."

The stitch kicks in despite my breathing, and I have to slow to a walk.

"Molly?" Anne-Marie slows down to match me. "Are you okay?"

I stop to touch where the pain has set in fully, sharply. Emma? I ask. And what is she, the weird haughty one? I breathe deeply again; as the sun rises and the air warms, it is a little easier.

"Molly?" Anne-Marie's voice soft, patient. "Do you want to talk?" That makes me laugh, tuck up your sleeves and loosen your talktapes. I start to run again, spurting ahead of Anne-Marie.

When she catches up to me I tell her, Emma has a lovely voice, like a mermaid's. I do not think she will sing with me. "What do you want to sing, Molly?" Anne-Marie asks quietly.

I tip my head to listen, first hearing *Lucia di Lammermoor*, then Bessie Smith. Then I find a song I sang with Shana and Susan.

Come, I say, sing Pearlstone songs with me. *On a wagon bound for slaughter / There's a calf with a mournful eye . . .*

Anne-Marie's voice wavers, Is' wobbly singing. I lean down and scoop handfuls of snow, messages from Chatham on the clean university walls.

TRUE BELIEVER to make it on their own. recovery 38 mi. (A marathon and a half.)

My hands are wet on the walls, the messages melting as I write them. I look for you, to see if you are the one breathing them away, into the cool water of my Christian name.

Hush now, don't explain
   You're my joy and pain
The club is dark and stinks of cigarette smoke: the smell of Marlboros is mixed with Camels, Gauloise and clove cigarettes, which is why Felicia and I can bear it. The singer is nearly old enough to have known |—she could be an African goddess carving, with her thick shoulders and large breasts, the wrinkles a lacy filament across her rouged face. Her scarlet lips match the sequins on her red dress, match the comb in the hair of the blonde at the front table, as well as the red loincloth on the tiny rust-brown baby hidden away under Felicia's dress.

Rachel is covering her eyes from all the smoke. Leo leans forward, his chin cupped by his hand, in his other hand a glass of wine. I am drinking wine too, a really nice Corvo—so long since I had good wine, late dinners with Colin, interludes before good sex or broken windows. (Hearsay in paradox lust.)

I am also eating very salty peanuts, they only make me want more wine. Felicia is smoking, and I hold one of her cigarettes between my fingers. I breathe in her smoke the way the sax player breathes in his reed, his young face screwed up with the effort of yearning out the next few notes.

When you're brokenhearted an' your man is out of town . . . I light the cigarette and suck deeply, bringing the smoke deep inside. The pain in my lungs is carried forth by the singer's voice. *Go to the river. . . .*

Babbo has warned me that smoking will hurt my voice, but I know it only makes it deeper, richer, just like hers, the skinny singer in her slinky blue dress. I exhale black smoke and watch the door: I am waiting for Jack, an American painter I met at the Pavillon Royal in the Bois de Boulogne.

The pianist is tall, lean, like Emile, who first brought me here. He could be Emile, the same long and slender fingers that rolled a smooth boogie-woogie between my legs, to my moon star. Emile has gone away, a long time ago. I do not know Jack's last name.

An' if he don't come back to you I'll tell you what to do
Just jump right overboard, 'cause he ain't no more to you

Then I see them, Samuel Beckett and Peggy Guggenheim, close up to the singer. I have not seen Mister Beckett since he helped me find Number Seven Eccles Street, carrying me through the Dublin blizzard to your face of frozen snow. *An' that's the reason why I've got those weeping willow blues.*

Down the street from the club, I am throwing up out the window of Rachel's Volkswagen.

"We probably shouldn't have let her drink," Leo is whispering. "And since when does she smoke?"

"No," Felicia murmurs back, "we should have just finally let her kill him."

I can barely hear them through the thunderstorm in my head, the sounds of the passing cars, one of which is Gary and Denise's Toyota.

I finally stop hiding my face when we get to the house. Leo helps lift me up the stairs. I huddle next to the heater and look out the bay window. You are not watching me tonight, and in the street-light I watch melting ice drip from the branches of the oak, from the trees we have hanged our hearts upon.

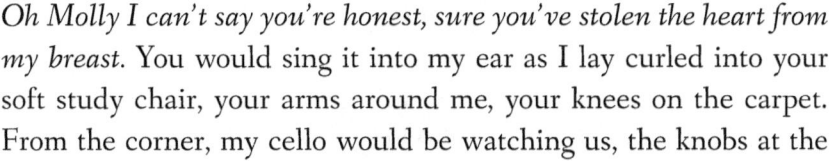

All are washed in the blood of the lamb.

Christmas at Shana's church is different, no candles or nuns, no Mozart. Instead we sing together, *Go tell it on the mountain / That Jesus Christ was born.* Shana's baby has her big brown eyes and sings along in his grandmother's arms, except without any words.

| and Emile would sing and sway with Shana, *Go tell it on the mountain!* Anne-Marie sings in their place, holding my hand. Today she wears a dress, the first time I have seen her in a skirt since I left the hospital.

Since we left the hospital. Shana holds my other hand.

Crucifix missing from the altar, only a huge square cross. I miss it, I miss the bleeding body, Christ soaked in the blood of the lamb. It's why you're not here: no bloody crucifix, no Will. Even though you can't see it you crave it, just as you crave the smell of the tapers and sacramental wine. No sacraments here, only songs, even communion is a song.

In this church you would not sing, Will: you would stand silent, your back straight, unseeing eyes fixed on the cross as though your inner vision could make it bleed. God wants blood victim.

Your touch could do it. I look around for you, although I know you are dead, that I am safe.

That you live not is my grief.

And my salvation.

Amazing grace, how sweet the sound / That saved a wretch like me.

Oh Molly I can't say you're honest, sure you've stolen the heart from my breast. You would sing it into my ear as I lay curled into your soft study chair, your arms around me, your knees on the carpet. From the corner, my cello would be watching us, the knobs at the top an insect's eyes. Downstairs, strangled TV music, Margaret watching General Hospital.

You would stay in me for a long time after you came, and then whisper Shem, do you remember where the towel is? Strands of my hair twirled around your fingers as I ran the damp towel over your skin and then my own, absorbing fluid and smell. We would sing Mozart, erotic little arias, Papa-pa-papageno, until we were both dry.

God has joined us, Lucia sang to her lost lover, her hands covered with her new husband's blood. Nothing can divide us. Sender: Boston, Mass.

The day after Christmas the bay window is frosted, hiding the snow. I wake up and draw my name on the glass. Felicia helps me dress to come downstairs, asking gently, "Are you ready for them?"

"All are washed in the blood of the lamb," I answer.

"Them" is my family, surrounded by big and little boxes in glittery paper, jewel-colored. (Those are jewels that were my eyes.) Shaun and Barry sit on either end of the sofa; Barry holds little Stephen, who is crying the tired and frustrated wail of the three-year-old.

Margaret sits in the middle, her makeup careful, her hair dyed a smooth dark auburn—sheltered on either side by Anna and Emma. My little sister had no. If I could say Mother. Mother

She rises to meet me, puts her arms around me. She is saying something but I cannot hear her over Stephen's cries. "Molly," I finally hear, "my dear sweet Molly," her voice full of the heavy slow drama of her soap operas—the ones that masked the clarience of the childlight in the studiorum upstairs. Emma urges little Stephen to come and greet me, but he is still crying (besides, Helen and Giorgio were too afraid to risk letting me hold him). As they all chatter I don't even distinguish the voices, I stare at the boxes. My body hurts from holding it still.

"He's so tired . . . it's a long drive."

"Let me try." Leo approaches Stevie, crouches to face him. The tiny hands reach out and pull at Leo's long hair, curiously; Leo shakes it off, Stevie tries again. The game calms him; my little nephew, will it be you who tries to obliterate my memory, someday? Or will you be too busy tattooing yourself, to hide the burns from Margaret's hot coffee?

Shaun shifts position on the couch, he is uncomfortable and stiff, Shaun MacIrewick is still a shame and a sham. I lock eyes with him and he looks away.

"Molly, we got you some presents, do you want to open them?" Emma tries to hug me but I swing away from her.

"No I have had too many presents already," I say, feeling cross. I ignore the tears in her brown eyes, and instead ask about midnight Mass. Did the crucifix bleed?

Emma looks to my mother, who lowers her eyes. "Anne-Marie said you wanted to sing," Emma says, her voice low.

"What did they sing Christmas Eve?"

Margaret's voice wobbles as she sings with me; Emma looks younger than her baby, her mouth round and wide so the notes can escape. I feel my arms stiffening, I do not want to face her baby eyes. I wonder what step she would call it, the twelve (thirteen? seventeen?) steps of dementia praecox.

They have brought a songbook with pictures, so Stevie can sing along: we sing about the Christ child, about Frosty the Snowman, about going over the river and through the woods to our grandmother's house. My throat tightens with each song.

Finally I stand up and stop the sing-along, the same way I did at JPI.

Anne-Marie whispers to Barry and he leaves, pulling Margaret and Stevie into the kitchen. They are afraid, just like Giorgio and Helen, and they have good reason, this time.

By the time they leave all the Christmas boxes are broken and Leo's arms are tight around me. I am tired, my hands are tired, my fingers stiff. As Felicia puts me to bed, soft voices on the other side of the door: Anne-Marie and Leo. *You know Kepler will want her back . . . just read the court order.*

I've already had it out with Shaun, I can get him not to report this. I think he's content to leave her to me, though I doubt we'll see my mother here again.

What about Emma?

I stand up, wrestling with the bedclothes. Felicia holds my shoulder but I cry to them, Blood will suffer blood to die hungry! My voice is loud enough to shout through the door, but I want it to echo further, over the snowy buildings and straight up to Boston. The door to the studio opens and Leo and Anne-Marie surround me.

As I start to speak I feel the truth between my teeth.

"She got my castoff devils, all right," I tell them.

Leo wants me to talk, not cry myself to sleep. He holds me tight and murmurs into my hair, "let it out let it out," but I just keep crying.

Felicia and Leo are moving Rachel's furniture out of the house, helped by a group of artists singing loud songs. Anne-Marie wears jeans and a flannel shirt to help them. Rachel is moving out for the rest of the year. "I'm sorry," she said to me. "But I need peace."

She is not the only one. Shanti shanti shanti. Shanty slanty scanty.

Every night I watch the window, for your face: if you do not come I stare at it, until I am nearly blind. Blind me, beloved enemy of my will.

It was men invented virginity not women, invented it so they could kill it. And it is like death. Ours is a mistery of shame, Babbo. So many years.

Come, smooth of my slate to the beat of my blosh! Cello practice always ending the same, a reward for good work a punishment for inattention. *yes, Shem. oh. yes. doesn't that feel fine? we're helping your breasts bloom.*

For my fifteenth birthday I gave you the virginity men invented: we had awaited this, naming the day we could be closer than hands and mouth and soft pressures. The pain started in my cunt and traveled upwards, it split my head open but you could not see it.

Not a proper skin, Bab wrote: *lesions internal.* Underlining "internal," to explain pain from mysterious wounds. Music fucks me; I'm sure it's bad for me.

Babbo did | feel you inside, whenever she played the piano?

Vision clearing. arms lighter: my body finally free of the drugs. Leo is making me eat but I still throw up a lot; when I am done vomiting Felicia and Anne-Marie take turns massaging me, until I can feel my skin again.

New Years' Eve we stay up and watch television, crowds in New York watching the ball of lights drop. I was there with Colin the year someone was stabbed; we read about it later in the newspapers. This time I watch carefully for the person who will die tonight, but the picture is not clear enough.

After midnight I want to run in the night air, like I did in the summer, before I died. Felicia will not let me: "It's too cold," she says, wiping my tears. "It's much too cold."

Not too cold for me to feel you again, the ghost hands inside of me, licking and sucking at my hindmoist. I get up and run out the back door; I crouch in the cold mud, wait for the cold to freeze you, for Felicia and Leo to pull me back inside.

Felicia sleeps next to me that night, both of us encased in long underwear: blankets below and above us like a tent. I do not get up to look for you in the window; your face is well enough imprinted inside my eyes, your touch burned into the skin of my inner thigh.

"Happy New Year," Felicia mumbles, falling asleep. Her body is warm next to mine. I can feel my skin burning.

Papa Is goes to bed in silks | tells men = love
    go to hell—but not the hell of the damned
    my summer dream, I am a naked teenager carrying your coffin
    laughing in the Texas heat, I wish I had done that.
    I did do that.
That Bloomsday month, every day the temperature was over 100 degrees, just like Baltimore. We took air-conditioned taxis the four or five long blocks to the conference; I wore little sundresses and shivered in the air conditioning, and just like ten years later everyone thought I was your wife. "Is your husband's podium tall enough?" "If there's anything I can do let me know" of course they thought that, that you were like the rest of them, trading in on a new grad student every year. "I admire his work so much, your husband." and every time I heard it my skin grew even colder.

By the end most of them knew me, *oh isn't O'Donnell's daughter so sweet.* Sweet sixteen and been kissed far too often. Kissed and beaten and caressed and eaten, in Paris London Dublin Zurich.

Until that night, the last night of the conference, when for the first time I would not let you touch me.

I do not belong to you I do not belong to you I do not my face soaking wet from saying it over and over, resisting your deep sighs, your careful tears, your beautiful voice singing your love for me your dark chocolate voice speaking authority to me, *don't you want access to your passion? Do you want to ruin yourself as a musician?* You also tried to rouse my body as only you knew how, all the touches to make me scream: but I ran instead crying from the room, slept outside in the grass behind the hotel.

You did not force me: that much is true. (Did you force me, at five and six and seven? Did I resist? I don't remember, only remember fingerkisses and semen-smell in my curls, you would rinse it out and rub my head with a hot towel. I was ticklish, it made me giggle.)

I do not belong to you For she must walk out. And it must be with who. Teaseforhim. Toesforhim. Tossforhim. Two. Else there is danger of.

 memb (?) of Is naked is accevable (scribble) my love to procure
Ti abbracio, Babbo. Ti abbracio.

Three a.m.: Leo sound asleep on the tiny futon, Felicia is spending the weekend in Washington with some friends.

I go to the window and you are there, waiting patiently.

You tell me where I can find what I want: in the bathroom trash can, at the bottom. Felicia used it to shave my legs last week. | helps me crush the plastic handle, quietly, using the heavy porcelain toilet cover.

I am down the hall from sleeping Leo so I must be silent. I run the water, keeps my blood from clotting inside me.

You had blood in your eyes.

And I did not console you.

Life is good. In another place the sun is hot and the watery gold glows and fades, it is alive.

I look in the mirror and your eyes glow blue, fill the bathroom with blue light, like in my dream. The sink blue-tinted white, specks of color dancing where the porcelain is chipped, the water bubbling pink.

The blade is dull; if I could feel it, it would hurt, the digging and scraping. Birth, hymen, martyr, war, foundation of a building, sacrifice, kidney burntoffering, druid's altars, Anna Liffey's red here.

In the mirror you smile serenely, Bach in your smile, the blues in my ears. *Death was here, he didn't stay long / I looked in the bed and my daddy was gone.* (I looked in the bed and my daddy was there.)

Then it is Leo behind me in the mirror and he is pulling at me, blood on his hands as he throws the razor down. He lifts me bodily and buries my hands in towels, carries me over to the tiny futon.

With one hand he is calling Felicia in D.C., with the other he swirls gauze round and round and round my wrists. It is the first time I have seen him cry.

∾

Things are not as simple as you think, said Kundera, even though he was not talking about my virginity.

But in truth, breaking my virginity was not a one-step process. It took three or four tries, each exquisitely painful. *We're getting there, Shem.*

Just like you told me when I was starting my dissertation.

I am getting there, Will.

Cold like air conditioning, crystallizing my tears into rock solid rage.

∾

Felicia has found a way to feed me—protein drinks, not the disgusting ones they used at Pearlstone but something she makes in the blender, sweet and pineapple-y, like those big tall Hawaiian teenage-girl drinks. Where's the little umbrella? I ask and she laughs; the next thing I know she's stolen tiny umbrellas from work. She drinks them too, lately she cannot eat either, my sister in stomach rage.

Leo has given up trying for the moment, no more gourmet feasts. "How do you expect to be able to run again?" he wants to know, Anne-Marie wants to know.

But I can see the burning baby in Felicia's eyes now. I am bringing him to life inside her. She is getting thin again like last summer. I try to say I'm sorry and she hands me my glass, I toast her baby she toasts my fever dreams.

Then Anne-Marie comes and we go running, or try to. My ski suit keeps me warm and it is easier now that the snow is gone, you are no longer splattered all over the streets of Baltimore. But my legs are stiff all the way up to my hips, even though Felicia massages them often.

Anne-Marie wants me to call Emma, who is afraid of me now.

I want to, but every time I try I feel your hand on my lips. Our secret, Shem. Our secret. Did you say that to Emma too? But I cannot pick up the telephone.

Bitter cold again: I cannot even open the windows without my hands freezing. (*Io gelo ad ardo! Io manco!*) Too cold to run, even in super winter spandex—so I do not try to call Emma.

A letter from Shaun and Anna, it comes inside a long envelope, Shaun's new stock firm in Boston. Without reading it I bring it upstairs, slide it between the metal grates of Felicia's space heater. Who tears up letters she never put pen upon?

The smoke alarm is prompt, and Leo follows it: for the first time, he is angry with me. *set fire in room.*

"Don't be stupid—I know you're angry, but you have no right to burn us down in the process. The hospital put up with this shit, do you really want to go back there?"

Leo's fire made smoke trail into Will's study: I was holding my tiny cello, Will his violin. We had to stop "Twinkle, Twinkle Little Star" so that Shaun could bring Will downstairs, so they could shout at Leo. Emma came upstairs with her Barbie dolls, I put down baby Mamalujo to instead play with her.

"Sure I wanted to burn him down," Leo says. "But he's dead now, Molly. And you didn't make him dead." The sentence inside my head an explosion of marigolds. *I also think it's better if you and I just not communicate for the rest of this year; I know you understand my reasons. I thought I had made matters clear to you last summer, in Texas—but your recent actions show that not to be the case.* words made of marigolds, *your recent actions.*

Thanksgiving you greeted me with airport roses, spoke softly into my ear over dinner *oh look how sweet, Molly and her dear father are still so close* pulled at my dress late at night, your touch strong and forceful. I twisted away and fled downstairs, sharing Emma's bed that night. Emma never asked why: because, I think, she knew.

Oh Danny Boy, the pipes, the pipes are calling every blow of Colin's accurate punishment, the day he burned me I laughed as much as cried.

The first day of February and I am able to eat breakfast, sweet runny omelet with tiny pieces of cilantro and broccoli, carefully chopped and edible with a spoon. Solid food a new weight on the tongue, a scary weight inside my chest.

Felicia still can't, she shrugs before making another protein shake. I see something else in her eyes; I think she is drinking at work, the lethemuse that washes off at bedtime. Drink enough and you can forget anything.

Leo and Anne-Marie unearth one of my old CDs, Tchaikovsky's Violin Concerto: Colin's sharp blue eyes and quick English grin—a bit of an advanced Beatle. I remember when we chose the photograph, sifting among dozens of head shots. In Tchaikovsky's fury every ounce of Colin's erotic violence, poured into huge passionate double stops. "So young," he said to me that first night, "yet so skilled . . . and where did you learn to do that?" but he never waited for the answer.

I show Leo and Anne-Marie my tiny burn scars, almost invisible now after two years.

Drink enough and you forget why you deserve the blows.

You only know that you do.

Until you spend mornings in bed waiting for your hangover to clear, then run off to teach a few stray cello lessons, killing time until he needs you again.

"How can I share you?" kissing me that night in Ohio as my cracked rib seared from inside. *I do not belong to you I do not belong to you* those words foreclosed now, inside the mystery of shame.

I'd rather my man hit me than git up and quit me / T'ain't nobody's business if I do

Did Emile teach that to diaphanous L?

I lie on my side on the floor as Felicia draws me, the tape deck yielding the slender clarinet opening of *Rhapsody in Blue*. She says she will name this drawing after the music. I try not to think of *Manhattan*, watching it at Pearlstone, or holding hands at the movies with the beloved enemy of my will.

Instead I watch little kids chase each other down the street, on lunch break from the elementary school half a block away. I watch Felicia and her eyes are dry, I think she may have slept for perhaps three hours; she got in at four from the late shift, and I could hear her fussing upstairs as early as eight this morning. She will not tell me about her dreams.

The music is too gentle, I break pose and stand up, the calm saxophone and sexy piano are too gentle for the way I feel. Felicia puts in the tape that taught me to dance, Lucia B's song, *Take me to the river, drop me in the water*.

We start out dancing the way we did at St. John's Church that night, the night I ran away from Pearlstone; she takes my hands and we sway and kick, at first laughing and then more furious. Take me to the river, drop me in the water, hot water on her face and shoulders.

Then Felicia puts in a tape I always hated, some British band screaming and screaming and screaming. Now we stomp up and down like pogo sticks; Lucia you would never do this, you who curved so gracefully for *Rythme et Couleur*.

Leo comes upstairs, his face flush red from the cold. "What's all this?" he asks, a grocery bag still in one hand.

"I think we're dancing on graves," Felicia shouts over the music, her eyes less dry, her face flushed. Her baby is dancing inside her as if she were pregnant, I jump higher and harder and don't say much.

Leo sits on the floor and watches us. When the music is over Felicia collapses against the wall, out of breath. I lean my face against the cold window pane.

"Whose grave, Molly?" Leo asks, softly.

"Maybe mine," I say.

At his concerned look I explain, "Until I Wake, like Finnegan!" Even Leo knows the song, I must have been an infant when Will first started singing them to us. *We'll all dance a jig at Finnegan's Wake*.

So when will it be time for us Finnegans to wake, as L and Bab commanded? Not so long as I still see your face in my bay window at night, *Kept late hours/Pop's back home*. That night I try to break the glass, but it is too strong for me: I end only with bruised hands.

∾

After failing with the bay window, I succeed in breaking all my plates, the way you did, Will, the way | did | *breaks plate/cries* Leo makes me wear rubber gloves while I do it, Felicia collects the shards and throws them away.

That night the radiators are going full blast, no need for the space heater. I snuggle in my sleeping bag and watch the cars go by outside. Then I see your reflection in the window, I rise to meet you both.

You stand side by side, sad by sad with twin white canes, Will and Bab: Will wears dark glasses and Joyce his round wire-rims. What do you want? You don't answer, but I know.

No more, Babbo. No more, Will.

I take back from you all the hot afternoons and sweaty mornings, the prick of the spindle that gave me the keys to dreamland. I take back from you my music and my words.

But of course I cannot, they are already given, already lost.

I take back from you my body and my soul.

She did not believe in God and ignored the existence of her neighbors.

By the time Felicia comes downstairs I have been throwing up into the bathtub for half an hour. She and Leo clean my face and put me to bed.

As soon as they leave I look around, ready to hide. But the fathers are nowhere to be seen, I have screamed them away.

Up all night I watch the glow from the streetlight, patterns of leafless branches against the floor of the studio. Through my tears it blurs, diffuses, like the sun through the windows of the main building at Pearlstone. In therapy groups I sometimes got lost in that light, drowning myself in my own defense.

∾

Then the hunger starts. For the next few weeks I am murderously hungry, like after a track meet or at a funeral. Leo cooks huge vats of pasta, polenta, grills large tasty fish. I eat like three of me.

Felicia still can't, and it doesn't seem she can sleep, either *era una piccola bambina che rideva il giorno e non dormiva durante la notte*. Many nights she goes upstairs to her attic room after the late shift, but I wake with her beside me, some ten-year-old crawling into mommy's bed to cure her bad dreams.

Anne-Marie is here more frequently; she has started to date Felicia's friend Philip again, years after they broke up. She eats Leo's food more delicately, complimenting a spice here, a presentation there. I am too busy eating to say anything.

A cool rain blessed February thaw. Anne-Marie and I sit on the back porch by the kitchen, watching the rain curtains sweep along the back alleys of 27th Street and soak the tall garden boxes, liquefying the dirt.

From one of the boxes rises Lucia, in her silver fish costume. She swims out and onto the ground in slow, careful, angular motions, the rain washing off the mud. Because of the rain, it is hard to tell at first that she is crying.

I move down the stairs toward her, letting the rain into my skin, opening my mouth to drink it. (Let me rain now, she is swimming in me hindmost, my fellow daughterwife.) The rain dissolves her fish costume and she is naked, except for the burn scars on her back.

I lean down and kiss every scar; then I stand up and put my face close to hers. *I love you, Lucia. Ti amo, je t'aime. Let the raised name of love every person thrill.* I lick the tears from her cheeks.

She brings me back into the box with her and we lay down, deep in the mud, creatures unto that element. The mud is warm, her body warmer. We fall asleep in each other's arms. I wake alone in the box, staying there until Anne-Marie rouses me. Leo cleans up after dinner. while she and Felicia walk me upstairs and turn on the shower.

∽

Jessie Berger arrives with false spring, little buds beginning to open up, forgetting that there is at least a month left of winter. She says she is dedicating her novel to me. "To all of us." All of us? I smile. Then you had better include Lucia.

"I was Lucia too, you know that. . . . I was Issy and Christine, both. And maybe Nicole Diver."

"And maybe Molly O'Donnell," I reply, laughing as we cross North Street and pass the Charles Theater, which is playing some German movie, a poster of a silver Berlin statue glowing safely behind glass. I tell her to dedicate it to Lucy Doe.

We pass the conservatory and I instinctively look for the other Lucia, even though I know full well she is not there. She is back behind the walls.

"Ruth Kessler," says Jessie, "I know her. She liked me, I think. She tried to sell me condoms." We head down into East Baltimore; as we cross Greenmount Avenue a passing car splashes mud onto my sweatshirt, clotted grey with snow.

We slow to a walk at the corner where I met the car, the long black Oldsmobile with a teenage driver that sent me to Pearlstone. And then my gut understands, by the time I saw him I had begun to remember, not seeing it but feeling it, my body finally telling my mind what it felt. I remember the driver's face, he was more frightened than I—I was busy feeling your fingers inside me, hearing my own voice over and over again, *I do not belong to you.* Jessie and I walk slowly as I look for the rain gutter decorated with graffiti—the one I stared at that summer night, singing Lucia.

When I find it, I sit down, clearing the gutter of damp newspaper to read the most recent verses in the antiphony: SAM R., DAKOTA '94, FUCK THE POLICE. I hear the few cars on the street slow down and drive around us, as I keep reading. Jessie squats next to me. "Oh man, the words of the prophets *are* written on the subway walls." BY ANY MEANS NECESSARY takes up about half the length of the block.

| *loves street signs on TMH street* Bab would write the words down in his tiny square notebook, after diaphanous L told him what she had seen.

I ask Jessie if she has ever managed to forgive her father.

She wrinkles her nose. "It took a long time . . . and what you end up with isn't exactly forgiveness."

I tell her about breaking plates and Christmas boxes, and ask if that will ever stop. She laughs, an unexpected sound even in these balmy aired streets. "Raves of wage, I used to call 'em . . . they get gentler, but I don't know if they ever stop."

It begins to rain as we swing back up north, past the reservoir, another favorite spot for Lucia B a/k/a Ruth Kessler. I try to read the no forgiveness in Jessie's face as she speaks into the air in front of her, giving out the bald facts of her childhood.

Not distance, not even peace. In German you could do it, just stick them together, rage + acknowledgement of the past + love, love have I on my back spine. *Liebschmertzbösespilltmilk* or something like that. I wonder if I will have to do it first for Bab and then for Will.

As we reach North Charles Street, a car stops behind us. Leo reaches out from inside the car, pulls both of us into the back seat. Anne-Marie is behind the wheel, a small black cat curling next to her. "He was at the vet," she says softly.

I pick up the cat and start to laugh, burying my face in its fur. "They said you were a doctor," I tell it, "but as long as you are a cat it is different."

~

Tomorrow is Saint Valentine's day
All in the morning betime
And Leo is going home
To be with his Valentine.

He has let his hair grow the whole time here, and his ponytail reaches behind him, an auburn-gray horse's tail. I hold him for a long time; there are no words to thank him for being here with me. I mention the food instead, I tell him he will have to ship some of Oliver's delicacies across the country, since he taught me to eat again.

He asks again if I want to come with him. "San Francisco is much warmer, even at this time of year—and all my cooking you can stand."

Not now, I tell him. Maybe later. When I stop having dreams while I am still awake.

Today Anne-Marie wears a long wool skirt. The people at her new job understand, she says, they have given her time off to be with me.

The harsh rain feels like the tail end of a hurricane, like the one that crushed homes in North Carolina last October. The highways are covered in sheets of rain, the grounds to either side swelled, bubbling, as if febrile. We listen to the radio; Anne-Marie chooses the station and sings along. *Baby, baby, where did our love go?* The scared/sacred name of love. I remember running this route with Emma: but never in the rain.

The parking lot at Pearlstone is paved with umbrellas; doctors and nurses and aides get out of their cars umbrella first, then only pulling the rest of their bodies out to follow. I am no longer looking for Zelda.

Dr. Kepler's office is sparkling clean, as if the rain has eaten all the mess. He is quick, impatient, but then the gel in his hair is wilted and he needs to go fix it. The lawyer from my hearing stands at the back of the room. He looks tired.

"How are you feeling, Molly?" the doctor asks. The question brisk, almost offhand.

I want to laugh, I want to sing *I'm forever blowing bubbles*, but I know this is serious and they can keep me here, so I do neither. I am much better, I tell him.

Kepler keeps looking at his watch—this one is different, the band is gold. (HURRY UP PLEASE IT'S TIME). I ask him about Susan, about Karen, about Barbara. He shakes his head. "Confidential." Only doctors know those secrets, Kate Strong with her keys to the castle.

Chatham is harder: I start to shake seeing the bare walls, the floors hard-scrubbed with antiseptic. I have never signed in at the front desk before, and my wrist feels suddenly naked without the half-inch strip of plastic round it. The nurses tell us that Ruth Kessler is just out of seclusion.

As we pass the front dayroom I see José, still here (here again?). "I pray every day," he is telling a volunteer. My Lucia B is on the smoking porch, looking through the tall grey fence that bars all exit, onto the grounds pelted with rain. Her hair has grown longer and she wears it in a ponytail, like Leo's: she no longer looks so much like Lucia, except for the squint in her eye.

When she notices me, she laughs. "Well if it ain't the girl with the running shoes." Anne-Marie leaves us alone, and I ask why she was in seclusion. She laughs some more. "I busted some stuff," she said. "You ever do that? Just bust some stuff?"

I nod, thinking of the Christmas boxes and my plates. I look beyond her, through the metal grating, watching the clouds, waiting for the thunderstorm.

She takes a long drag on her cigarette and is Lucia again, inviting all comers into her little cottage at Bray. "This place," she says, "sometimes it makes you crazy."

"Oh yes oh yes," I say.

She turns away from me, reaches out an arm and curls her fingers around the metal lace of the cage. "What do you care," she says, "that lawyer got you out."

On the way home I make Anne-Marie turn off the radio, and we sing all the way home. *Go down, Moses! Go down, Moses! Go down, Moses! And let my people go!*

I also learned from Dr. Kepler that Jim Keene has died.

That he lives not is my grief, I told him.

But they couldn't keep me for saying that.

Words words words.

After a battle, Kepler also gave me back my lettrines from art class, and my notepads. The words echo | 's, Bab's, echo my Shakespeare madwomen bleeding inside of me.

My father had blood in his eyes.

He is dead and gone, lady, he is dead and gone.

No Molly voice, I was lost to the other voices, those dances I dreamed. | you sang my pain for me.

Slip me inside of you.

Is love worse living?

I am so tired.

Yet my body is stronger now, stronger than my soul. Anne-Marie and I have been running every morning, even in the rain, even on days when I could otherwise not move. I am able to reach over and tear out some of the pages with musical notes, tape them to the walls of the studio—between my lettrines and Felicia's sketches of me.

Mirror reflects variously, I tell Felicia and start to laugh. At Pearlstone I used to say that all the time, and not remember whose those words were. After sound, light and heat comes memory, will and understanding.

Memory, Will and understanding? My throat still hoarse, my arms still ache from blinding you in dreams.

That night Felicia comes home from a long day serving drinks in high heels, men trying to pull at her skirt. "I ache all over," she says.

For the first time, she lets me massage her back.

I try to remember what has felt best to me: deep pressure, the tense muscles like little air bubbles that pop under my fingertips. But I cannot help but reach for the screaming baby, no smoke rising from her back this time. I move my hands in small arcs, wipe tears from the tiny eyes. I sing softly, *Era una piccola bambina.* When I lean on her lower back I feel her shudder, and I release her quickly, afraid I have hurt her. But she twists her head around and says, "No no it's fine, Molly." Her voice a little thick, and there are tears on her cheeks.

"It's good, it's okay."

I kiss her shoulder, gently: I feel her tense a little so I kiss it again, this time leaving my mouth on her skin. A long sigh from Felicia, deep exhale.

The skin on her shoulders is butter-soft under mouth and hands, especially compared with the tattoo-rough baby below it. The rain batters at the window and I try to protect the babies; I hover low enough that my hair brushes the small of her back. When I place my other hand on her hip, she moans softly.

So this is where we were going, her in my bed all those mornings.

I trace the larger baby's face with my lips and tongue, run my hands along her sides, first gently then roughly. My skin is burning but not like before, I can feel the swelling and heat deep in my center.

My lips surround her shoulder blade: then she tears from my grip so she can turn and face me. Her soft tongue tastes faintly of cigarettes, its probing is not gentle; nor is there gentleness in the way she claws at my T-shirt, buries her fingers underneath it. I am kept busy tasting the tears in the hollow of her collarbone; then she takes my right hand and places it between her legs, so I can feel the wetness there too.

"Jeff knew," she whispers, "he always said I had the hots for you. Even before."

Before is forever ago: I kiss her mouth again, hugging her tightly against me. After a few minutes she raises up, turns me on my back; her hair is soft, vestigial curls nuzzling my belly as she gently spreads my legs.

Her tongue draws white heat, white light that is mine, the shouts and screams are mine are ours the little breaths and climbing color are mine.

I have been given my body back just in time.

Scribbledehobble!

Anne-Marie still wants to know what that word means. I am still her "client" so I try to explain, to show her a little of diaphanous L and Bab's journey to dreamland, though Wonder-lawn's lost forever. My notebooks and papers are spread across the floor of the studio, like in my blinding-Will dream. The sun glares through the bay window, Anne-Marie's sunglasses hide her eyes from me.

Photos of Lucia dancing, of the Joyce family in stiff pose. L not so diaphanous in her fur coat and crossed eyes, Nora with that smug smile. I bet she was smiling like that the exact moment that Lucia threw the chair at her.

My life and Lucia's spread out across the floor in pages and pages of scribbled writing, measured out in coffee spoons and cryptic sigla, < > [| . I walk along the carpet of my notes until I find the notebook I want—the notes of Babbo's 1924 dream, the cry of shame/ and horror I have now been howling for half a year.

Suddenly I am a scholar again, trying to show Anne-Marie L and Bab's co-creation, the whirling dream-nightmare too rich to give up. My original copy of *Finnegans Wake* still bears Will's handwriting on the front title page, his notes in my handwriting crossing my notes for | .

One day Anne-Marie brings her own *Wake*, carefully high-lighted and color coded: yellow for things she heard me say, blue for what my journals made her notice. *Speaking of incestuish salacities among gerontophils. . . . Me as with you in thadark.* Not so simple, my friend. So hath been, love: tis: and will be: till wears and tears and ages. Spelling my yearns to her, to him. To you, Will.

Running by myself, glorying in the sun-filled spring morning: baby green tree leaves gracing the gold and white buildings of the univer-sity. No ivory tower, not even the huge sandstone tower that shows Lucia's library in Texas: the smaller squarish buildings remote to me, inaccessible. I do not recognize any of the students, nor would they know me. Somewhere in there is Gary, his leg long since healed, sharing Shakespeare and sex with another earnest student.

The baseball stadium is empty, slumbering now that the base-ball games have themselves moved downtown. I run into the center, wishing I had Ruth Kessler by the hand to show her this sad grandeur, Athena's empty temple after Christianity banished the goddess.

The goddess is a madwoman, breathing angels through the cross on her forehead, her believers burned as witches. Now witches drugged as madwomen: it crops out in your flesh, heavy limbs wet mouth, the angels healing from Susan's mind. No wonder Ruth always stood here, staring her Lucia eyes at the stadium.

In third grade Emma and I named all her Barbie dolls after goddesses, we parked Athena in the living room. Will laughed, asked how we planned on cutting off Artemis' breast. All I know now is Artemis would be tattooed, like the one-breasted woman at the half-marathon.

And I know that it is time to call Emma.

I run on to the reservoir, singing to them both in my head. The water glimmers in the afternoon sunset, blue mixed with rose; elderly couples eye me suspiciously as they circle the lake in their sweat suits.

On the way home I am newly in love with the trees, their leaves gold yellow near-green. Virginia knew it: trees are alive, they send their golden streams into our blood streams if we will only let them. If only we cannot be locked up for saying so.

At Charles Street I finally stop, run my hands over the branches of a low oak near the art museum. Too beautiful—Ophelia, Septimus, Issy, Caddy and numerous Lucias all equally entranced, the trees far too beautiful for us to listen.

Seven a.m. and the sun is rude, demanding my attention: I perform a sun salutation, as I sometimes did on the Pearlstone grounds. Stretching my back, my arms to the tin ceiling; then down, one knee on the hardwood studio floor. My head raised to the watery gold light as it glows and fades.

I have to be careful not to disturb my papers, still scattered and pasted around the room, a luxuriant if incomprehensible carpet.

When the door opens without a knock, I know who it is: Anne-Marie called ahead of time. She and Felicia on either end, twin bodyguards against the fear in my little sister's eyes. Her mouth is pressed tight, trying not to cry; I stand up and move toward her, my mirror of mirror.

After a moment she extends her hands toward me, palms forward, reminding me of that first time at the hospital. We touch fingertips, as we did then. "Hello, Emma," I say.

She swallows, hard. "Hello, Molly."

Welcome to my blue: season.

The book of the opening of the mind to light.

The book of the dark.

Which do you have in your hands?

Note from the Author

My bluish season

It feels a little like time travel.

You know those movies where someone meets their much-younger self? It's much more dizzying than the films . . . sound.

That former self is in her late twenties: let's call her Christina, the name I was using for resumes and legal documents. Unlike the lesbian journalist writing this essay, she identifies as neither: after a brief marriage to a boy she adored ended with a crash, she finds herself newly living in San Francisco, getting used to being single[1] and trying to find an agent for her first novel, *Every Day is Remembrance Day*. Christina came to California after a few years in Baltimore, the city she'd moved to when her marriage fell apart. That city would stay in her heart and become the home for her next novel. The characters in *Remembrance Day* will stay with her for decades, even after she abandons the book as her "practice novel."

Because having finished the first one, she's already planning the second, addicted now to the novelist's double consciousness: living one life while the one she's creating thrums inside her. The new one, she decides, will be based on the life of Lucia Joyce, daughter of the iconic Irish writer. She'd spent happy college years immersed in the multilayered language games of Joyce's novels and was weirdly unsurprised to learn that his daughter had spent most of her life in mental institutions. No less than Carl Jung told Joyce that he was swimming in a river that was drowning his daughter. Could twentysomething Christina do justice to *her* story?

So she writes to the professor with whom she studied Joyce in undergraduate school, Suzette Henke[2]. Henke warns her that Lucia's story is controversial, that Joyce's grandson burned her letters and declared his aunt off limits; Henke sent Christina a copy of the suppressed final chapter of the biography of Joyce's wife Nora, which author Brenda Maddox had had to agree to delete lest the estate deny her permission to quote Joyce's well-copyrighted work. Christina decides *not* to try to tell Lucia's story, but to weave one that pings off it, with a contemporary character who starts by studying Lucia but ends up in a mental hospital herself. In Baltimore she knew a lot of people in the "recovery" community, members of groups like Adult Children of Alcoholics; the central character who soon whispers to her, Molly O'Donnell, has father issues quite separate from Lucia's.

Still not realizing she's a journalist, Christina immerses herself in other biographies, as well as books on abnormal psychiatry. She spends hours going through the psychiatric bible, the DSM-III (Diagnostic and Statistical Manual), and can't stop laughing at the definition of narcissistic personality disorder—she even reads that aloud to friends who knew her ex-husband. Struck by what feels a permeable border between "schizophrenic speech" as described by clinicians and pioneering poetry and prose, she also picks up popular denunciations of psychiatry: Kate Millett's *The Loony-Bin Trip,* Thomas Szasz' *The Myth of Mental Illness.* When she's laid off from her job and goes on unemployment, she also signs up to volunteer at the Jacob Pearlstein Psychiatric Institute.

This being 1991, Christina—this younger version of me—is

surrounded at JPPI by news of "The Decade of the Brain," and treatment plans that seem to consist of choosing the right drugs to treat patients' distress. She doesn't last long there, after she's cautioned about "boundaries." Those experiences then form her second protagonist: the social worker Anne-Marie, whose efforts to treat Molly make the spine of the hospital story. By the end of those chapters, Anne-Marie will fight the hospital in court for Molly's release.

For her novel, in place of JPPI, Christina creates a Baltimore psychiatric institution housed in a former boarding school—where her protagonist ends up after a car accident, talking only in Joycean riddles. Baltimore, because that was where Christina went to heal and spent a year-plus in therapy digging into her own upbringing and failed marriage. (She steals the locals' pronunciation and calls it "Balmer.") The hospital chapters alternate with Molly's journal in the year before the accident, as she tries to write about "Madness in Joyce" and ends up obsessed with Lucia, unearthing her own memories of childhood abuse by her very beloved father. Christina sees Molly's illness as a retreat from those memories and tries to tell the story of how she fights her way past them.

In the three years she's working on the novel, Christina swims past JPPI and visits the Joycean world. She force-marches herself through a reading of *Finnegans Wake,* with its dominant daughter-figure Issy; when she learns that nearby Stanford University houses copies of Joyce's notebooks for the *Wake,* she goes there and secures the mentorship of one of its top Joyce scholars, Robert Polhemus. She goes to Texas to see Lucia's notebooks there, where representatives of Stephen James Joyce tell her that while they can't prevent her from reading them, she certainly can't expect to quote them. *I can't, but my fictional madwoman can,* she thinks.

She even develops her own theory, Molly's theory, about how the *Wake* might be a crime scene for father-daughter incest. She names the book *blue: season,* a phrase from the notebooks. And when the annual Joyce conference happens in California, where

Christina is coincidentally living, she goes to the conference and presents an excerpt of the novel, from a chapter titled "Diaphanous L and Bab working at c&d." Christina also meets a Philadelphia professor named Carol Shloss, who is working on a biography of Lucia that will celebrate her brief career as a dancer, and posit Lucia as a co-author of the *Wake*. Schloss never says what she thinks of "Diaphanous L," in which Christina shared Molly's incest theory. She does hear from Dutch scholar Christine van Boheemen that if the scholars accepted her theory, "It would deconstruct the profession!"

30 years after that Joyce conference, I can come from behind the curtain and speak in first person. Over the years I spent working on "my Lucia Joyce novel," I let San Francisco midwife my coming out as a lesbian; upon coming back East, I became a journalist and ended my career as a faux-Joycean. I never had to experience, as Carol Shloss did, a years-long legal battle with Stephen James Joyce, one that ultimately became its own story[3] when Shloss finally published her book in 2003, *To Dance In the Wake*. By then, Joyce scholarship had nearly shut down after years of the estate's intransigence: there were anthologies where entire chapters were printed in blank, journals junked for lack of permission to quote. By 2006, when the Modern Language Association convention was held in my wife's hometown of Philadelphia (my new hometown), I dropped by a panel that discussed all this. It was led by Shloss, who by then was at Stanford and married to Rob Polhemus (the same guy who'd helped me a decade earlier). I'd sent Polhemus at least one draft of *blue: season,* but I didn't dare ask Shloss if she'd read it.

Shloss and I are now "Facebook friends," and she's still writing about literary fathers and daughters; her upcoming 2023 book[4] is about the hidden daughter of Ezra Pound. She also moved back to Philadelphia a few years ago, and I asked her to coffee. "That would be WILD," she answered but never said yes. She knows I'm a journalist and about my nonfiction book, probably knowing I no longer spend my time dreaming of Issy, the Wake's daughter figure.

So whatever became of *blue: season?* It was rejected by a slew of major publishers and a few less-major ones, though it won an award at the City College of New York, where I'd fled East thinking an MFA would help. I left my agent (who herself left the profession), and found a new one who loved it and garnered another round of rejections. I'll spare you most of my subsequent "failed-novelist-turned journalist" story and move on to why, decades later, I'm thinking of finally publishing *blue.*

In the Amazon era, such indie publishing doesn't have the stigma it once did. I watched as dear friends who've gone that way garnered Kirkus reviews, bookstore appearances, and many of the trappings normally associated with traditional publishing. Meanwhile, I still believe in my book.

As I was deciding to publish now, one of my beta readers called it "clear, gripping from the first sentence, illuminating, and more than a little heartbreaking." I hold that sentence close, along with some from a high-school classmate, now teaching at Lehmann College, who'd done his dissertation on Joyce:

> I am blown away. A voicing of silent voices on so many
> levels. The marathon running was such a fascinating coun-
> terpoint/thread. Really brilliant. And deserves to be read
> by others!! Completely away from the deeper truths of the
> book, it made me realize that academia has changed in the
> past 20 years more than madhouses.

After those words from my professor friend, I tried to get the agent who got me through *Ain't Marching* to read and think about repping it, but no go; he'd told me he wouldn't rep my fiction. So I went back to my journalism wormhole and finished my nonfiction book, *I Ain't Marching Anymore: Deserters, Dissenters and Objectors to America's Wars.* But *blue* stayed in my heart, and I never stopped noticing when other Lucia-inspired works emerged: The decades since my immersion have produced at least three Lucia

Joyce novels, two dance performances and more than one movie. Just this week, Edna O'Brien premiered at the Abbey Theatre "Joyce's Women,"[5] starring Lucia. Artists and storytellers can't resist her.

Meanwhile, 2017 marked 75 years since James Joyce died, placing his work in the public domain. And in 2020, as noted by *The New York Times*[6], Stephen James Joyce died, no longer a "fierce gatekeeper" of all things Joyce. But do I really want to subject Molly and myself to the pushme-pullyou of the literary market? At 60, long past my twentysomething certainty that I was *meant* to be a famous novelist, I'm striving for something both more and less certain.

Lucia Joyce died on December 12, 1982. I don't know if the 40th anniversary of her death will make a splash; doubtless other writers/filmmakers will try. And now, *blue: season* will join that stream. Among the voices no longer silent is that of twentysomething me, whose hopes I smothered for so long.

Endnotes

Note from the Author

1. "San Francisco in the 1990s." *Failbetter,* #16, (February 9, 2005), failbetter.com.
2. Henke's iconic works include *James Joyce and the Politics of Desire* (Routledge, 1990) and *Shattered Subjects: Trauma and Testimony in Women's Life Writing* (St. Martin's Press, 1998).
3. D. T. Max, "The Injustice Collector." *New Yorker,* June 19, 2006.
4. Carol Shloss, *Let the Wind Speak: Mary de Rachewiltz and Ezra Pound* (University of Pennsylvania Press, 2023).
5. Max McGuiness, "*Joyce's Women,* Abbey Theatre review — Edna O'Brien's play offers its heroines visceral freedom." *Financial Times,* September 24, 2022.
6. Sam Roberts, "Stephen Joyce Dies at 87; Guarded Grandfather's Literary Legacy." February 7, 2020.

Afterword

Reviews are the lifeblood of independent publishers and authors. If you liked meeting Molly and Lucia and travelling with them on their journey, please leave a review on Amazon or on Goodreads, or both. Please also consider signing up for the Mumblers Press newsletter, where you will find news on our authors and future books.

Warmest thanks,
Mumblers Press LLC

About the Author

Chris Lombardi's fiction has been shortlisted for the Pushcart Prize and won both the Lowell DeJur Prize and the Germaine Griffin Moore Prize at City College of New York. *blue: season,* a meditation on memory and grief, spins around the story of Lucia Joyce, daughter of the Irish writer. Excerpts from the book were presented at California Joyce in Irvine, California, after which Lombardi was warned that her thesis about Lucia "could deconstruct" Joyce studies. Decades later, Lombardi's also a veteran journalist and advocate, and author of the nonfiction *I Ain't Marching Anymore: Deserters, Dissenters and Objectors to America's Wars* (New Press, 2020). *blue: season* speaks equally to lovers of literature, abuse survivors and advocates, and anyone wondering what "mental health" really means.

Her fiction has been published in *minnesota review, Anything That Moves, Lurch, The Pearl, Living Room,* and assorted anthologies, including *Hey! Paesan: Lesbians and Gays of Italian Descent.* Her journalism has been published by *The Nation, Ms. Magazine, Poets & Writers, Women's Enews, ABA Journal, American Book Review, Inside MS, Medium, The New York Times, Al Jazeera English, Seattle Times, The Mercury News, Guernica Magazine* and the *Philadelphia Inquirer.*

Lombardi's novel *The Suicide Project* was one of 12 finalists for Barbara Kingsolver's Bellwether Prize. In the fall of 2002, she appeared at the New York James Joyce Society to present excerpts of her novel *blue:season.*

facebook.com/ChristinaLombardi

twitter.com/CrisAintMarchin

instagram.com/chrisaintmarchin

Also by Chris Lombardi

I Ain't Marching Anymore: Deserters, Dissenters and Objectors to
America's Wars (New Press, 2020)